Maya Blake's hopes of becoming a writer were born when she picked up her first romance at thirteen. Little did she know her dream would come true! Does she still pinch herself every now and then to make sure it's not a dream? Yes, she does! Feel free to pinch her, too, via Twitter, Facebook or Goodreads! Happy reading!

Millie Adams has always loved books. She considers herself a mix of Anne Shirley—loquacious, but charming, and willing to break a slate over a boy's head if need be—and Charlotte Doyle—a lady at heart, but with the spirit to become a mutineer should the occasion arise. Millie lives in a small house on the edge of the woods, which she finds allows her to escape in the way she loves best: in the pages of a book. She loves intense alpha heroes and the women who dare to go toe-to-toe with them. Or break a slate over their heads…

Discover more at millsandboon.co.uk.

PREGNANT AND STOLEN BY THE TYCOON

MAYA BLAKE

THE CHRISTMAS THE GREEK CLAIMED HER

MILLIE ADAMS

MILLS & BOON

First published in Great Britain 2023
by Mills & Boon, an imprint of HarperCollins*Publishers* Ltd,
1 London Bridge Street, London, SE1 9GF

www.harpercollins.co.uk

HarperCollins*Publishers*, Macken House, 39/40 Mayor Street Upper, Dublin 1, D01 C9W8, Ireland

Pregnant and Stolen by the Tycoon © 2023 Maya Blake

The Christmas the Greek Claimed Her © 2023 Millie Adams

ISBN: 978-0-263-30698-9

10/23

PREGNANT AND STOLEN BY THE TYCOON

MAYA BLAKE

MILLS & BOON

CHAPTER ONE

'SEND THE NEXT ONE IN, Lily. Please.'

Genie Merchant remembered to tag on the courtesy, despite her brain firing off in a million tangential directions.

Social cues are important.

Her childhood therapist's words echoed at the back of her head.

Why? she remembered asking.

A wry smile from wise eyes.

They oil the wheels of evolution.

She remembered silently snorting back then. That sound, too, echoed at the back of her mind now. No number of courteous words tagged onto hard facts and sophisticated, groundbreaking coding had been enough to secure her what she wanted.

Instead, it'd only resulted in drawing unwanted attention from men in suits who wanted to steal years of her hard work.

Her *life's* work.

Which was why she was reduced to this…farce.

Why she'd swapped her favourite lounging co-ords and Ugg boots for a cream jumpsuit, uncomfortable heels, and itchy jewellery the online stylist called 'on trend'. Why she'd exchanged her utilitarian glasses for contacts that made her blink like an electrocuted owl, left the sanctuary of her basement tech lab and home, and travelled up to the twenty-first floor of the building overlooking the east London ribbon of the Thames.

She barely looked up to catch her assistant's reserved smile as the woman nodded and stepped back out of her office.

Four meetings down, one to go.

Four *very disappointing* meetings.

She was running out of time. At her last check on the dark web this morning, there were six questionable entities closing in on her, ready to force her hand or take her intellectual property by force, two of them security forces of so-called democracies.

She had a week, maybe ten days, at most.

And if she was successful…

Genie sucked in a long, shaky breath, attempting not to dwell on that thought. But it was no use. With her dream tantalisingly close, it was impossible not to skim past it one more time. Maybe even to linger longingly for a few seconds.

To imagine what it would *feel* like to—

'Mr Graham to see you, Miss Merchant.'

Genie schooled her features and posture into the stance she'd wasted precious time perfecting in front of the mirror this morning and turned.

Shoulders back. Steady eye contact. Lips stretched a half-inch on either side but no showing of teeth. Hand outstretched ninety degrees from her body.

'Mr Graham. Thank you for coming.'

The short, thin man with small, beady eyes looked her up and down. 'No, thank *you* for making the time to see me. And call me Frank.' His toothy smile stretched even wider as he blatantly appraised her. 'Had I known what a vision you were, I would've reached out much earlier.'

Her reservations, already severely tested from having to go down this road, hardened into rejection as his sweaty hand grasped hers and subtly tugged her closer.

She resisted and pulled away from him to link her fingers

in front of her. 'I hope my gender isn't the determining factor of our negotiations?' she enquired, her cold tone icing between them.

He eyed her in wary surprise, before he laughed. 'Of course not, Genie. May I call you Genie?'

'No. Miss Merchant will be quite adequate. Thank you.'

His face dropped and her ire rose. Was he really that deluded? Did he believe this was a social exercise? That sexist informality was his gateway to acquiring her most prized possession?

She watched him examine her office, taking in the stark icy blue minimalist decor with faint disdain before lingering for several seconds on the velvet grey sofa.

'Well, shall we make ourselves comfortable, Genie?' he asked, his American twang thickening as he waved her towards the sofa instead of the small conference table she'd opted to use for her other meetings.

His blithe refusal of her request stiffened her spine and made up her mind. 'No. I don't think this is going to work, Mr Graham.'

His face morphed from condescension to anger. 'Excuse me? You haven't even heard my offer.'

'Do you even understand how my algorithm works?' The beauty of her highly sophisticated predictive algorithm was that it could work wonders for a farmer in Peru in accurately projecting weather patterns, long term soil viability and a plethora of advantages. The bad news was that in the wrong hands, it could also be weaponised to give military advantage to a ruthless dictator. Hence her being at pains to ensure it didn't fall into the wrong hands.

He shrugged. 'Not in its entirety, but I have a few dozen clever geeks back in Silicon Valley who are very excited about it and ready to put it to great use. So why don't we talk numbers?'

'No.' She considered the social cue. Then disregarded it.

Frank Graham didn't deserve her *thanks for coming*. He'd wasted her time. Precious time she'd never recoup.

Anger reddened his face. 'Now, look here. I flew in from California especially for this meeting. You can't just dismiss me without hearing me—'

'I can and I just have.' Striding to her desk, she pressed the button for her secretary, then another one that automated her office door.

It swung smoothly open, and Genie breathed a sigh of relief to see the two burly guards standing in the doorway.

Yes, she had been reduced to employing bodyguards because in moments like these, and as she'd discovered in the last six months, it was effective in deterring the men in suits who didn't have qualms about taking what was hers.

Frank Graham looked ready to force the issue, until he saw the security and changed his mind. It didn't stop him from sneering, 'Little girls who think they can play in a man's world get what's coming to them, eventually. Mark my words.'

'I won't. In fact, I've already forgotten them. Good day, Mr Graham.'

She kept her posture and her expression intact despite the knot of despair tightening in her stomach. But the moment the door shut behind the odious man, she sagged into her chair, then twisted it around to stare unseeing out of the window.

She registered neither the tourist boat floating lazily down the river nor the unseasonally bright blue skies overhead. Neither the acrobat entertaining passers-by on his tiny unicycle nor the group of young students sharing a joke over their lunch.

But the young mother pushing a stylish little pram caught her eye. Pulled agonisingly hard on her heartstrings.

Her dream. Her one wish. Now even farther away than it'd been this morning.

Her posture deflated further until Genie suspected she could disappear into the giant chair she hated but which the decorator had insisted was the right symbol to project power and dominance.

Genie had declined to point out that she didn't need outward trappings to demonstrate her worth. Her power and dominance came from her superior brain power. Her Rhodes Scholar accolades and the Girl Genius label the media liked to crow about, despite her being twenty-eight instead of eight, spoke volumes for themselves.

She should've taken her business team's advice and let them broker this deal on her behalf. But wouldn't that have been more painful than putting herself through the torture of social confrontation with strangers? Wouldn't sitting in her lab downstairs, blissfully surrounded by her super computers and out of the way but having others decide on the fate of her life's work, have been even more excruciating?

A breath shuddered out of her, her forlorn gaze resting on the mother who'd paused to coo at her baby and following them until they were out of view.

Yes, it would've been excruciating, but she wouldn't be here, taking a front-row seat to her own failure.

Affirm the positive. Don't dwell on the negative.

This time her snort ripped free, tinged by a dart of guilt.

Dr Douglas wouldn't have approved. He would've called it 'an unfortunate social miscue'.

But Dr Douglas had retired a long time ago, and then shortly after that, her Christmas card had been 'returned to sender' because he'd passed away.

She was on her own. Alone and circling the drain of failure.

The soft whine of her door made her grit her teeth. Was she to be denied even this rare moment of self-pity?

'We're done for the day, Lily.' She scrambled through her morose thoughts and summoned further socially accepted words for her assistant. 'I am…grateful for your help. We did, however, fall far short of our goals, so—'

'Don't be ready to throw in the towel just yet, Miss Merchant.'

Genie swivelled around at the sound of the voice.

The deep rumbling volcano of a voice.

Not hyperbole.

The man striding with supreme confidence into her office had the voice that could rival the soundtrack of that volcano that had erupted in Hawaii recently. And it was accented. Not thick but blended with something else. Enough to make it distinctive.

South America. Spanish. But not quite Chile. Not quite Argentina. Off the coast. Smoke. Fire. *Samba*.

'Cardosia,' she murmured.

He paused, his eyes narrowing a fraction, then gleaming, before he inclined his head. 'Indeed. Not many can tell.'

Genie shrugged. 'I can parse thirty-seven languages and dialects.' She wasn't entirely certain why she felt the need to share that information and on some level she knew she would be disappointed when she arrived at the reason why. Because it strongly suggested she was intimidated by this stranger.

This towering force moving through her personal space.

She tilted her head and examined him clinically.

He was hands down the finest male specimen she'd ever seen. Considering she rarely left her building, she might be sorely lacking in source material with which to compare him, but if she placed him in the category assigned by her favourite TV characters, he was a 'banging ten-ten studly stud'.

Had he taken a wrong turn to a photoshoot for those far too large billboards that dominated the skyline and seemed to slap her in the face whenever she ventured out? Because he really was too much to behold.

She looked past him to her assistant. 'Lily.' The older woman had worked for Merchant Labs long enough to decode the question held within her name.

'I'm sorry, Miss Merchant, I don't have Mr…um…'

'Severino Valente,' the stranger supplied, the intensity of his voice deepening further.

Lily's eyes widened, then her face flushed. Genie categorised the reaction and deduced that her assistant had registered the 'studly-studness' of her unwanted visitor.

'I don't have Mr Valente on the schedule, but he said you'd be interested in taking this meeting with him, and since Mr Graham left early…'

Genie kept her gaze on Lily, faintly registering that perhaps she was staring too long, perhaps even displaying her displeasure with this uncharacteristic action by her assistant. Was that…fair or unfair? 'Did he?'

Diverting her attention from Lily, she met a pair of unwavering slate-grey eyes, her question, also meant to ridicule his assumption, bouncing off his wide shoulders.

He moved towards her, and the most peculiar thing happened.

Her skin began to tighten. Not in flight-or-fight mode. She knew those two well enough. Had experienced both in the past six months and beyond that in the not so distant past, when she'd questioned her true value to the people who should've cared about her. When she'd believed she might be better off on her own.

No, this was different.

It felt almost like…anticipation. *Stimulation.* Although why she should…*oh.*

Oh. Goodness.

Her body was straining towards him of its own volition. And her hand was extending towards his in answer to the large one he held out to her.

As if he had some sort of…*power* over her.

Alpha-male posturing.

She'd read that somewhere. The logical thing to do to negate stimulus was to separate the stimulant from the object.

She started to drop her hand, even contemplated stepping back but that would be a red flag he wouldn't miss.

'My assistant is correct that my last meeting was cut short. But I'm afraid I don't have time for another, especially with someone who walked in off the street.'

He dropped his hand and Genie felt an odd disquiet that he hadn't pushed for a handshake. 'I'm not a random visitor, Miss Merchant. My people have been trying to set up a meeting with you for weeks.'

'Then that should've been a firm indicator that I wasn't interested in whatever this is about.'

He shoved his hand into his expensive coat pocket, the action widening the gap between the lapels to show the bespoke suit he wore underneath. The dark navy shirt threw his deep olive complexion into strong focus, emphasising every masculine feature he possessed. 'If I were in the habit of allowing every small hurdle to stop me, I wouldn't be where I am today.'

Genie wasn't sure whether she bristled at the 'small' or the 'hurdle' part.

Before she could respond, he continued, 'Besides, I have it on good authority that your initial short list has been a total failure. Perhaps you should rethink the parameters of your selection.'

'I don't need advice on how I conduct my business, Mr Valente. *My* people will be compiling the next list. Feel free to speak with them, although I can't guarantee you'll be successful next time either.'

He sauntered past her as if she hadn't spoken, prowling to the very window she'd been staring out of a few minutes ago. After a charged minute—which she spent far too engrossed in his riveting profile when she should've pressed the button for her security to escort him out—he turned to her. 'You're running out of time. Are you going to waste more by dismissing Valente Ventures' bid without even hearing what I'm proposing?'

Valente Ventures.

The very name screamed predatory capitalism with a capital C. 'Everyone I've met with so far has been a great fit.' On paper at least.

'And yet you've come up short. Zero out of five as of ten minutes ago?'

Another unpleasant jolt careened through her. 'How do you know—?'

'I do my homework, Miss Merchant. And I'm extremely thorough with it.'

'And does that homework include spying on my company?'

He angled his head at her in a way that made her feel…inadequate. A feeling she'd experienced…rarely. And only where it pertained to her relationship with her late parents. She was dealing with that bolt of unnerving surprise when he answered.

'Come on, now, don't be naive. If companies went around wilfully blind to each other's activities, there would be no healthy competition. Besides, didn't I hear you say just now that you've fallen short of your goals?'

Genie pursed her lips, reluctant to hand him the win. 'That still doesn't mean I'm willing to meet with you.'

He watched her with those far too intense eyes for a minute. If he hoped to make her squirm or uncomfortable, he was going to be disappointed. She was used to being an oddity. A creature people whispered about, sometimes within earshot. She'd long since thickened her skin against being distressed by such things.

'You're accustomed to thinking outside the box, are you not?'

'I am but I don't need to with you. You're firmly in the *no* box, Mr Valente.' With a neat pirouette, she turned towards her desk to summon her assistant, and her security, if need be. As she did, she was struck by the odd desire to see this man grapple with her guards, perhaps even best them. He might be adorned with the trappings of power and influence, but she sensed that, underneath it all, Severino Valente could be ruthless when he needed to be. From her recollection of his people, Cardosians were proud and formidable.

And why on earth was she thinking all this?

She reached out her hand to her intercom.

'You want your algorithm to help people. I have a whole country in desperate need of something brave and bold to change their lives. Surely you won't deny them that because the body seeking that help falls under the umbrella of venture capitalist?'

She froze. Turned her head to meet his gaze over her shoulder. 'What people?'

'Mine,' he answered, his tone grave and powerful. 'Cardosia is in the middle of an ecological and economic crisis. The predictive precision of your algorithm for things like weather patterns is nothing short of astounding but I'm sure I don't need to tell you that. It could change the fortunes of an ailing nation. We're not quite teetering on the brink yet but it's only a matter of time. If you think I'm exaggerating, I'm sure you can find out the truth for yourself with a few keystrokes.'

She dropped her hand. She wasn't changing her mind. Not by a long chalk. 'How do I know this isn't a ploy just to get your hands on my intellectual property? If you've done your homework as you say, then you'll know that two of the entities I met with today outright lied about their true intentions for my algorithm.'

A flash of furious affront whipped across his face and the hairs on her nape stood up. Not because she was afraid of his reaction but because she was riddled with curiosity as to the depths of his passions.

Another hugely troubling first.

She really should've let her business director act on her behalf, saving her from this disturbing interaction. But again Genie felt the oddest sensation in her belly. The one that rejected the idea of missing this…whatever it was.

'I've never needed to lie my way into getting what I want, and I'm not about to start with you. But I'm willing to accommodate a measure of oversight if that will sway to selling your algorithm to me if that's what it takes.'

Oversight.

Maybe he *had* done his homework. Because he was making the very proposal that the previous four candidates had rejected outright. She stepped back from her desk and fully faced him. Only to once again be hit by the veritable force field of his presence.

Had he moved closer?

Because the air was redolent with the scent of sandalwood and spice and warm skin, a curious combination that made her want to take a breath. A *very* deep breath.

'How much oversight?'

'The algorithm will be mine outright and you will not interfere with its day-to-day usage, but I'll allow you a review once every year for the first five years.'

'Just once? A lot can happen in a year, Mr Valente.'

'What I'm offering is more than you received from your other prospective buyers.'

True. And it'd been a concession she was reluctantly willing to negotiate down, as long as she verified beforehand that she was handing her precious property into the right hands. But now he'd opened the prospect of more oversight, it was hard to discard it. Her breath snagged in her midriff when he stepped closer. 'Since I didn't get what I wanted, they too left empty-handed.'

A deep gleam lit his eyes, turning the grey alive and mercurial. 'I'm confident we can both walk away from this with exactly what we want.'

About to respond, she paused when he glanced at his watch.

'Do you have some other pressing matter to attend to?' she snapped, then immediately regretted it. Display of heated emotion was unlike her. Was it because she'd been ready to call this day a loss before this man walked, uninvited, into her office? And now that she'd let herself be intrigued, he was backing away? Was it a tactic?

She met his gaze when he raised his. Again, he studied her for far longer than Genie suspected was polite. She knew because she'd wondered that about herself on a few occasions.

'As a matter of fact, I do,' he responded, his gravel-rough voice causing an unwelcome sensation inside her. 'But I will return this evening. You'll have dinner with me so we can finalise this deal. I'll pick you up at eight.'

The hollow sense of loss when he'd said he was leaving now clashed with the irritating assumption that she would welcome him back or that she would be free to have dinner with him. 'You're getting ahead of yourself, sir. My time is quite regimented, and it doesn't include—'

'You'd rather go back to the drawing board and attract unsuitable buyers to waste your time than spend a few hours acknowledging that I was the best buyer to start off with?'

His argument was irritatingly logical. But the thought of spending more time with him, with his intuitive eyes fixed on her, made her...unsettled. 'We can have a discussion without the dinner.' Quick. Clinical. *Safe*.

He looked around him, his gaze tracking every sterile surface and impersonal ornament before returning to her. 'I've followed your career. I know there must be a specific reason you wish to let go of your work now. You have a few hours' grace to decide whether you want to sell or not. I suggest you get your people to do their due diligence before this evening. As for the timing, I have dinner reservations I'd rather not go to waste. Unless you have an aversion to eating?'

'I don't,' she snapped. 'But I'm picky about whom I eat with.'

'Then I hope you'll make an exception for a future business acquaintance.' With that he strode towards the door. 'You don't need to leave your cave for longer than three hours,' he mused, the faintest stench of mockery on his face.

Genie was working up a comeback searing enough to make Dr Douglas turn in his grave when Severino Valente paused.

'And, Miss Merchant?'

She contented herself in raising a caustic eyebrow.

His gaze lingered on her face, dropping to her mouth before rising. 'I meant what I said. I will walk away with what I want. I always do. Nothing else will suffice.'

Genie absently noted that the quivering in her belly had spread all over her body as she watched him saunter through her office door and disappear from view.

She took his advice and pulled up his name the moment she'd changed back into her favourite lounging attire. Although it stuck in her craw the whole time she munched on a carrot while her fingers flew over the keyboard of her beloved supercomputer.

She'd built the first one from scratch when she was eleven and gifted herself the joy of reincarnating one every birthday since she turned sixteen.

While another computer performed a deeper dive, she speed-read through his life.

He was a multibillionaire. *Of course.*

He'd started his venture capitalist outfit at a young age although not as young as she'd been when she'd been forced to survive on her own. But young enough to raise a few eyebrows. Every sign pointed to a superior intellect. One that other notable corporate figures called on for guidance; one that earned him several industry accolades and invitations to keynote positions in conferences where he gave…engrossing speeches.

Genie told herself it was part of her due diligence when she clicked on one of those speeches, only to switch off minutes later when that peculiar tingling sensation returned at the sound of his voice. For whatever reason, Severino Valente's voice caused a distinct reaction in her.

But more and more, she found herself lingering over the details of his personal life. It didn't take much effort to confirm that Seve Valente was also skilled in his pursuit of the opposite sex. Was perhaps even an aficionado. Page after page of his liaisons attested to that, although the man was reportedly very much attached to his *most eligible bachelor* status.

He was healthy. He'd run a few marathons in his younger days.

His blood type wasn't rare enough to be a problem. His family tree was robust enough not to raise any red flags. And he wasn't interested in attaching himself to any particular female.

He's compatible.

Genie wasn't sure when the idea grew from a whisper into a kernel, then into a fertile seed.

Perhaps this—her subconscious working on the problem— was why she'd experienced all that nonsensical tingling and quivering while in his presence.

The reason behind everything she was doing in the first place.

Her next birthday was in ten months. This time she planned on giving herself an altogether different gift.

A life-changing one.

I'm confident we can both walk away from this with exactly what we want.

His words held much more weight now, not that the man knew it himself.

Five minutes of his time; maybe less if her brief previous sexual experience was an indication. That was all she needed.

Provided of course that the remaining digging didn't unearth any nasty surprises.

It didn't. Which was why she stood in another outfit—one only slightly less comfortable than the last—outside the private entrance to her building at five to eight.

Severino Valente pulled up at eight on the dot in a sleek black sports car, the purr of its engine distinctly electric. If his choice of fuel consumption was designed to impress her, Genie reluctantly admitted it worked.

He stepped out and Genie felt that rush again. It was because of the decision she'd made, she told herself. Nothing else.

That assurance gave her permission to watch him approach. He'd changed too, swapped his formal shirt for a black one, open at the neck minus a tie, over which he wore another bespoke but more casual jacket coupled with matching trousers. His hair looked a little windswept but it was his face that arrested her scrutiny.

Grey eyes watched with impossibly more intensity before swinging past to the two burly guards positioned a few feet away.

'Dismiss your bodyguards. You won't need them tonight.'

Genie started, then berated herself for her lapse in concentration. She opened her mouth to do as he bade, but held her tongue for several seconds. Dr Douglas would perhaps describe it as childish but she didn't want to show this man how eagerly her senses jumped to accommodate him. Without her express permission.

When he raised that sardonic eyebrow, she turned and nodded her dismissal.

She followed him to the passenger side of his car, where he hesitated before opening the door, his gaze tracking her body shamelessly from head to toe.

'After the way we parted, I was convinced you'd come out in a tracksuit. You look stunning, Genie.'

The whirlpool in her belly spun faster. 'This isn't a social outing, Mr Valente. You don't need to fall into predictable platitudes.'

One corner of his mouth lifted. 'I don't think you want me to stray outside predictability, Genie. Otherwise, I risk being intensely inappropriate.'

Sensation akin to mild electricity flowed through her veins as his gaze lingered on her mouth. To combat it, she grasped at the first defensive straw. 'If you're thinking of making juvenile rubbing lamp or wish jokes about my name, don't bother. I've heard them all.'

He pulled the door open with smooth, suppressed force. Waited until she was installed in the bucket seat before shutting the door.

She watched him round the low bonnet of the car, his leonine glide impossible to resist watching. When an oncoming set of headlights lit up his face, the static intensified.

She continued to watch him once he slid in beside her. And then even as he reached across and secured her seat belt, reminding her that she'd forgotten. Reminding her of his focus-altering scent when she inhaled.

'I'm many things, Genie. Juvenile isn't one of them.'

She believed him. From what she'd learned of him, he'd vaulted from pre-puberty straight into adulthood. Her search for those few vital adolescent years had come up empty in the time she'd had. As much as she didn't want to be, she was intrigued by those missing years.

'And it's okay to admit you find me attractive, too,' he added as he slid the car into gear and accelerated from her sanctuary.

Genie shrugged, eagerly falling back on firm and solid logic. 'It's a physiological reaction to the opposite sex. I'm confident I could line up fifty men on the street right now and guarantee I will have a similar reaction to at least two of them.'

From the dashboard lights she caught something distinctly... primitive flash in his eyes. 'You're sure about that?'

The tingling in her body escalated and that scent seemed to reach out to her, demanding that she breathe it...*him*...in... 'Oh, yes. The very structure of our society has primed us to find more than one individual compatible enough to have sex with. Otherwise there wouldn't be almost eight billion of us walking the earth.' She tilted her head, allowed her gaze to trail him up and down. 'Surely an exemplary specimen such as yourself wouldn't conform to the archaic thinking that there is only one person for every human being on the planet? The proverbial soulmate?'

His nostrils flared, as if she'd touched a nerve.

Don't pick on the weak.

She pursed her lips and gave it few moments' thought. Was she stepping out of line? She didn't think so.

She'd weighed up her opponent before embarking on this skirmish and she was sure—hell, she was confident—he had the mental dexterity to keep up with her.

'For their sake, I'd advise you not to summon those fifty men in my presence. I won't be responsible for my actions otherwise.' There was a scalpel-sharp edge to his tone. A tightening of his grip around the steering wheel.

She frowned. 'You're...not pleased with my response.'

A short laugh grated from his throat. 'I will let it slide just this once, *pequeña*,' he rumbled.

His clenched jaw suggested the proposed 'slide' wasn't an immediate thing, so Genie chose to remain silent for the rest of the short journey.

Silence continued to reign as they were seated in a private booth in a secluded part of the Mayfair restaurant that boasted three Michelin stars on a discreet plaque at the door.

But after he'd ordered wine and their first course had been delivered, she clasped her hands on the pristine napkin in her lap.

Time to lay a card or two on the table.

'I struggle with social cues. You should know that.'

He looked up from his veal starter and fixed his eyes on her. Silence thudded between them for a long stretch. 'Most geniuses do,' he responded eventually.

There was that peculiar fluttering in her stomach again. She looked down at her scallops.

Maybe she should've stayed away from the molluscs. But...

she'd never had an adverse effect from eating them before. Therefore the logical conclusion was that something else...or *someone* else was responsible for the sensation.

She looked up.

He was watching her with those leonine eyes. Was she expected to thank him? Was his response courteous or merely observatory?

Several minutes passed before she realised they were staring at one another. That his mouth, while unmoving, held the minutest hint of amusement.

'Is something wrong with your food?'

'I haven't decided yet.'

'Explain.'

Her grip tightened momentarily on her fork. 'There's a sensation in my stomach that I can't apply a source to. Well, no, that's not true. I mean, I'm not sure if it's indigestion or...'

'Or?'

Mild shock waves rippled through her. 'I don't think I have a precise name for it.'

This time his lips developed a distinct curve. A smile. A... transformative smile that held her attention completely. She'd known that he was a handsome man. But she hadn't taken into account just how compelling a simple smile could be. How... *enrapturing*.

Then she frowned. Because that smile looked entirely at her expense. 'Am I missing something, Mr Valente?'

'I dare say you are, *pequeña*,' he said cryptically.

Which rattled her cage even further. 'I don't like mysteries.'

'You don't? Isn't chasing mystery what fuels your work?'

She shook her head. 'You're confusing drive with mysterious.'

'At the risk of sounding simplistic, your brain has informed you that you're attracted to me. Your body is merely catching up.'

She blinked. 'By giving me indigestion?'

'When you get used to it, you'll be able to differentiate it from indigestion.'

'You're assuming that this feeling will last longer than I wish it to.'

'While it's your choice whether to act on it or not, some things are beyond your body's control. This is one of them.'

'I disagree,' she snapped immediately. This felt like something she needed to defend herself from.

This time the movement of his lips was more pronounced, redirecting her attention from his eyes to his mouth. To the near perfect symmetry of the thinner upper and the fuller bottom. To the divot dissecting the top lip in a riveting V-shape and—

'First lesson in this new realm you find yourself in, Genie. Don't stare at a man's mouth like that unless you wish to provoke a specific reaction.'

'What sort of reaction?'

A sound emitted from his throat, one she couldn't quite decipher immediately because it was animalistic in nature. 'That of the carnal kind. You stare at my mouth and all I can think about is how much I want to taste yours.'

A pulse of heat surged from the very place she was experiencing the sensation. No, not quite accurate. It was lower. In her pelvis. Between her thighs. She crossed her legs but the hot tingle didn't dissipate. So she dragged her gaze upward. But then she was confronted with eyes that didn't look quite the same as they had a few moments ago. They were heated, narrowed. Laser focused on her in a way that made her thighs clench tighter.

'Understood. I will endeavour to not stare at your mouth, Mr Valente.'

Another sound surged from his throat again, more animalistic than before. It sounded like…a growl. It was primitive enough to make her grimace inwardly. But not enough to stop another intensely physical reaction.

Wetness between her legs.

Stiffening and pinching of her nipples.

Slow drag of heat through her pelvis.

Reactions of the carnal kind.

Inconvenient while it lasted but perhaps advantageous where it counted.

Setting her fork down, she linked her fingers once more. 'I've come to a decision, Mr Valente.'

That fierce light she was beginning to attribute to heightened emotion lit his eyes before he penned it once more. 'I'm eager to hear it.'

Unexpected emotion clogged her throat, demanding she clear it before she could speak. It was perfectly rational. This was everything she'd been working towards. A lifelong wish guarded and nurtured through her solitary and neglected childhood. It was right she gave it due gravity.

So she took another breath. 'I'll consider selling you my algorithm on one condition.'

'Which is?' he prodded.

'Which is that you impregnate me.'

CHAPTER TWO

SEVE HAD CHOSEN this restaurant for its privacy, pleasing ambience and excellent cuisine.

He'd spotted a few business acquaintances on his way to their table but the ultimate reason he'd wanted to come here was because discretion was guaranteed.

There were no raucous birthday celebrations or hen dos deafening everyone else.

Which was why he *knew* he hadn't misheard her.

So it was most likely the shock that made him demand, 'What did you say?' in tones that sounded like the crunch of broken glass.

The stunning genius in front of him merely pursed her lips, immediately drawing his attention—as had happened aggravatingly often since they'd first met this afternoon—to plump crimson lips that stood out like a neon sign on her otherwise pale face. Coupled with her astonishing green eyes fringed by thick black lashes, they made her face resemble a fairy-tale character come to life.

It was the first of many revelatory shocks when he'd impelled his way into her office this morning. Before then, he'd only seen grainy pictures of the child prodigy turned innovative genius who'd written the unparalleled ground-breaking code with the ability to significantly combat the global climate crisis, amongst many things.

Nowhere on that list of astounding revelations had he anticipated…*this* reality.

I struggle with social cues.

Abrupt but vulnerable. Honest. A brief glimpse behind her impressive titanium armour.

Dios mio. How on earth could five random words immediately give him a hard-on? Five words that should make him hurry up and be done with this so he could get on with the important business of helping Cardosia, but instead made him want to know everything about her. Like how she'd even arrived at her absurd demand.

She'd floored him completely—a feat most would pay hard-earned money to witness when it came to Seve Valente.

'Ideally, I'd like it to happen before our deal is concluded. I wish to give birth before my twenty-ninth birthday. If it helps, my ovulation window is from next Wednesday to Saturday.'

Seve was glad he hadn't taken a bite of food. He feared he would be writhing on the floor choking on his veal by now.

'Eugenie.'

She froze, her green eyes widening to saucers. 'You know my given name,' she muttered before she shook her head. 'Of course you do. If it helps progress things, I'll allow you to call me that. No one else does though.'

'Why not?'

She blinked. Then a tiny spark he hadn't even been aware of died in her eyes. Immediately, illogically, he wanted it back. 'My parents forbade anyone from calling me that. They said Genie was more appropriate. Because it sounded a lot like—'

'Genius?' he guessed.

Another spark died and he bit back a growl.

'Yes.'

He inhaled long and deep to establish some semblance of calm. 'When we're more…comfortable with each other you'll tell me which one you prefer. For now you'll repeat what you just said about…wanting a…' He paused, not sure why he couldn't even utter the word.

She couldn't know that on his list of things he intended to avoid in this life was fathering a child. That the still vivid horror of his own childhood demanded that the label never be pinned on him.

'A child, Mr Valente. I want you to provide me with the requisite equipment to create a baby.'

The requisite equipment…

Was it possible to be punch-drunk having consumed only a few drops of alcohol? He had to give her her due, though. It wasn't often he was this astounded by anything any more.

At the ripe old age of thirty-six he was severely jaded. Nothing and no one had surprised him for a long time. People were predictably greedy, cruel and selfish, and not necessarily in that order.

On paper, Genie Merchant had been just another run-of-the-mill eccentric genius who smugly believed that the world revolved around her. He'd encountered more than his fair share in his line of business. They often laboured under the wrong belief that their wish should be everyone else's command and when they discovered that Severino Valente didn't intend to jump, they tended to throw a strop, then postured before quickly capitulating to his will.

He'd waited for *weeks* for Genie Merchant to fall into line. Had watched her attempt to align herself with a trove of unsuitable candidates. Hell, he'd had to slyly step in once or twice to ensure the more deplorable runners on her list didn't progress past the initial consideration stage.

After weeks had gone by, and after he'd had to admit that this time *he* was the one destined to capitulate, it'd chafed for a while before he'd set the unfamiliar feeling aside for the greater good.

For Cardosia.

'I'm a man who's unequivocal about stating what he wants. And yet I'm under the impression that I've skipped several rungs of this conversation without due process.'

A pink tongue slicked over her Snow White lips as she shook her head. 'You're not. You haven't. I'm also a woman who doesn't hold back from stating what she wants. I've told you what I want. Mindless chitchat isn't necessary.'

Slowly, an unnerving sensation wound its way like a dark underground river through him. 'Tell me you didn't make this proposal to anyone else. Is this a contingency that was attached to all your meetings today?' Why did that matter? And, *Dios mio*, why did the very idea of it fill him with such fury?

True, he hadn't expected the near-reclusive genius to be so intensely...feminine. Alluring and breathtakingly beautiful. Not the gangly teenager wearing regulation nerdy glasses with mousy dark hair, oftentimes hiding behind her more publicity-seeking parents.

The reality of her had been so shocking that, for several seconds, he'd believed he'd walked into the wrong office.

No one had warned him the genius with the jaw-dropping IQ inhabited the body of a nineteen-fifties pin-up. That the ropey, lifeless hair was in fact lustrous tresses that invited a man...*him*...to sink his fingers into the heavy mass, grip it firmly to nudge her head back so he could plunder those sinful lips. To learn her taste and savour her essence.

And yes, his initial reaction after seeing her in the flesh for the first time had been...visceral. He was a red-blooded male with vigorous passions and a healthy libido, after all. But—

'I did not,' she replied crisply.

A layer of that furore subsided at her answer, but he still remained highly out of sorts, a baffling and irritating condition.

All he had to do was utter the *no* lodged like a heavy stone in his gut. Redirect the conversation back to the pertinent and pressing reason they were here. And yet all he could think of was that once he denied her with that 'no', she would seek the next candidate. That *he* would be consigned to the reject list.

So what?

He didn't want children. Definitely not for the sake of procreating to fulfil the cachet objective the way his parents had. And most definitely not as a manipulation tool or a bargaining chip to be peddled for power. His whole childhood had been a joke, a cruel game of false affection, abject neglect and quid pro quo no child should be subjected to.

It was an experience that had, if not damaged him, at least psychologically scarred him. The risk that he could pass it on to his child, that he might unconsciously visit that same cruelty on an innocent offspring?

No. *Never.*

The searing reminder burned away the peculiar sensation swimming in his gut, attempting to move that stone. And when he exhaled next, it was with the reassurance that common sense had reasserted itself. 'The answer is no, Miss Merchant.'

Her shoulders stiffened for a fraction of time, then deflated a little. Before she gave a curt, dismissive nod. 'Very well.'

His eyes narrowed and that furore returned, twice as incendiary. '*Very well?* What does that mean?' The intensity of his reaction shocked Seve.

As it did Genie, if her sharp intake of breath was an indication. For several seconds, she merely blinked at him. Then, she reached for her glass, taking a sip of water and setting it down in precise motions before she glanced at him. 'I sense that I'm supposed to either beg, convince you to change your mind or take your answer at face value. Option number three seems the most logical. We're both pressed for time, and you stated a few minutes ago that you're an unequivocal man so it stands to reason that you wouldn't say no just to play games with me.'

Seve was…nonplussed. And he hated it. This woman was drawing emotions from him he deeply resented.

Then get back on course. Be done with this.

He forced a reluctant nod. 'Good. This dinner is to discuss you selling your algorithm to me. You haven't lost sight of that, I hope?'

Her lashes swept down for a moment but when she lifted her head again only the faintest shadow in her eyes reflected the peculiar conversation that had just taken place. 'No, I haven't.'

A growl rose in his throat, but he quickly killed it. 'You're not what I expected.'

'I've heard that often enough before, Mr Valente.'

'Seve.'

'Excuse me?'

'Call me Seve.'

The pulse leapt faster at her throat and his fingers itched to trace it. 'I would rather not.'

'Why do you want a child?' *Dios*, why was he pursuing this?

She stiffened, then waved an elegant hand. 'That's none of your business. You refused my request. I don't owe you an explanation.'

His insides clenched. It was the same sort of dismissiveness he'd been subjected to as a child. The sort of treatment he'd tried—and succeeded—in throwing into a vault and tossing away the key. Now that unpleasant box was rattling, threatening to fly open and throw up all his bitterness and resentment about his childhood.

Only if you allow it. Only if you dwell on this.

Deeming him dismissed, she started to quiz him about his plans for her algorithm.

The subject was close enough to his heart that he could rattle away answers without guise or reservation. Her algorithm would direct the scientists and environmentalists where to focus their energy in reversing the ecological damage being done to Cardosia. Amongst many other advantages. But even as he rattled off his country's many needs, his unanswered questions loomed larger as they ate their main course, then the dessert Genie ordered and the espresso he chose for himself.

By the time she sank her silver spoon into the strawberry and cream concoction and lifted it to her mouth, Seve couldn't hold back any longer.

'You're going to sell to me. We both know that.'

Her green eyes sparked and something ignited within him. 'I wouldn't be so presump—'

He held up a halting hand. 'If this was going nowhere you wouldn't have ordered dessert.'

She looked down at the concoction as if surprised it was in front of her. 'Perhaps I have a near-addictive sweet tooth that needs servicing.'

'Which you can indulge in the privacy of your home once you get there. You're not that undisciplined.' She opened her mouth again but he beat her to it once more. 'This is a social cue I can help you out with, Miss Merchant. You're lingering because you're not ready for this dinner to end. You've done your homework on me, and it was more than satisfactory because you would've cancelled if you had deep enough reservations. Don't forget, I know you threw Frank Graham out within five minutes. You know I'm the most viable candidate. So it begs the question, why are you holding back from giving us both what we want?'

She set her spoon down and folded her hands in her lap. Seve was beginning to recognise that cue, too. She did it to guard herself from the gravity of her needs. To collect herself before she gave too much away.

It stood to reason that a woman with her level of intelligence would need to, otherwise she would be taken advantage of. And why did that *too* send a pulse of fury through him?

Perhaps he needed his own head examined.

'This is my life's work thus far. It's logical that I give it more than a meal's duration worth of consideration, don't you think?'

Something snagged in his chest, but he dismissed it. He was done with entertaining peculiar feelings. 'Yes, it is. And while you do I have questions of my own.'

Shock, then wariness filmed her eyes. 'You do?'

He shrugged. 'I have some burden of responsibility too. One of which is to know why a young woman like you is eager to offload her life's work. And before you say it's none of my business, I must insist that your answer is contingent on whether this deal goes forward, of course.'

'Why?'

'Because I'd be a fool to go in blind only for you to turn around and build a similar code a year from now and sell it to my competitor.'

Affront quickened her breath, causing her breasts to strain against her dress. It was enough to flood him with red-hot desire. Enough to thicken his shaft and trigger potent craving he hadn't experienced in a long time.

'I would never do that.'

'I haven't got this far in life by taking people at their word, Miss Merchant. I'm sensing you have experience of the same.'

She swallowed and, again, he couldn't stop himself from following the graceful line of her throat, wondering how that curve in her neck would feel beneath his lips. On his tongue. Her scent filling his nostrils.

Por l'amor de…

'I can put that in writing if you want.'

They both held still.

Because, in that moment, the gravity of her words, her capitulation, needed its presence acknowledged.

After a full minute, she exhaled, her shoulders relaxing a fraction. She looked away momentarily before her bold gaze met his again.

Still, she said nothing.

He hid a smile. She was formidable. Enough to tweak and

hold his interest. It made him wonder in what other ways she could achieve that. And he silently shook his head.

Theirs *should* and would remain a transactional relationship. He didn't have the head space to deal with the untamed emotions she triggered in him.

'You will sell me your code.' He needed the words spoken out loud so he could finish this and move on to more important things. Like helping his people. Like stopping his uncle from stripping his beloved homeland of every last resource.

'Yes.'

The affirmative answer he'd wished. And yet...

Suddenly, he wanted to be somewhere else. Somewhere the presence of others didn't intrude on this moment.

'We'll take your dessert to go,' he said, shocking himself once more. Hadn't he promised himself one minute ago that he'd move on?

'Go where?'

Our separate ways. Now that I have what I want.

'Somewhere quieter where we won't be interrupted. The English weather is being uncharacteristically cooperative. Inside or outside. We can go anywhere you want.'

Her nose wrinkled cutely. 'I'm not an outside type of person.'

He shrugged. 'Because you haven't been exposed to the *right* type of outside.'

'I'm not sure what that means.'

He fished out his wallet and tossed a few hundred pounds on the table. Summoning the waiter, he gave his request.

A minute later, her dessert was boxed up and the *maître d'* was wishing them a good evening.

But when they stepped outside, a spurt of misgiving sprang up.

He'd never mixed business with pleasure and he was certain he wasn't about to start. But almost instantly, he was flooded by the unsettling sensations that had been driving him all night.

Seve wasn't a man who liked to admit weakness, but as he sped through the streets of London towards his destination, he couldn't fail to register that he was helpless against the compulsion pounding in his veins.

Compulsion that had nothing to do with the fact that he now had within his grasp his most effective tool of toppling his uncle's power and setting Cardosia back on the right track.

And everything to do with Genie Merchant.

Somehow he wasn't entirely surprised when he pulled up to his private parking space in the underground garage of his duplex.

'Where are we?' Genie asked.

She'd remained silent throughout the journey. Now she looked around for a moment before turning her gaze to him with one eyebrow raised.

'Somewhere you can finish that—' he nodded at the box in her hand '—while we finalise the terms of sale.'

Her fingers spasmed on the box, a tiny betraying movement he caught nonetheless. Because everything about her interested him to the point of slavish intrigue.

He realised he'd held his breath when it rushed out at her eventual nod of consent. He unfastened her seat belt with more alacrity than he'd intended, and with every click of their footsteps towards the private elevator that shot them up to his penthouse, he ignored the inner voice demanding to know what he was doing.

The East London residence he used when he was in England had been constructed to impress men of his business stature and influence. Every sophisticated amenity was within reach. But what had sold the vast, luxurious space to Seve—as was the intention—was the view both day and night.

At almost eleven p.m., the carpet of lights and distinct icons of the bridges that dissected the Thames drew Genie past the soft dove-grey walls interspersed with some of his favourite art and sculptures, past the sumptuous matching sofas and lofty ceilings, past the Italian marble floors and the specially commissioned Swarovski crystal chandeliers.

To the outside.

He watched her make a beeline for the wide outdoor sofa facing the spectacular view, something inside kicking wildly as he witnessed her unfettered interest in *his* view. He hid a smile as she took it all in.

Then, he went indoors to his kitchen, returning with a silver spoon, which he held out to her.

She looked up, a touch surprised. 'Oh. Thanks.'

Her thumb brushed over his knuckles as she took the utensil from him. Her breathing faltered, a tinge of colour staining her cheeks at his unabashed interest. Again, he tried to smother his wild senses when her gaze swept down, depriving him of the vital connection.

Stepping around the sofa, he took the opposite end, and watched as she ate her sweet.

Two bites in, Seve crossed his legs to hide the effect of what the spoon continually disappearing into her mouth did to his libido.

Dios mio. Perhaps it was time to call up a past flame, take care of his physical need with a night of vigorous sex so he could think more clearly.

His last visit to Cardosia four months ago had driven home the urgency of his actions, and left room for little else. But now he had a solution within reach he couldn't be distracted by—

'Six months.'

Although he knew what she was referring to, he still raised his eyebrows. He told himself he wanted to make sure they were on the same page, but underneath that prompt, there was a burning need to hear her voice. To keep her engaged. 'Six months?' he echoed.

Her green gaze flitted over to him, then rushed over his

body before returning to the view. But he hadn't missed her quickened breath when she glanced at his torso and crossed legs. She took her time to swallow before she spoke.

'The oversight period. I want to review it every six months.'

He shook his head. 'Fifteen months.'

Her eyes returned to his filled with more fire. 'No. Ten months. That's six times over the course of five years. That's non-negotiable.'

He would see this intriguing creature every ten months. Possibly pick her incredible brain on ways to better improve the dire conditions in Cardosia. Keep the lines of communication open.

It was a sensible option he would be a fool to dismiss.

Are you sure that's all it is?

He gritted his teeth, intensely irritated with the unrelenting inner voice. 'I will agree to ten months, as long as it's done on site.'

Her spoon, holding another delicate concoction, paused halfway to her mouth as she considered his addendum. It shouldn't have been sexy. He didn't have a sweet tooth in his body, and yet he found himself leaning forward, swiping a crumb off the corner of her fork with his thumb and tasting it. 'Just so we're clear, that means I want you in Cardosia. In person. No exceptions.'

Her hand trembled a little, her eyelashes fluttering as she raised the morsel and closed her plumps lips over it. By the time her tongue flicked out, Seve was fully erect, the pressure in his groin unbearable and every square inch of his body on fire.

God, he needed to get laid. Like yesterday.

Again, she chewed and swallowed before she answered, keeping them both waiting. 'I can do that. Cardosia is in a beautiful part of the world.'

Pride and determination burst to life in his chest. '*Sí.* I in-

tend to do everything in my power to ensure it stays that way.'
From afar, though. Returning home roused his demons to life.

Seve knew that was the moment he had her total agreement. It was also probably when he should've ended their
meeting. Driven her home or, better yet, called his twenty-
four-hour car service and placed some vitally prudent distance between them.

Instead, he pulled out his phone and dialled a familiar number. He finished the five-minute conversation to find her staring at him.

'You're getting the contract documents drawn up right now?
It's almost midnight,' she stated in surprise.

'I have lawyers on retainer in several time zones in the
world. My New York lawyers are standing by to get started.'
He paused, his gaze drifting over her face with a hunger he
was unaccustomed to. 'Do you wish to get the ball rolling or
do you need to get your beauty sleep?'

Her chin went up, mild outrage in her eyes. 'Don't pigeon-
hole me with stereotypes, Mr Valente. Do *you* require beauty
sleep?'

The way his senses were rampaging, sleep was the last thing
on his mind right now. 'Not at all, *pequeña*,' he murmured.
'I can go all night.'

He stifled a groan as colour rushed freely and enthusiastically up her neck and into her cheeks. He clenched his fist
tighter, fighting the need to stroke her skin, feel that gush with
his fingers. 'So can I,' she tossed out in a defiant, breathlessly
husky voice.

Seve dragged a hand through his hair, sadistically tugging
on the strands to better concentrate his mind. The sexual chemistry between them was insane but Cardosia was more important.

'Good.' He sent a quick text before putting his phone away.
'Then let's talk numbers. I know your highest bid was eight
hundred million. I'm prepared to top that to one billion dollars

if you throw in your building and all relevant staff as part of the deal. I need your tech experts to configure the algorithm to suit my needs as soon as possible.'

Her jaw sagged, her luscious lips dropping open as she inhaled in shock. 'I... A billion dollars?'

'Yes. That's how badly I want you— Your algorithm.' He allowed himself a smile. 'And it's not without pleasure for me to welcome another woman to the billion-dollar club.'

'I don't care about that,' she stated primly, her eyes flashing again.

He believed her. He'd studied her long enough to know money wasn't what drove her.

So what did?

Unbidden, his gaze dropped to her flat stomach. The belly she intended to fill with a baby as soon as possible if her statement at dinner was an indication. With a billion dollars she'd never have to work another day in her life. She would be free to have an entire brood if she wanted.

Without him...

'What do you care about, then?' he asked before he could stop himself.

She started, her attention drawn from the stratospheric figure he'd tossed into her lap to his question.

'I thought we agreed to leave personal business alone?'

'Did we? I don't recall agreeing to anything of the sort. You said it wasn't my business.'

'It still isn't—'

She paused when she saw movement behind them.

The text he'd sent was to the twenty-four-hour concierge service. The attendant wheeled in a sterling silver tray with glasses and a bottle of vintage Dom Perignon set in an ice bucket.

Seve directed him where to put it then nodded his thanks. Once they were alone, he popped the champagne, poured her a glass and took one for himself before he sat back.

'What shall we drink to, besides the obvious?'

Her nostrils fluttered. 'You're determined. But you must know this isn't going anywhere because I'm equally determined.'

'Think of it less as prying and more like...humouring me.' It was a deeper, more visceral need than that, once whose source he couldn't quite fathom.

Or could he?

While, on the surface, Genie Merchant had exemplary qualities stemming from her brilliant mind, she was the last person he would've laid a maternal label on. Which was why her demand had knocked him sideways. But it had done more than that.

It'd unearthed unwanted memories of his childhood, and the reasons why he didn't want children. And, perhaps equally importantly, why not everyone who wanted to procreate should.

His own parents were a typical example.

While his childhood had been hellish, not once had he wished for a sibling to alleviate that loneliness. Because even as a small child the last thing he'd wanted was for a brother, even worse, a sister to suffer the way he had. To live in fear of the wrong word or look inviting corporal punishment, which was gleefully doled out under 'character building'.

It would've been unbearable to watch another child sentenced to his father's and uncle's brutal fists at the smallest infraction. Even worse to see his mother do nothing while her son was abused.

It was a small crumb of comfort in a hellscape he'd thought he'd put behind him until Genie Merchant unearthed the memories.

'Maybe I want the same thing you claim you do. To leave the world a better place than I found it,' she said, blithely unaware of the churning within him.

'By filling it with babies?' he gritted out with more bitterness than he'd intended to reveal.

She stiffened, her skin going pale as she stared at him with pained eyes.

A flash of regret fired through him but it wasn't deep enough for him to issue an apology. Because he felt strongly about this. Perhaps too strongly.

'I think we should stick to business from here on out, Mr Valente,' she said stiffly.

But the boy turned man who wore the scarred consequences, and understood what an ill-thought-out plan to procreate for the hell of it could produce, wasn't ready to let this go.

'So you can get to the more urgent business of asking another man to give you a child?' Again, his whole being reacted violently to Genie Merchant repeating her request to some other man. To offering her body to another to take, to touch. To fill with his seed.

With a barely stifled snarl, he launched to his feet, the untouched champagne spilling over his fingers as he stalked to the low glass wall bordering the terrace. He wasn't even aware he was growling until she cleared her throat behind him.

'I believe your social cues are abandoning you, Mr Valente.' The sharp click of her setting down her glass on the coffee table made him turn around. 'Perhaps we should take this back up in the morn—'

'No!' Her eyes widened at his tone, and he forced himself to inhale slowly. 'No.' He modulated his voice. 'Consider the matter dropped.' *For now.* It wasn't…shouldn't concern him what she did with her new-found wealth. Or her body.

She tilted her head, studying him like a new strain of code she found interesting. When his body started to react to that too, he surged forward.

'The subject of children…unsettles you,' she murmured, open curiosity stamped on her face.

He clenched his teeth. 'The frivolity with which people pursue parenthood does, yes.'

Her eyes shadowed and, after a moment, she looked past him to the view. 'I'm not a frivolous person, Mr Valente.'

'Seve.'

Her gaze swung back to him. 'What?'

'Another request for you to call me Seve,' he pressed with biting insistence alarming in its intensity.

She blinked. 'Why?' The question was filled with genuine curiosity. And burgeoning self-awareness that flared renewed heat in her cheeks.

'Because it will please me.'

Her breath feathered out in a little rush. 'Why would I want to please you?'

He shrugged. 'Call it an experiment. Do it and see the result.'

She frowned. 'Why—?'

'Don't overthink it, Genie.'

'I rarely overthink. I give every matter an allotted amount of time. Then I move on.'

His lips twitched and once again he acknowledged how much he enjoyed their verbal jousting. It was almost enough to soothe his ruffled nerves. *Almost*. 'That's not true, is it? You were dwelling on your disappointment when I came to your office this morning.'

Her throat moved and he vaguely registered that she was nervous. 'You're mistaken, I'm sure.'

He stared down into the bubbles in his drink for several moments. 'Let's make each other a promise. Let's always be honest with each other.'

She considered it, her gaze once again flitting to the view before meeting his. 'That's acceptable.'

'That's acceptable, what?' he enquired mildly, his tone at variance with the jangling nerves performing acrobatics within him. This was yet another absurdity he couldn't figure out. And yet the compulsion raged without cease.

Her nostrils fluttered and for the longest second, he thought she would refuse. And then, 'That's acceptable, *Seve*.'

Perhaps the fates knew why he'd insisted. Because something clenched decadently inside him when she uttered his name. When she tilted her head, exposing the sleek, graceful line of her neck and asked, 'Did I say it right?'

'You know you did,' he responded thickly. 'Your perfectionism won't let you get it wrong. Say it again,' he commanded, pretty sure he was skirting some dangerous line but not caring in that moment.

'Seve,' she whispered, unconsciously sultry in a way that he suspected she wasn't aware of, which made it all the more desirable.

'Dios mío. Qué demonios está pasando?' he muttered, half expecting his inner voice would mock him for asking what the hell was going on.

'Dígame usted,' she replied in perfect Spanish. *You tell me.*

His head reared up. 'I forgot you speak my language.'

'And several others besides,' she reminded him without fanfare.

Witnessing her being so comfortable in her utter brilliance? It was irresistible.

But there was one language she was untutored in. She couldn't quite hide her arousal.

Her body all but *trembled* as she stared at his mouth then his body with blatant hunger that only fuelled his own. That chipped away at his already failing resistance.

'We seem to have lost sight of our toast.'

'Nothing has followed a predictable pattern this evening,' she answered, picking up her glass.

He clinked his glass to hers, took a healthy gulp of vintage champagne, then uttered more wildly unpredicted words. 'Maybe it's a sign to just go with the flow.'

She sipped her champagne, then shook her head, bewilder-

ment mingling with her arousal. 'But…why can't I resist this…
pull? It's quite infuriating, but I can't stop.'

Seve groaned. With every cell in his body he wished she
hadn't uttered those words. Hadn't been unabashed about what
she was feeling.

Because the next flood that surged washed away the last
of his resistance. Made him set his glass aside and spear his
fingers through her hair the way he'd been fantasising about
all evening. Hell, all damn day!

And heaven help him if the strands weren't as silky and
luxurious as he'd imagined. She didn't pull away. *Dios*, she
stared at him with such unfettered and curious desire, he wondered how innocent she was. Whether she knew what such a
look did to a man.

Leaning down, he gave into the urge and brushed his lips
across hers, featherlight and flame-stoking. 'Does that pull
hunger for this?' he breathed against her satin-soft mouth.

She swayed closer. 'Yes.'

'And this?' He nipped at the corner of her mouth.

She gasped and her eyes fluttered closed, her body surging closer. 'Yes.'

Seve licked the sting he'd caused, then continued licking
until her lips parted for him. But before he could delve in to
devour the way his senses screamed at him to, a splash of cold
wetness stopped him.

They both looked down to see her champagne spilling over
her fingers.

Seve relieved her of the glass, then, capturing her fingers,
he drew them to his mouth, licking the tart liquid from them.
And with each lap of her smooth skin, the blood pounded
harder through his veins, her hitched moans lighting further
flames to his senses.

'How infuriated are you right now, Genie?' he mocked teas-
ingly.

'Extremely,' she returned huskily, her beautiful eyes limpid with desire, her breath emerging in pants. 'But please don't stop.'

Lust raged free, the restraint he'd placed on himself all night unshackled. He sucked on her fingers until her knees gave way.

He caught her in his arms, sealed his mouth to hers and finally delivered the kiss they both craved.

Then because he knew in his bones it wouldn't be enough, that nothing but complete possession would do, Seve swung her into his arms, turned and strode purposefully indoors.

CHAPTER THREE

SHE WASN'T DRUNK, at least not from alcohol. She'd only taken a sip of champagne and spilled a significant portion of the rest.

Yet, her senses were in free fall, floating through sensation she'd never experienced before. All created by the man she'd agreed to sell her life's work to.

The man who'd refused her brazen request and should therefore be on her *strictly platonic* list. The man who had arrogantly spelled out her attraction to him and should therefore be on her *thinks too insufferably highly of himself so stay away* list.

And yet he was the same man her body strained against, the one around whose neck she tightened her arms as he walked them towards goodness knew where. Whose eyes devoured her like a raging forest fire without mercy. Who made every cell in her body tingle although even she knew that was scientifically unlikely.

The spaces he walked through were lit by low lamps that gave her brief glimpses of impeccable taste and decor. And even if they were fully lit, she wouldn't have taken proper note.

Because the drugging effect of his lips on her neck made her eyes too heavy to keep open, every self-preserving instinct paused while she drifted through nirvana.

But when he reached his destination and set her down, she roused long enough to note they were in a vast, supremely masculine bedroom, the greys and whites and chrome from before echoed throughout the space.

And then Seve was commanding her attention again, sensual promise in the hands that drew her to his body, in the fingers that spiked back into her hair, and in the lips descending on hers.

A fleeting thought *un*-paused her consciousness for the briefest moment.

Was she really doing this? Agitating an already unsettling evening with sexual chemistry?

Yes.

A brush of his firm lips on hers. 'These lips have driven me crazy all day.'

Genie hung onto her cogency long enough to challenge him. Because she'd learned something new this evening. She *enjoyed* sparring intellectually with him. 'Why? Because you don't like what they had to say?'

He laughed, and the sound filled her with even more impossible yearning. 'On the contrary. I relished every word because they intrigued me. Far too much. They also made me want to do more of this.'

He swooped down and recaptured her lips, stoking the fervour already churning in her midriff. She'd had minimal health issues in her life, but Genie recalled one particularly virulent fever she'd had one winter. This sensation was like that but in a much more *exciting* way. A way that made her crave more of it. Made her want to burn with it. Because every logical deduction promised an explosive outcome.

And she so wanted to explode.

'More,' she gasped when he lifted his head.

He didn't deliver. Instead his eyes narrowed, his blazing gaze promising things she couldn't quite fathom but actively craved. 'Beg me,' he commanded gruffly. 'Beg me for what you want, Genie.'

It should've been nonsensical. Illogical.

He was denying them both what they plainly wanted. She wasn't delusional enough to have conjured up the need she saw stamped boldly on his face. And yet he was asking her to degrade herself. To lower herself…

So why did she want to?

Why did the very thought of it send further flames leaping through her bloodstream, intensifying the chemical reaction to this man?

A slow, conceited smile spread over his lips. Lips reddened and slightly swollen from devouring hers. 'The idea turns you on, doesn't it?'

Self-preservation dictated she deny it, but she hesitated.

Let's always be honest with each other.

'Why does it?' she asked instead.

'Because your instincts tell you it will heighten your experience. Both our experiences. You yearn to say it. I need to hear it. Sometimes it's as simple as that.'

Was it?

She'd never begged for anything in her life. Not even the affection and regard her parents had cruelly denied her. Despite it being the hardest thing she'd ever done, she'd smothered those impulses until they were buried deep. Not deep enough to rescue her from the pain of their actions but enough so no one could guess her torment. Her abject loneliness.

Would it have been as simple as voicing the words? Pleading for what she wanted?

Or was she slapping a simplistic solution on a deeper problem? Didn't the textbooks and renowned experts state that affection should be freely offered, not fought or shamed for?

Fingers trailed down her neck and she shivered free from her unsettling wondering.

This *was* different.

This was sexual desire.

And as Seve had already shown her, it had different rules. Different parameters.

For starters, this was fleeting. Between consenting adults. And one night only.

Perhaps it was that simple. A giving and taking of carnal pleasure.

His searing gaze compelled her, his body poised in arrogant expectation.

'Please,' she tested, then felt a loud rush in her ears as his eyes lit up, his fingers stroking the leaping pulse at her throat. 'I want you. Please,' she whispered again.

A guttural groan of satisfaction was her reward. A feral sound she wouldn't have attributed to deepening her pleasure before tonight.

'It's my turn to demand more. Tell me what you want me to do to you, *bonita*.'

'Why?' she demanded again.

And that innocent query, that thirst for knowledge, made him harder than he'd ever been before.

His voice was barely coherent as he responded. 'Because it heightens *my* experience. Call it a primal thing if you want. But I need it.'

Wide eyes stared at him for a handful of seconds before they dropped to his mouth.

Seve could barely control his groan when she slicked her tongue over her lips and said, 'Please, kiss me again, Seve. I'm begging. I need more of everything you have to give.'

He was certain he slipped into temporary madness in that moment. Time, space and thought fled his consciousness.

He only *felt*. Experienced a depth of sensation he'd never considered possible.

With hands that shook from pure need, he peeled the dress off her body.

And was rewarded with a vision that siphoned every ounce of air from his lungs. *'Dulce cielo, eres hermosa,'* he praised, in a voice he didn't recognise.

His knees nearly buckled as he saw the surge of colour beneath her skin. As he gave in to the wild need and traced the flow with eager fingers. Revelled in her gasp as she begged some more.

With each lust-stoking plea, he kissed and licked and sucked, attempting gentleness that quickly fell by the wayside, propelled by primal hunger that demanded he leave his mark on this moment. On this woman.

She cried out when he suckled her pert, rose-tipped breasts, the Snow White replication of cream and rose driving him higher up the peak of insanity.

And when he'd kissed his way down her body and finally parted her thighs, the slick pink heart of her drove a pure, animal sound from his body. 'Every inch of you intoxicates me,' he confessed.

Her fingers curled into the rich coverlet, her back arching to his words. 'Show me, then. Please show me, Seve.' The tiny slur of her words, the rich Cardosian intonation of his name nearly undid him.

Like a starving man presented with a feast, he dropped onto his elbows, his arms shackling her supple thighs as he lowered his head. And feasted.

For as long as he lived, Seve suspected he would never forget the taste and feel of her, his plain-speaking genius with the untapped sensuality. A sensuality that unravelled into his waiting clutches, her husky cries a symphony he would remember long after this night.

Eager for more, more, more, he drove her from one peak to the other, her feminine core his priceless treasure.

'Please, I can't,' she protested weakly when he tried to command another release.

Drunk on her, he forced his head up, already missing the taste of her. 'Yes, you can. You will. I insist.'

The aftershocks simmering through her were a vision in

and of themselves. He watched her hair ripple like a seductive river as her head thrashed on his pillow.

Allowing her the briefest respite, he rose and padded to his bedside table. The sensation of her eyes on him powered his unsated hunger as he tore open the condom and sheathed himself.

'You like what you see, *pequeña*?'

Her gaze dropped to his manhood and stared with unabashed wonder. 'Logic tells me you'll fit but I'm still a little…awed.'

Prowling back onto the bed, he arranged his logic-driven beauty so her sweet backside was tucked against him, one leg splayed over his and wide open to him. Wrapping one arm around her, he caught her arm and tucked it over his shoulder. With unfettered access to her front, Seve caught her earlobe in his teeth, his shaft throbbing when she shivered.

'Screw logic, *mi precioso*. Feel. Just *feel*.'

With that he hooked his arm beneath her knee and surged inside her. Her scream was a blessing and a curse. Because he wanted to hear more of it while lamenting that, like everything else about this captivating woman, it would remain imprinted on his psyche for the rest of his days.

Feel. Just *feel*.

Genie did nothing else for the next three hours. One moment blended into the other until she feared the fever possessing her would never break. That she would remain submerged in this alternative universe until she stopped breathing.

She discovered that the key code to unlocking Seve Valente's passion was to plead for pleasure. And she tapped it shamelessly.

A part of her suspected she revelled in this success because she'd failed in her primary goal, and his refusal still smarted. But the majority of it was because sex with Seve was unlike anything she'd experienced before.

Just as she knew it was something she wouldn't…*couldn't* repeat after this unique night was over. Like a rare comet streaking through the sky, this was as close to a once-in-a-lifetime event as she was likely to experience.

She'd witnessed first-hand through her parents how impossible it was to satiate thirst-based pleasures. She'd watched from the sidelines as they'd sought high after high, each act more desperate than the last, the child they used to fuel their proclivities forgotten.

It was why she'd vowed never to fall prey to such addiction.

This…chemical reaction to Seve was one she would wean herself from.

Now.

She forced her eyes open, stifling a moan when the delicious heaviness in her limbs threatened to send her into stupor once more.

He was sound asleep, his hair falling over his eyes.

Objectively she assessed him, willing her brain to figure out why she'd reacted to him in such a *primal* way. It wasn't because he'd provided for her in the archaic sense. Her attraction to him had started long before he'd astonished her by offering her over and above her asking price. And as she'd said, this wasn't about money.

Maybe this was one of those inexplicable enigmas. Like why she loved the scent of patchouli but detested the smell of lavender.

But, contrary to what he'd said before, she didn't like puzzles. And he was a giant puzzle she needed to set aside.

She had more important things to do.

So why was she lingering, fighting the urge to rake back the lock of hair draping over his eyes? Why was her gaze consuming every inch of tanned skin she could see, reliving the feel of him beneath her touch?

Enough.

Their business was finished. Once she turned over the sale to her lawyers she was done dealing with Seve Valente.

For ten months at least.

A lot could happen in that time. If things went according to plan, she would have everything she'd dreamed of.

A pang in her chest made her blink, and still she couldn't drag her gaze from him.

If only he'd said yes…

The futile thought finally propelled her limbs into motion. She told herself she didn't care whether he woke or not but the very idea that she'd have to search for the appropriate social cue, which she was entirely unaware of, prompted her into stealth mode as she dressed and went to fetch her clutch.

The code he'd imputed in the underground garage lift was easy to recall and she used it to return to the lobby. A few minutes after that, a taxi was ferrying her away from the most stimulating night of her life.

Towards a future whose lights should've shone bright but was inexplicably dimmed around the edges.

Nine weeks later

'The car is here to take you to the airport, Miss Merchant.'

Genie nodded, then tagged on her thanks, but she didn't stop her progress through the sub-basement room that had been her home for almost a decade.

For whatever small time remained, she let her gaze wander over the almost empty space. She'd had her computers placed in secure specialised storage until she was eventually settled. But the memories were still vivid. Some were agonising—like the weeks she'd been sure her very freedom was at stake— while others were exhilarating—like when she'd completed the first life-changing algorithm and test-driven it.

The remaining years had been sheer hard work, but it was

work she'd relished with every fibre of her being because she'd
believed every string of code would serve a greater good.

And she'd done it.

She had achieved one long-desired goal. She'd ticked items
off her years-old to-do list.

The contract with Valente Ventures was done and dusted.

Silicon Valley and the world media had lauded her achievement with superlatives. She'd been welcome into the Ten-Digit
Club with more offers than she could count. Several megalo-
maniacs had immediately attempted to hire her, just so they
could harness her power.

She'd ignored them all.

Only to be stuck at the final hurdle. She'd allowed her assistant to keep the flight booking only because she hadn't been
able to wrestle her whirling thoughts long enough to formu-
late a new plan.

Her current situation had fully stymied her and forced her
into suspended animation. She couldn't make firm plans until
she knew. And with each day she delayed finding out, the
deeper she sank into inertia.

To say she was disappointed in herself was an understatement. Especially since within that understatement existed an
electric current of trepidation, humming and buzzing its presence that wouldn't leave her alone. Because if she did confirm
what she suspected was happening, she'd have no choice but
to act on the data. Specifically—

'Miss Merchant, sorry to disturb you but there's someone
here to see you.'

She didn't need to turn around to *know*. It was almost laugh-
able that it should happen like this. Just like last time.

Except this time, she was deep in her natural habitat. A
place she deemed sacred. Her sanctuary. If only for a short
while longer.

But Seve Valente's air of entitlement was total. He strode
into her tech lab as if he owned it. Because he did.

She watched him walk around, broad-shouldered and viscerally masculine, those piercing eyes stripping every corner, every socket and cubbyhole as if he had the rights to its secrets. To *her* secrets.

Part of her was thankful he'd never ventured down here when she was surrounded by her treasured possessions, devices that had saved her from a life of apathy and abject hopelessness.

He would've seen too much then. *Still* saw too much now.

Probably labelled her pathetic hermit, more attached to gadgets than to human beings, the way her father once scathingly did. All because she wouldn't embrace financial success the way he thought she should.

Reminding herself that those times were behind her, that this connection with Seve Valente would also soon be behind her, she forced composure into her body and turned, attempted to stare him down.

Despite the complete lack of readiness for the atomic impact of him.

Despite wanting nothing more than the freedom to relive every single moment of their time in his penthouse.

A freedom she couldn't afford.

'You have no right to be here.' She didn't add *not yet* because it was elementary. She'd signed the papers two weeks ago. His fourteen-day grace period ended at midday.

It was now eleven fifty-four.

But she suspected the remaining six minutes weren't what was uppermost in his mind when his gaze scoured her from head to toe before returning to her face.

'Oh, I have every right. As part of our contract, I now own this building. Which gives me the right to be inside it.'

Heat flooded her body. Was he playing with her by using those words?

'But you don't own everyone *in* it. You don't own me. You

could've waited a few more minutes and I would've been gone. Why didn't you?'

Something raw and primal shimmered over his face, sending shivers through her body. 'I'm here because as much as I want to ignore the possibility of what may have occurred, I've recognised that only direct communication will serve in learning the truth. So here I am.'

Her heart dipped, pretended to fail then righted itself again. 'I'm not a mind-reader, Mr Valente. You're going to have to spell out what you mean.'

The smallest fraction of a smile twitched one corner of his mouth. 'Of course. As you wish, *pequeña*.' He sauntered closer, bringing his scent with him, along with proof that, in some instances, chemistry could be replicated with the same astounding results.

Because she was breathing him in, relishing the uniquely pleasing scent.

'The last time we were together, we made love for hours in my bed. I have no reason to believe the contraception failed but the experience was more...intense than I expected. With resulting recklessness.'

Heat punched through her at his words, vivid reminders exploding across her brain like the fireworks she sometimes watched from her bedroom window on New Year's.

'We would've discussed it if you hadn't chosen to leave without the courtesy of saying goodbye.' He eyed her with something close to condemnation, a flicker of something almost...harrowing passing over his features before he continued. 'Now, I'd like to believe that nothing came of it and your silence since then suggests so. But some things I'd prefer not to leave to chance. So I'm here to ask you, Genie. Is there something I need to know? Are you leaving with something that belongs to me?'

'Everything that is exclusively yours is already signed over to you,' she returned heatedly, well aware she was evading the question.

Seve Valente was equally astute, perhaps even more than her genius IQ since he had the backing of worldly experience she readily admitted she sorely lacked. So she wasn't surprised when his eyes narrowed. 'I assure you, this isn't the time to play semantics with me. If you have something I have rights to, Genie, now's the time to confess it. Do you?'

Seve watched nerves take hold of her for a few seconds, but as expected, and as had so intrigued him about this breathtaking creature, she didn't back down. If anything, she stepped up, her chin angling up so she could flay him with her gaze. It was fiercely enraging—and furiously unacceptable—that the move aroused him to the point of breath-stealing intensity.

'I have nothing to confess, since I don't know myself.'

His eyes narrowed. 'You don't know? It's been nine weeks. Which makes your ignorance deliberate. Because you're hoping that by staying in the dark, *I'll* go away?'

Her heating cheeks betrayed her.

He laughed, a low, hoarse sound that made her eyes widen. 'You're not that deluded, Genie, surely?'

She bit her lip and the wildness straining through his veins threatened to explode. For weeks he'd dismissed this sensation every time she crossed his mind, steeped in his unshakeable belief that it was only a matter of time before it dissipated. But here he was, confronted by the unwavering truth.

He still wanted Genie Merchant. Desperately. Ferociously.

Once hadn't been nearly enough.

Hell, not even the prohibitive thought that she might be carrying his child, a notion he'd never wanted but could now not go more than five minutes without obsessing over, could kill his rampant lust for her.

'I have a plane to catch, Mr Valente.'

Her glib dismissal turned his mood darker, the hollow in

his gut at the thought that she might *not* be pregnant bewildering him now as when she'd issued that absurd condition weeks ago. But she still *hadn't* denied it. 'You'll do well to cooperate with me, Genie.'

'My social cues may be lacking but that sounds like a threat.'

He smiled. 'It's an offer of advice I suggest you take.'

'I told you I don't have any news for you, and I meant it. When I learn otherwise, I'll let you know. That's the best I can offer. Besides, you weren't interested in aiding me in having a baby. I'm assuming this is just a cursory interest that will wane with time.'

'You assume wrong. Refusing to participate in creating a child is one thing. Creating one anyway regardless of circumstances is another.' And if they had…if his child was, even at this moment, growing in her belly…

Cold sweat prickled the back of his neck as disturbing memories threatened to crowd in again. Was he resilient enough to stop past trauma from staining a new, innocent life?

The question was still quaking through him when she nodded briskly.

'Understood. Goodbye, Mr Valente.'

For far longer than was polite, he stared at her. Genie didn't need a string of source code to decipher that she wouldn't like whatever was brewing in his formidable mind.

But since she didn't intend to be around for it…

Clutching her bag to her body, she headed for the door, making sure to stay out of arm's reach of the man who continued to dominate far too much of her thoughts. With every step, she felt his gaze boring deeper into her.

She didn't breathe until she was safely ensconced in the lift. Even then she remained wary, her gaze darting around her when she reached the lobby. All the way to her car, she expected large hands to grab her, shackle her to his hard, warm body.

But she wasn't stopped.

Forty minutes later, when a smiling stewardess approached her in the first-class lounge to inform her that her plane was boarding, she breathed a sigh of relief.

And mild disappointment.

For all his bluster and stern pronouncements, Seve Valente had let her slip free despite suspecting she might be carrying his child.

For weeks, he'd lived with the possibility that she might be pregnant and done nothing about it. He might have felt obliged to bring it up but he'd effortlessly let himself off the hook at her smallest resistance.

In the end, his new acquisition was all he'd been interested in.

Just as the financial rewards of her genius had been all her parents craved.

Logic stated that she should be relieved with this outcome.

Except *logical* was far from what she felt as she followed the attendant down a surprisingly deserted ramp.

With illogical and emotional thoughts crowding her mind, she barely noticed that the plane was far smaller than the one she'd expected.

That the interior was plush to the point of luxury. That it, like the ramp, was devoid of passengers. But most importantly, that the attendant was shutting the door and the engine was already powering up.

By the time logic rushed in and lit up neon signs in her brain, the attendant was disappearing into a galley.

A door was opening at the back of the plane.

The figure walking towards her none other than Seve Valente, fire and brimstone and ruthless determination stamped into every inch of his body.

Her gaze whipped around her before returning to his. 'Wh-what are you…? What in heaven's name is going on?'

He stopped two feet from her. Slate-grey eyes consumed her from head to toe, as if he hadn't seen her less than an hour ago. After an eternity, he reached out and relieved her of her bag, tossing it aside. Then he wrapped his hands around her arms and urged her shock-riddled body into the nearest club seat.

With quick, efficient motion, he secured the seat belt.

Only then did he lean close and murmur in her ear, 'I told you I always get what I want. You should've believed me.'

'No.'

The single word injected her with adrenaline that punched the shock right out of her. Unfortunately, it was too late. The plane, which she now registered was a very sleek, private jet, was already in motion.

'*Sí, pequeña.* We've been given permission to take off. There is no going back.'

'Stop calling me that. I'm not your sweetheart.'

His jaw clenched, his eyes gleaming in a way that said her self-preservation instincts needed to be at peak performance. She'd illogically assumed her sharp exit had concluded their business and lowered her guard.

The reminder of her flawed thinking made her hand scramble for her seat belt, belatedly spurred into action.

With lightning-quick reflexes, he surged forward and placed his hands over hers. 'Stop. We're about to take off. You will remain seated.' His tone was unbending steel.

'Subterfuge, then throwing commands at me. I guess now you have my algorithm there's no need to hide your true colours, is there?'

One eyebrow cocked. 'How have I deceived you?'

She waved a wild hand at the window and the view trundling past at speed. 'Are you serious? You're in the middle of kidnapping me! Stop the plane right now!'

His smile was lethal. And pulse-shredding. 'I will not. I

gave you ample warning,' he murmured almost softly, as if he pitied her for not heeding him.

'And this is the solution you came up with? To detain me against my will?'

'Until I find out whether you're carrying my child or not? Yes.' His eyes narrowed. 'Tell me why you haven't taken a pregnancy test yet.'

She swallowed. 'I don't owe you an explanation.'

His lips thinned. 'Then prepare to not be let out of my sight until we know one way or the other.'

'What?'

'Your hearing is perfectly fine, Genie.'

She looked out of the window at the swiftly disappearing landscape as if it would give her insight as to how deep his madness went. 'Where are you taking me?'

'That depends on a few outcomes.'

She laughed but the sound abruptly cut off when his gaze dropped to the hand she'd placed unwittingly on her flat belly. 'You mean you'll drop me off in Paris and you can go on your merry way to wherever once we verify I'm not pregnant?'

His gaze shot up to her. 'You think you're not?'

The laser-sharp intensity to the question made her breath catch because it held notes she couldn't quite decipher. Notes that sounded like disappointment…*but not quite*. Like the merest hint of loss…mourning…*but not quite*. 'I told you, I don't know.'

As was becoming customary in their interaction, he let the silence stretch out for uncomfortable seconds while his gaze roamed over her face. Her hair. The tightly woven fingers in her lap. Then back up to her mouth.

Genie wanted to scream at him that she wasn't a museum oddity to be examined quite so thoroughly. But…she'd never experienced anything like it before they met nine weeks ago.

She still hadn't.

And social cues or not, the way this man—vastly worldly,

visually arresting and far too arrogant with it, who knew he commanded female interest just by breathing—watched her was…addictive.

After minutes had passed, during which the aircraft soared into the skies, setting her heart racing faster, he looked over her shoulder.

Following his gaze, she saw the attendant who'd walked her onto the plane emerge from the galley. The attendant nodded at Seve and smiled at her.

'Can I get you anything, Miss Merchant?'

The tart, intensely antisocial response rose and died on her tongue. She couldn't take out her angry panic on an attendant doing her job.

About to shake her head, she glared at Seve when he murmured, 'Some water would be great, Agnetha. Thanks.'

With another courteous smile, the attendant hurried to do her master's bidding.

'I commend you for holding your tongue,' he drawled.

She glared harder. 'I don't make a habit of attacking people who don't deserve it.'

His teeth bared in a breathtaking caricature of a smile. 'That's good to hear. We may have room for peaceful negotiation yet.'

'Any negotiation between us was forfeit when you kidnapped me, Mr Valente.'

'Seve,' he insisted with a glint in his eyes that sent shivers over her body.

'We're not friends. I won't pretend otherwise.'

Another slow scrutiny of her face and body. 'But we've been much more, *pequeña*.'

'A mistake you'll recall I was eager to put behind me by leaving before morning.'

His face hardened, but his words were still silky smooth when he responded, 'Are you sure that's why you left?'

She snorted. 'Why else?'

'Because you found our night as stimulating as I did, perhaps? I was there, remember. You were insatiable, *bonita*. Breathtakingly so.' One hand rose from where it'd been resting on his hard-packed belly to his lips, his fingers tracing over his lower lip.

As if reliving their kiss.

Heat swelled and pulsed between her thighs as she watched, unwillingly mesmerised as his finger moved back and forth over his velvet-smooth lower lip.

Whatever pithy answer she'd tried to conjure up withered under the force of sensation pummelling her and, in its place, a traitorous moan started to rise. Genie swallowed quickly, dragging her gaze away to notice that they'd levelled off.

She was further saved from answering when the attendant returned with a crystal-cut glass and a carafe of water.

Just for something to do, Genie took the drink, murmuring her thanks before raising to sip, keenly aware of Seve watching her every move.

She drained the glass, then, that vexing compulsion striking again, she glanced at him. To find him watching her with unabashed satisfaction.

'What?' she barked, the sensation that she'd done exactly as he'd wanted swirling through her.

He didn't respond immediately. His gaze went to the window, then the moment a muted ping sounded in the cabin, he rose and held out his hand.

'Come with me.'

She remained seated. 'Not a chance in hell, Mr Valente.'

He dropped his hand, and she breathed a sigh of relief. Only to have it snatched away when he stepped close and dropped into a smooth squat before her.

Standing tall, he'd been formidable, a pillar of masculinity that drew unfair attention to him.

Crouched before her, in a diminishing position that didn't diminish this man even one iota, he made her want to do the unthinkable. To reach out and cup that marble-hard jaw. To experience the heat and power of him. Chafe her skin against the delicious stubble springing to life over his vibrant olive skin.

Before their meeting nine weeks ago, she'd had minimal human contact. Went out of her way to avoid it unless strictly necessary.

Seve Valente had delivered a feast on which she had gorged until her every sense was saturated. After which she had gone back to hungering.

Now, like an addict, she was desperate to feel again. He'd opened her eyes and her senses to a world she couldn't sever herself from. With each moment in his presence, it grew impossible.

His words slammed into her memory.

Screw logic. Feel. Just feel.

'Let's not prolong this any longer, Genie,' he said with heavy finality.

Cold reality rushed in. While she'd been lost in their torrid night together, he'd leaned in closer, his gaze devouring her once more. His hands were positioned on either side of her hips without touching, and, that absurdly, it made her yearn for contact all that much more.

He's *kidnapping* you.

The forceful reminder brought welcome clarity of thought. As much as she wanted to refuse, she knew he was formidable. Seve wasn't about to let this go until he had her cooperation.

She could protest all she wanted, but the only way she'd rid herself of him was to bend a little while she was forced on this flight with him.

Once they landed however…

'Fine,' she said, thankful when her voice emerged even, betraying nothing of what she'd been feeling for the last few minutes.

Just as quickly, he disengaged her seat belt and rose. This time he didn't hold out his hand to her, the absence of which she felt distinctly as she stood and followed him at a slower place to the back of the plane.

When she realised he was entering a sleeping cabin, she froze in the doorway.

Did he think…? Surely he wasn't that deluded?

She opened her mouth to ask the very same question, ignoring the flash of heat and anticipation zipping through her body as he came towards her.

'These weren't the circumstances under which I imagined we would conclude this conversation, but here we are,' he drawled.

She felt the blood drain from her head when she saw the packages in his hand. 'You're not serious.'

CHAPTER FOUR

HE MERELY RAISED an eyebrow, delivering a pithy answer with that smooth motion.

'You want me to take a pregnancy test right now? Absolutely not!' Raised voice. Elevated heartbeat. Vivid sensation pulsing through her. All signs of unstructured overstimulation.

Absently, Genie wondered why she wasn't more alarmed. Why she felt weirdly...*alive*.

Granted, she'd also never been pregnant—a possibility she suspected was most likely. Nevertheless, she blamed him entirely for her destabilised state because, according to the information she'd consumed, pregnancy hormones wouldn't kick in for another week or two.

'This plane's travelling range is thirteen and a half hours. I'm sure you'd like to finish this business long before then.'

She balled her fist. 'I have a right to do this in my own time.'

'Then why haven't you done it yet?' He raised a hand when she opened her mouth to shut him down. 'Before you say it, this no longer falls under the "none of your business" banner.'

She bit her tongue. As much as she wanted to hate him, he was right. Hell, she had the same superior brand of test he held in his hand burning a hole in her handbag.

'Tell me why,' he urged.

She hated him even more because he didn't demand or command. There was genuine curiosity in his tone. A need to know that urged her to confront her own reasons why.

She was afraid.

Afraid that, despite wanting this more than she'd ever wanted anything else, she would fall short as a mother. That the same lack her parents had found in her would curtail her full potential as a parent.

She was different. She knew that in her bones. An oddity in a world that rarely celebrated idiosyncrasies unless they directly benefitted or entertained, and even then, preferring the benefits to be delivered from a distance. As much as she hated to admit it, that difference had chipped away at her self-esteem over the years.

Enough to make her put this off even after two missed periods.

She couldn't tell Seve any of this, of course. The raw power he exuded and the conquer-at-all-costs persona demanded that she keep her fears under lock and key.

So she cast her gaze around the room. Then forced a shrug. 'I wasn't ready.'

His eyes narrowed and his body turned stiff as marble. 'You weren't ready?' he repeated with zero emotion. 'You asked me to father your child as part of our deal nine weeks ago.'

The memory burned and chafed inside her, the bold attraction that had led her to issue that request still disarming. 'I did. And had you said yes, we would've discussed the appropriate time for scheduling a baby.'

Impossibly, he grew stiffer and, from the corner of her eye, she watched his face turn dark with condemnation. '*Scheduling a baby?* Like scheduling a coffee run or a test drive on a string of code?' he bit out, his tone arctic.

Like last time, she'd evidently struck a nerve. Again, she tried to see beneath his surface to why he felt so strongly about it.

Since he'd said no.

'Well, not as unfeeling as all that but—'

'But what? You would've found time to schedule in some emotion too?'

Despite deliberately seeking the distance from emotion, Genie felt her insides sting at his words. 'How I feel about the child I may or may not be carrying is—'

'Let me guess, none of my business? That's where you're wrong. Because now more than ever, I'm convinced right here is where I need to be,' he stated with rigid reproach. 'Let me state again. I'm not going anywhere, Genie. Not until we confirm whether or not you're carrying my child. So what's it to be?'

Get it over and done with.

She wanted to deny the voice echoing in her head.

But she'd strung this out long enough. Her life was going to change whether she liked it or not. Hell, she'd already adopted her eating, sleeping and exercising habits to accommodate the possible pregnancy. If she was preparing her body for the biggest event of her life, then she couldn't bury her head in the sand any longer.

Her heart hammered with mild panic as he held out the packages to her.

In less than five minutes she would know whether she was going to be a mother.

They both would.

Her hand shook as she took them from him. She barely saw him motion towards the door that led to the plane's bathroom. But she was searingly aware of him following a few steps behind her until he stopped himself, his hands forcibly shoved into the pockets of his trousers.

Genie didn't need to look over her shoulder to know that his gaze was boring into her, its intensity very much heightened.

Contrary to what she'd thought, he was heavily invested, she realised. Or else he wouldn't have taken such drastic actions.

Shutting the door behind her, she shook her head. It didn't matter. Her plans about her child had never included its father. She was sure she could negotiate Seve out of this too, if it came to it.

Is that wise?

She bunched a fist over the sink, avoiding her own gaze as she shook her head once again. It didn't matter. Single parenthood had been the plan all along. Once she got over this alarm, the merits would be just the same.

Running her gaze over the instructions twice, she tore the box open and took the test. After washing her hands, she sat on the lid of the toilet, every cell in her body shaking as the endless seconds ticked by.

Five minutes later, she stared at the thick cross that positively confirmed what she already knew deep in her heart.

Uneven waves of panic, awe and disbelief washed over her until she wasn't sure which emotions she was drowning under. Raising her eyes to the mirror, she caught sight of her glazed eyes, her pale face, the breaths puffing out of her stunned mouth.

She was pregnant.

'Genie.'

The naked blade of his voice, edged with simmering emotions she couldn't name, cut through the euphoric fog of her brain.

She was pregnant.

She fumbled for the door. She expected him to rush in, but he remained aloof a few steps away. An omen, perhaps?

Maybe not, if the fever blazing in his eyes was any indication. He didn't even need to voice the question. It was a towering neon sign growing larger by the second.

'Yes. I'm pregnant.' The words fell like tiny, explosive miracles from her lips.

A loud rush followed, drowning out all sound. The plane pitched. Or maybe it was her.

Genie wasn't entirely sure as she took a step and fell forward into pitch darkness.

When she blinked awake, she was in the king-size bed, fat pillows propped behind her, and thick luxurious covers thrown over her body.

Seve sat on the edge, tension vibrating from his body as he stared down at the test confirming the altered course of her life.

Of *their* lives.

No. She had enough to contend with. She wasn't going to allow her brain to accommodate what this meant for Seve too.

She raised a hand to her temple, struggling to sit up. 'Wh-what happened?'

Sizzling eyes shifted from the stick to her face, conducting a quick scrutiny. 'You announced you were pregnant, then passed out,' he gritted out.

Pregnant...

The power of that word was…indescribable.

Her hand trailed to her stomach. He followed the movement, his face clenching as he exhaled.

'Dear God, I did *not* just swoon like a pathetic Victorian maiden,' she muttered.

He heard her, of course. He was attuned to her in a way that should've been uncanny, and yet, the more exposed she was to it, the more she accepted it.

'Let's blame it on turbulence,' he rasped. His face remained grave but she had the absurd urge to laugh. A broken sound escaped before she could stop it.

His eyes latched onto her throat, as if he yearned to hear it again.

Shaking her head, she reached for the covers, ready to throw them off.

'Stay.'

It wasn't an arrogant command like before; nevertheless it was a directive that made her bristle. She needed solitude to properly absorb the news. To talk herself through this trepidation so she could make careful plans for her baby. 'Haven't we achieved the objective of all of this?'

He rested his elbows on his knees, subtly blocking her exit from this side of the bed. 'We've merely verified the foundation on which we stand.'

'What does that mean?'

He didn't answer. Instead, he reached for a sleek little gadget on the bedside table. She watched him press the button labelled 'cockpit' with growing alarm.

The crisp voice answered, echoing in the room. 'Yes, sir?'

'Flight option one, please,' Seve responded.

'Of course, Mr Valente.'

He released the button, then eyed her in a way that made the hairs on her nape stand up.

'Flight option one?' Even as she repeated it, Genie suspected she wouldn't like what it meant. 'For your sake I hope that means you're delivering me to my original destination.'

One corner of his mouth lifted but there was no humour in the motion. 'I'm sorry to disappoint you, but no. We flew over Norway about half an hour ago.'

'Then turn back!'

The tic in his jaw gave her his answer even before he said, 'No. You're carrying my child. That changes things.'

'What things—?' The question snagged in her throat as the aircraft banked with a definite course adjustment that made her heart lurch. 'Why is your pilot changing course? Where are we going?'

He rose from the bed, and she noticed the pregnancy test was still in his hand. He stared down at it for a long moment, his chest rising and falling in heavy breathing. Then he speared her with ferocious eyes, his stance giving no quarter as he answered. 'We're going to Cardosia. Where my child will be born.'

Several thoughts charged through her brain as she stared at him.

The primary one was that *this* was why she didn't like human interaction. Because half of the time she wasn't sure whether they were the faulty creatures, or *she* was missing vital clues of fairness and decency.

'You're quite insane if you think I'm going anywhere with you, never mind staying for the better part of a year.'

Her scathing response didn't faze him one iota. 'As far as I know, insanity doesn't run in my family. Which is why I can assure you with one hundred per cent certainty that that's exactly what is going to happen.'

She swallowed the unhelpful panic scrabbling at her throat. 'Enlighten me, please. Is this usual behaviour for men like you?'

'I don't speak for other men, nor do I care how the general male population feel about anything. You're my main concern. And you, Genie Merchant, are in the unique position of being the only woman who has affected me enough for me to lose my head in bed. Just as you are the unique woman carrying my child.'

Her nails dug into the covers, seeking an anchor in this mad tempest. '*Our* child. If you must make proprietary assertions, have the decency to include me.'

'Perhaps I do so because I suspect that if you had your way, you would put the distance of half a world between me and what's mine.'

She couldn't deny it. Nor could she stop the treacherous heat that confirmed his words. 'Well, calling it your child doesn't make it so.'

He gave a slow, eloquent shrug that emphasised every step he was taking to stake his claim. And in that shrug, she learned something else.

Seve Valente wasn't about to budge an iota.

He surged forward when she threw her legs over the side of the bed and stood up, but he didn't touch her. He watched her like a hawk however. And she realised he'd stayed close long enough to ensure she wouldn't topple over again.

It shouldn't have chipped at a small fraction of her fury. That it did bewildered her even more. This man was making declarations about her life while keeping her prisoner on his airborne palace. Every cell in her body should be incandescent.

Yet several of those cells strained towards him as she passed him. Even more infuriating, a significant portion of her senses delighted in his scent, the aura emanating from him, as she noted that the delicious stubble had grown even more. Wondered how deliciously it would chafe if she—

No!

She was absolutely not going down that unhinged path. It was what had landed her here after all.

One night. It was only meant to be one night.

She realised she'd said it out loud when his whole body tightened, turning even more marble-like than before.

'But a night with consequences, evidently.'

'Why are you doing this? You don't even want a child. You said as much.'

His eyes glinted, his incisive gaze tracking her as she paced the small cabin. 'What I felt a few weeks ago no longer matters.'

'That's absurd. Of course it does.'

He gritted his teeth. 'Let me rephrase. The child you're carrying…my child, is now my number one priority. I'm not taking eyes off you until he or she is born.'

Something inside her cracked against her will, and without her permissions started to melt. Since she couldn't fathom what it was, she immediately took steps to shore it up. To separate it from clear, logical thinking. She couldn't afford anything else.

Couldn't afford to wonder how her life's trajectory would've changed if only her parents had made her their number one priority.

They hadn't. They'd put her last on their list every time.

Until she'd taken herself off it completely. Until she'd emotionally emancipated herself from the two people who should've given her unconditional love and support but had only zealously loved her bank balance.

They'd helped themselves to her millions, citing that they'd given their lives and livelihood for her dream and therefore were entitled to it.

'And what happens after that? Your end goal currently seems to be delivery.'

'That will be a matter for later discussion.' Although he didn't break their stare, Genie got the singular feeling he'd already made up his mind. That he was several steps ahead of her and was keeping that vital move to himself. 'For now all you need to know is that you're going to be in a place where you're provided with a healthy diet and strict monitoring that doesn't include living in an underground tech dungeon where you ignore the existence of sunlight and human interaction for weeks on end.'

The wave of desolation and hurt that swept through her took her literal breath away. She managed to snatch it back, as she whirled around and headed for the door.

'Where are you going? We're not done talking, Genie.'

She grasped the door handle and rapidly blinked away stupid tears. 'Logic tells me that if I find your words hurtful and disrespectful then we shouldn't engage in conversation.'

'Or, contrarily, we should keep talking until there's no room for doubt.'

His deep voice right over her shoulder indicated he'd followed her. And really? There was nowhere to go. Her only option was to have this conversation within earshot of the attendants.

When Genie turned he was, as expected, only three feet away. She grasped at the last tendrils of composure and went to the nearest seat set next to the window. 'I don't owe you explanation on how I live my life but, if you must know, I exercise three times a week and have been exceptionally prudent with my diet the last few weeks.'

Perhaps she was mistaken but his shoulders relaxed a tiniest fraction at her words. '*Bueno*. But you fainted a little while ago. This baby is already making demands on your body, so I need to know how you feel. And not just physically. Emotionally too.'

'I could tell you that. I could also shout and ask where you get the nerve to ask me that. But why would I hand you the advantage of any of that? You said unapologetically that you're not above using my feelings to manipulate me into giving you what you want.'

He didn't respond, merely crossed his arms over his sculpted chest, leaned back against the door and watched her.

Genie considered sitting in silence right along with him. But Dr Douglas's voice chose that moment to gently chide her. *Take the high road.*

Casting a glance out of the window so he wouldn't see how much the words affected her, she kept her gaze on the fluffy clouds as she answered. 'Okay. I feel lonely. A lot. All the time, actually. Even when my parents were alive.'

A furtive glance out of the corner of her eye showed his arms had dropped, a disarmed look on his face.

She'd shocked Seve Valente with her unguarded honesty.

It wasn't a terrible feeling. So she went further. 'I felt lonely even before I was old enough to understand what that feeling meant. It hasn't gone away.'

Seve prowled closer, emotion in his eyes she couldn't quite decipher. 'That's why you wanted a child?' he grated out.

'Partly.'

'What other reasons are there?' he pressed, not giving any quarter now she'd cracked the door open.

'Because I'm aware of where my parents went wrong, and I'm well equipped to not repeat their mistakes.'

'Doing the opposite of what they did wouldn't automatically guarantee the results you require,' he countered, a bite in his voice.

She turned from the window to face him. 'I wasn't planning on using the exact opposite template. Just doing things differently.'

His nostrils flared in irritation. 'You could still go wrong elsewhere, unless you have the answer to every question being a parent entails. And that's impossible.'

'I know being a good parent doesn't come from books. It comes from within.' She knew that deep in her soul because that was where the most anguishing hurt had resided. 'What about you? You're so busy labelling me an unfit parent five minutes after discovering you're going to be a father. What experience do you have to show that you'll do any better?'

His jaw tightened when the accusation hit the mark. Shadows of bleakness and bitterness charted over his face, but he tossed them off almost instantly. 'Unlike you, I'm willing to admit I don't have all the answers—'

'And yet you're determined to emerge the winner.'

His nostrils flared in displeasure. 'For starters, I have a better support system. And this isn't about winning—'

'Of course it is. You see the child I'm carrying as yours. You're taking it away because you believe you're better equipped to take care of it than I am.'

'As opposed to what? Having it brought up on some grey corner of your AI lab where you can nip in and check on it in between building algorithms?'

The sting in her midriff intensified. 'Your views are based on nothing but assumptions.'

'Prove me wrong, then. Show me how wrong I am.'

'You're baiting me into showing my hand again.'

He shrugged. 'You have to reveal your cards at some point, Genie. You can't hold them to your chest and expect me to take you at your word. What were your plans to bring up my… our baby?'

'What are yours? Beside kidnapping and holding me hostage for the duration of my pregnancy?'

Purpose rippled from him in waves. And somehow, she wasn't at all surprised when he merely rasped, 'You'll find out soon enough.'

He was doing the right thing.

Whenever the tiny pinpricks of guilt lanced him, he pushed back. *Hard.* Because he couldn't afford even an ounce of softening. Not when the stakes were this high.

He glanced at the closed cabin door and tightened his resolve.

Genie had coldly frozen him out once it became clear he wasn't changing his mind about their destination or revealing his plans for the baby she carried.

For his child.

He clenched his gut against the next shockwave that surged at those three words. But even more shocking? The fact that, watching her walking into the bathroom to perform the test, he'd felt a punch of dismay at the possibility of the result being negative.

Nine weeks ago he'd dismissed her request for a child as insane because the notion of fathering a child had been anathema to him. A deliberately abstract occurrence he'd been certain he wouldn't mind if it never came to pass.

Waking up the morning after their night together to find her gone, he'd convinced himself that it was for the best, too. Hell, he'd been saved the firm but awkward disentangling from clinging expectations.

That flash of disgruntlement that had lingered far longer than he'd wanted it to? It'd weirdly been allayed when, replaying their night together in the shower, he'd been jolted by the possibility that the protection had failed beneath the vigour of their coming together. He'd remained in that shower far longer than usual, alternately shocked and alarmed by the thought that he was in no hurry to chase after Genie Merchant to verify.

Even the primal urge to ensure she made the choice he preferred had disappeared at the certainty that if she was pregnant, she would keep the child.

His child.

He'd been in no hurry because *that* had meant he'd see her again, one way or another. If only to verify that their night together had left no consequence.

It was that very unsettling notion that refused to dissipate, urging strongly that theirs was unfinished business, aside from the algorithm contract, that had conversely kept him away until the very last moment.

Had he known subconsciously that this life-changing event was on the horizon?

He shook his head. What did it matter now? The only material thing going forward was that he was going to be a father. With the crushing weight of history a jagged spear in his chest.

Would he fail his child just as his parents had done? Would he at some point in the future lose his way so badly that he wouldn't care whether his child was harmed by another so long as it benefitted *him*?

It might seem unthinkable to him *now* but what of the future when he didn't know how his twisted childhood would manifest itself?

His lungs constricted again with deep apprehension but he pulled himself past it.

It wouldn't happen. Not if he took the steps he was planning.

For a start, it was even more imperative now that the future stability of Cardosia was ensured. Disabling his uncle's hold on his homeland was one way of ensuring his flesh and blood had a future home and legacy. Something to be proud of if all else failed. One thing that wouldn't make Seve a failure in his child's eyes.

Glancing at the door one last time, he rose and went in the

opposite direction, towards the plane's conference room. As much as he would like Genie's cooperation in all this, he was prepared for there to be a little turbulence before the path smoothed out.

He was used to adversity. And between the baby growing in the womb of the woman in his cabin and his determination to save Cardosia, he would have a battle on his hands.

Accepting that, he opened his laptop and brought up the latest weekly report on his uncle's activities.

The very first page darkened his mood.

Between last week and this, Lorenzo Valente had brokered two more deals that would strip essential resources from Cardosia's ecosystem. Even worse, Seve knew every cent of that deal would be funnelled into his uncle's private bank account in Luxembourg.

By the time he reached the end of the twenty-three-page document, fury blazed through his bloodstream.

Snatching up the phone, he punched in the far too well-used numbers. The moment it was answered, he barked, 'Have you seen the latest report?'

'We have, sir. We're attempting to stall the deals he's making but we won't be able to do so for ever. He's the head of state.'

His fingers tightened around the phone. '*Dios mio.* Try harder! This is unacceptable.'

He'd been used as a pawn as a child and, even as a successful man, Seve knew Lorenzo still flaunted his name about in order to secure deals for himself. His wily uncle continued to pillage his homeland ceaselessly.

No more.

The team he'd put together to monitor his uncle's activities—and to stall his intentions to bleed Cardosia dry—comprised scientists, economists and a few key figures serving in his uncle's government.

The oldest of them was the one who bore the misnomer

of a conscientious politician—Alfredo Santiago. He cleared his throat and Seve pinched the bridge of his nose because he knew what was coming. Alfredo never failed to bring it up at least once in their every interaction.

'You know what you need to do, son. The window of opportunity is fast closing.'

'And I've told you, I'm not going to run for president.'

'Can you afford not to? Soon there will be no Cardosia left to find on a map. Hell, he was heard floating the idea that our beloved country should become a province of one of her larger and more powerful neighbours.'

His chest clenched. 'What? Are you serious?'

'I'm an old man, Seve. I can't afford jokes when the stakes are this high.'

'And I'm telling you to focus your energies in that regard elsewhere. Cardosia will be in more capable hands than in mine. Politics bore me to death.'

The old man snorted. 'Says the man who's livid at what's happening to his homeland. If that isn't what pure passion of a patriot looks like, then I've led a very wasted life thus far.'

Pure passion.

He hated that those two words threw up a different image. That of having Genie Merchant underneath him, of pumping into her tight sheath as she screamed her pleasure. Unadulterated pleasure expressed without an ounce of manufactured performance.

Seve shifted in his seat when his blood rushed south and awoke senses he didn't need awakened right this minute. Clearing his throat, he forced his focus on the conversation. On the utter abomination of what his uncle was doing to Cardosia. 'Tell me who Lorenzo has been speaking to. I need to know who to put on my red list.'

'A red list is all well and good, Seve. But you're attacking the symptom instead of the disease. I know you don't want to consider it, but you really are our only hope. Time is fast running out.'

His nape tingled with dread at the finality in the man's tone.

Long after that conversation had ended, Seve was reminded that one of the reasons he liked dealing with Santiago was because he didn't exaggerate or overdramatise a situation. Which meant things were as dire as stated. Perhaps even more so.

Gritting his teeth, he placed the next call on his list, making no bones about the consequences for those who supported his uncle in his efforts in hastening Cardosia towards perilous straits. His last was to the private bank he knew his uncle used. But even as he threatened fire and brimstone, he knew there was only so much his threats would achieve.

Which was why he was still locked in full frustration mode three hours later when he ordered lunch for Genie and, tray in hand, retraced his steps.

She was sitting up in bed when he entered, her hair a little tousled and the remnants of sleep in her eyes. Slivers of sunlight slanting through the windows formed a halo around her and his gut clenched against the enticing picture she made in his bed with his covers and pillows tossed around her.

It would have been no effort at all to set the tray to one side, to prowl onto the bed, nudge her back against the pillows and take his fill of that satin-soft mouth. Would she gasp and moan as she had nine weeks ago? Would those bottomless green eyes reflect every facet of her pleasure as she clung to him?

Sí. She would. He was sure of it. Her unfettered passion lurked just beneath her no-nonsense surface, waiting to be reignited to life.

Except if he attempted such a thing, she would probably claw his eyes out, considering the glare she was directing his way. For now, he needed her less…stressed about his intention to install her fully in his life. At least until the baby arrived.

'You're awake. *Bueno.*'

Striding across the room, he frowned down at the tray.

Nothing looked particularly harmful to a newly pregnant woman, but then what did he know? Was he failing his child even now? So soon?

He would remedy that lack of knowledge before morning, he vowed silently. Hell, he would consume every report ever written on pregnancy and parenting, if necess—

'You look…distressed.' Her head tilted to one side and he couldn't stop his gaze from tracking the smooth line of her neck, a place he'd thoroughly explored during their night together. A place he yearned to explore again. 'Is it socially unacceptable to say I hope your guilt is eating you alive?'

Seve was stunned by his first instinct to laugh. Hell, he couldn't help cracking a smile, which made her eyes widen to alluring pools that roused his libido.

'You never have to be circumspect around me, *pequeña*. In fact, I would prefer you not to even try. I can handle raw honesty.'

'Can you? You don't believe in practising it yourself.'

His mood soured further and he didn't appreciate the pangs that irritated his insides. 'You need to stop insisting I lied to you. I showed you my true colours. You chose to disregard it. That's on you, not me.'

Her lips pursed and he bit the inside of his cheek to stop him from surging forward, tugging the plump curve into his mouth. She would probably claw his eyes out *and* leave her gouges on his skin if he tried.

So why did that make his blood thicken even more in his veins?

He would definitely have some serious explaining to do to his grandmother if he landed in Cardosia with claw marks on his face. Even more than he anticipated was coming his way.

'What's so funny?' she griped, and he realised, despite his mood, his lips had curved at the thought of what awaited him in Cardosia.

'I'm looking forward to you meeting my grandmother,' he said before he could process the wisdom of it.

'You have family there?' she burst out, the napkin she'd picked up suspended in the air. Then she frowned, possibly because, like his, the statement had slipped out without permission. 'Of course, you do,' she muttered a moment later. 'Do they condone kidnapping too?'

The last of his humour washed away. 'I would rather you don't air our personal business in front of the staff or my grandmother.'

'I think you have *personal business* confused with cross-border crime.'

'You think taking my seed into your body and growing our child in your womb isn't as personal as it gets?'

He'd intended to be earthy enough to remind her of their frenzied coupling, and he knew he'd succeeded when blood rushed into her face. Her eyes grew a little dazed, as if recollecting how they'd got here was as sensually visceral to her as it was to him.

He reached forward, tucked a strand of hair behind her ear, then drifted his knuckle down her heated cheek. 'You wanted a clinical conception. Instead you got a mind-altering experience that is set to change both our lives. No one needs to know the details of how this baby was conceived or how we plan to raise it.'

'We?' The word shook out of her. There was sceptical curiosity in the question, but he didn't blame her. He had a million anxiety-laced questions too.

There was a reason he chose to battle Cardosia's problems from afar. A reason he hadn't come face to face with his uncle for half a decade.

Until now.

Too much hung in the balance. Not least of all his unborn child.

'Oh, yes. We.' He didn't elaborate beyond that. There would

be more than enough time to unveil his further plans once they were in Cardosia. 'Eat your meal. Then come join me in the lounge. We land in forty-five minutes.'

Genie ate more out of necessity than appetite.

Sleep had done nothing to calm her roiling nerves. She was still lugging them like unwanted baggage when she set the tray aside and went into the bathroom to refresh herself. Once again she met her gaze in her mirror. This time she looked poleaxed with a peculiar shine to her eyes she couldn't explain.

Shock, maybe? Anticipation of the fight ahead?

Because she wasn't going to just lie down and take Seve's diktat on what the next months of her pregnancy were going to be, was she?

No, she assured herself forcefully when her brain dared to ponder the answer. She hadn't come this far just to hand the reins of her life to someone else.

Not even a man who had such strong possessive feelings about his child? Feelings that if honed right could benefit their chi—?

Dear God, she wasn't making excuses for him, was she? When he'd all but proclaimed her an unfit mother?

She turned around and marched out of the bathroom and suite and down the narrow corridor that led to the main lounge.

Whatever fighting words brewed on her tongue vanished at the sight of him.

He was staring out of the window of the plane, lost in thought. It gave her valuable seconds to examine him unnoticed, although in the next breath she realised her thoughts were severely lacking in value when her senses obsessed over tracing his astounding, almost formidable good looks. With the sun's angle beaming worshipfully on his profile, picking out the dark gold flecks in his brown hair, he was almost too profoundly beautiful.

The strong forehead, the aquiline perfection of his nose

and—just as arresting as it'd been weeks ago—the sensually potent curve of his lips all served to deliver a potion kick to her senses.

There was also no value in daydreaming about whether their son—if their child turned out to be male—would inherit his father's magnetising good looks and overpowering personality, but she found herself doing so anyway. Found herself speculating if, by dallying with this man, she'd saddled herself with a life-long reminder of him in her child.

Of course, you have. This exceptional DNA wouldn't allow for anything less than total domination.

His head swung around, hawk-sharp eyes zeroing in on her with a ferocity that snatched her breath. It said he could read her every thought; knew his impact on her. Probably *revelled* in it.

That real possibility paralysed her for a second before Genie forced herself to move.

To pretend his effect on her wasn't alarming. 'I can't force you to get your pilot to turn this plane around. And for the sake of this pregnancy, I don't intend to zip across time zones with gleeful abandon. I will stay in Cardosia for twenty-four hours only. Anything beyond that and I will report you to the authorities for abduction. Are we clear?' she snapped with, she hoped, enough bite to distract her from noticing everything sinfully attractive about her captor.

But as one corner of his mouth quirked with amusement at her ultimatum, an inner voice was echoing one question across her brain.

Just how do you plan to stop him?

CHAPTER FIVE

TWENTY-FOUR HOURS.

HE HAD NO plans to agree to that, of course.

But it bought him time without anticipating that she would do something foolish, like attempt to throw herself out of the SUV transporting them from the private airport to his estate. Or flee in the middle of the night.

She was extremely wealthy in her own right now, thanks to his purchase, and had the means to vanish if she so wished. Not without a trace, of course, because he simply wouldn't allow that to happen. Not with his child in tow.

But a lot could happen in twenty-four hours. So he curbed his satisfied smile and watched from the corner of his eye as she tried to hide her awe at the surroundings.

Cardosia's beauty was soul-stirring, and it wasn't just because it was the country of his birth. As a young boy, he'd often wondered how cruelty could exist in such a magnificent place. As a man, he knew humanity's brutality needed very little kindling to ignite.

Did such a kindling exist in him?

He pushed the chilling thought away and forced himself to look around too.

Cardosia rivalled its onshore neighbouring Argentina and Chile in dramatic soaring mountains, world-class wineries and thoroughbred horses royalty and billionaires vied for.

But there was one resource that set it apart on the world stage—Cardosia's deep, priceless diamond mines. Cardosian diamonds were a rare deep purple not found anywhere else on earth. A resource that turned covetous eyes on his country.

That he had personally had a hand in elevating Cardosia's standing was a source of inner pride. But that pride had been severely dented in the last decade, especially when that exposure had led to exploitation by his uncle, serving only to fatten the older man's greed.

His smile dimmed at the reminder of why he needed to do better before his beloved homeland was decimated economically and ecologically to the point of no return.

Not just for him and his people, but for his unborn child.

She leaned forward to catch another view of yet another striking landmark and he took the opportunity to observe her closer. Her flawless profile. The curve of her breasts. Her flat belly where his child was resting and growing. And every last tinge of guilt melted away.

He was doing the right thing.

At the very least his *abuela* would be happy once he delivered the news. After years of her despairing quietly over him, he was returning with news that would win him mega points.

'Unless you possess X-ray vision, I fail to see why you're staring at my belly.'

His gaze shifted up to meet hers.

Despite her curt tone, her face was flushed and her breathing was a little elevated, no doubt at his blatant scrutiny of her body.

Seve restrained the wanton need prowling through him and shrugged. 'I should warn you to prepare yourself for more of it, *pequeña*. My seed is growing inside you. I find that a singularly primal experience and I won't apologise for revelling in it.'

A light quiver took hold of her bottom lip before she drew it between her teeth, making him stifle a groan. 'I would never have taken you for the primitive type. My research said you're an ultra-modern man who thrives on forward thinking, and yet here you are, talking like a Neanderthal.'

A smile curved his lips, surprising him. 'I'm multi-dextrous in my thinking. I can be many things without losing who I am. And you really shouldn't believe everything you read online.'

Any response was halted when their SUV drove through the tall Valente-crested iron gates guarding the entrance to his estate. Although she tried to feign boredom, her gaze swung left and right, taking in the tall cypress trees lining the long driveway, and the rolling pastures beyond, and in the far distance the beach where his yacht was moored.

She glanced to her left, her breath catching faintly when she spotted the horses grazing half a kilometre away.

Seve knew that were he to ask in that moment if she loved horses, she would've denied it, just to be contrary. But he made a mental note to introduce her to his favourite stallion.

He watched as she finally looked forward to the sprawling villa that was his favourite place on earth. The home he'd built for his grandmother after years of enforced estrangement by his parents, who'd forbidden his *abuela* from seeing him because she'd had strong views of their shortcomings.

Seve was bitter about a lot of things regarding his childhood, but the deliberate shattering of his relationship with his grandmother would cut deep for ever.

The good thing was she was fully installed in his life now.

He held up a staying hand when his driver alighted and reached for Genie's door. 'Before we go in, there's one thing we need to establish. My grandmother. She's made of stern stuff but I still don't want her to be upset by any of this. Whatever is happening between you and I stays between us. Is that understood?'

Stunning, intelligent eyes regarded him with a hint of smugness. 'You do realise you've just handed me leverage, don't you?'

He allowed himself another smile. 'No, I haven't. Because

I did my research too. And I'm fairly confident you don't go around upsetting old ladies just for the fun of it.'

Her long lashes swept down, guarding her expression, but he didn't need to see it to know his assessment was accurate. Of course, she came back fighting. 'Since I'm going to be here barely a day, it shouldn't be a problem. But…' her head tilted imperiously, her eyes narrowing as she stared down her pert nose at him '…misfiring social cues or not, I won't lie or cover up for what you're doing. If you're in hot water with your grandmother, you're there of your own making.'

Amusement and attraction for this little lioness swelled within him. He nodded at the driver to open the door before he did something foolish, like drag her into his lap and devour those Snow White lips. 'Warning duly noted.'

He watched her alight, her long, shapely legs outlined in the dress flattened to her body by the light breeze. When she lifted her hand to tuck away a curl disturbed by the same breeze, Seve swallowed a groan. He needed to keep his head in the game, not salivate over her like some hormonal teenager.

The towering front doors opening behind Genie helped him put aside the need rampaging through him. His grandmother rushed out, curiosity snapping in her dark brown eyes as she reached the top of the steps.

'Severino! I was only informed of your arrival a few hours ago. Why didn't you tell me you planned to come home?' she snapped, but the warmth in her eyes belied her tone, soothing some of the ruffles inside him.

Going to her, he caught the hands she held out and kissed the soft, lined cheek she tilted towards him. 'My plans changed unexpectedly,' was all he said.

Her lips pursed but her gaze darted past him. 'And you've brought a guest, I see?'

He turned to where Genie stood, her fingers clasped demurely before her. '*Sí.* This is Genie Merchant. Genie, meet my grandmother, Julieta Valente.'

The two women eyed each other for a long second before Genie held out her hand. 'A pleasure to meet you, Señora Valente.'

His grandmother immediately waved her away. 'I don't respond to "Señora Valente", child. Everyone calls me Lita, short for *abuelita*. And so will you.'

Genie looked startled for a moment, then she frowned before her gaze darted to his. At his nod, she glanced back at his grandmother. 'I will.' And after a moment, 'Thank you,' she tagged on.

The old woman smiled. '*Buena.* Now come, get out of the sun. I have refreshments ready in the *salon*.'

For a moment, Genie wanted to protest.

To remind the man walking beside her with his arm tucked courteously around his grandmother's that she wasn't here for a social visit.

But she'd granted him twenty-four hours.

For her baby's sake, those hours included rest and sustenance. And, as Seve had annoyingly and accurately pointed out, she wasn't in the business of upsetting old ladies. And his grandmother was as darling as they came.

The diminutive woman packed a punch but every glance she cast her grandson was filled with warmth. The kind Genie hadn't experienced in a very long time, if ever. So she bit her tongue and accompanied them down a gorgeous, warmly lit corridor, decorated on either side with art and artefacts bearing heavy South American influences. It was clear Seve took pride in his Cardosian home with the sheer number of renowned artists' work that graced his walls.

Despite his wealthy status there was no Rembrandt or Monet flouting his prestige, just golden-hued tones that made one room flow into the other, ending in a sunlit salon where a veritable spread awaited them on a sleek table set to one side of the room.

A buxom woman introduced as Sofia, the housekeeper,

waited alongside a butler. The two older women exchanged a few murmured words before she hurried off.

Lita took a seat in a wide rocking armchair that looked out of place in the opulent room.

'Help yourself to some grilled shrimp, Genie. Sofia uses a dash of Cardosian spices that are simply heavenly. And serve your guest some Cardosian wine, *cariño*. We make the best reds in the world,' she boasted with a pride-filled smile.

Genie opened her mouth but Seve beat her to it. 'Genie can't take wine, Lita. Or shellfish.'

Lita's eyes widened, then her face started to fall before the coin dropped. '*Santa María*, that can only mean…' Her gaze darted from Genie to Seve. A look passed between them before she clasped her hands over her heart. '*Sí?*'

'*Sí*, Lita,' he confirmed with deep, solemn tones, his face betraying nothing but the news. 'Genie is carrying my child. You're going to be a great-grandmother in a little under seven months.'

The old lady jumped from her seat, completely belying her age by rushing forward to engulf Seve in a hug. He leaned down and allowed himself to be kissed on both cheeks.

And then Lita turned to Genie. Her effusiveness was a touch reduced but her smile was no less warm. 'You've made an old woman very happy, *carina*,' she said in accented English.

Genie opened her mouth to speak but, a little terrified she would say the wrong thing, shut it again and merely nodded.

Lita bustled over to the table, waving the butler away when he stepped forward. Muttering excitedly under her breath, she heaped a plate full of heavenly smelling food and hurried over to Genie. 'You must eat, child. Valente mothers make fat, beautiful babies but we can't rely on just nature to get the job done.'

The image of herself with a swollen belly months from now made Genie's breath catch. Filled her with such overwhelming feelings she could only nod again and accept the plate of food. Studying it, she noticed that Lita had picked everything a pregnant woman could safely eat.

And surprisingly, her appetite was ready for the delicate pastries, the stuffed peppers and vegetable kebabs making her mouth water.

She was mostly ignored as Lita chattered excitedly to her grandson.

But when the room fell silent, she glanced up to see two sets of eyes on her. Lita's dropped fleetingly to Genie's left hand, a hint of a question in her eyes before Seve rose to his feet.

'Give her time to adjust. This is all news to Genie too.'

Lita frowned. 'News to her? But you said she's two—'

'I know what I said, Lita,' Seve interrupted firmly, faint warning in his tone making the old woman's lips purse. 'The priority for Genie now is to get some rest. We crossed several time zones to get here.'

'But we will have dinner together tonight, *sí*?' Lita pressed.

'If Genie is up to it, yes.' He reached her and glanced at her nearly finished plate. 'Are you ready to be shown to your room?'

A chance to be alone? To take all this in?

Hell, yes.

Setting the plate aside, she rose.

Lita approached them with a smile. 'Are you sure you've had enough? I can have another plate brought up to your room?'

Seve glanced sternly at his grandmother. 'You need to eat too, and rest.'

She made a face and waved him away. 'I'm only seventy-five, not a hundred and five. Besides, I can sleep when I'm dead.'

'Technically, being dead isn't sleeping. It's ceasing to exist,' Genie retorted.

Lita looked startled for a moment, then she threw her head back and laughed.

Genie looked bewildered. Adorably so. So much so Seve wanted to run his knuckle down her flushing skin.

He locked his knees and frowned at himself.

Since when was he obsessed with finding excuses to touch a woman? Normally, the reverse was what occurred. Except in this moment, he couldn't think of any other woman he wanted to touch more than the one staring at his beloved grandmother as if she were a cipher she dearly wanted to decode.

'I like this one. But I get the feeling she doesn't like you very much,' Lita said to him.

'I don't,' Genie responded in perfect Cardosian, making his grandmother's eyes sparkle even brighter in pleasure as she smiled wider in delight.

'You speak Cardosian?' she asked, approval brimming in her voice.

Genie nodded briskly. 'I do, and if you want to know why I don't like him, your grandson—'

'Would like nothing more than to get himself and his guest settled. So shall we?' The warning tone in his voice was hard to miss. By both women. As much as he loved his grandmother, he didn't owe her an explanation for why he'd turned up with a pregnant stranger who was carrying his baby.

As for Genie...

She got the hint well enough to purse her lips as the housekeeper stepped forward and ushered her out.

His grandmother watched everything with shrewd eyes, and when he caught her gaze, she raised an eyebrow. He shook his head, prompting the old woman to stay her words once more.

Genie eyed him the moment they stepped into the corridor.

'You two always speak to each other in sign language?'

'When you know each other that well, it helps. Who knows, you and I might develop a unique language of our own.'

A blush flew up to envelop her cheeks, but, of course, her eyes remained rapier sharp with displeasure. 'I wouldn't hold my breath if I were you.'

He stepped close enough to say his next words directly into her ear so they wouldn't be overheard. 'But there could be fun in that. There's a reason erotic asphyxiation exists, *pequeña*.'

He caught her elbow as she stumbled over her feet. Her blush bloomed into a full-blown flush he wanted to explore with his hands. Then his lips.

'You…you're outrageous. I would never indulge in such… proclivities!'

His gaze traced her graceful, voluptuous body, lingering on where his seed was growing, where his baby would bask for the next several months. Something about that earthly, primal knowledge only served to heighten the arousal that lurked so close to the surface when he was near her. 'Not in your current state, obviously, but who knows what will happen in the future, hmm?'

'Nothing remotely like that you…you pig!'

'Don't knock it until you try it. Remember how good it was between us? Tell me you had anything even close to that and I'll call you a liar,' he challenged.

Her nostrils flared but Seve, with every sinew strained towards this woman who fascinated him more than any other creature on the planet, also noticed that her eyes sparkled in that thirsty, experience-seeking way they had before.

'One experience, no matter how…noteworthy, doesn't mean I'm all in to throw myself over the edge of a cliff, Mr Valente.'

'Seve,' he insisted. Then when he caught a glimpse of her mutiny on this small issue too, he changed tack. 'Or you can call me Mr Valente. But know that that will trigger even more evocative scenarios of me disciplining you in the most deliciously decadent possible way.'

She gasped once more, further outrage bristling through her frame. But her nipples still puckered, her chest rising and falling in sweet, tormenting agitation. 'You really are a Neanderthal, aren't you?'

He smiled. 'You're outraged, maybe even genuinely, but it's not stopping you from being extremely interested in the possibilities. Your heartbeat is elevated and your pupils are dilated. I may not be a scientist but I'm well versed in body language.'

She shrugged. 'That doesn't mean anything. Human beings are programmed to learn through experiences but that's not to say I want to dip my hand into a fire just to see how hot it burns.'

He realised his fingers were caressing the velvet-soft skin of her arm. For the life of him he couldn't bring himself to stop. 'Oh, yes, you do. You thrive on it.'

Her lips parted on a scathing put-down, but then her eyes widened as she accepted the unvarnished truth. But a blink later and she was scrambling for composure. 'Not enough to do…that with you, I assure you. In fact, I would be obliged if you took your hand off me.'

Reluctantly, Seve dropped his hand, and resumed walking down the hallway. From the corner of his eye he saw her flit him a glance and he curbed a smile. As unexpected as it'd been, he'd enjoyed yet another skirmish he hadn't even consciously instigated.

Their brief history had taught him that Genie drove a hard bargain. Always. And he was beginning to relish every fight with her.

The next months would be nothing if not entertaining.

What on earth was wrong with her?

He'd mentioned sex—the serious risqué kind she imagined only took place in dungeons and racy BDSM clubs—and she'd immediately gone up in flames. Had shockingly imagined it for a nanosecond before fleeing from the thought.

She was pregnant, for heaven's sake!

Being pregnant doesn't mean sex—of any kind—is off the table…

She exhaled in exasperation as the housekeeper, who'd patiently waited a discreet distance away while Seve had rumbled on about his insane proclivities, nudged open elegant double doors and stood to one side with a gentle smile.

Genie stepped through the doors and her senses were engulfed by a different kind of overwhelming.

It was starkly different from the room she'd called her bedroom in her building for the better part of a decade. This was… magically beautiful.

Soft dove grey blended with the barest hint of blush accents, right down to the grey and blush carpet, the same colour theme on the art and decor gracing the room. Even the bedding carried on the scheme, although the pillows and covers held more blush pink than grey.

Genie had the most peculiar urge to run her fingers over everything, feel the textures beneath her fingertips. Let some of the calm tranquillity seep into her soul. She gave in, her senses settling a little when the inviting coolness made her sigh.

Of course, all of that calmness evaporated when she looked up to find Seve watching her, his gaze moving from her face to her fingers and back again.

Sofia murmuring that her things had been unpacked and pointing to the adjoining dressing room thankfully disrupted the sure path to further agitation.

A nod from Seve and the housekeeper left the room. When his gaze dropped back to her hand, now clutching a clump of bedspread, she refused to react.

'Get some rest, *pequeña*. Your personal maid will be on standby to draw you a bath if you require. We will speak further later.'

'I fail to see what about. I'm leaving in—'

'T minus twenty-one hours. Yes, I'm aware you're counting down. But until the time is up, you'll indulge me. *Sí?*'

He was walking away before she even responded, as if her answer didn't matter. As if his mind was already made up. Weariness and the need to avoid another verbal skirmish—although thus far each one with Seve had been absurdly stimulating—made her bite her tongue.

And berate herself when she got her wish to be alone and

immediately wanted him back. Wished back that invigorating force field that reminded her with every second that she was *alive*.

She sagged against the bed, let out a long exhale and kicked off her shoes. She wanted a shower. Needed to gather her thoughts. Contact the contractors who'd been expecting her in Norway to tell them she'd been unexpectedly delayed.

But weariness was dragging down every cell in her body.

And the bed was *so* inviting.

So she gave in, crawled under the sheets, and let sleep take her.

'He's a Cardosian Blanco.'

'Indeed.'

Seve watched as Genie ran her hand down the stallion's forehead and felt something intensely needful kick in his groin. She'd found him in his study after a two-hour nap and—from the scent of shampoo and alluring perfume torturing his senses—a bath. Her hair was coiled in a loose knot atop her head, leaving the elegant line of her neck to his full view.

He'd made the wise choice to start the tour outside so Lita wouldn't bombard Genie with the questions she'd fired at Seve for a full hour before he'd taken refuge in his study.

Of course, he hadn't taken into account that Genie would enthral his favourite stallion, too.

'What's his name?' she asked.

'Cyclone, so named for his terrible temperament before he learned the error of his ways.'

She hummed under her breath as she caressed him, her gaze moving over the other six horses in the paddock.

'They're breathtaking. *You're* breathtaking,' she whispered to the horse, a world removed from the woman who'd laid down the law on the plane a few short hours ago. The woman who had fought him with words every single step.

Like everything about her, her many facets intrigued him

far too much. And yet he couldn't draw his gaze away from her fingers, from the soft wonder on her face as she caressed the horse.

His horse. Which he was in danger of feeling peevishly jealous of.

'You'll have to admire them from afar for the time being, I'm afraid.'

A layer of softness receded when she glanced at him. 'You mean in the…' she glanced pointedly at her watch '…eighteen hours and nineteen minutes I'm here.'

He shrugged. 'If it pleases you to keep reminding me of the ticking clock, sure.'

Her hand slowly dropped from Cyclone's muzzle, a thing that didn't please the stallion, who attempted to nudge her touch back. And wasn't it a hell of a thing to now feel a kinship with his horse?

'I'm getting the impression that you're simply humouring my intention to leave tomorrow.'

'And there I thought I was giving you a tour.'

'I've seen your stables, your beach, your swimming pool and the admirable recycling project you've got going. I know your estate runs on an eco-safe fuel system. I would've thought a man of your position would have better things to do than devote so much time escorting me around his home.'

His jaw clenched. 'You keep making the mistake of not taking me at my word. I said you and the baby you're carrying are now my priority. You will do well to start believing me.'

'But what has it got to do with all this?' She gestured to the paddock and the stables beyond. 'Unless…' Wariness crept into her eyes. 'Unless you're humouring me because you don't intend to let me leave?'

He turned from her, striding to the electric buggy they'd used for their tour. 'Get in, Genie. We'll talk inside.'

From the corner of his eye, he watched her hesitate, then walk to the vehicle.

She remained silent for a full minute before sending a searing glance his way. 'You can't keep me here. I have plans for my future that don't include...whatever it is you've got up your sleeve for me.'

Seve nodded. 'You'll have a chance to tell me what those plans are when we get inside.'

He sensed her surprise, then her wariness. 'Is this a trick?'

'I promised you a discussion when you woke up. We're going to have it now.'

Minutes later, he watched her march into his study as if she owned the room. And, hell, if he wasn't captivated by her fighting spirit. When she went to speak, he stopped her. Crossing the room, he poured her a glass of blended juice Lita had sent Sofia with when she saw them returning. No doubt his grandmother would be monitoring Genie's food and drink intake with the fervour of a brooding hen.

'Drink this or Lita will have both our heads.'

She accepted the glass from him, her breathing wavering a little when their fingers touched. She took a sip, no doubt to be polite, then, eyes widening a fraction at the delicious taste, she gulped down the refreshing juice. A little self-consciously, she licked her lips and set the glass down.

'These plans of yours. Tell me about them,' he said.

'Bring me a laptop and I will.'

He crossed the room and returned with a sleek, brand-new device. Taking a seat next to her on the wide sofa, he watched her fingers fly across the keys with mesmerising efficiency. Ninety seconds later, she turned the screen to him.

It showed a sizeable piece of land about the size of his west paddock. In the pages that followed were elaborate plans of her intentions for the land. The more he read, the more the mixture of pride and fury stirred faster through him. Perhaps he was searching for a conclusive excuse, one she'd just handed him on a platter. But he took it and let it erode the last of his guilt.

'Everything on there is self-sustaining. Even the electricity.' Her tone was prideful. A touch defensive.

'You planned all of this?' he asked, even though he knew she did.

'Yes. It's been a year in the planning. The only thing keeping me from making it a reality is this imposed prison sentence.'

'Impressive. Your plan for one hundred per cent sustainability is highly commendable. But it's still not good enough. You're yet to put this all together and it's not advisable to take on such a project in your condition. Besides, it's too isolated. There are no medical facilities for hundreds of miles. What if something happens to you or the baby?'

She gritted her teeth. 'I had contingencies in place for that.'

'You don't need to have them here. You're surrounded by staff, some of whom have medical experience. And a doctor can be summoned within minutes. All that aside, our goals might just align in theory if not geographically.'

Against her will, curiosity bit her. 'What do you mean?'

He didn't answer immediately. Instead, he went to the laptop he'd been using on the plane and activated it. A few clicks later, he turned it towards her.

The file was detailed, with long pages of enticing offers that made her eyes widen.

Doctor's appointments, an elaborate diet plan she could approve or alter at her whim, a workspace of her choice. Yoga or Pilates instructors to attend her in person or remotely, the use of his Olympic-size swimming pool any time she wished. In fact, the whole estate was at her disposal. She would want for nothing and she could work as much or as little as she chose.

In essence, it was eerily similar to the plans she'd made for herself, the only difference being the location. And her freedom. 'It's my turn to ask if *you* planned all this all along.'

He answered without an ounce of guilt. 'Oh, yes. Everything down to the last detail. While you've been counting down the time until you leave to become an eco-warrior while pregnant with my child, I turned my life inside out. Not for me but for the baby. And therefore for you. You're the vessel keeping him warm and healthy. For now, you're important too. And this is the best place for you to remain. Nothing you've shown me convinces me otherwise.'

For now.

He couldn't have spelled out more explicitly how expendable she'd eventually come to be to him if he'd tried.

'Except it's not what I want,' she said. Then watched as his eyes gleamed with the fire of determination that announced that he was about to bring out the big guns.

'You see me letting you go as the only viable solution when I've presented you with several ways we could make this work,' he drawled. Whether he kept his voice low because it was a prelude to pouncing or not was neither here nor there.

It affected Genie as strongly in sending tremors through her body.

'None so far that are good enough. Name another.'

He paused for a fraction of a second. Then laid down his final card.

'Marry me.'

CHAPTER SIX

GENIE FELT HER eyes blink in comical slow motion.

Once. Twice. Then twice more. 'What?' The word gushed like a chain-smoking screen siren's whisper. Equally comical. She just couldn't seem to make her voice work properly.

'Marry me. Be my wife. Join me in full parenting of our child.'

She blinked again, her nostrils fluttering with emotions too illogical to name. And because she feared she couldn't contain them one second longer, she expelled them in a firm, 'No.'

The billionaire venture capitalist who'd dated some of the world's most beautiful women obviously wasn't used to being denied.

Seve's eyed widened. Not as comically as hers had, she imagined. But still, there was distinct surprise, then a tensing. As if a sucker punch to his gut had winded him.

Not that he let it show for long. 'Why not?'

Why not?

There was no need to beat about the bush. Hell, she wanted to lay it all out there in the hope that this unnerving sensation would dissipate by exposure. 'Because I don't like the way your proposal makes my insides feel.'

Something wicked and dangerous gleamed in his eyes. 'Describe it. In detail.'

'Unnerved. Elated. Then deflated. I think the common term is roller-coaster emotions. And they are a sign of weakness.

For the sake of this child, I can't be weak.' There. That was plain and stark enough.

His eyes glinted even more, pure relish entering the dark depths. 'Or it's a sign that you simply need time to let it settle, to get used to the idea.'

'Why? It'll change nothing.'

He shrugged. 'It'll give you time for clearer thinking. Roller coasters don't go on for ever. When they end, it's the abiding feeling that remains that is the most important. You're describing feelings based here...' he trailed his fingers between her breasts, then below over her swollen stomach '...rather than here.' Now his fingers caressed her temple.

Her skin reacted predictably. Chasing the chemical sensation his touch triggered. Then further plummeting her emotions when he dropped his hand.

It wasn't productive or wise to keep chasing that reaction.

And yet...she couldn't think of a counterargument, especially not when his sensual lips were moving again, forming words she needed to concentrate on.

'But should you require a little of the roller-coaster effect, we can have that too.'

'But that's...illogical. I just said it was counterproductive.'

'Not everything needs to be experienced in those terms, *pequeña*. A second helping of ice cream is sinful, but you do it anyway.'

'Just so we're clear, is ice cream a euphemism for sex?' she blurted, then continued to hold his gaze, even as her face flamed.

'I don't need to hide behind euphemisms. Marry me. Agree to joint custody and live in Cardosia. Have sex with me if that's the roller coaster you want to jump on. We both know you enjoy sex with me. And when that inevitably wanes, we'll devote ourselves to our child's upbringing.'

The purest strain of wicked temptation shivered through her before she pushed it firmly away. 'No. This wasn't part of my plan. I don't need a man to be the best parent I can be for my child. Nor do I need sex.'

His jaw tightened and his eyes narrowed into formidable slits. Genie expected him to breathe fire next, as anatomically impossible as that was. But then he'd shown her that there was far more to human interaction than just words and actions. There were…feelings. Indescribable sensations. Yearning as powerful and palpable as loneliness.

'Plans change,' he said eventually. 'You didn't plan on selling your algorithm to me and yet you did because I presented the best outcome you needed.'

'You're not comparing an algorithm to a child, are you?'

'You enjoy reducing everything to logic. I'm putting it in terms we can both work with.'

She opened her mouth to debate that, but he held up his hand. The gesture made her bristle, even as his elegant fingers evoked memories of how they'd felt just now on her body.

Seriously, what was wrong with her?

'Take the rest of your hours to decide, *pequeña*. Let that clever brain of yours weigh the pros and cons of having a two-parent support system.'

'I've already told you I had two parents who claimed to do their best. That logic is flawed.'

'They claimed it without putting in the work. Will you put in the work?'

She didn't need to think about it for even a nanosecond. 'Of course, I will.'

'So will I. You made the mistake of assuming the father of your child wouldn't want to be involved in your decisions. You need to readjust that thinking. Then go further and explore the logic and advantage of doing it together rather than apart.'

'My original plan was to go a different route.'

His eyes narrowed and Genie got the feeling he wasn't pleased about that. Why did that send such a decadent thrill through her? Was she a closet masochist too? She swallowed, a little perturbed by these layers of herself she was uncovering. What would she discover next? That she craved more of those little terms of Cardosian endearments he tossed at her with seemingly effortless ease?

No. She didn't.

'Then you shouldn't have planted that thought in my head, then taken me into your body so enthusiastically, should you?' he rasped with sizzling conceit.

'Are you blaming me for the protection failing?'

He shrugged. 'It doesn't matter how it happened. It happened.'

And now you're here. You're mine, his ferocious gaze seemed to growl.

'We're getting nowhere.'

'No. We're getting exactly where we need to get to. You're just being stubborn about seeing the merits of it. But you have a little time—'

'Sixteen hours and fifty-seven minutes isn't enough time to consider changing every single plan I have for you.'

'You wound me, *querida*,' he said, although he appeared the least wounded person she'd ever seen. 'Most women I know would jump at the chance to put a ring on me.'

'I'm not most women,' she pointed out, just because she felt a vital need to.

Only to draw an even more devastating smile. One she felt all the way to the last nerve in her small toe. 'I'm bracingly aware of that, Genie.'

And yes, there went another traitorous shiver.

One she cursed herself for reliving in the hours that followed, long after their discussion had ended, and she was hiding away in her room with her laptop.

Dinner was a stilted affair, which seemed to bewilder Lita into filling the silence with chatter, to which her grandson responded with near monosyllabic grunts.

Genie was too frazzled to parse through which social cues she needed to observe to engage with them, so she kept mostly silent, cringing a little inside every time the old woman sent a furtive glance her way, then blamed Seve under her breath for their guest's joylessness.

It would've been almost endearing to see the interaction between grandmother and grandson…if she weren't still reeling from the sharp right turn of Seve's proposal.

As night fell over the estate, the sound of cicadas and the pine-scented breeze through the open doors leading to the terrace outside the dining room calmed her a touch.

Still, she couldn't wait to escape, and the moment she was done with the heavenly slice of *chocotorta* drizzled with warm honey, she placed her napkin on the table.

'It's been a long day. I think I'll head off to bed.'

For a moment, Seve's jaw clenched but he stood and came around the table to hold her chair, an almost outdated courtesy that nevertheless made her feel that same strange rollercoaster sensation in her belly. Not to mention the effect of his aftershave with him so close.

'Before you go…'

She paused in the doorway, partly glad he'd halted her exit. She wasn't looking forward to spending hours with her thoughts spinning around in circles. And, she suspected, not even the usual thrill of coding would grab her attention.

She turned to face Seve, who'd crossed the room to lean against the giant stone-hewn mantel, one ankle crossed casually over the other. 'The doctor is coming in the morning for a check-up. Unless you have a particular objection?'

Her first check-up as an expectant mother. With the father of her child in attendance. Not how she'd expected any of this to unravel. But she could hardly say no, could she?

Her hand trailed to her stomach, the thought of seeing her baby for the first time, if only in sonogram, a touch overwhelming. 'Not at all.'

It wasn't until his shoulders relaxed fractionally that she realised he'd been tense awaiting her answer. Perhaps thought she might object.

Because that was all she'd done so far, wasn't it? She stiffened at the censorious voice.

'Good. Sleep well, *querida*.'

Another casual, terribly affecting endearment, which sizzled right through her.

Which made his grandmother produce a small, indulgent smile as she added her own goodnight wishes.

Genie nodded and fled. Then spent the better part of the night tossing and turning. Her mind whirling back to Seve Valente. And his proposal.

She woke at the crack of dawn no closer to escaping her churning thoughts. In a bid to quiet them, she grabbed her laptop and, going out onto the stunning terrace, lost herself in writing code until the sun kissed the horizon.

When birdsong replaced the chirping of cicadas and sunshine beamed down on her face in warming welcome, her fingers slowed on the keyboard.

Around her the estate was coming to life and, for the first time ever, Genie felt the all-encompassing loneliness recede a touch. Distant laughter and horses neighing lured her to the low wall. She leaned on it, taking in the sights and sounds of the estate.

It was breathtaking…for a prison?

No. She had several hours left before she found out if Seve would truly let her go or if, indeed, he was humouring her. Several hours she could use to progress her initial plans in Norway.

And yet she lingered, breathing in the incredible air and basking in the South American sun. Several minutes later, when she realised she didn't want to move from the perfect spot, Genie forced herself to do just that.

She couldn't afford to get attached to Seve or his beautiful home.

Back inside she took a shower, attempting to ignore the way her senses leapt and shimmered in anticipation the closer the breakfast hour approached. The clothes she'd packed for a temperate Norwegian summer were just as good for what passed for a Cardosian winter, so she dressed in a wispy light cotton shamrock-green sundress and a pair of flat mules and left her hair flowing free. Smoothing on a sun-blocking moisturiser, she grabbed her mobile phone and left the room.

To find Seve stepping out of his own suite halfway down the corridor.

His unapologetic stare made the already excitable butterflies flutter even more frenziedly, and, for the life of her, Genie couldn't stop scrutinising him as intently as he was watching her.

God, it was almost as if it was a silent competition to see who could stare the longest.

Her breath caught when he sauntered towards her. *'Buenos días, pequeña. Dormiste bien?'*

'Realmente, no,' she replied, before it dawned on her that she'd responded in his mother tongue. There was no taking it back.

Nor was there stopping that smug glint in his eyes or the whisper of amusement curving his lips as he stopped before her. 'You should've come to find me. We would've found a cure for your restlessness together.'

'There was no need. I knew exactly what caused it.'

Her accusation bounced off his white linen-shirted shoulders. Combined with the loose palazzo pants, he looked the picture of indolent virility and she was irritated by the effort it took to drag her gaze from his chiselled jaw and bronzed perfection. For the way her fingers itched to comb back the damp lock of hair kissing his forehead.

'The doctor will be here in an hour. Hopefully by that time, breakfast and a walk in the sun would have put you in a better disposition?'

She wanted to say there was nothing wrong with her disposition. But he was holding out his arm and her brain was short-circuiting at the thought of the sustained stimulation of their skin touching.

Get yourself together, Genie.

Sucking in a breath, she took his proffered arm.

A few minutes later, they were stepping outside onto the wide terrace on the opposite side of where they'd dined last night. The early morning sunlight bathed the space and a smiling Lita was already seated at the table.

She waved Genie to a seat after accepting a kiss from her grandson. The conversation was light and general, a vast difference from last night, much to Genie's relief. She helped herself to fruit, muesli and tea, then, at Lita's nudging, a helping of warm, buttered bread baked fresh by Sofia. She was enjoying her second cup of tea when Lita glanced over at her.

'You're still so pale, child. Don't worry. In no time at all, that pale skin will be glowing. The little *niño* will love it too, you'll see.'

Genie's reaction was visceral and immediate. 'But I'm not staying.'

Lita's eyes widened with confusion, then slowly darkened with distress. Her gaze shifted to her grandson. As did Genie's.

His earlier congeniality was gone. He was watching Genie with a chilled message in his eyes.

Don't upset her, it warned.

As recently as yesterday, she would've ignored him. Stated exactly what was on her mind. But Lita had welcomed her with nothing but warmth. It wasn't her fault that her grandson was a Neanderthal who went around kidnapping women to his gorgeous South American estate.

Not women. Just you.

And it was probably in that moment, when outrage should've been her reigning emotion but instead there deigned to be a swelling for this special exclusivity, that Genie realised she was dangerously close to losing her way. To buckling under Seve Valente's demands.

'What does she mean?' Lita asked her grandson.

Seve's jaw gritted. 'Nothing for you to worry about, Lita.'

The old woman glared at him. 'I'll be the judge of what I need to worry about, *mijo*.' She turned to Genie, skewering her with a look so much like her grandson's, Genie's breath caught. 'Are you planning to leave?' There was mild accusation in her tone. And, absurdly, guilt stung Genie.

She glanced at Seve, but he wasn't inclined to save her now she'd upset his precious grandmother and placed herself in the old woman's crosshairs.

Genie licked her lips as he reached for the carafe of orange juice, poured her a glass and proceeded to pour himself some heavenly smelling coffee.

He took his time to sip it, his eyes mocking her over the top of the expensive china.

'I had…have a project that I'm working on that I need to return to.'

'Do you?' Seve enquired with deceptive mildness.

'Yes,' she insisted, struggling not to scowl.

'Perhaps you should double-check those plans before you make hasty decisions?'

A chill washed over her neck. 'What are you talking about?'

He shrugged but before she could push for an answer, the butler stepped onto the terrace. '*Señor*, the doctor and his team are here.'

A different sort of tension swept over the table. The only one who looked excited was Lita. Seve pinned Genie with a look as he came around to grip the back of her chair. Under the guise of helping her up, he murmured in her ear, 'We'll pick this up later.'

'We most certainly will.'

Their march back indoors was far more strained than when they'd come down half an hour ago. Genie kicked herself for feeling bereft for it. And even as she was introduced to the middle-aged female doctor with her all-female crew, something churned in her chest that closely resembled desolation.

The portable gurney set up in one of the smaller siting rooms was comfortable, yet Genie couldn't bring herself to relax. The series of questions Dr Dominici asked her didn't help, conscious as Genie was of Seve's domineering presence beside her.

As one of the doctor's team made notes on a tablet, Genie felt fingers caressing her temple. 'Relax, *pequeña*. All this tension isn't good for the baby.'

The words were low and evenly spoken against her ear, but they held the tiniest edge that did the opposite. Seve felt it, and she sensed his displeasure as he straightened again. But in the next moment, her belly was being exposed by Dr Dominici, and Seve's fingers were wrapping around hers as the screen flickered to life.

And then an alarming thing happened.

Awe filled her as she saw the bundle of cells that was her baby for the first time, just as Seve's fingers brushed soothingly over her knuckles, making her spine ease against the bed and the tension ooze right out of her. Genie couldn't have separated the two emotions if her life depended on it. And when strong hands tightened around hers, she tightened hers in return. She told herself she couldn't look away from the screen because she didn't want to miss a thing.

But deep down she knew she wasn't ready to see the same emotions weaving through her reflected in Seve's face. Or worse...*not.*

And weren't pregnancy emotions truly the worst? Because now her jumbled emotions were making her eyes prickle and the blood rush into her ears, and the insidious voice asking if she was truly ready to go off to Norway, continue this journey on her own when she could stay right here. In the sun and warmth and mercurial but, oh, so stimulating presence of her infuriating captor.

A peculiar sound escaped her throat before she could stop it. More alarming reaction to add to the suddenly mystifying code that was her life.

'Everything all right?' Dr Dominici asked.

Genie cleared her throat. 'I believe I…we should be asking you that.'

The doctor smiled. '*Sí*. Everything is as it should be. The heartbeat is strong and the measurements show you're almost ten weeks along. We will be able to tell the sex of the baby on the next scan if you're interested?'

Genie felt Seve's gaze boring into her, compelling hers. Unable to resist, she glanced up at him. And there it was. The formidably powerful range of emotions she'd been too terrified to confront. It was right there, swirling through his eyes, and in the slightly elevated rise and fall of his chest. In the eyes that left hers for a brief moment to cling to the screen, his fingers spasming a touch before firming again.

Oh, he was affected as much as she was, and she was one hundred per cent sure he'd want to know the sex. But for some reason, he quirked one eyebrow, leaving the decision to her.

To butter her up? To make her feel in control of a situation *he* ultimately controlled?

Genie didn't care. *Couldn't*. Because all this was suddenly too much.

'I prefer to wait. *Gracias*,' she tagged on.

Dr Dominici nodded briskly, then went through a list of caretaking advice. Finally, she hit a button on the screen, then held out two squares of glossy paper, one to each of them.

Genie took it, heart hammering and throat clogging when she looked down at her child. Seve scrutinised his intently, then slid it into his pocket.

Five minutes later, they were back in the hallway and the tension was creeping back.

'I need a moment…' she started, then realised it sounded as if she were asking permission. She cleared her throat. 'I have things to do. I'll come and find you when I need to talk.'

'Genie.'

Again that wave of suppressed emotion was evident in his voice. Her belly clenched, half in alarm and half in anticipation. But layer by layer, the emotions dissipated, leaving his face as smooth as cold glass.

'I'll see you at lunch.'

He walked away without a backward glance.

And she escaped to her bedroom, pacing the living room as she clutched the photo of the child growing in her belly.

When she eventually flopped down onto the sofa and dragged her beloved laptop close, Genie wasn't surprised to find an email from the project manager in Norway. She barely went past the Due to unforeseen circumstances… before she closed the email.

Whether Seve Valente had a hand in disrupting her project or not didn't even matter. The traitorous relief flowing through her unlocked the cipher of her decision. She had a handful of hours until her self-imposed deadline ended, but it didn't matter any more either.

Staring down at the ultrasound picture, she took a breath.

And made a decision.

Four months later

Genie would be reluctant to admit it openly, but she loved everything about Cardosia.

Four months and thoughts of Norway had receded so far, she struggled to recall why she'd felt so strongly about going there in the first place. Yes, her ambition to discover new and improved ways for communities to realise a sustainable future burned bright, and the auspices under which she'd arrived in Cardosia still stung a little, but her perspective had shifted somewhat.

For starters, because Seve had never made her feel like a prisoner. And because once she'd got the full picture of what needed to be done in his country, she'd known that her plans could be shelved for the moment. Cardosia was on the brink of ecological disaster.

Maybe all this had happened because Seve knew her better than she knew herself? Knew she wouldn't try to escape? It was a recurring thought that lately triggered mild panic in her. One in a series of alarming fluttering every time she thought of the man whose baby was growing healthy and strong inside her.

And that was the other thing.

Where was her feminine outrage? And why was she referring to their child as *his baby* now, when she'd been spitting nails on the plane when he'd done the same?

She hated to admit it, but he'd been clever in slowly drawing her into the plans he had for using her algorithm for Cardosia. When he'd shown her the scale of devastation the mining and agricultural plundering was causing, she'd been shocked. Then she'd got to work.

Her algorithm had predicted and devised shortened steps to reclaiming the land, much to the delight of Cardosia's scientists.

Even more impressive was discovering that he'd been secretly buying the desecrated land and handing it over to a nature trust after guaranteeing it would be ecologically maintained. But there were still astonishingly large areas where urgent help was needed.

Finding out during the course of her work that the man responsible for the shocking state of the Cardosian economy was Seve's uncle, Lorenzo Valente, had brought her up short. And when she'd mentioned his name at dinner and received a frosty response from Seve, she'd known to leave the matter alone.

Seve and the team he'd gathered to implement his plans were in a race against time. She was better off concentrating her energies on her contribution to his essential project.

And if she liked it a little bit too much when he praised her for the work her algorithm had achieved, it was a reaction she wisely kept to herself.

What was occupying more and more space in her mind was the trouble she was having analysing why he'd *stopped* asking her to marry him.

For the first month, he'd steadily demanded she give him her decision. Aided and abetted by an eager Lita, who freely expressed that she would love nothing more than for them to wed.

And then he'd stopped. Cold turkey.

Which, of course, had triggered her agitation.

Did he not want to marry her any longer?

The heated eyes that followed her around and the drift of his fingers over her arm, her back of her neck, and, oh, God, her growing belly, said otherwise.

The worst of it was when he travelled to San Martina, the capital city of Cardosia, or even overseas for a few days. It was illogical to torture herself with thoughts of who he was seeing, whether it was of the female persuasion. They owed each other no fidelity after all.

And yet…she missed him with a fervour bordering on insanity.

And when he stalked into her tech studio in search of her on his return and his gaze ran feverishly over her as his chest rose and fell in a deep exhale, her heart leapt, even as she convinced herself it was normal. That there was a rational explanation for it.

They shared a child.

It was one such time that he lingered on his return, sprawling his six-foot-three-inch frame on the long sofa he'd insisted was placed in the basement studio so she could take breaks.

Once he'd conducted that thorough scrutiny that involved

running his eyes all over her body, then lingering on her belly, he looked around her work space.

'I have countless rooms in this house and on the estate you can use. Or I can have one built to purpose for you. Why do you choose to hide in the basement?'

She started to shrug but the eyes boring into hers stopped her. Over the past four months, she'd discovered they shared an interest in many facets of their lives. More than she would've thought possible. She'd seen first-hand how much he cared for his country and the environment.

Equally significantly, they were sharing the most important event possibly of their lives.

Certainly of hers.

And while his first barb about her previous basement-dwelling had stung, he'd done it out of ignorance. No one on earth knew what that previous space had meant to her because she'd never shared it.

So enlighten him. So he'll think better of me?

She swallowed the *yes* that rose far too readily to her throat.

Those instances were arriving far too frequently. She'd need to watch that or—

'The longer you take to answer my question, the more intrigued I become.' His languid repose was deceptive. Yet she was drawn to it like prey to a majestic jungle cat. The misleading conviction that she could sidle up and stroke him was all too real and, no matter how much her logical brain tried to warn her that she was straying into dangerous territory, she still couldn't resist the intoxicating danger of baring herself to him. Of basking in that magnificent aura he exuded so effortlessly.

But this feeling—so intense, so raw—was out of her comfort zone. God, everything about Seve Valente had been way out of her sphere of comfort from the moment they met.

A furtive glance at him showed him still relaxed. Intensely alert—because that was his natural state—but giving off an air of recreation that was…soothing. She almost laughed at the description.

Soothing and Seve didn't go hand in hand. Was he making an effort?

Should she?

She frowned inwardly at her own flailing. 'I'm at a loss as to where to start,' she confessed reluctantly.

He nodded. 'That suggests there's a deeper meaning behind your choices?'

She shrugged, still unsure she should be baring herself like this. 'Isn't there always?'

'No. Some nerds just prefer the stereotype,' he said with a trace of amusement, which dissolved as he continued to watch her with hawkish eyes. 'You're not one of them.'

'Probably because I'm not a nerd.'

'No, you're not. You're much more,' he said with the kind of matter-of-factness kings and gods tossed about with conceited abandon.

And, damn him, it had the desired effect. To know that he recognised the special circumstances behind her previous and present actions…mattered. So before she could think further on it, she blurted, 'My parents used me for power and prestige from when I was six to fifteen.'

CHAPTER SEVEN

HE STIFFENED, his posture no longer as relaxed as it'd been seconds ago. He didn't move much, but the intensity in his gaze increased, searing and searching, demanding more.

And Genie had no choice but to give now she'd opened the forbidden box of memories.

'At first it was signing me up for quizzes and maths contests they said would help with bills and to pay for my educational equipment.' She paused, the lump in her throat making it hard for her to swallow.

Superfluous emotion.

She wanted to bat it away but for the first time since Dr Douglas died, Genie found herself readily steeping herself in his counsel. Or was it because it closely echoed Seve's own words the first time they'd been together?

'Let yourself feel. Don't try to rationalise it. Whether it's pain or pleasure, feel it. Both heal.'

Yes. The voice started off as Dr Douglas's and curiously grew deeper, accented, with distinct tones of the man watching her. Waiting for her to bare herself further.

She shook her head free of the muddling sensations. 'It then grew to radio shows and TV appearances and international chess matches.'

A tic rippled through his jaw. 'They were using your genius to line their own pockets.' It wasn't a question but a rapier-sharp statement.

The naked disapproval and quiet rage made more emotions unravel through her. 'Yes. They had no clue how my brain worked or how to have the simplest conversation with me, but they were quick to brag about how much money my intelligence had made them in a particular financial quarter. And because I was a child, they controlled everything. So they could get a big house and employ a full-time minder to look after me while they travelled the world, spending the money they'd made off me.'

'They neglected you,' he confirmed through clenched teeth. 'Completely.'

Again, Genie suspected she was letting herself down by basking in his righteous indignation on her behalf, but in that moment, she didn't care. It felt...*good*. Hadn't Dr Douglas urged her to accept that positive emotion in those rare moments it happened?

'Yes, they did,' she responded, sucking in a breath when something cracked in her chest. Perhaps it was finally speaking it out loud.

'What happened when you were fifteen?' he pressed.

'They died in a boating accident. They were testing out a speedboat they'd leased during a holiday in the south of France when it overturned at high speed. They both drowned.'

A rumbling volcano blazed in his eyes. 'Where were you? Tell me you weren't with them?'

She shook her head, then shivered in recollection of the fear and abject loneliness she'd felt when the two policemen had delivered the horrible news. 'I was at home, in the basement, writing security code for a Swiss bank they'd made a deal with. I couldn't even stop to go and see my dead parents because they'd locked me into an impossible deadline. I finished it in time to attend their funeral.' She paused, a part of her stunned that she was peeling back so many painful layers. But she was on a course she couldn't abandon, like a string of code she had no choice but to see through to completion. 'But that wasn't the worst of it.'

His eyes swept down for a moment, then rose to pin her. 'What was worse than burying your parents when you were fifteen?'

She couldn't sustain the eye contact; his was too penetrating and Genie suspected hers probably showed far too much raw emotion. She hadn't quite perfected the knack of hiding her feelings like him. Her gaze dropped to the gentle swell of her stomach.

At six and a half months, her stomach was well pronounced. Resting her hand on it, she sucked in a long sustaining breath.

'It's burying your parents when you're fifteen then finding yourself in foster care before the sun sets on the same day.'

He jerked forward, his elbows landing on his knees as he cursed darkly in Cardosian under his breath. 'They didn't provide for you?'

She exhaled shakily. 'No. They didn't bother to put a guardianship in place should anything happen, so I was destined for foster care. I also discovered the house was rented, not owned, and they were in rental arrears. Much like with every other luxury they'd helped themselves to. They'd perfected the art of living excessively beyond their means. In fact, the only thing I owned were the clothes in my wardrobe and my laptop. Even the more expensive tech equipment was on lease agreement.'

'What about the deal with the Swiss bank?'

'They'd already collected on it and the money was gone.'

Eyes filled with banked fury rested on her. '*Dios mio*, Genie…'

She looked away because something in his eyes promised far more danger. The kind that *warmed. Comforted.* Made this sharing almost…*okay.*

This should've been an information-delivering exercise. A means for him to see why she preferred the workspace she preferred. Even if, inherently, the choice was based on emotion?

She shrugged the probing voice away while attempting to push away the warmth burrowing inside her. He evoked far too many of those feelings in her lately, and it was becoming too convenient to blame it on pregnancy hormones. 'Pity isn't useful. I found a way around my situation.'

'It wasn't pity. Trust me, I know what that feels like.'

Her head snapped up and their gazes collided. His shadowed a touch, as if he regretted his revelation. Before she could ask him to elaborate, he asked, 'How did you get around the situation?'

'By shortening my time in foster care to one single month,' she said, striving for the same matter-of-fact tone he'd used earlier, and missing by a mile. Because that month had been the most miserable of her already miserable life thus far, and what had come afterwards had been a mix of terror and loneliness, the residue of which she hadn't ever shaken off, despite Dr Douglas's help.

'One *month*? How? What happened after that?' Seve bit out.

She allowed herself a smile, even though she usually hated gloating, especially over those circumstances. But she'd come through the harrowing ordeal stronger. If not fully in control of her life—because she'd never been quite successful in ridding herself of the abject loneliness—at least with the final say over who she let beneath her guard. 'I ran away from my foster home and started a company that bought the building that eventually served as my head office.'

'How?' he rasped again.

'I'm determined. I'm sure you know that about me. And it's astoundingly easy when you've just written code for a Swiss bank. I hired myself out to companies wanting similar work who didn't bother to ask how old I was. I used the money to acquire shell companies and used *those* to buy a building.'

The slightest widening of his eyes was the giveaway that she'd impressed him. 'And then what?'

'A few keystrokes when you know what you're doing is all

it takes. I erased myself from most databases and hid from the system in the basement of the same building I bought. Even then I'd had enough of well-meaning men in suits who claimed to have my best interest at heart but insisted my continued well-being would proceed smoother by letting them help me hone my intellect. I disagreed. So I made myself a home in the basement of my building and I stayed there until I turned eighteen.'

Shock shrouded his face and the hands hanging down between his knees bunched for a few seconds as he said sharply, 'You lived *alone* down there in that square box for three years?'

A peculiar mixture of pride and shame fizzled through her. 'Just about. I was a few weeks from turning sixteen when my parents died. And my choices were limited. I didn't want to be an unwanted burden on anyone or let anyone else dictate my future. Especially the government.'

His nostrils flared and he raked his fingers through his hair. 'Because the two people who should've made your welfare their priority didn't.'

More emotion shook through her. 'Yes.' Her voice quivered with her answer.

He rose from his seat and approached, slowly, prowling languorously as if he didn't want to spook her.

For the longest time, he just stared down at her.

She struggled not to fidget but it was hard when she could almost feel the atomic particles colliding from their proximity. Did every couple who had created a child between them feel this way? This constant edginess as if something seismic was about to happen?

No, she answered her own question. She was certain this was unique to them. Unique and ultimately detrimental if left unguarded against.

And yet she didn't protect herself when he lifted his hand and caught a strand of her hair between his fingers. When he toyed with the silken tresses for an age before transferring that riveting gaze to hers. 'You are a formidable creature, Genie Merchant. But while this is familiar territory and comforting for you, you don't need to hide any more. You have more than earned the right to step out into the light now.' His gaze raked her face intensely before he added, 'And in the light is where you belong.'

The words were low and deep, rumbling through her like a seismic event until it stopped precariously close to her heart. Until it made her so weak, she raised her hand, braced it against his chest as he continued to play with her hair, to stare deep into her eyes, absorbing her every reaction.

Her fingers curled into warm, solid muscle. That weakening intensified.

And before she knew it, she was surging up onto her tiptoes, straining for more of that warmth, that connection, that *feeling* she'd avoided for so long because she'd equated it with weakness, but now craved above all else. For good or ill, she wanted it.

And she would have it.

He met her need, tunnelling his fingers into her hair to cradle her skull, while his other hand braced beneath her body, easily supporting her as his wickedly sensual lips claimed her with unfettered passion.

She was moaning long before his tongue swept past her willing lips to tangle with hers. To stroke with such sensual mastery, she lost her train of thought.

'*Dios mio.* You're intoxicating,' he stated hoarsely when they separated. His fingers drifted down her temple to her cheek, then he traced the outline of her mouth. 'You glow with our child and your joy is enthralling to watch.'

'I was terrified when I found out I was pregnant. It felt… daunting,' she found herself confessing. She'd already bared so much of her secrets, pain and loss. Why not one more?

'But not so much any more?'

She shook her head. 'Not lately, no.'

'Good. You can rest in the assurance that we will always do what is right by our child.'

Something shrivelled inside her at his words. Genie couldn't quite pin it down, but a cool breeze swept over her, dampening her fervour.

It grew colder when, with one last feather-light touch, he stepped back. 'I'll let you finish your work. But from now on, I'll escort you upstairs to lunch every day, and you'll take more breaks to eat and relax. *Entendido?*'

A sliver of that warmth crept back. When was the last time someone cared enough about her like this? *Never.* 'If you insist.'

Dark eyes gleamed with immovable intent. 'I do. Very much.'

And it was as he was leaving that it struck her that she could do something about this feeling. At the very least, she could ensure she wasn't left with these yawning feelings of uncertainty whenever he went away.

Because surely as a wife she would have rights?

Besides the kidnapping their dealings so far had been above board. Deep inside she knew he was a man who held himself to a high standard.

Enough to abstain from sex indefinitely?

Have sex with me if that's the roller coaster you want to jump on.

The thought sent shivers through her, which were doused when thoughts of the end impinged. Dear God. Was she really considering marrying him just so she could ensure he didn't stray into another woman's arms? When she'd explicitly stated that she had no intention of falling into his bed again? What did that make her?

Selfish. Self-centred. Self-absorbed. Human?

That last plaintive question echoed in her own voice, not Dr Douglas's. And when it trailed away, she was no closer to satisfying herself that she was making a sound decision. Which unfortunately threatened her concentration for the rest of the day and in the days that followed.

Days when Seve arrived mid-morning, at lunch and mid-afternoon, as promised, to ensure she took breaks. To walk outside with her, where cool drinks appeared as if by magic at vantage points. And at one spot under a large Cardosian mesquite tree, a picnic had been laid out.

She was enjoying a glass of her now favourite drink—which she'd discovered was a combination of guava, mango and a dash of alcohol-free Cardosian *hierbas* poured over tons of ice—when she felt his gaze on her.

'The doctor is returning tomorrow. Are you still determined not to find out the sex of our child?' His deep voice was laced with amusement.

Dressed in loose linen trousers and a white polo shirt and relaxing with his back against the tree, he was the picture of masculine health and vitality, made even more potent by the impressive bulge between his thighs accentuated by his crossed ankles.

Her face heated when she realised she'd been staring far longer than was polite. Clearing her throat, she attempted to get her brain to track. 'There's nothing to be gained from knowing. It won't make the pregnancy go any faster. My only concern is that he or she is healthy.'

'You know Lita will take it as a personal affront that your refusal is blocking her from making a list of suitable names, don't you?'

The laughter that burst out of her surprised Genie. Seve too, if the fierce glint and fixed stare were indications. But then his grandmother had become a delightful fixture in her day. She shared at least one meal with the old lady and although she was close-lipped about her grandson's past—because Genie had attempted to garner a few titbits after his reaction to his uncle's name—they got on very well.

So much so that Genie had started to embrace the idea that

not all family was all bad. That maybe there was something worth hanging onto regardless of what happened with her and Seve once the baby was born.

'She'll make the list regardless. Just as I'm sure she's secretly designing nursery and christening gowns.' Her statement held a question.

Which Seve blatantly ignored with a shrug. 'I reserve the right not to incriminate myself.'

She continued staring at him as her curiosity mounted. 'Will I have to fight you on names too when the time comes?'

The mood altered a touch, his gaze growing cool when he answered, 'I'm not one of those men who insists on their child taking their name to perpetuate some lofty idea of worthiness or virility.'

She sat up against the half a dozen cushions laid out for her comfort, tugging the light blanket around herself. 'You're named after your father.' She'd discovered as much in her research but not much beyond that. 'It's not a stretch to believe your reasoning stems from this.'

He stiffened and once again Genie suspected she'd strayed onto a red zone. But while she mourned the loss of their easy conversation and laughter of minutes ago, a newly discovered yearning wanted to keep transiting through this danger and discomfort. This…roller coaster.

Dr Douglas would call this progress. And hadn't Seve himself claimed that roller coasters eventually ended, leaving abiding feeling?

Her abiding feeling before she'd stepped on the path was that she wanted to know him more. She'd bared herself to him against every self-preserving caution.

'If there was ever a blatant example of a man using his offspring to over-inflate his ego, then I was it for my father. Hell, both my parents.'

The words were tossed out with icy contempt but Genie suspected he wasn't even aware of the bitterness coating his voice. His gaze was trapped in the middle distance, his languid pose replaced by pure tension.

'Lita doesn't seem like the kind of woman who would sit by and let you be treated that way.'

His face hardened further, as if this truth was even more caustic. 'She isn't. Which was why they cut her out of their lives and by extension mine until I went to find her when I turned eighteen.'

'They deliberately kept you two apart?'

One corner of his mouth lifted but his expression was humourless. 'She didn't hesitate to make her feelings known about how her son and daughter-in-law were mistreating her grandson, only bringing him out to display him to their guests when it benefitted them to play the parental role. At some point, she begged them to let me live with her permanently. They refused of course. It didn't suit my father to be seen as a neglectful parent, even though he fitted the label. And once he passed, my mother attempted to pick up where he'd left off. I'd made my first ten million and she felt it was time to leverage her son's accomplishments for social elevation. I hear she still does with her Z-list friends in Buenos Aires.'

Genie gasped. 'Your mother is alive?'

'Very much so. But since the only use she had for me were bragging rights she could gain from having a billionaire son, we parted ways a long time ago.'

Silence reined over their picnic, Genie fighting the strong urge to reach out.

She'd gone with her instincts far too much lately. And these raw emotions were too potent to trust. For all she knew, it was the wrong social cue.

Screw logic. Just feel.

'I don't know if those traits attracted them to one another or whether she was corrupted by my father later, all I know is that family was secondary to him. His primary raison d'être was to elevate himself first and foremost, by whatever means necessary. Fully endorsed by my uncle.'

A jolt went through her at his volunteering this morsel. 'Lorenzo?'

Chilling bleakness entered his eyes. 'I don't know who influenced whom about my upbringing but the worst of it came from him.'

Her mouth dried. 'What did he do?'

Tense moments ticked by when he said nothing, his mouth a thin, forbidding line. When his fingers tightened, she wanted to reach out, to lay her hands over his in reassurance. But she held still, gave him the space he needed.

'He couldn't father children of his own, so I became his surrogate son with my father's blessing. He was rich and influential enough to sway my parents to his thinking about my upbringing.' His tension ratcheted up until she feared he would snap from the force of it. 'Including administering routine corporal punishment when I was deemed to have misbehaved.'

Genie gasped. 'No.' She didn't realise her hand had shot out to cover his clenched fists until he looked down.

For an eternity they remained still, then his nostrils flared in a loud exhale. 'Oh, yes. They believed being belted on a regular basis would make me a proper man.' The words crackled with bitterness.

Something in her chest cracked as puzzle pieces slotted into place. 'Is that…is that why you didn't want a child of your own?' she ventured softly.

Shadowed eyes rose to meet hers. 'Lita is the only family I trust. But she's not going to be around for ever.' He shrugged. 'The human psyche is a labyrinth. Some things are worth the risk. I didn't think bringing a child into a family plagued by dysfunction and abuse was one of them.'

Her heart lurched. 'Do you still think that?'

His features darkened further. A muscle ticked in his jaw and his gaze lowered to the blanket. 'Like you, I don't accept failure as an option,' he said, his voice driven with purpose. Perhaps even a determination to prove he could succeed where his father and uncle had failed?

It wasn't the resounding *no* she'd hoped for. But then didn't she have her own misgivings about her looming role?

His trauma wasn't on par with what her parents had done to her, but it resonated, making her wonder if this was what had drawn her to him.

They both carried scars from a past filled with hurt.

The very possibility of such a kinship cracked something tight and hard inside her, a firewall against her loneliness that she realised had been battered and softened in the months she'd been in Cardosia.

Long after the picnic had ended, Genie couldn't harden herself back up again.

On her return to the suite she'd grown ridiculously attached to, she paced. At a much slower clip than before but the vastness of the rooms and the added square footage of the terrace served their purpose.

She'd agreed to stay until the baby was born.

But she was also locked in contractually with Seve's project for the next few years. A project she believed in. Why not take the last step?

They'd both witnessed the deep flaws in their upbringing. Enough to avoid the pitfalls in their own parenting. And as Seve had repeatedly pointed out, weren't they better doing this together than apart?

As if agreeing, Genie felt the softest kick in her womb.

Breath catching, she sank down on the bed and cradled her bump.

'Is that what you want, little one?' It wasn't illogical to talk to her baby. Not when the science had proved it was an effective means of communication. Encouraged even.

So...forget logic. Just feel.

But not too much. Because feelings of bonding love with her baby were one thing.

Letting her firewall be completely eroded and baring herself to emotional desolation from Seve—a man accepting father-hood because it'd been thrust on him—was another.

CHAPTER EIGHT

SHE MADE SURE to keep as much emotion out of it as possible by lingering after breakfast and sharing another cup of tea with Lita until after Seve left for his study, before following him.

She swallowed the nerves eating at her and barely waited for his prompt to enter after knocking before stalking in, and promptly stumbling to a halt.

Genie was sure he didn't plan it that way—the man she'd come to know didn't chase after vanity—but once again he was bathed in worshipping sunshine, the rays lovingly detailing every perfect sinew and curve, every symphony of movement.

She was frozen in rapt appreciation when he looked up from the documents he was studying, his pursed lips easing when he saw her. But that look reminded her of the formidable powerhouse behind the Valente name. That he had a global empire beyond the borders of Cardosia, one maintained with an iron but very successful fist of his stock value, was an indication.

'Genie, did we forget to discuss something?' he asked, although his tone implied he'd forgotten nothing.

Prodding herself to move, she approached and stopped at a sensible distance where, if she was lucky, she wouldn't have to breathe in his enticing masculine scent on top of everything else. 'We didn't. This is an unscheduled visit to tell you that I've made my decision. I'll marry you.'

She had the pleasure of witnessing Seve caught in wordless shock for a handful of seconds.

Then the usual characteristics flowed. The gleam of triumph in his slate-grey eyes. The imperial nod that suggested he was pleased she was finally seeing things his way.

Then of course that smooth uncoiling of his body from his chair, the well-oiled symmetry of his stride as he ignored her silent plea and brought all that power and sexiness and heavenly scent into her space.

Surrounded her with it.

'This is unexpected excellent news, *pequeña*,' he rasped, his gaze raking her intently as if he hadn't seen her at the breakfast table ten minutes ago.

Feeling all kinds of salacious heat prowling through her, she folded her arms, ignoring the mild discomfort of doing so over her protruding belly.

'My project is on hold for the foreseeable future but I can still work on many more that aren't mine.'

'With mine a priority of course,' he inserted, his eyes still doing that laser-beam thing on her face, absorbing every reaction.

'As per the contract, yes.'

'And those are your only reasons? You don't need to rush off somewhere else to save the world?' Was that an edge in his voice?

She shrugged, even though her heart was beating faster than it had a minute ago. 'Your argument had merit. I'm not averse to trying to do this together. With the option to dissolve the partnership if it proves fractious.'

His lips compressed. 'How very...clinical. Are you sure there are no other reasons?'

She frowned. 'What other reasons could there be? I'm not intoxicated on high emotion, if that's what you're getting at.'

His eyes darkened, but he nodded a moment later. '*Bueno*. The important thing is that you've seen sense. You're doing what's best for our child.'

For the first time, something chafed and snagged inside her.

The tiniest hint of resentment that shocked and horrified her. Because it struck her hard that, for a millisecond, she hadn't wanted to be doing this *just* for her child. She'd wanted to be included in the equation that made the whole, not a tossed-aside fraction with no relevance.

'Genie?'

She shook her head, berating herself for the unforgivable flaw. But was it truly a flaw to consider herself a little?

Is there no room for me, *too?*

'Genie.'

The firmer, commanding voice refocused her. Made her aware that he now stood before her, eyes narrowed on her face.

'Yes?'

'What are you thinking?'

She couldn't tell him her thoughts, of course. She hadn't forgotten his cutting words about her basement and how totally absorbed she could be in her work. Mention that she'd been selfishly thinking of how she wanted some attention too, and she'd be proving him right.

She licked her lips, hunting for a feasible answer, acutely aware that with every second his gaze grew more probing.

'I—' She stopped and gasped, the firm kick in her middle snatching her words, saving her from scrambling for an answer. 'Oh!' Her hand flew to her belly, her gaze darting up to meet his suddenly intense one.

Firm hands gripped her upper arms, his eyes racing over her. 'What is it? Is the baby okay?'

Again that abrasion bruised, but, thankfully, the joy of feeling her baby move soothed it. Momentarily.

'No, nothing's wrong. I just felt the baby move.'

His gaze dropped to her stomach, his attention riveted on the pronounced swell. 'Does it hurt?'

For some reason it provoked soft laughter. 'No. Of course not. It's not even uncomfortable. Only a little…unfamiliar.'

His eyes darkened. 'But beautiful, *si*?' he prompted hoarsely.

'Oh, yes. Very much so,' she murmured, her voice equally hushed, as if terrified to break the moment.

The feeble kick came again and, at her gasp, Seve leaned even closer, watching her hand trace the movement with almost awed eyes. 'May I?' he rasped.

Struck by the profound moment despite having felt several flutters in the past, Genie could only nod.

His hand dropped to hover over her stomach, his gaze rapt on her belly. The moment she felt another movement, she took his hand and guided it to the location. For several seconds, they waited, breathless.

Then the third kick came. His intake of breath snapped off halfway and he made a choking sound. *'Dios mio, eso es increíble,'* he rasped under his breath.

'I've been feeling a bit more movement but the textbooks say the kicks will get stronger,' she offered, why, she couldn't exactly say. It felt like something she needed to share.

He nodded but his gaze didn't leave her stomach for an age. And of course, because it was Seve Valente, he was rewarded with two more kicks.

When he raised his head, his eyes were molten with overpowering emotion. Emotion she wasn't averse to opening herself up to. To sharing with him because he was directly partnered in this phenomenal event.

The cadence of his caress shifted, the hand moving over her stomach less searching, more…targeted at a different kind of exploration.

'Wh-what are you doing? Is this another social cue I'm unaware of?' Her voice was breathless because they were still wrapped up in feeling their baby kick. Not because…not because other sensations were swirling around them, intensifying with each passing second. Sensations she wanted to dive headlong into, they were so alluringly potent.

'I should hope so. What is happening is that I'm a redblooded man, *mi dulce.* The sight of the woman who has just agreed to take my name—*my woman*—ripe with my child, turns me on. I'm not going to apologise for it. Especially when you're this breathtaking with it.'

'Seve…'

'Si?' he drawled as his hand moved to her hip, slowly bunching up the flimsy material of her dress in his strong fist and drawing it up her body. 'Tell me you don't like this,' he demanded as he walked her a short distance to the bare wall of his study.

'I…can't.' The unvarnished truth. Because she liked his hands on her. It was mind-altering. Comparable only to the euphoria of spinning an elusive code into being.

He tilted his head, aligning his face against hers until his stubble teased her skin, his steady exhale brushing her earlobe. 'Tell me you don't want this,' he breathed, starting a delicious shiver that shimmered down her neck all the way to her toes.

'I… I…' She moaned when his fingers whispered over the top edge of her panties. 'I do. I want it.'

With a gruff sound of satisfaction, he dragged the blunt edges of his nails over the skin above her panty line, eliciting a shaken gasp. Her eyes squeezed shut as decadent sensation washed over her.

'Another first for us, *pequeña*. I too have done my research. Pregnant women are extra sensitive. And I've been dying to experience that first-hand.'

Before she could respond, his fingers were delving beneath the soft cotton, seeking her very needy, very wet centre. Finding it, he released a torrent of Cardosian her brain translated as praise and satisfaction and sheer pleasure at her unfettered response.

Genie sagged in his hold, her back braced against the wall and her head falling forward to rest on his shoulder as his fingers boldly explored her. Minutes passed when he teased and tormented with shallow thrusts and feathery touches.

'Seve,' she half moaned, half protested.

'Shh, *mi hermosa flor*, you will be allowed to bloom in due time,' he growled against her ear, then caught her lobe between his teeth. 'For now, let me explore. Let me pleasure you.'

She trembled, her breaths gasping as two fingers breached her feminine centre, stretching her channel as he finally satisfied her craving.

'Seve!'

'Ah, *querida*. You're just as gloriously tight as I remember. I can't wait to feel you again when you beg me to claim you.'

The *please* trembled on her tongue right then.

Genie didn't know where she found the strength to bite it back. Perhaps she didn't. Perhaps she was rendered mute by the fingers thrusting inside her, finding and stroking that secret bundle of nerves deep inside, at the same time his thumb circled her clitoris and the arm holding her up relocated to her neck, firmly tilting her head up to meet his fiery kiss.

The triple sensation was too much. *Far too much.*

With a muted scream he swallowed as his due, Genie came apart in his arms, succumbing to the transcendent chemistry cascading through her body, transporting her to bliss.

Eyes still shut, she realised a long minute later that the floating sensation was Seve carrying her across the room, spreading her out on his sofa. When she dragged her eyes open, it was to find him poised over her, his ferocious gaze devouring every twitch and shiver.

'You're so beautiful when you come,' he said thickly. Then stunned her by reaching for her sodden panties and dragging them off her body. 'One more, *querida*. I need one more.'

And swift on the heels of one climax, Genie found herself racing towards another when he dropped to his knees and delighted her with his mouth. She was still gasping in release when he disentangled her fingers from his hair and kissed his way up her body.

God, what he did to her was addictive.

Too addictive.

She couldn't fall under this spell, too. 'This can't happen again,' she blurted.

His eyes darkened. 'What?'

'This. Sex. It can't be part of our marriage.' She needed to retain *some* control.

His nostrils flared and she watched him gather his control with something close to amazement. This was why Seve Valente was a veritable bulwark in the venture capitalist world.

'You have my word that I won't touch you until you beg me to. But bear this in mind, *pequeña*. When you do get around to doing so—and don't bother arguing with me, it will happen—there will be no going back. The next time I spread your thighs and claim you, it will mark the beginning of your permanence in my bed.'

He tucked her hair behind her ear, and she caught a whiff of her essence on his fingers as he trailed a hand down her cheek.

Dear God, but that scent alone was enough to make her consider surrendering *now*. To tell him there was no need to wait, that she was ready to jump—or waddle—into his bed right now.

But that would be illogical.

That would be succumbing to the base needs of her body when her mind should be the only consideration tool at play here. Wouldn't it?

As her thoughts whirled, he crooked a smile, that wicked, decadent, I-know-you-better-than-you-know-yourself smile that should've infuriated her but only made her weaker, made her lean into him. Further branding her with his touch.

Those hands continued to mould her flesh with unapologetic bold caresses. As if the magic he'd just wrought on her had given him free access to her.

Hadn't it?

'Battle with yourself if you must, Genie. But don't keep us both waiting for too long.'

'Is…is that a threat?'

His smile deepened, snatching yet another lungful of air from her. 'Not at all, *mi corazón*. But think how…exceptional it would be to take advantage of the next few months until our child is here to indulge.' He leaned closer and whispered in her ear. 'To be a little selfish and take what you want and not feel guilty about it.'

She gasped, her head rearing back so she could stare into his eyes.

He knew. Of course, he did.

The man had near-sorcerer levels of intuition. And when he followed her retreat, brushed his nose with hers then tormented her by hovering his lips over hers without quite making contact, she suspected she was doomed.

'Let me make this easy for you. We will marry next week. On our wedding night, you will come to me. And we will gorge on each other the way a husband and wife are perfectly entitled to.'

Once again she jerked away, another ripple of shock shaking through her frame. '*Next week?* We can't get married in a week!'

His teeth bared in a breathtaking white smile. 'We are two billionaires with every available resource at our fingertips. Even if I hadn't anticipated your acquiescence and put plans in place months ago, it would've been far from impossible.'

'You…what?'

'Don't act so surprised. Your stubbornness in accepting that this was inevitable didn't stop me from doing what needed to be done.' Still reeling from his words, his proximity, her orgasm, and countless other seismic shifts, she could only whimper when he finally brushed his lips over hers, stared down at her mouth for a ferocious few seconds, then resolutely stepped back. 'My grandmother has spent the last three months making your wedding dress. She's been instructing her favourite dressmaker to keep adjusting it once a week.'

'Your grandmother has made my wedding dress?' Yes, she

was aware she was rabbiting his words as if her brain cells weren't firing properly. Could anyone blame her?

She'd walked into this room confident of what she intended to happen next. Instead, he'd pulled the rug from beneath her, starting with two mind-bending orgasms, the aftershocks of which she still experienced every minute or so.

'*Sí*. She, like I, lived in hoped that we would marry before the baby arrived. But she also fully accepts that if it isn't to your liking, the final decision is yours.'

No, she *wasn't* melting inside. It was just the prudent coming to terms with her decisions. But as Seve slipped an arm around her waist and led her from his study towards the *salon* where his grandmother spent most of her mornings, she couldn't help but feel her heart swell with…gratitude. With…*love* for the old woman.

And when the old woman took one look at them, quirked an eyebrow at her grandson, then burst into a torrent of Cardosian at his subtle nod complete with clapping and wild smiling, she told herself the tears prickling her eyes were pregnancy hormones.

When Lita patted the seat next to her and picked up the bell to summon the housekeeper, Seve nudged her forward.

'I will leave you to it,' he murmured in her ear, his breath— deliberately, she suspected—wreaking final havoc on her senses.

But she rallied fast before she was completely railroaded. 'Two. I'll marry you in two weeks.' Hopefully by then this insane roller coaster feeling would've stopped long enough to reassure her that she was doing the right thing.

For the longest moment, he stared her down, imposing his will over hers. When he realised she wasn't going to back down, he exhaled and nodded. 'Two weeks.' Then with a hard, firm kiss, he walked away.

And that was how Genie found herself drowning in mountains of gorgeous tulle, silks and priceless pearls.

And a clutch of irrational jealousy.

Would Lita have made this for any woman Seve had intended to marry or…?

She looked up to find the old woman eyeing her with a knowing look. 'You're his choice, child. No one else.'

The words, murmured low and deep in Cardosian, pierced through her jealousy to soothe something inside her.

'Because of his child,' she said, attempting to stave off the swell of emotion rushing at her.

She shrugged. 'I can't change your mind if you want to believe that. You're one with tall walls no one else can break but you. But I also know my grandson. As much as it pains me, he too has walls no convention will break. But he's breaking down a part of it. For you. I don't take that lightly.'

Neither should you.

Genie heard the unspoken words but could only swallow. Because what could she do? She couldn't offend the old woman, who seemed steeped in her belief, by telling her that she was wrong about her grandson. That, yes, while convention didn't matter to Seve, this one where his child was concerned mattered to him. And that it had nothing to do with her.

You're the vessel keeping him warm and healthy. For now, you're important too.

The reminder echoed with bracing force. One that made her gasp despite her every effort to mask it. And when the old woman reached across to clasp Genie's hand, she attributed the resurgence of tears to more hormones.

'Enough talk of walls and conventions. Let's talk instead of colour schemes and guest lists, *sí*?'

Throat still clogged, Genie nodded. And was introduced to the sheer genius Seve's grandmother could conjure up with a needle and thread.

More tears threatened when Genie saw that the dress had started its life with a smaller waistline and had been let out several times to accommodate her growing pregnancy. With clever stitching, she saw that there was even more room should she decide to wait.

But she wouldn't be waiting. For good or ill, she'd made up her mind.

Despite his rough childhood and rigid stance not to be a father, Seve had committed himself to this. Collaborating with him in bringing up their child was the most logical course of action.

For now.

And if that commitment altered in future? If he regretted it?

She ignored the inner voice, and when she looked down to find her fingers lovingly caressing the pearl-studded tulle skirt, she ignored the deep emotion moving through her too.

What was harder to ignore was the indulging and knowing look in Lita's eyes. 'You like it?' she asked, nodding to the dress.

Swallowing, Genie nodded. 'I love it.' At the woman's continued stare, she added, 'And yes, I will wear it for the wedding.'

The housekeeper, maids and Lita broke into excited chatter. A mobile phone was produced and suddenly they were neck-deep in caterers, designers and assistants making lists.

It carried on for days, and before her very eyes, Genie watched the estate transformed into a stunning wedding showpiece.

The path to the jetty that would be welcoming guests was lined with large bunches of assorted flowers that resembled wedding bouquets. Mini chandeliers were hung from strategic branches in the garden and gazebos.

Long benches stood waiting, ready to be decorated. A team of gardeners clipped, pruned and spruced up the garden until it was just that fraction of an inch past perfection. Where the whole thing seemed like an impossibly beautiful vision.

And that was before Seve appeared at her bedroom door

two nights before the wedding and imperiously asked to be invited in.

She'd only seen him from a distance during the day, striding around the grounds with the butler and estate foreman, issuing instructions that were immediately executed.

Genie wasn't sure why it surprised her that a powerful man whose time was literally worth billions was getting involved in his own wedding preparations.

Maybe because she'd thought such things were beneath him? That he'd leave everything to a delighted Lita to take care of? What did it mean that he was taking personal interest?

'The socially acceptable thing is to invite me in, *querida*,' he drawled lazily after several beats, making her bracingly aware that she'd been standing there blocking the door with her body and staring at him with wide-eyed interest.

After a moment's hesitation, she stepped back and nudged the door wider in silent invitation.

He shut the door behind him before turning to her. Heated eyes took in the silk robe she'd changed into after her long soak in the bath, lingered for a spell before dropping to her bare feet, making her toes curl into the deep, soft carpet.

By the time his gaze rose to meet hers again, her body was reacting with alarming predictability, heating in places, dampening in others and hardening in telltale spots that required her to fold her arms across her chest before she gave herself away completely, and she hurried into her living room, perching at the end of one sofa.

'Did you want something?' she asked, then cringed at her breathless tone.

He watched her with knowing eyes, his nostrils flaring in primitive pre-scenting that absurdly made her hotter as he took a seat.

Without answering, he took in the foot spa Sofia had set out for her use. Although she wasn't on her feet most of the day, Genie was tasked enough with sifting through the various interactive social cues and her work on her own code that she barely had time to put her feet up.

The housekeeper's suggestion that she use the luxury spa had been a godsend, although Lita had pursued her lips and muttered about having a perfectly capable grandson who could perform the same duty better.

Genie had pretended not to hear her then, but now, with Seve's attention again on her bare feet, she could barely rip her mind from images of what that would look like.

Just when she imagined her nerves couldn't be stretched any tighter, that her body would betray her completely by thrusting itself into his arms, he reached into his pocket and drew out an oblong velvet box. The kind she knew contained shiny, expensive things because, over the years, several CEOs and wealthy individuals had tried to woo her services by gifting her similar things.

She'd returned every last one. She had no interest in owning baubles. Had never imagined herself in any circumstance where she would be required to don jewellery.

Until now…

Because she was reaching out for it before she could think twice, her fingers caressing the soft velvet.

'This is yours. I would've given it to you tomorrow but Lita has expressly forbidden me from making contact with you from midnight tonight.' There was wry exasperation in his voice but it was lined with affectionate indulgence.

The kind she'd come to yearn for from Lita and shamelessly gorged on during her interactions with Seve's grandmother.

She tapped on the box, prolonging the moment until she opened it. Fighting—futilely, she expected—the surfeit of emotion she would feel once she did.

'You know I can afford whatever is in here, don't you?' she said, because the constant battle between giddiness and danger raged inside her. She couldn't bear to acknowledge that she might be on the losing end.

'Perhaps you can. But the effect wouldn't be quite the same, would it?'

It was a simply stated truth. Bare and unavoidable. 'No. It wouldn't.'

He nodded. 'There's usually intent behind the offering of a gift that makes it have deeper meaning, no?'

She couldn't exactly pinpoint why she blurted out the answer, 'I wouldn't know. The gifts I've received so far have been driven by ego and the need to gain competitive edge.'

'Then be rest assured, this one is not.' A light gleamed in his eyes as he nudged his chin at her, silently commanding her to open the box.

Genie did, fully expecting to see a cascade of gems tossed into an elaborate creation by the latest in vogue master jeweller. Instead, the single, albeit sizeable teardrop diamond, bearing the proud hallmarks of Cardosian purple, was nestled in a deep yellow gold that spoke of its age. The chain was delicate but strong, the kind you saw in period portraits. Matching earrings glinted on either side of the necklace.

She gasped at the simple beauty of it, her fingers drifting over the chain before brushing the dazzling diamonds. 'It's… beautiful.'

'It belonged to Lita. She wore it on her wedding day. You will wear this on our wedding day. It will please her,' he said, then, after another of those volcanic glances, he rumbled, 'And me.'

Perhaps she was mastering this social cue thing because those last words tipped her into pleasure. Into exhaling shakily before giving a simple, acquiescent nod. 'I will.' Then, with a smile because this was getting easier, she added, 'Thank you.'

Now his gaze was riveted to her mouth, making it tingle and quiver. Making her whole body yearn unbearably.

Her baby kicked as if egging her into doing *something* to alleviate this ache. Was she bold enough? Foolish enough? She'd drawn a line in the sand in his study two weeks ago. Crossing it so soon would be ludicrous. Wouldn't it?

'Have you used that yet?'

She startled a little at the gruff question, and glanced at Seve to find his attention on the foot spa.

'No, I was just about to,' she replied.

He plucked the bottle containing the oil she normally infused the water with and examined it. Then he did something that yet again made the breath leave her lungs.

Seve Valente sat back on the sofa and patted his strong, muscled thighs. 'Allow me?'

And because every muscle in her body attempted to strain towards him in total compliance, she folded her arms again and raised an eyebrow. 'You're an expert on foot massages?'

'Why don't I let you be the judge?'

She was aware her eyes had grown comically wide. That her pulse was racing much faster than it had moments ago. The baby kicked again. She dropped a hand, laid it on the swell of her stomach, but there was no calming her boisterous baby.

'I see I have an ally,' he said with supreme smugness, his eyes lingering on her belly.

Then, without waiting for a response, Seve rose, picked up the spa and walked out of the room with it towards her bathroom.

The thought that he meant to conduct the massage himself settled in deep, making that tingling a full-bodied event that had no logic whatsoever. But, goodness, it was…addictively good.

By the time he returned to the sofa, sat down and patted his thighs once more, Genie had stopped battling with herself.

Intensely aware of her breathlessness, she angled her body and raised her legs.

Strong fingers curled around her ankle to settle her lower limbs on his legs. The scent of geranium and marjoram drifted through the air as he poured a measure into his hands, warmed it up in his large palms. Then glided them over the top of her foot.

Genie caught her lip between her teeth, barely containing the moan before it slipped free. From the first, his touch had aroused and excited her. Despite this being a stress-relieving kindness on his part, this time was no different for her.

More, it quickly turned into an erotic adventure she hadn't had a single inkling about until the sight of his oiled hands on her feet threatened to induce hyperventilation.

She blushed when the next moan slipped free.

Eyes like molten mercury met hers, the slight parting of his lips making her wish they were devouring her. Dear heaven, what was wrong with her?

Her brain was tired of answering the question so all she heard was the rushing of blood through her ears, and all she could do was grip the edges of her robe with one hand, and surreptitiously bite down on her fist as his expert fingers dissolved the tightness in her with acupuncture accuracy.

It was so good that when her spine melted, she didn't protest. When her nipples tightened, she didn't bother to hide them. It was no use.

Seve knew his effect on her.

'You look like a very fertile enchantress,' he observed thickly. 'A lesser man would be begging for you to cast a spell on him.'

A shade of disappointment threatened to douse the pleasure zinging through her body. 'You're not one of those, of course?'

His barely there smile looked strained around the edges. 'We agreed that any begging between us would be done by you, *querida*. Not me.'

'And you're set on not straying from that course, *señor*?'

He glanced down at her feet, a pinched look invading his features as he stroked his thumb between her first and second toes.

A rough sound left his throat as he followed the movement and shifted in his seat.

It was then that she got a better idea of what was happening to him too. The hard bulge in between his legs against the arch of her foot. The breath hissing between his teeth. The heavy rise and fall of his chest.

With clear reluctance, he caressed her arches one more time, then rose from the sofa. Watching him wipe off his hands, she prepared herself for his departure, but he only dragged fingers through his hair before striding to the other side of the room.

'Should I ask if something is wrong or wait for you to volunteer it?'

'There's something else you need to know. My uncle is attending the wedding.'

The uncle who'd made his childhood hell and was intent on damaging Cardosia just as badly? Genie stiffened. 'Why? You owe him nothing. Am I missing something? I can tell you're not particularly thrilled about it.'

'I'm not,' he bit out, his jaw clenched. 'And I didn't invite him. Lita did. I can't uninvite him without causing unnecessary drama.'

Genie frowned. 'But she knows what he did to you. Why would she?'

His gaze met hers with solemn contemplation, long enough for her to squirm.

'Is it a social cue I'm missing? A rule that says you have to endure someone you dislike?'

Something hard chased across his face. 'It's not that simple.'

'Isn't it? You don't like him, so don't invite him.'

'Sometimes circumstances demand we put our emotions aside.'

As he'd done with her? Was there a logical conclusion she was missing? Something deeper?

'Are…are you trying to prove something to yourself, Seve?' she asked.

He stiffened. 'What if I am?'

Her heart lurched then ached for him.

He'd listened to her past without judgement. Told her it was time to step into the light because she deserved it. Wasn't it time he did the same too? If that meant confronting his uncle, then wasn't she selfish to protest? If this thing they were doing was ultimately to succeed, mutual support was imperative.

She nodded. 'Then let him come. If only to witness first-hand his failure to subjugate you.'

A jolt went through him, as if her words had shocked him. When he started to frown, she rushed on. 'Besides, with the number of guests attending, spending minimal time with him shouldn't be hard at all.'

His mouth quirked without humour. 'Your faith in me is touching, *pequeña*. Unfortunately, he isn't a man who likes to be ignored.'

'If you're telling me to act a certain way around him, I can't guarantee I will.'

For the first time in the last few tense minutes, his lips quirked in a genuine smile. 'I would prefer you to be exactly who you are.'

Genie's spine melted again and she realised she'd started to tense up again. Resisting the absurd urge to smile back, she nodded. 'I will. Thank you.'

Seve watched her for a few more charged minutes. Then he inclined his head. 'Sleep well, *mi dulce*. I will see you at the altar,' he said.

She nodded, her emotions too overwhelming to form words.

With sure strides he went to the door. Opened it. Then looked over his shoulder. 'A lot can happen in thirty-six hours. Ensure that you not turning up isn't one of them.'

Far from being annoyed by his high-handedness, she caught the barest hint of vulnerability in that statement. It was what kept her buoyed that night, and the next.

Right up to the moment Lita kissed her gently on her cheek

on the morning of her wedding, told her to take a moment if she needed it.

Right up to the moment she stepped out onto the terrace, dressed in her wedding gown, ready to marry the father of her child.

And the tendrils of uncertainty set in.

CHAPTER NINE

'NO NEED TO start a war yet, friend. She's only nine minutes late. I'm told an hour, even two, is standard operating procedure for a bride's tardiness. Of course, that's a theory I never intend to test.'

Seve shot a glare at the man he'd chosen as his best man. The man who was gently teasing him because of that one flicker of his gaze to the terrace doors. Fine, perhaps it'd been more than one.

He could count the number of his true friends on the fingers of one hand.

Alessio Montaldi was one of them.

Although their paths crossed in person only a handful of times in any given year, the flint-eyed Sicilian had an outlook on life that Seve found…agreeable. He possessed a familiar single-mindedness, and by all whispered accounts he'd pulled himself up from dire circumstances as a child to become a formidable businessman.

But what impressed Seve most was that Montaldi held his past close to his chest, just as Seve did. Somehow they'd formed a friendship from behind their individual impenetrable walls.

He'd arrived on his superyacht mid-afternoon yesterday and insisted Seve spend his last evening of freedom onboard the vessel. He'd refused, of course. For some reason spending the night under a different roof from Genie felt…undesirable.

'You have time to mock when you've also been checking your phone every five minutes? Tell me it's not a woman behind that frantic checking.'

'Frantic? Hardly. And no, it's not a woman. Well, at least not the type of female that attracts my attention.'

'I could pretend I care, or I can—' He stopped, his breath leaving his lungs when he saw movement on the terrace. But it was a member of the catering staff.

His jaw gritted as Alessio laughed under his breath and Lita shot a worried look over her shoulder.

Eleven minutes.

He'd make it a clean dozen before he...what? Did the unconscionable thing and hunted down his pregnant fiancée and forced her to the altar? In full view of a watchful Lorenzo, whose presence speared jagged knives of fury and bitterness through him? Perhaps he should've listened to Genie and uninvited him. Was he misguided to pick this occasion to look the devil in the eye and show him he was...what? Better than him? That he intended to succeed where his father and Lorenzo had failed?

Yes.

He ignored the tinge of guilt that came with it. Didn't want to examine if his vigour in persuading Genie to remain in Cardosia had partly been because he'd needed to prove to himself that he was...impervious to letting past trauma and Lorenzo's shadow damage his future.

He shifted as the guilt intensified, but, alongside it, determination to see this through burned steadily in his chest.

Lorenzo didn't matter any longer save as an obstacle to be disposed of for the betterment of Cardosia. Nothing more.

His presence here was a good opportunity to show him his 'failure to subjugate'.

Genie's words intensified the flame. Re-grounding him.

Dios, where was she? She hadn't changed her mind. She'd given him her word.

Hadn't she?

As he thought back over their conversation two nights ago, a stone lodged in his chest. She hadn't actually given the promise. Considering he was marrying a renowned genius, had he allowed himself to be tricked? Perhaps the courtesy of two weeks had been a mistake on his part, considering he'd bided his time for over *four months.*

He should've swept her into his arms and found the nearest church the moment she'd stormed into his office and announced she would marr—

Another movement stopped his chaotic thoughts, and every muscle froze in his body.

'She's here. Maybe it's time to throttle back the murderous intent on your face?' Alessio quipped under his breath, but Seve barely heard him.

He was far too riveted by the sight drifting down the lawn towards him. He wanted to say Lita had outdone herself with the dress, but it was the woman wearing it who created the breathtaking vision. The low scoop of her gown and cinch of the high waistline highlighted her very pregnant state, and Seve was certain he'd never seen her more magnificent.

She carried no flowers in her hand but a circlet of white and purple flowers rested on her crown, her hair elaborately braided and pinned away to leave her swanlike neck on display. Her face bore minimal make-up, and her skin *glowed* underneath the Cardosian sun. And—

Barefoot. She was *barefoot.*

A dismissing of norms or because Genie Merchant, soon to be Valente, was confident enough in her power to simply do as she pleased?

Who cared? She was here.

He took a breath. Then another. But the clamour didn't ease inside him. It'd been building for weeks and, for the first time in his life, he couldn't exactly pinpoint the source of it. All he knew was that he…*yearned.* And while he pondered father-hood often enough, the totality of that yearning wasn't centred around his unborn child but rather the woman carrying it. The rage and kinship he'd felt that day when she'd confessed why she clung to her basement workspace. His shock and elation when she'd blatantly confessed what he made her feel.

He'd wanted *more* of that, he realised.

Had he deluded himself into believing he was marrying for one reason when the reasons were manifold?

The soft green grass only accentuated her bare feet, expanding her allure until it consumed him whole. Until he knew, deep in his bones, a fundamental shift had occurred. That he did not want just a connection with this woman through their unborn child or their shared dysfunctional upbringing. He wanted...*more*.

And he didn't have a clue how to get it.

'Seriously, you're beginning to terrify *me*, and I'm the one who triggers terror in others,' Alessio rumbled quietly beside him.

Genie's gaze was momentarily on Lita, who was blowing her a soft kiss. Seve throttled back his rioting feelings, arranged his stance into a less...feral pose, channelling his thoughts into less of his marauding forebears who took without reserve and more of the modern man the world believed him to be.

A deep breath. Less concrete shoulders...

'Much better. Now I suggest you put a ring on it before you show her your true colours.'

His true colours.

His gaze shifted past Genie back to Lorenzo, the man who'd imprinted his merciless scars on him. Were those his true colours? Or could he find it within himself to eject any traces of trauma from his soul?

The older man, who bore an uncanny resemblance to Seve's father, watched him with chilling warning, as if he knew

Seve's thought. One eyebrow rose, asking a question Seve had no intention of answering.

Not now.

Not when Genie was three feet away, her eyes set unwavering upon his.

His fearless genius.

'I'm here. Now what?' she asked softly in that defiant way he now knew covered a multitude of vulnerabilities. Vulnerabilities he would ensure were eliminated soon enough.

Beside him, Alessio snorted under his breath.

Seve ignored him and held out his hand to her.

She took it and stepped up beside him. And despite the tremble in her hand and the nerves that made her cast furtive glances his way, Genie Merchant made her vows.

He followed suit, the shifting in him intensifying.

Resetting his life in ways he couldn't quite fathom yet. But he allowed it to happen because, as terrifying as it was, it felt…right.

She was married.

Genie nursed an apple spritzer in place of the overflowing vintage champagne and tried not to stare too hard at the glittering Cardosian diamond on her finger. Its setting was far more modern and sophisticated than the necklace and earring set Seve had gifted her, but it was no less magnificent.

All around her people laughed and chatted, occasionally casting furtive glances her way.

She supposed it was normal, people taking an interest in the new bride. Or maybe it wasn't, and they just wanted to gape at the obviously pregnant woman Seve Valente had saddled himself with.

The one who'd attended her own wedding without shoes.

She told herself she didn't care. But years of isolation had a way of sinking their claws into one's psyche and it wasn't easy to shake off. So she'd dug deep to find socially acceptable responses to the guests' well-wishing. And once that had dried up, she'd chosen silence.

Seve was talking to his best man, Alessio Montaldi, the man whose intensity rivalled that of her husband, and who tugged out his phone with alarming frequency to scowl at the screen, as if he was willing whatever he was waiting for to materialise. So far without success.

A strong arm curled around her thick waist, and she startled. *Seve.*

She thought he'd forgotten about her.

'You're either completely enamoured of your wedding ring or you absolutely hate it. Which is it?' he murmured in her ear, and, curiously, something eased inside her. Because just like with his parting statement two nights ago, there was a touch of uncertainty in his voice that awakened the feeling again.

The feeling that he *cared*. That she *mattered*.

'It's certainly…unique,' she hedged, even now afraid to embrace it. Even though her strong emotions warned her that it might be too late.

That this was a culmination of weeks of her foundation being chipped away by Lita's acceptance, Sofia's soft words, Cardosia's beauty. But most of all, by this man…*her husband*…who evoked feelings inside her no one person on this planet could.

As much as the illogical term confounded her, she was… falling in love with Seve. Probably already had.

'That doesn't quite give me the answer I require,' he pressed, his voice deep, insistent.

She looked up into his eyes and everyone in the room ceased to exist. 'What would you like me to say?' Her voice wasn't as steady as she would've liked, what with that seismic shift creating impossible waves inside her.

'Tell me how it makes you feel,' he said, the words packing more of a punch than she'd expected.

'Why?'

He faced her with his broad back to the room, blocking everyone else out. 'Because I find I like knowing how you feel, Genie Valente.'

'Genie Valente-Merchant. I haven't made up my mind if I want to give up my name yet.'

His nostrils flared but along with it came a whisper of amusement darting across his face. The small crack in his facade again caused emotion to swell. Enough to soften that vulnerable place around her heart.

Enough to make her glance down at her hand and murmur, 'I love the ring, Seve. Very much.'

'And?' he demanded tightly.

For a fraught few seconds, she didn't know what he meant. Then she saw it emblazoned, wild and demanding in his eyes.

I won't touch you until you beg me to...next time...it will mark the beginning of your permanence in my bed.

But would it be demeaning if it was what she...what they *both* wanted? They were married now. She had a right to her husband's body just as much as he had a right to hers. If emotions had crept into the picture, surely it wouldn't alter the fundamental reason for marrying?

The tiny void in her heart said different. Genie ignored it. For now. Instead she opened her mouth to answer. To offer what they both wanted.

But the words locked in her throat when Seve stiffened. She followed his gaze and met the slightly darker grey version of Seve's eyes in the older man who'd kept his distance but watched them since his arrival.

Lorenzo Valente was suave and polished, his suit bespoke and sharp. But it was all a carefully cultivated veneer, like his neatly slicked back hair.

He would never attain the sheer *presence* his nephew possessed. Seve didn't need to announce himself when he entered a room. Lorenzo might inhabit a space, but no one felt his existence until he was right in front of you. Which was probably a dangerous thing.

Judging from the cold lifelessness of his gaze and his reptilian smile when he reached them, she'd do well to remember that.

'I haven't had the chance to personally welcome your bride yet, nephew.' His gaze lingered on her face, then deliberately dropped to her belly. 'Or to congratulate her on the happy addition to our family.'

'Your wishes are noted. But as to my wife and child being part of your family, that'll never happen. You had your chance and you failed at it. Also, your gift will be returned. My wife adores Cardosian diamonds. The tennis bracelet you sent, while beautiful, has questionable sources we'd rather not accept.'

Genie stiffened, then melted against him as her heart swelled. How well he knew her. She hadn't even seen the gift yet but she would've done exactly as Seve was doing.

Even as Lorenzo's face hardened. 'You'd do well to show some respect. And while you're at it, to not poke your nose into matters that aren't your business. I'd hate to have to engage in unnecessary public squabbling with my own flesh and blood.'

'Cardosian business is my business. And respect is earned. Enlighten me in what ways you've earned mine, Uncle?'

Lorenzo gave a humourless smile that chilled Genie. 'You've been overseas too long. Clearly you've forgotten how to respect your elders.'

Seve turned into a pillar of stone. 'Trust me, I've forgotten nothing. Perhaps it's you who should bear that in mind.' His arm circled her waist once more and, despite the warmth of his proximity, a shiver raced through Genie. 'Things have changed and *will* continue to change. How you deal with it is your problem. Enjoy the rest of the reception, Uncle.'

As he steered her away, Genie couldn't shake the inkling

that she'd just been used to make a specific point. But just what the point was, she couldn't determine.

Before she could question him, Lita was making a beeline for her.

'Time for a little rest before the evening's events, child.' She cast her grandson a quizzical smile and Genie saw Seve shake his head from the corner of her eye.

Again, she wanted to demand to know what was going on. But he was brushing a kiss on her temple, a second and third on her cheek and corner of her mouth, effectively scrambling her brain.

'See you shortly, *pequeña*,' he murmured, but the edge remained in his voice, the tension in his body.

By the time she'd regained the power of speech, he was halfway across the room, his gaze narrowed on his friend. Again, a silent conversation took place and Genie watched the two men stride towards his study, the tingling at her nape intensifying.

'Come, *muchacha*. Let's get you upstairs.'

She let Lita and her retinue lead her out of the room and by the time she reached her bedroom, Genie was grateful for the breather. Her back ached, the size of her stomach seeming to have grown since she woke up that morning.

Her baby, wanting to make its presence felt, kicked, distracting her from her thoughts. But they soon came crowding back. And since she was installed on her sofa with Sofia gently lowering her aching feet into the spa, Genie cradled her cup of tea, glanced at Lita and went for it.

'What's going on between Seve and his uncle?' she asked. Now wasn't the time to edge her way into the subject.

For a second, the older woman stiffened, but then she gave a smile tinged with sadness. 'A past I'd hoped could be put behind us once and for all. Lorenzo and Seve's father were as thick as thieves, unfortunately not in a way that would make any mother proud. It would be easy to blame Lorenzo for leading my other son astray, but a man creates his own path.' Her eyes speared Genie's and held with that core of steel Lita displayed when she made a point. 'Trust that your husband will not forget who he is,' she added cryptically.

'What do you—?' The question was cut off when Lita, deciding the conversation was at an end, strode away, bustling the other women into their designated roles for the evening party. Genie pursed her lips, attempting to stem the rising disquiet within her.

It didn't work as efficiently as she wished, and by the time she'd changed into the deep champagne-coloured gown with thin gold stripes that made each step she took shimmer, the disquiet had only grown. Low gold pumps were manageable after her foot spa and after a quick refresh of her lip gloss, she was ready.

The first thing she saw when she rejoined the party was that Seve had changed too. His morning suit was swapped for a more casual but bespoke one that matched hers. Hard on the heels of that, she noticed that his demeanour hadn't changed. If anything, his face held that same determination from the day he'd walked into her office demanding she sell him her algorithm.

Her algorithm…

Was that what his uncle had been referring to? No doubt the older man would be aware of what Seve was doing by now.

Unease building inside her, he'd barely reached her when she blurted, 'What's going on? What did your uncle mean earlier?'

Something dark and forbidding flashed in his eyes but a moment later, he'd blinked it away. 'It's nothing for you to worry about, *querida*.'

'I'd be reassured if you enlightened me so I don't make assumptions.'

Again something flashed in his eyes and this time it stayed. Something that surprisingly resembled bleakness. 'You don't trust me, Genie?'

That brought her up short. Not once in her life had trust been demanded of her. Her parents hadn't wanted or needed her trust. They'd simply desired a cash cow they could milk. The authorities she'd had the misfortune of dealing with had merely required her compliance so they could take advantage of her.

But these last few months, she'd lowered her guard and let others in.

Because of Seve.

The rush came again, drowning out an echo of the disquiet. 'Yes, I do.'

The light now burned a different shade, almost consuming her as it stayed on her face. Then he held out his hand. 'Then believe that everything will happen as it's supposed to.'

Genie swallowed the next dozen questions. She might not be built to simply accept a cipher and patiently wait for it to unravel itself, but, with Seve, she was learning that she could bend whichever way he wanted her to without losing herself. It was a tightrope she was learning to navigate.

Her questions could wait. It was her wedding day.

And while her baby bump stopped her from exerting herself too much, she could sit at the banquet table set out in the garden and watch the sun go down while guests she didn't know laughed and danced. While Lita affectionately pushed tiny dishes Genie's way in a bid to fatten her up, and Seve helped her up when she needed to stretch her legs and rubbed her lower back just when she needed it.

She breathed a sigh of relief when Lorenzo abruptly left but Genie couldn't totally relax because Alessio strode up a minute later.

'It's time for me to say goodbye too.' He reached for Genie's hand and, ignoring the rumble of warning from Seve, pressed a kiss to her knuckles. 'Until we meet again, *dulce.*'

'Did what you were looking for arrive?' Genie asked, indicating the phone clutched in his hand.

Alessio's face morphed, a mixture of harshness and intrigue glinting in his eyes. 'Not quite. But cast your net wide enough and all manner of interesting things get caught in it,' he replied cryptically.

He held out his hand to Seve. And like with many of the people her husband was close to, a secret conversation passed between the two men that set Genie's hackles on alert all over again.

'I will keep you apprised, friend,' Alessio said in rapid Sicilian.

To which Seve replied, 'I am in your debt.'

With a nod, the other man strode away.

CHAPTER TEN

'SHOULD I BOTHER asking why you're indebted to your best man or does this conveniently fall under the trust umbrella too?'

For an age, Seve simply stared at her, then he calmly held out his hand. 'Dance with your husband and tell me which other languages you speak beside Sicilian and Cardosian so I can be on guard. I also find that I'm in dire need to pick up on another conversation.'

'You are avoiding the subject.'

'I'm rescheduling it for when the time is more appropriate.'

His hand remained between them, and, like a puppet on a string, hers rose to slide into his grip. 'Is it accepted to say that being cryptic can be sexy to other women but it just makes me want to grind my teeth?'

A flash of teeth delivered a dazzling smile that didn't quite reach his eyes. 'We've established that you can say whatever you wish to me, *dulce esposa*. But I don't quite believe you about the singular reaction. You can find me sexy and grind your teeth at the same time. In fact, I bet that's what's happening right now.'

He wasn't wrong. The slide of his hand in hers was making her breathing jump and skitter in her chest. And as they reached the dance floor, something else occurred to her. She stared down at her feet. Well, she tried to but her belly was in the way. 'I'm not very good at dancing. Nor am I sure how we're going to do this with my—'

'Hush, *pequeña*,' he rumbled in her ear. 'Leave the logistics to me.'

Whether by design or coincidence, the sultry beat of a Cardosian samba tune thrummed through the air. In the waning daylight, light and shadows whirled around them, fireflies awakening to join the festivities as Seve took both her hands and moved in loose-hipped, mesmeric rhythm. The first few steps were easy enough to follow and they were soon in sync.

The soft whisper of her gown, the warm breeze, the heated intensity of Seve's eyes and the hands gripping hers…the trust…all interlocked into a divine expression of everything she was feeling inside.

The…love she'd craved for so long and despaired she'd ever find.

The astonishing realisation that the harsh binds of loneliness that had lashed her had unshackled and fallen away without her taking note of it.

That should she choose to, she could wake up every morning and be a part of a true family. With her baby. Because, surely, that was what Seve had meant when he'd demanded permanence?

Was it truly within her grasp?

It felt too powerful, too awe-inspiring to fully accept. Like the heart-stopping moment before the final string of code fell into place and you realised something phenomenal was about to occur.

Could she—?

Her thought froze when Seve slid a finger beneath her chin and raised her gaze to his. '*Mi preciosa*, what troubles you?'

She realised her eyes were prickling with the power of her emotions. 'It seems I'm back on the roller coaster again.'

His nostrils flared. 'Experiencing it in a good way?'

She nodded. 'In a great way. I… I…'

Love you.

She wasn't sure why the two words collapsed and died on the tip of her tongue. Perhaps it was a social cue thing. Neither of them was overly flamboyant. So perhaps this was a pointer that she needed to say it in private.

Later?

The twang in her chest suggested otherwise.

But Seve was lowering his head, brushing his lips lightly over hers, twirling her around and nudging her close, so her back was to his front. And her breath was stuttering all over again because he was raising her arm to twine it around his neck, trapping it there with one hand, while his other sneaked around her waist to cradle her belly.

'Oh…'

His hips nudged hers, guiding them into a sensual sway. 'That's it, *mi esposa*. Sink into it. Let it wash over you.'

He held her like that through three songs, until her back protested and the baby's kicks grew too distracting. Then Seve swung her into his arms and gave a very brief speech to their guests before striding with her towards the far end of the lawn.

Where a helicopter waited.

'We're leaving?'

'For the next several nights, yes.'

'I can't help but think you're kidnapping me again.'

'Technically, I haven't freed you from captivity yet,' he said dryly, the teasing glint in his eyes setting her alight.

Her lips curled in a smile, and as she stared up at him the last of her resistance melted away.

She was in love with Seve Valente.

What better way to celebrate her wedding night than in his arms? In his bed. Where she could confess…as much as her limited knowledge of these things would allow…what she felt for him.

He caught her smile and something shifted in his eyes. A

question? An acknowledgement? A flash of primal acceptance of his due?

Whatever it was, it thrilled and left her breathless, making her cling to him all through the twenty-minute ride into the mountains.

To the sprawling cabin set in the middle of dense woods that made it all the more perfect. From above she saw soft gold light scattered throughout the sprawling structure.

The air was cooler up here. When they alighted from the chopper, Seve shrugged out of his jacket and draped it over her shoulders, infusing her with his warmth and scent.

Hand in hand, they walked up the stone path that led to solid oak doors.

The moment the doors shut behind them, she heard the rotors of the chopper again. 'Are we on our own?' she asked.

He nodded, guiding her further into the vast living room, which had oak beams, sumptuous seats and a gentle fire roaring in the hearth.

Seve's hands drifted down her middle and traced over the swell of her stomach before he responded. '*Sí.* If you're worried about being away from civilisation, the pilot isn't going very far, and the butler, doctor and a few staff are minutes away.'

She hadn't fully taken in that there was a niggle until he volunteered the information. Then her shoulders relaxed. Kicking off her shoes, she turned and slid her arms around his neck, an act that was getting alarmingly easy and addictive. The circle of Seve's arms was beginning to feel like…belonging.

Like home.

'I'm not worried,' she replied, then realised it was true. She'd admitted her trust and she knew Seve would do anything to protect their baby.

His lips curved against her neck and his hands moved from her belly to her hips, kneading firm circles into her flesh that made her moan. 'Good. It's been a long day. I should let you rest,' he said, but she caught the thick need in his voice.

The same need echoing through her.

'Yes, you should,' she said, her attempt to tease sending a shiver through her own body. But he responded, his breathing a little erratic as he pressed a kiss to the sensitive skin beneath her ear. 'But I'm guessing you'd rather keep me up for a little longer?'

'*Sí, mucho,*' he growled, his hands digging deeper.

Genie was fairly sure he wasn't aware how firmly he held onto her. She didn't call his attention to it because she liked it. Liked him being so intensely enthralled. Liked being needed this much.

It was so new that she was still discovering the unique facets of it with far too much enthusiasm. So she turned, presented her back to him, and swept her hair to one side. 'Help me with my zip?'

His nostrils flared and her skin tingled where his eyes feasted on her. Confident fingers drew down the long zip until it bared her back, and she cupped the dress to her chest to keep it from slipping to the floor.

When she glanced at him, the look in his eyes was ferocious. Earthy and primal. Devouring every inch of flesh he could find. 'Cease the torture, *mi esposa*. Say the words.'

'I want you, Seve. I need you to take me.'

His chest expanded on a heaving breath that stayed locked, making him almost appear a beast. *Her beast.* 'And? Tell me you know what that means.'

Emotion shook through her, solidifying her decision. This wasn't a frivolous one-night stand. This was a commitment. For life. 'I do. I come to your bed, I stay in your bed.'

The breath expelled from his lungs as he prowled around to face her, his chiselled features tightening as his fevered gaze roved all over her, stamping his complete ownership of her.

Firm hands grasped her arms, lifted them away so her gown pooled into a silky froth at her feet, leaving her in only her white lace panties.

For an eternity, he stared at her ripe body, his throat moving convulsively as he swallowed. '*Dios mio*. You're a goddess. *Mi diosa perfecta.*'

'Hardly,' she tried to counter, but her hitched voice betrayed her thrill at his words.

'Oh, yes. Your belly is swollen with my child and it's the most perfect sight I've ever seen.'

Genie couldn't help it. Tears filled her eyes, words of love tripping to her tongue.

He made a rough sound. His hands cupped her face, brushing away the tears before they fell. Then he swooped, sealing her mouth with his before she could speak the words. And then she was lost in sensation, clinging to him even as he shed his clothes, a mixture of frustrated laughter only building the blaze of lust and connection between them.

When he fetched fat cushions and laid her down on the thick rug before the fire and proceeded to kiss every inch of her body, Genie buried her fingers in his hair, closed her eyes and lost herself to pure sensation and magic created by his hands and lips and tongue.

She was delirious by the time he propped her up on her hands and knees, her senses on fire. Genie moaned when his hands glided down her spine, thick words of praise falling from his lips.

'I need you,' she whimpered at the feel of his touch caressing boldly between her thighs, stoking her wet centre.

'Aren't you forgetting one last thing?' Seve rasped, his body hard, warm and primed for her.

Her brain lagged for a few seconds before she gasped. 'You're not really going to make me beg?'

'A deal is a deal, *pequeña*,' he stated hoarsely, his tongue gliding out to lick his lower lip as anticipation carved his features into perfect stone.

'Please, Seve. Please take me,' she obliged breathlessly, too far gone to equivocate. Then took pleasure in watching him shut his eyes on a groan as he grappled for control.

Then he was surging into her, the skill and intensity of him making her cry out in sheer bliss. Perhaps it was the weeks upon weeks of roller-coaster emotions she'd been through that had brought her up to this point, or it could've been the sheer bliss of taking him into her body without protection, but Genie felt the power of the moment. More tears flowed and she didn't bother to stem them.

Her life was no longer a desolate landscape. She had a husband and a baby.

What more could she ask for?

Just one final thing.

Seve accepted what needed to be done as he curled his body around Genie's, his heart still racing from the transformative sex they'd just had.

He'd stalled for long enough.

They'd been in his mountain cabin for seven days. One glorious, uninterrupted week he'd been uncertain he'd settle into—because he rarely took vacations—but had quietly relished nonetheless. Days when, every time he caught a glimpse of Genie's belly or the flash of the Cardosian diamond on her finger, or, hell, even saw her bare feet, it produced a wild kick in his chest he repeatedly had to clench his gut to absorb.

And Genie…

He enjoyed indulging her. She made him feel…*lighter.* And he would feel lighter still once he exorcised Lorenzo from his life once and for all.

Genie's intelligence had gifted him the means to save Cardosia. The unreversed gift of her body in nurturing his child and delighting him in bed had lifted dark shadows he'd feared he'd live with for the rest of his life.

It was time to let go of the past. To embrace the challenges and rewards of the future.

On cue, his phone buzzed. He disentangled himself from his wife…his *wife*…chuckling when she protested in her sleep, and reached for it.

The message from Alessio removed all traces of amusement.

Rising, he fired back a response as he went into the bathroom. A quick shower later, he selected more formal attire than he'd worn in a while.

He was slipping on his favourite watch when he entered the bedroom.

'Why are you dressed? Are you leaving?' Her puzzled, sleep-roughened voice reached him from across the room.

He tensed, then forced calm into his body. Raising his head, he almost groaned at the sight of her. Tousled, sexy, a fertile goddess draped in tumbled white sheets that barely contained her beauty. The urge to tear his clothes off and slide beneath the covers with her was so strong, he had to mentally shake his head to regain his focus.

He was doing this for her.

For their child.

For Cardosia.

He couldn't lose sight of that. He'd tried to find a different solution, had fought the path he'd been urged to take for so long, but enough was enough. The critical mass had been reached. His uncle could no longer be allowed free rein.

'*Sì.* I have something to take care of.' He approached the bed and leaned over, unable to help himself, to taste soft lips still swollen from his kisses. She blushed, still shy despite everything they'd done to each other in the last few days. Minutes later, he groaned and leaned his forehead against hers.

'I have to go, *dulce*. But you have two choices. I can send the chopper back to bring you home later or you can stay here. I'll be back tomorrow, maybe the day after.'

Her beautiful, astute eyes searched his. He knew she read

in his eyes the resolution that pounded in his veins. After a handful of seconds, she nodded tentatively.

'I'll decide later. I have my laptop with me. I'll get some work done,' she replied.

Pride warred with this new extreme possessiveness he couldn't stem. He would be the last person to stand in the way of her work, but he didn't want her consumed with anything else but him. As irrational as that was.

'As long as you promise to take care of yourself?'

A slow smile spread across her face, the siren she was becoming rousing to render him even weaker. *'Sí, mi esposo,'* she responded with sultry seductiveness.

Dios mio. He shuddered to think how powerful she would be a year…ten years from now, when the shadows of desolation faded completely, and her confidence grew in spades.

Knowing he would be there to experience it set his veins alight. Just as her face, her body, her beautiful mind did.

With another, rougher groan, he tore himself away, stood looking down at her for an age before striding for the door. Teeth gritted, he grasped the handle, just as her voice reached him again.

'Seve?'

'Sí—' He turned and froze.

She'd thrown off the sheet. One arm was flung above her head and her back arched ever so slightly, her blooming body on full seductive display. 'I'll miss you.'

'Dulce cielo.' As he pivoted and reversed direction, he knew he was going to be late.

Very late.

It was impossible to be this happy. Illogical, even. And yet here she was.

Delirious.

She'd taken her time to leave their bed after Seve's departure. She missed him even as he reluctantly dressed after ravishing her. Lingering in bed, breathing in his scent had made her heart swell even bigger. While she had reminders of him everywhere in the cabin, their bedroom was where she felt closest to him. So she'd stayed, lazily enjoying the breakfast tray delivered by the butler soon after Seve's chopper had taken off.

That was the other reason she'd stayed in bed. As she'd known he would, Seve had instructed the staff to descend on the cabin, his unapologetic protectiveness allowing no argument.

Well, she was just over eight months pregnant after all. So she'd gone from having just her husband for company to having a staff of six, including a doctor and two bodyguards, secreted in and around the cabin, keeping a discreet eye on her.

She sighed.

She wasn't really complaining. Seve was a busy man. A possessive one too, she was discovering. Why that sent a thrill through her, she wasn't going to question because she welcomed it. It fed a previously dried-up well where there should've been love and fulfilment but which instead was fractured with loneliness and desolation.

Which was why she was perfectly happy to dwell in her happy bubble all day and the next, taking a short walk to the wide, clear stream that ran a few hundred feet from the cabin. She even managed to ignore the guards who remained close but out of sight as she sat on a high rock next to the stream and raised her face to the warming sun.

Sadly, she couldn't outrun the chafing disquiet. And there by the stream, faint unease grew into a distinct pang.

She still hadn't told Seve she loved him. Because something was holding her back. Self-preservation because he hadn't expressed his own emotions?

Was she so shallow that she needed him to declare his feelings first?

The baby rolled as if mocking her. Genie smiled as she caressed her belly. 'The heart wants what it wants, doesn't it, darling?'

A firm kick. She laughed. Then slowly sobered.

What if Seve never said it? What if he was okay with the sex and the possessiveness and the whole Neanderthal hunter-gatherer moves but that was as far as it went? Would she be satisfied with that in the long term?

Her heart lurched.

No. She'd endured too much unhappiness to accept diluted devotion.

It was all or nothing. And if she had to fight for it…?

She pushed the thought away, rose and made her way back to the cabin. Its solid ruggedness was reassuring, her fondness for the time she'd spent there blowing away the uncertainty as she stepped inside and followed the sounds and smells of cooking. Dinner was an hour away but her walk had made her peckish.

Conversation stopped when she walked into the kitchen.

The guard and butler from the estate, who'd made an appearance with the rest of the staff, murmured greetings. But she knew something else was going on, couldn't miss the excitement in the air.

'What's going on?'

Both men appeared hesitant. But Sofia, elbow-deep in flour, looked up, her eyes shining. 'It's the *señor*. He's making the announcement. Finally.'

Finally.

One simple word. And yet it sent icy cold shivers racing over her body.

'Wh-what do you mean?'

The housekeeper, clueless to the speaking glances being cast her way by the men in the room, continued, 'It's on all the TV, *señora*. Do you want to see?' She nodded to the tablet set on the kitchen island, but the butler stepped forward.

'Or perhaps I can get you something to eat, *señora*?' he said.

Her appetite gone, Genie shook her head. 'No, I want to see.'

Her shaky voice gave her away. Sofia's excitement dropped, her eyes widening as she finally read the room. Before she could speak, Genie snatched up the tablet.

Her first thought was that it was a good thing she could speak Cardosian. The second was that it wouldn't have mattered at all because the press conference was large enough to convey the importance of the event. Not to mention the helpful subtitles running along the bottom of the screen that screamed *Breaking News!* with a countdown clock promising said news in less than three minutes.

The venue was the Cardosian Parliament Building.

And there was Seve Valente, her husband, his features stamped with fierce intent as Alfredo Santiago wrapped up his heralding speech.

Rousing words flew from the older man's lips.

'Self-made billionaire… Beloved by his people… A selfless Cardosian with his people's interests at heart who returned home to devote himself to his country. A newly minted husband with a child on the way. Everything Lorenzo Valente was not and would never be!'

The rush of blood in her ears almost drowned out Santiago's voice. But the subtitles kept coming. Wave after wave of dread inundated Genie. She vaguely registered concerned voices and firm hands taking hold of her, hustling her out of the kitchen and into the living room. But she still didn't let go of the tablet. Or take her gaze off Seve.

Behind him were some of the men who'd attended her wedding. Men she recollected had been part of his uncle's administration. And to the side, looking almost cynically amused but for his equally calculating expression, was Alessio Montaldi.

Her gaze returned to Seve, her heart hammering harder as she refocused on his face, his words. As he announced that, following his uncle's resignation, he was standing for president.

To his credit—or by design—he didn't viciously malign his

uncle. Hell, he barely mentioned him at all. And perhaps she would've forgiven him, had the lingering niggle not finally revealed itself as the betrayal she'd subconsciously feared as Seve stared into the camera and delivered his speech.

'Cardosia deserves a different vision. A better vision. The road ahead is tough and will require difficult choices, hard work and sacrifice. I'm not a stranger to any of those things.' He stared into the middle distance for a moment, shadows crossing his face before he refocused. 'Challenges will arise and seek to derail us. I've had a few of my own recently. But we will meet those challenges and turn them into advantage.' The crowd roared until he raised an imperious hand. 'You will be pleased to know I've already started the groundwork...'

The rush in her ears grew louder.

The groundwork...

Her algorithm? Their marriage? *Their baby?*

As the vice around her heart tightened, Genie registered that she wasn't even upset that Seve had procured the algorithm as a stepping stone to gain political power. She knew first-hand that her algorithm would do good.

But he'd deliberately kept her in the dark about his end goal—usurping power from his uncle. Using her as part of his plan to take his ultimate revenge. While she'd been gleefully basking in happy ever afters and love and family, he'd been scheming on how to turn the accidental pregnancy of his one-night stand into political gain.

Everything had been one giant ploy orchestrated by Seve to get her onside.

Her vision went ashen.

Sofia made a distressed sound and pressed a glass of water into her shaky hand. When she pushed it away, shaking her head, dizziness washed over her.

Then a wave of darkness swept it all away.

CHAPTER ELEVEN

'THIS WASN'T WHAT we agreed.'

Seve had said that a few times and was well aware he was repeating himself. Could he blame the euphoric catharsis of finally confronting his uncle and driving the old man out of his life as an excuse for being swept into a hasty decision? One he'd made without consulting the most important person in his life?

'We needed to seize the momentum. Strike while the iron was hot.'

Alessio quirked an eyebrow at Alfredo Santiago from across the room. 'Any more idioms up your sleeve you wish to toss in, old man?'

Seve glared at his friend, then transferred his gaze to the minister who'd orchestrated the press conference without Seve's approval.

'That wasn't how I planned on doing things, Santiago.'

Santiago managed to look contrite for a moment. But he perked up a moment later. *'Sí, el presidente.'*

'Don't call me that.'

Santiago snorted, contrition replaced by ebullience. 'Did you not hear them out there? They're ecstatic. The polls are on fire for you and the stock markets are already trending upwards. This is the best news our country has had in decades. Why aren't you celebrating?'

One word came to mind.

Genie.

He'd gone about this all wrong. While others were to blame for jumping the gun a little, he'd taken the familiar route of playing his cards close to his chest when the very person who was responsible for him finally taking the right action was kept in the dark.

This life he was leading wasn't about him any more. He'd known that in the weeks he'd spent on tenterhooks waiting for Genie to accept his proposal. In the visceral soul-connection he'd felt with her since he brought her to Cardosia.

I should've told her many more things. Like I love her.

Something shook to vicious life in him.

There it was. The final puzzle piece he'd been looking for since he could remember. The one thing that made utter and complete sense. The one thing his billions couldn't buy.

He strode from his desk to wide windows in the minister's office. Behind him puzzled silence reigned.

They didn't know. They probably never would if they weren't as lucky as him.

But had he gambled with that luck with his actions? A strain of terror so debilitating gripped him he had trouble digging for his phone.

'*Señor?*'

'It's time to leave, gentlemen,' Alessio said. 'The circus is over for now. Give the man some space.'

'But—'

'I must insist,' Alessio intoned, his tone coated in titanium.

This was why he was his friend. Why Seve had trusted no one but him with the final investigation into his uncle, ensuring Lorenzo didn't get away with any more atrocities. Alessio Montaldi was a man of many dark and dubious talents.

'You want me to stay?' Alessio asked once the room had cleared.

Seve sensed his friend's restlessness. Hell, he was surprised the Sicilian had returned considering the situation *he* had brewing back in Europe.

'No. I'll handle it from here, *gracias*,' he said, despite the dreadful weight in his stomach that said he'd screwed up. Big time.

He'd emancipated himself from the dark shadows of the past. Finally.

'We may bear the same surname, but I will never call you family. You're out of my life for good.'

Lorenzo had had the audacity to looked shocked at Seve's parting words. But in putting his past ghosts to rest, had he thrown his future into jeopardy?

Alessio clasped him on the shoulder. *'Buena fortuna*, friend. You know where to find me if you need me.'

He nodded but barely heard his friend leave. His heart was stuttering in his chest as he listened to the phone ring and ring and *ring.*

The past twenty-four hours had been beyond hectic, but he'd received reports that Genie was fine. She'd chosen to stay at the cabin instead of returning to the estate.

So why wasn't she answering?

He redialled his security, every bone in his body locking when that phone too rang endlessly. About to give up, he exhaled in relief when it was answered.

Then he was grateful for the glass wall's support as the strength leached from his body. 'Repeat that,' he snapped, one hand braced against the window.

'I'm sorry, *señor*. But your wife fell unconscious. The doctor is with her. We're about to board the helicopter—'

'What happened?' he shouted, terror eating him alive. The urgent voices in the background made his fingers tighten on the phone and his stomach churn.

'She was watching your press conference, *señor*. And she got a little distressed.'

Horror dredged harder through him. 'Is she…is she okay?'

Genie was strong. Wilful. Highly intelligent. And utterly beautiful. But so far she'd fainted at one other key moment. When she'd discovered she was pregnant with his child. How utterly idiotic of him to believe he could make such life-changing decisions without considering how it would affect the most important person in his life.

'*Señor?*'

He powered through the soul-shrivelling self-recrimination to focus on the voice seeking his attention. The doctor. 'What's wrong with her?'

'I don't know for sure yet, sir. Her vitals are a little erratic so I think it's best she's taken to the hospital.'

'Where are you taking her?'

'The private facility where the birth was to take place is best.'

'*Dios mio.* The baby…'

His recklessness might have put not just his wife but his child in danger.

For eight incredible days, he'd had everything he wanted. Had he thrown it away with his recklessness?

No. Not while he had breath in his body.

'I'll meet you there.'

He hung up and sprinted for the door, startling the small crowd gathered outside.

'Get the hell out of my way,' he snarled when one brave soul attempted to approach.

But even as he staggered out of the building and attempted not to bellow his agony, he knew the totality of the anger and guilt he felt was directed at himself. Just as he knew should anything happen to his wife, he would never be the same.

The swim up to consciousness was long and terribly unpleasant.

Genie knew something awaited her. Something that would set her back months, *years*, throw her back to the place she feared and detested most.

Loneliness. Desolation. Despair.

And this time, it would be a million times worse. Because now she knew the difference between pure love and parental indifference and selfishness. She'd scaled the ultimate high. Now she was heading for the darkest low.

The machines continued to beep, diligently dragging her from the shadows, beep by beep into the light of false hope.

'Turn it off,' she mumbled, as if by the sheer act of speaking the words, she'd get her wish and return to sweet oblivion.

But when had any wish of hers been truly granted? She'd believed in a false fairy tale with nothing but disappointment on the last page.

A sob caught in her throat. A rough sound echoed in the room.

It took several moments to realise the other noise didn't come from her.

Seve?

No. He was busy turning *his* dream into reality. He'd plotted his fairy tale with no mistakes or flaws. Unlike her.

'*Dios mio, mi amor.* Don't cry.' The far too familiar voice, deep and low, last heard whispering incredibly sensual words in her ear as he made her soar with bliss.

Blissed out and ignorant.

'Don't tell me what to do,' she mumbled around a constricted throat. 'You should leave. I don't want you here.'

Another sound, much like jagged anguish, echoed again. 'Open your eyes, Genie.'

The punch of steely authority almost made her chuckle. Which was the height of absurdity. Maybe they'd given her meds that were making her delirious.

Would they though, considering she was…?

Her baby!

Her hand launched off the bed, another sob crowding her throat when she touched the hard, full swell of her belly, more tears, this time of relief, pouring from beneath her eyelids.

'The baby is fine, *pequeña*. Healthy and doing well. But please. Open your eyes. Let me see that you're okay.' One warm hand gripped the hand not on her belly.

She snatched it away. 'I'm not okay. But that's none of your business. Not any more. Go away.'

More sounds that were a weird mix of aggravation and misery drifted low over her ravaged senses.

Seve was there, yes, but perhaps the sounds were from Lita?

The old woman must be distressed by the possibility of her great-grandchild in distress. Genie wanted to open her eyes and reassure her but she was terrified because Seve was here, too. Even now, through the beeping and desolation and utter hopelessness, her awareness of him was insane.

She wasn't ready to face what the rest of her life looked like. Not yet. Maybe her instincts had been safeguarding her from this by keeping her unconscious. Because the sharpness of the agony was unbearable.

So she turned her head away.

The baby was fine. Somehow, she believed Seve when he said *that*.

Everything else, she would deal with…later.

'What do you mean there's nothing wrong with her? My wife is in a hospital bed. She won't talk or eat more than a few bites of food!'

Seve was aware his attitude was terrifying the staff. Prowling up and down the halls of the private hospital sent people scurrying for cover.

He didn't care.

All he cared about was Genie. Who'd been hospitalised for a week and had barely spoken a word to him. Or Lita. Or her doctors.

When she'd finally opened her eyes, the sheer misery and desolation in the blue depths had taken him out at the knees. Hell, he'd half wished she'd remained sleeping because he never wanted to see that expression again. Especially knowing he was the cause of it.

But any attempt to talk to her had been met with silence and apathy. It was the apathy that was driving him insane. The woman he knew fought tooth and nail for the smallest cause.

That he was responsible for her dejection terrified him more than he was willing to admit.

It didn't help that Lita, keeping vigil outside Genie's room, glared at him with unabashed recrimination every chance she got.

'We were a little worried about her blood pressure but that's stabilised in the last few days,' the doctor said.

'So what's wrong with my wife now? Why can't I take her home?' he pressed, that ever-growing stone of terror in his gut crushing the life out of him.

The short, bespectacled doctor squirmed for a minute before sighing. 'We've already discussed this with Mrs Valente. She's aware she can leave but she…indicated that she would rather remain here.'

A lesser man would've reeled from the shock. Seve clenched his gut and called on every ounce of self-control, past, present, and future, to keep him from crumbling.

'If there's nothing else, *señor*?'

The moment he dismissed him, the doctor scurried away, leaving Seve staring at the swinging door to the private waiting room.

He faintly registered that the hand he was dragging through his hair was shaking. Hell, his whole body was shaking.

Genie would rather remain within the soulless grey walls of a hospital than return home?

Grey walls…like her tech dungeon? Had he ruined things so spectacularly that his wife preferred the desolation of her past life?

Before unwanted answers could eviscerate him, he was striding down the hall.

He'd just reached her room when his hand was snagged in a firm hold. He glanced down at his grandmother, impatience rifling through him.

'Lita, I need—'

'I know what you need,' she said in a firm, urgent voice. 'And *I* need you to understand that the only way forward is to truly open your heart. Show her who you truly are. I want to go home, *mijo*, and I'd really like to take my family with me.'

Seve nodded, the rock in his throat preventing him from speaking.

Resolution pounding through his blood, he opened the door to Genie's room.

She'd showered recently. Her drying hair was brushed and hung around her shoulders, and she was propped up by several pillows. The scent of her shampoo hit him and he curled his fingers against the desperate urge to stride over to the bed, scoop her up in his arms and bury his face in her throat until the world stopped its insane spinning.

Instead, he stood there, enduring her dismissive silence, until, perhaps sensing his intent, she angled her head towards him.

'Seve.'

His name on her lips punched him hard in the gut. 'Yes. You want me to go away. But I'm not leaving. Not today, not ever.'

She stiffened and cast him a look filled with misery and a fraction of the fire she usually showed. But it was fire, nonetheless. And it gave him much-needed impetus.

'I screwed up. Big time. I know. But, *mi amor*—'

'I'm not your *amor*. If you care even a little bit about me, you'll stop calling me that.'

'You are so I won't.'

She inhaled, shakily at first, then she rallied, her fingers linking under her extended belly. Like the exquisite goddess she was, her chin tilted upward, her eyes glancing over him before she looked at a point over his shoulder. 'I'm not going to debate that with you. It's not worth my time.'

He sighed. Ventured closer. 'Why haven't you touched your laptop?' he asked, nudging a chin at the neglected gadget on her bedside table.

She cast an uninterested glance at her favourite device and shrugged despondently. 'Nothing on there that can't wait.'

'Wait for what exactly? For me to do as you wish and leave? Because, in case you didn't hear me, I'm not going.'

'Then what do you want?'

'For you to come home. With me. With Lita.'

Her chin wobbled for a handful of seconds before she controlled it. 'I don't have a home, not any more. I probably never did.'

'You did. You do. Always.'

Another wave of pain, then she shook her head. 'Don't you have a *presidency* to step into?'

The word was a curse that flayed his skin. Deservedly. Teeth gritted, he replied, 'No, I don't.'

Surprise slid through the despair. 'What do you mean? I saw you and your people on TV making an announcement. Proudly citing your *groundwork* and how you turned your recent challenges into advantages. Tell me you didn't mean me. That you didn't mean our baby?' she shot at him, daring him to refute it.

Shame gripped him, the ground beneath his feet shifting dangerously. 'I did,' he confessed gruffly.

Her pale face whitened and he cursed himself to hell.

'Genie—'

'No. No more. I can't…' Her voice wobbled but she rallied. 'It may not have been part of your plan, but you used me… us…as a tool to battle your uncle, didn't you?'

His jaw clenched. 'Not as a tool. As an armour. My armour. Because that's what you've been for me.'

She laughed and his insides ripped to shreds at the bitterness he heard. 'That's great for you, I guess. But using me as your armour left *me* vulnerable. Do you know how it feels to know you didn't want me or a child but used us anyway because you saw us as an *opportunity*?'

He rushed forward, then stopped at the foot of her bed. It wouldn't do to rush this, as much as he wanted to. He needed to explain himself. 'That's not true. I've wanted you from the moment I saw you.'

Her lips turned down. 'Well, I'm glad it all worked out for you, Seve…' She paused, a wave of pain washing over her face before she shook her head.

He braced his hands on the footboard. 'Just before our wedding I got wind that my uncle was striking a half-a-trillion-dollar deal to sell off every single diamond mine in Cardosia to a foreign government. If it had gone through, the country would've been begging for scraps from other nations for the next five generations. I couldn't let that happen.' He paused, took a breath. 'I couldn't let what he did to me go unanswered either. I needed to confront him. On all fronts.'

A sliver of softness washed over her face, but she still shook her head. 'I get that. But I had to find out via the news. And what Santiago said, about you becoming a family man giving you the advantage… It all sounded so calculating.'

'It was mistimed, misguided and not at all what I intended when I left you that morning, *pequeña*.'

'But you happen to have the very tools you need,' she replied, scathing condemnation in her voice. 'How very convenient.'

'If you're talking about the presidency, Santiago is about to announce that it was all a misunderstanding. I've told him to withdraw my name with immediate effect.'

Shock widened her eyes. 'You have?'

'I told you. All this snowballed out of control before I could stop it.'

'So you don't want to be president?'

Unable to resist, he crept closer and perched on the edge of her bed.

This close, her scent washed over him, renewing him as surely as food and water. 'I never wanted the position. And especially not if it drove you away. You're the most important thing in my life, Genie. You and our baby. And don't forget, I have an insanely successful venture capitalist empire to run. I know you feel I've betrayed and used you and our baby, but I meant what I said. You empowered me to do what I should've done two decades ago. To stand up to my uncle, and not let his brutality shadow my life. I love my country but, before I brought you here, I only helped it from afar because the memories were too harrowing for me. You deserved better than a man stuck in the past, residing in bitterness, licking his wounds. I wanted to give that to you.'

'You didn't have to fight him alone.'

'It's a flaw I will work on, but I'm used to doing things on my own. Genie, you conquered your demons long ago. I was ashamed I'd let mine get the better of me for so long. I wanted to make myself whole. For you.'

Her nostrils quivered but again she shook her head, terrifying him even more. 'Don't you see? You were always whole to me. Our scars remind us of what we've been through. How far we've come. They're what make you the man I...'

His heart lurched when she stopped. 'The man you what, Genie?'

'It doesn't matter. Not any more.'

His fists bunched but he forced himself to relax them. 'Please, my love. Forgive me. I'm so used to doing things on my own. I've been so busy fighting to make things right in Cardosia that I didn't stop to consider what this would do to you. To us. But what you've shown me these past few months... I never want to jeopardise that.' He sucked in a deep breath and reached out to cup her delicate jaw. 'I love you.'

A shudder ran through her, and she visibly shook as she inhaled. 'You do?'

'*Dulce cielo, si.* With everything inside me. I worship the ground you walk on, *mi amor.* That incredible brain of yours. This insane body nurturing our child. You're everything to me.'

'Oh, Seve. I thought… I thought…'

'I know what you thought. I swear I will never betray or mislead you.'

Wide beautiful eyes stared up at him. 'I was crushed, Seve. After everything we've been through, I felt like an afterthought. I never want to feel like that again.'

He swallowed as he leaned forward and brushed her lips with his. 'I'm sorry. Forgive me.'

Her hands rose to grip his wrists and she nodded. 'Yes.'

Joy tore through him. But as he went to kiss her again, she placed a finger on his lips. 'I think this is where you ask me why I was so crushed.'

He frowned. 'What?'

She rolled her eyes. 'I love you too, Seve. Only love can make things hurt this deeply. I've been in love with you for weeks. Months. I've been dying to tell you, but I think I needed to hear how you felt first, just in case—'

'*Te quiero mucho. Siempre.* You never need to wonder again.'

A long, moan-filled kiss later, he pulled back. 'Have mercy and tell me I can take you home now? Before Lita sends in the army?'

Her smile sucked the air from his lungs. Dear God, she was so beautiful.

And mine.

'Yes,' she said simply.

Rising, he plucked the phone and called his driver. Then he whirled around as Genie made a choking sound. She was standing next to the bed, clutching her belly.

'Oh…oh, my God! I think Lita's going to have to wait a little longer.'

His lungs emptied as a new burst of terror exploded in his chest. Tossing the phone aside, he gripped her arms. 'Why? Tell me what's happening, Genie,' he rasped, his voice breaking with the fear pulsing through him.

Her eyes filled with trepidation…and wonder. Then, miraculously, another smile that set his world to rights. 'Seve… the baby… I think it's coming.'

He shook his head fiercely, as if the act could reverse her words. 'But…it can't. You have two more weeks…'

'I don't think our baby wants to wait that long.'

'Dios mio,' he muttered, then bellowed for the doctor.

A long time later, he would wonder how he'd managed to keep breathing. To keep reasoning. To keep from losing his mind when every cell in his body was either frozen in shock or marvelling at the strength his wife possessed.

Because watching Genie bring their daughter into the world floored him and changed him on a fundamental level he never wanted to reverse.

Seve knew he held on because her eyes were no longer shuttered. They blazed with love and determination and power.

For him.

For their baby the moment she was placed in her arms.

He was a risk-taker who'd come within a whisker of losing the most important thing in his life.

'What are you thinking?' Her voice was a little hoarse from her labour but all the more breathtaking for it.

He looked up from the sheer wonder of his beautiful daughter, Angelina Valente, into the equally captivating face of his wife. The woman who owned his very existence. 'Promise me you'll never let me screw this up? If I come within a whisker of making you or our children unhappy, you make my life hell until I fix it. Promise.'

Tears filled her eyes and spilled over but the smile that

bloomed on her face made his heart swell so big he was terrified it would burst. 'I promise,' she whispered, then held out her arms.

He walked into them willingly, placed their baby back in her arms before enfolding them close.

'*Dios mio*, I love you. Both of you. So much.'

'*Yo también, mi corazón,*' she whispered. Then she raised her face to his. 'Now kiss me, my darling husband. Then take us home.'

* * * * *

THE CHRISTMAS
THE GREEK
CLAIMED HER

MILLIE ADAMS

MILLS & BOON

This book is dedicated to
my love of all things Christmas.

May the magic and joy of the season
light you up like a Christmas tree.

CHAPTER ONE

"AND SHE LIVED happily ever after."

Maren grinned as she headed up the stairs to the glorious palace she now called her home. She was beside herself with the joy of this moment.

Yes. This truly was remarkable.

Every room was perfectly set up to her satisfaction. She peeked in each and every door on her way to her bedroom.

And then she pushed open the door.

Two things registered for her once. The first was that the bed was very large and very pink, and was in fact exactly the bed that she had specified to be put in her room. The bed that she had always dreamed of.

A princess bed.

To go with a princess castle.

The second was that there was a *man* on it.

Lounging.

He was—she could see even though he was lying down—very tall. And he was wearing a black suit, and his black hair was pushed off of his forehead in a devilish fashion.

His eyes were black and far too sharp. And she knew

beyond a shadow of a doubt that she would remember this moment, and this image, with startling clarity forever.

There was something intense that radiated from him.

Something she could feel, burning deep within her chest, but not something that she could name.

She froze.

It was like looking at a predator. A small voice inside of her whispered run.

But another voice, just as compelling, whispered stay.

So she did, immobile. Inert. When she'd flown in on the helicopter this morning everything had finally made sense.

This? This didn't.

She hadn't known quite what to expect but it wasn't this. Nothing that had happened up till now had prepared her for this.

"Hello, Princess," he said, his voice a silken thread that wound itself around her.

Or perhaps a silken threat.

One letter made quite a lot of difference in this instance, and yet she was far too beset to tell the difference.

"Hello… Hello."

She was acutely aware, just then, of how isolated she was. She'd been feeling isolated in an emotional sense already, but not…cut off.

There were many members of staff in the palace, all around them. Iliana, the household manager, was lovely, and she knew if she screamed people would come running.

And still. In this moment she could hear nothing but her heartbeat.

There was no land to speak of around the palace. It was set entirely on a craggy rock in the Aegean. Golden spires glistened in the sunlight, stretching up toward the sky.

It was the princess palace of her dreams. Resembling strongly both the castle her mother had given her as a child, and the place in her mind where she kept all of her memories.

Her mind palace.

Her sister, Jessie, also in possession of an eidetic memory, thought that the mind palace was fanciful.

Maren didn't see the point of being in charge of the creation of such a thing and having it not be fanciful.

Jessie had told her once that she kept all of her memories in file cabinets.

Maren thought that it was a waste of a brilliant mind.

With all of the details that they stored in their brains, all of the bright and brilliant images they had conjured up over the years, why would you put your memories in anything you could dream up—anything!—a unicorn stable, a fairy house, an enchanted suitcase that opened up to reveal a magical world—into…an office building.

Maren had always dreamed of castles. She'd always believed, hoped, dreamed, that she was meant for something more. Something better. Her mother had sat her down in front of her lighted vanity and let her try on makeup and fix her hair. They'd had the same red hair.

And she'd sang to her. Told her that she was a princess. That she was special.

When her mother went away, that had all gone away.

She'd had a privileged upbringing. Sort of. Growing up, they'd had money, Maren supposed.

Well, their father had. Because he had been a crime lord. They'd had shelter and they'd had food, but none of it had been about their comfort or what they liked, not with Marcus Hargreave. He'd been a monster.

He was dead now. Killed by gunfire exchanged with police when they'd tried to arrest him.

It was for the best.

Her sister, Jessie had a husband and a baby on the way. A girl, who would be Maren's little niece.

She loved the possibility of that future. And it would kill her to think that the baby might be in danger.

Yes, it was all for the best that their father was gone and couldn't hurt anyone ever again. She didn't care about her father.

He had been a horrible man. He had used his daughters to help run his criminal empire. Their minds had been a valuable tool for him.

Maren and Jessie both remembered everything that they saw. Everything. Down to the most minute detail. Jessie was especially good with numbers. Facts.

Maren was good with feelings. The expressions that people made, and the ones that they tried not to.

She was… Well, if she were feeling fanciful—and she often was—she would call herself an empath.

People's feelings seemed to radiate from them and into her.

Right now, his were moving through her like a velvet wave. Dark. Triumphant.

Sensual.

It was unnerving, but then, how could it not be?

She wasn't afraid of him. He was a dangerous man, or rather he could be. There were fractured, complicated emotions in him, she could practically taste them. But he wasn't cruel. Cruelty was an acidic tang on the tongue. Cruelty was what she'd sensed, felt, tasted, every day when near her father and any man who associated with him.

She knew cruel men. He wasn't one of them.

It was not strength, anger, or even an edge of darkness that made a man dangerous. It was whether or not he enjoyed the pain of others.

She knew instantly he did not, and in her life the difference between safety and danger depended on her ability to read people and to trust that reading.

He stood then. She had been correct. He was very, very tall. Broad-shouldered and well-muscled. His movement fluid, like a panther's. That impression only added to that disquiet/excitement rolling through her. The urge to run and the urge to stay.

"I trust that you found everything in the palace to your satisfaction?"

"Well, yes. So far. But…"

"Good. Have you been given a tour of the rooms and grounds?"

"I…"

She had been. As the helicopter she'd been in had descended toward the palace she'd been awed. But even more so when she'd seen it all up close.

The glorious palace itself was made of quartz.

That was why it shone so brightly. That was why it caught the sun in such a brilliant fashion.

The towers were capped in gold.

She'd wondered if they were real gold. Pure gold.

The windows looked like they were made of candy, all brilliant and colorful.

It was quite simply the most beautiful thing she had ever seen in her life, and photographs of it hadn't done it justice. Hadn't begun to show the utter brilliance of what had awaited her.

And the joy she felt…that she and Jessie had done it. That with that last poker game, that very last con, they had escaped their father's legacy, and they had made something for themselves, was overwhelming.

And if Maren felt slightly…undone by the fact that Jessie had found a family through all of this, while Maren had been further isolated, she wouldn't show it.

They'd both been affected by the loss of their mother, of course. Their dearly departed mother, as they sometimes called her.

Though she wasn't dead. She'd just departed.

But it had been her and Jessie against the world for so long. And now it was Jessie, and Ewan and their baby on the way.

She felt like a palace out in the middle of the sea.

Alone. Isolated.

Gleaming, though.

A *princess*, though.

She'd had to wait months to claim her own poker prize. And the timing was good. Because Jessie and

Ewan should have some time to themselves and they didn't need a lonely relation wafting around.

So now here she was. Ready to grasp what was hers.

But she had not just won the palace. She had won the royal seat of what was its own principality out here in the middle of the water.

She was a princess now.

Princess Maren.

She had always known that she was destined to be a princess.

Of course you're a princess, Maren.

The strong memory of her mother's voice, of her smiling at her, warmed Maren.

The most beautiful princess there is. And a princess ought to have jewels.

Her mother had loved to let Maren try on her jewels. Her dresses.

Her mother had been the most beautiful woman in the world. But she had been married to an ogre of a man.

And she'd had to leave.

Maren understood. She supposed.

Though it didn't mean that she didn't miss her mother terribly. Every day.

She brought her mind firmly back to the present.

It was both a blessing and a curse that she could remember those times with her mother with perfect, never fading clarity.

Sometimes, if she sat alone in a room, and went to that palace in her mind, it was like having a visit with her mother. Nothing new could happen, of course. But it was nice to remember.

It was nice.

And when she'd dreamed, she'd dreamed of a palace of her own...

And a child to share it with.

She couldn't have her mother back, but she could make a family of her own. Give all that love she had inside of her. She could *be* the best mother.

Jessie had gotten pregnant and hadn't even been sure she'd wanted a baby. That had made Maren feel slightly... It had hurt, was all.

She *wanted* a baby. She had for a long time. Her sister had gone and gotten pregnant on accident and it had been a huge drama for her. Which was fair. Jessie was different than Maren. But it had still made her feel a bit wounded.

She was closer now, though. To the life she wanted. The life she needed.

Sure, it had been accomplished through gambling. Which in any way she was philosophically opposed to, but she was also predisposed to being very, very good at it. And she had to embrace the idea of making a future for themselves using the resources that they had.

Plus, a fool and his money were soon parted.

It was not *her* fault that the men that sat down at poker tables with her had been fools.

And the old man that she had won the castle from had been very much a fool indeed.

He'd been raving about how if he lost it—and he'd been certain he wouldn't—it would at least keep that madman from...

A strange, cold sensation gripped her.

"Who… Who are you?"

But she had a feeling she might know.

She had a feeling this might be the madman.

The curve of his mouth did little to convince her otherwise.

"My name is Acastus Diakos. And I am your husband."

CHAPTER TWO

SHE WAS A VISION.

He could not quite believe his good fortune. Not that it mattered whether or not the Princess of the Palace on the Rock was beautiful or not. The woman could look like chewed-up leather and he would still be obligated to create an heir with her.

The terms of his family promise would be fulfilled.

He would give no quarter on this.

They had waited, all his life they had waited, for the Argos family to give them their due. And then Stavros Argos had given the Palace on the Rock away, and along with it had transferred his promise.

But that she was lovely…it was a nice surprise.

She was looking at him, shocked. "I… That… That makes no sense."

"Don't tell me you failed to read the fine print on the agreement that you signed."

"I didn't." She frowned. "It wasn't on the agreement I signed!"

"Princess, you should have received an almanac with all of this information. It was an addendum to your paperwork."

"I… I didn't though!"

He did know that. He'd intercepted the almanac. He hadn't needed her backing out of the agreement when it was important—essential—that the terms were fulfilled.

Stavros had been so against Acastus marrying his daughter that he'd gambled the palace away rather than see his promises fulfilled. Rather than see their bloodlines mix. He'd sought to undo the vows made between the families and to deny his family the honor they'd been promised.

The honor they deserved.

He'd worked in this palace as a boy. Scrubbed floors while Stavros put a boot on his back, and he'd done it because his father had commanded it. Because he had said they were earning their right to be royalty.

Stavros thought he was winning by passing the palace off, but in fact it was a total victory for the Diakos clan. Argos would be erased from the line at this moment, and Diakos would be the name that carried on.

The palace of myth and legend and story would finally belong to his family. They would be kings and queens. And his children would always bear the title they'd been promised, they would not clean floors. They would not debase themselves for a man who was just one in a long line of men who had made promises and broken them.

Acastus had vowed he would see this through to completion.

And Acastus kept his word.

"We are married," he said. "By taking up the throne you have taken a husband."

"But I thought that meant being a princess. And wearing a dress. I didn't say any *vows*."

"They were built into the contract."

"That can't be legal."

"This rock we are on is its own sovereign nation, as you know. It is not only legal, it is binding."

She blinked. "If I step off the rock, are we not married then?"

"No."

She looked around the room.

"What?"

"I'm looking for a hidden camera," she said. "I was starting to wonder if I was being pranked."

She was even beautiful when she was incredulous. "Sadly no. The Diakos family has been owed their place in the royal line for generations. We served the Palace on the Rock for five hundred years. In a great battle, all those years ago, an Argos saved a Diakos on the field of battle, and we swore allegiance. And we have been promised a place in the lineage for at least as long. And now time is up."

"It seems rather arbitrary."

"It isn't. I promise you. It is the law. As binding as your own agreement was, I have one of my own. An agreement forged in the blood of generations."

She wrinkled her nose. "Couldn't they have used ink?"

She did not fear him, this girl. It was a good thing, he supposed. If they were to make a child she could not fear him. But Acastus had never been…

Personable.

He was a ruthless businessman, brilliant in all things, in possession of a keen mind and not even a hint of modesty.

He had influence and power, he had no need of modesty or an engaging personality. Women found him sexy because he was remote. Who was he to question it?

He examined the expression on Maren's face. She did not seem to find him sexy so much as infuriating, but she would need time.

He'd known he was surprising her with the marriage. A gamble. But she'd gambled to win this place and he'd decided to take his chances as well.

"What does it mean… Does Iliana know that you're here?"

"Of course," he said. "She was well aware of the marriage agreement."

"I was not."

"A shame. It would've been nice if you would've been prepared."

"Well, don't go making it sound like that. That I somehow *shirked* my duties. Nobody *told* me. I did not get the almanac which apparently explained the 'duties' I was agreeing to."

"You signed papers."

"None of this makes any sense. I won the castle from a very old Greek man…"

"Yes. I know who you won the castle from. Stavros Argos. He did not wish for me to touch his daughter, and in fact, was so against my ever touching her, he was willing to lose the Palace on the Rock, his family legacy, to ensure I did not. He sought to end the obligation his family had to mine, he sought to ensure my family did not win, and yet, he did not count on me."

"On you doing what?"

"Coming here and fulfilling the terms of the marriage bargain. He thought I cared about marrying an Argos. I don't. I care about my legacy. I care about the titles. I care about what is owed."

She frowned. "Why…why would he do that? Why make the agreement if he wanted out of it?"

"This agreement is much older than we are."

"Well…why…" She cleared her throat. "You seem like a very nice man." She wrinkled her nose. "A nice man?" He glared at her. "A man. And a very tall one. So why is he so opposed to you marrying his daughter? I don't suppose it has anything to do with what she wants. He didn't seem like a man who would care about that at all."

"Oh, he doesn't. He's making me pay." He smiled. "He's a fool. He thought I wanted his daughter. I don't."

"She's well rid of you, isn't she?"

He laughed. It was funny, at least he thought that was what he felt. He so rarely found anything funny it was hard to say. "Yes. Undoubtedly."

"Woe unto me then."

"I suppose that all depends." He regarded her closely.

She looked quite alarmed. He almost would've felt sorry for her if he'd possessed that level of feeling.

But he was cold. Through and through.

Life had made Acastus that way. He had to be that way.

If he did not claim this now, the suffering of their generations would mean nothing.

The suffering he and his mother had endured would mean nothing.

And that meant, that it had to be seen through.

"So he gave the castle to *me*, a stranger, to avoid you?"

"Yes. He's a fool. He surrendered all to try and hurt me—he did not think it through."

"Well. He lost. He may not have planned to lose." She shook her coppery hair. "In my experience, men, particularly of a certain age, don't think I can beat them. They're invariably wrong."

He shrugged. "He did lose, whether he planned to or not. The legacy he lost for his daughter in his petty spite. Though Elena Argos has no great fondness for this place. I do not believe she wishes to leave her glamorous life abroad for a position here in the sea."

"In fairness, if I had a glamorous life in Paris I'm not sure I would have left it either."

"What a fool. And now the title will belong to me, belong to my children, my family will gain access to the royal line, through marriage."

She shrunk back. "That's quite archaic. My title doesn't even mean anything."

He lifted a brow. "Then surrender it."

"Absolutely *not*," she said, holding her hands to her breast as if she was clutching some imaginary thing. "It's *mine*."

She was like him. She wanted this.

Which was what he'd hoped. What he'd needed.

"Yes. And it doesn't work that way. You have married me by signing the papers and this cannot be undone. And we are to have a child."

Her cheeks went scarlet, like an innocent, and he felt his body respond. "I don't even *know* you," she said.

"You will know me soon enough."

Then she did something he did not expect. She threw her hands in the air and shrieked, and stomped. As she paced back and forth in the bedroom.

"This is unreasonable! I am a princess! How do I have less control now than I did before?"

"That is a hallmark of royal life, I'm afraid," he said, deliberately keeping his voice monotone to irritate her.

"I don't like it!" She stamped again for good measure.

He recalled a story he'd read as a child, *The Butterfly who Stamped*. She reminded him of that. All soft and fluttery, and then acute and sharp in her outrage.

She was emotional, this woman. The world would not be kind to her. Unless she stayed here, shut away, and she would have the luxury of doing so if she wished. He required little of her.

And then she leveled her gaze at him. "You did it, didn't you?"

"I did what?"

"You made sure I didn't get the almanac. So I wouldn't know. So I would sign everything and come here."

"Did I?" he asked, feigning innocence.

"Oh, Acastus Diakos. Don't try to con a con artist. You'll only embarrass yourself. I'm an expert at manipulation myself. You seem like a novice."

"And yet. Here you are, married to me."

She sniffed. "It isn't an elegant con."

"I'm all right with being perceived as ham-fisted if that means I win."

"Ooh!" She let out a sound halfway between a growl and a howl. "You are infuriating."

"And you're still here."

"Well, it's my castle."

"Fantastic. Then you are my wife."

She was so soft looking.

She was wearing a pale pink gown, her gingery red hair falling in a silken curtain around her face.

She had a smattering of freckles across her nose, and her green eyes tilted up at the outside corners.

Her pale pink lips were extraordinary. Her upper lip fuller than the one on the bottom.

He had not been with a woman in some time.

And he felt that now. Every night of his celibacy.

He was too involved in his work. That was the problem.

He had been taxing himself to get everything in order to make sure that all of his luxury hotel brands could run themselves effectively while he saw to his business here for the next month.

He would not remain on the island. Functionally, taking Maren as a wife would hardly change anything.

Having a child would hardly change anything.

All of it was symbolic.

But since his life had been filled with suffering that was more symbolic than he would like, he had decided that the symbolism mattered.

"The thing is," she said, walking toward him, her finger extended. "You're crazy. And nobody gets married for these sorts of reasons."

"You're incorrect. Royalty gets married for these sorts of reasons all the time. It is dynastic. And dynasty is what matters. My family is an ancient one. Our name is one filled with great pride. My father lived on the edge of a sheep farm for all of his days. He would take us by boat to the palace and we would work. Clean. He kept us in poverty. He kept us beneath the boot of the Argos family. He promised my mother she would be royal, and he failed her. He did nothing but wait. Wait for the promise to be fulfilled."

She shrugged. "I don't know what to tell you, this came with some money, but not an astronomical amount. Really, the value is in the property. In the title. I do like being a princess. But I'm bringing my own fortune, and I'm certainly not giving—"

He laughed. For the second time. It nearly startled him. It was so foreign, that sound, coming out of his mouth. Dark and not filled with humor the way that it might be if another person were to make the sound. But then, he himself was not filled with humor.

"I do not need your money. My *father* lived in poverty for all of his life. I did not. I'm a billionaire several times over, Ms. Hargreave. I've no need for money."

"Then why are you here?"

His life was a wasteland of broken promises and the pain they'd caused. The failures of his father. This was what his mother had wanted, what he'd worked so hard for—all for her. She'd wanted this title. She wanted to know the next generation was secured. Or rather, she wanted a grandchild. And he was willing to provide that, both for her and the legacy.

For all the work, all the suffering, it could not be only him who saw this palace in the Diakos name, finally. It had to be his children, and his children's children, and on down the line until they'd had their five hundred years restored and then some.

Life itself was fleeting. A legacy was what mattered.

His father's legacy was disappointment. Broken promises to the woman he'd married, and to the child he'd begotten.

Acastus's would be victory.

"I told you. I will have a royal heir. I will have a title. We will see the promises honored. A fulfillment of the sacrifice that they made. My great-uncle died fighting a war on behalf of the royal family. And before that, there were others. Lost children. Dead husbands. Sent into every conflict that the royal family of the Palace on the Rock deemed appropriate for them to fight in."

"Oh, I don't think we will be doing wars," Maren said, frowning. "I don't like them."

"I will be repaid," he said, intensity making his throat seize tight. "We will have recompense."

She took a step back. "I just think… I think that it seems a bit… It's a bit unorthodox."

"Indeed it is. But you're not in a position to negotiate. You signed yourself away."

She angled her head and squinted. "Did I *really*?"

"You did. The almanac you're looking for is under your pillow, Princess. Like a pea."

"That was under mattresses."

"Go ahead. Be off with you and look at what all that you have signed entails. The history of the country is there for all the world to see. Look at the marital promise between the Argus family and the Diakos family. Tell me what you find."

He straightened his black tie and walked to the door of the bedroom. "My chambers are down the hall. I will see you at dinner."

"I… What if I don't want a dinner guest?"

"That is no way to treat your husband," he responded.

"I have not decided if you are my husband."

"I already am. It is both simple and unambiguous. I will see you at dinner."

And then he turned and left her standing there, a sense of triumph beating in his breast as he walked down the corridor.

Finally, this place would be his. Finally, there would be restitution for all that had been lost.

He would uphold the promise made to his ancestors.

The promise he'd made to his mother. His mother had married his father on the understanding that she would someday be Queen Mother, an honorary title that would be given when Acastus married the Princess of the Palace on the Rock. That they would be wealthy, and all their needs met. That they wouldn't labor, but have people serving them.

What Acastus saw as the real failure on his father's part, was how he had poured everything into being obsequious to Stavros, and had not supported them. They'd been hand-to-mouth, always. Working in the palace and going home to a hovel.

Why had he not sought to better them at all? Why had he put everything into that future promise? That future marriage?

Acastus had not done so. Acastus had not rested. He'd picked up this burden, and every other, and had carried them up the hill to this moment.

Victory was finally at hand.

CHAPTER THREE

MAREN SPENT THE next hour reading the almanac. The bastard. He'd deliberately withheld this from her, she knew it. But she and Jessie had manipulated the world as con artists for years. It would be…dishonest for her to act shocked or wounded by this. What you put out in the world was what you got back.

This, she supposed, was her con woman karma. Complete with a castle and a husband.

Ascending the throne had seemed like a lark when she'd first won. It had been made out to be such a small nation when it had been presented to her. It had seemed rather…*inconsequential* that it was a country. The royalty part had seemed like such a formality that she hadn't even considered that there might be a secret marriage law bound up in all of it.

But indeed. She was now a full and complete expert on the history between the two families. Hundreds of years ago the Diakos family swore fealty to the Argos royals, and they in turn promised that at the end of a period of servitude, they would be grafted into the family through marriage. An eligible son marrying an eligible daughter, or a Diakos daughter to an Argos son.

But why? she wondered.

Why had the Diakos family served the Argos family like this? Especially when they had spent generations failing to live up to their promises.

There had been many Argos daughters that could've married Diakos sons, or in reverse. But they had not been given in marriage.

And on and on it went.

She wasn't an Argos. But still, she could see that it had passed to "the royal family of the Palace on the Rock."

She was a royal family of one.

But why not just give the title to…a man whose name sounded like a sneeze.

Acastus Diakos.

What sort of nonsense was that?

She looked into the room that had all of her finery in it, and her jaw dropped.

The room was well lit, with gowns on displays as if they were in a boutique. On mannequins, on lighted platforms, bags and hats elevated on shelves. Floor to ceiling glamour everywhere she looked.

Her mother would have loved this.

The thought made her stomach go tight.

She knew that it wasn't technically a formal dinner, but she decided to put on a pink, frothy gown that was fashioned from a spray of netting. It was so delightfully over-the-top and feminine and she'd always found a certain amount of power in such things.

When she and Jessie played poker they counted on a hyper-feminine appearance, on their beauty, to make men underestimate them.

She put gold makeup on her face, delighting in the items that she found in the glorious bathroom suite.

And when she went downstairs, she did her best to smile and look serene.

Because she was not going to allow this man to think that he had shaken her.

Even though she felt well and thoroughly shaken.

But she'd been in worse situations than this. She'd flirted and smiled and cajoled information out of random men countless times with her hair styled into bouncy curls and a dress that swirled around the tops of her thighs. Looking as sweet and vulnerable as possible, while being aware of every item around her she could use as a weapon if need be.

She'd grown up with a narcissistic sociopath for a father. She had learned how to protect herself, just in case. She didn't walk through life afraid because she was prepared. She paid attention to details. She was always alert.

She only looked soft.

Her mother had been soft, and so desperately in love with their father. And his betrayal of her had been so unendurable she'd had to leave.

He was a narcissistic sociopath.

Maren understood why a woman couldn't stay with a narcissistic sociopath.

Maren wasn't as naïve as her mother had been when she'd married Maren's father, because she'd been raised not to be.

She wouldn't be naïve now.

When she walked in, he was already seated there, at the head of the table, lounging.

Did the man do nothing but lounge?

"I have a question for you," she said as she walked in.

"Yes?"

"First of all, what is it you do."

He lifted a brow, the arrogant set of his jaw somehow intensifying even as he barely moved. "Do you not know who I am?"

And suddenly…she matched his face to images she'd seen before.

She felt her eyes pop wide. "Acastus Diakos? The billionaire real estate developer who routinely tops the lists of youngest self-made billionaires?"

"Oh, so you've read the write-ups."

"I've seen them. On newsstands. I can't forget things. It's sort of a quirk."

He frowned. "What sort of quirk?"

"An *actual condition* sort of quirk. When I say I remember everything, I mean I could recite the almanac back to you now."

"All of it?"

She sighed. "Here in this book, and in accordance with…"

"That's fine," he said, holding up a hand.

"So yes, I know who you are. Though I'm not sure you should be flattered by it. It's just a little hat trick I do."

He laughed. It was the same dark laugh she'd heard twice in her room, and it was…odd. It was not filled with humor. It made her feel cold.

She could read feelings easily, she could feel them. Taste them. Gauge their temperature. His were contrasts, and she found them strange. His laugh was a shard of ice. There was no humor in it. It sounded rich to the ear, but the quality of it…it was flat and sharp and the taste was acidic.

"It seems to me it's a card trick you do," he said. "Is that how you won the game?"

"Yes," she said, without hesitation. "I know it's frowned on but I can't help how my brain works. It's not intentional cheating, I don't have aces up my sleeve."

"And yet, I think if the men who lost to you knew…"

She batted her eyelashes. "How would they know? They'd have to admit that I might be smarter than they are, and I think we both know that would never happen."

He regarded her closely and she had the feeling of being a small butterfly, pinned down to a board. "What you're telling me is that I am to underestimate you at my peril?"

She nodded. "I suppose so. Though if you want to underestimate me, I won't stop you." She looked around the massive room. Her dining room, let it not be forgotten. This man might have installed himself here, but it was not his.

She looked down, and then back up, fixing him with her most intense gaze, which she'd been told before was quite unnerving. "Why do you think that this settles the score between yourself and the Argos family? I am not an Argos."

"You are not. But that isn't the point, the point is that I am after the title, the legacy, the Argos family means nothing to me, and he was narcissistic enough to imagine that being enmeshed in his disgraceful family was what I was after. He sought to deny me, but I am not denied."

"Why did he care so much? Why does he hate you?"

"It is…complicated."

She laughed, she couldn't help it. Her laugh was not flat, sharp or confusing. "Oh, come now. Humans are never complicated. Power, money or sex?"

"What?"

"Is the issue related to power, money or sex? I find it almost always is."

"You are wrong. Ego." He did not elaborate.

"Go on," she said.

"I see no reason to go on. The fact is, this is the only way. My father was an ineffective man. A man who was not brave enough to seize a life for his family. He was content to wait. I will not wait."

"I can understand the difficult father part."

"Tell me about your father," he said.

"Not yet," she said, feeling a pang of distaste at the idea of having to think about her father, and her life growing up in his criminal compound. "I want to talk more about this. Practically, what do you hope to achieve by having…a marriage into this…royal family of one. As I pointed out to you before, it isn't like I'm actually a member of the Argos family. How is that a legacy?"

"It doesn't matter. It is a matter of the history books. Of what will be written."

"Great. Does anybody write about principalities that don't have anyone living in them?"

"My family sacrificed and bled and gave for generations. Not for nothing. It will not be undone."

"And it's worth marrying a stranger for?" Maren had never given a lot of thought to marriage. She'd never thought she'd marry, and here she was.

She had loved Jessie's wedding. It had been so beautiful and romantic.

"It will not be a typical marriage," he said. "I have no designs on having a wife. Not in a real sense. We shall not share bedrooms or speak to each other over orange juice and toast in the mornings. I wish to marry into the family. I wish to have all the benefits of that marriage. And we shall have a child."

She felt her face got hot. "The thing is, a lot of people would argue that if we are going to have a baby, that would be a real…" She blinked. "Oh. Of course. We could do IVF."

"We cannot."

"Why not?"

"Maren," he said, his voice low and cajoling, as if he was speaking to a child. She didn't like it.

She frowned. "Don't talk to me like I'm a child. I'm not a child. I'm just not well-versed in this particular level of strangeness that I seem to have found myself enmeshed in."

"You have heard, I suppose, that there is no such thing as a free lunch?"

"Yes."

"But you thought there was such a thing as a free castle?"

"It wasn't *free*. I won it. Fair and square." Well. That

was overstating it. She had won it via counting cards and having an especially good ability to read the faces of those around her. But, it wasn't her fault that she could just do those things naturally. It wasn't like she had cards up her sleeve, now that really would've been cheating. She and Jessie cheated, sort of. It was just using natural methods.

"Fair and square," he said. "Okay then. Do you really think that things this big come this easily? Did you really think that a building this old, containing this many ghosts, would be given to you and you would suffer none of the echoes of the past? This is foolishness."

"It's foolishness to not realize that there was going to be a husband waiting for me in my bedroom. Also, why couldn't we do IVF?"

"You don't seem averse to the idea of having a baby."

"I'm not," she said.

If she was being objective the man in front of her was an absolute pillar of masculinity. He was well over six feet tall, broad-shouldered, his bone structure was stunning. Quite possibly, he was the most beautiful man she had ever seen in her life. If she was going to give genetic material to a child, she could certainly do worse. Shame about his personality, but as they were still on the fence about nature versus nurture, she was pretty sure that she could still work with it. He said that he didn't want a real marriage, fine. She didn't want to have orange juice and toast with him either. And there was no reason they couldn't…

"It is stipulated in the marriage contract that in order

for a child to count as an heir they must be conceived *ek fyeseos*."

"What?"

"By nature."

Maren nearly choked. "I'm sorry, what?"

"This was an old way of defining that they could not bring in a child that was not of their genetic material."

She couldn't believe what she was hearing. "That is *highly* offensive."

He lifted a dark brow. "It may shock you to learn the ancient peoples were not concerned with the offense of modern peoples."

"It's extremely offensive to adopted—"

He held up a hand. "Maren, no one cares. These are the rules. The stipulations. And it would be argued now, I believe, that any sort of unnatural method of conception would not fall under the parameters."

"This just seems very *medieval*."

He waved his hand as if to dismiss her concern. "It's a castle. Of course it's medieval."

Maren felt just slightly like hissing and spitting. He was so condescending. And he was suggesting… Well, what he was suggesting didn't even bear thinking about.

"I don't even know you."

"What does that have to do with anything?"

She regarded him for a long moment. And as she did so, two feelings, one familiar, and one disconcertingly unfamiliar, wound through her.

He was beautiful. There was no denying that. The impact of him was stunning, and it was a testament to that beauty the degree to which she could find herself immobilized by it even as she faced these extraordinary circumstances. The other feeling was a frightening familiarity. The sensation of looking at a man whose feelings were so buried, so remote, that she could not read them.

Her father had been like that. A man of inscrutable cruelty, who had seemed to make decisions about what he was doing without real thought. He simply acted. Simply did whatever seemed right and best. There was no emotional baseline that it seemed to come from. It just was.

He felt like that. Like something remote and far away.

But the mix of it with that bright burn… That was what frightened her.

Well, that and the fact he was standing there calmly suggesting that they conceive a baby.

She had never even been kissed.

She tried to imagine it. Tried to imagine this wild, unreadable creature moving to her. Lowering his head and claiming her mouth.

She liked romance novels. She liked romance. In theory. She had long believed that she might be able to put off some of her own romantic longings by consuming media that depicted love and sex. She had such a vivid imagination.

She had spent many long nights lying awake imagining a man trailing his large hands over her body. Kissing her. Possessing her. And even more importantly than that, holding her. Treating her like she was something special. Something precious.

He would not hold her like that.

But she knew that he would touch her.

His hands… She wondered if they would be expert.

He was gorgeous, glorious. She imagined that they would be.

That they would be skilled and knowing. That he could teach her things about her body, about lust that would set her on fire.

But did she want that?

Because that was the problem with a memory like hers.

The images didn't fade. The feelings. It was all disconcertingly present all the time.

Those moments with her mother, a blessing and a curse.

The fear of living under her father's thumb.

It was why when she and Jessie had run away Maren had made very strict rules for them.

She had been worried especially about Jessie, who had a wildness and a sharpness about her that Maren simply didn't possess.

Maren had always been soft.

She had always known that she could be easily broken. That if she loved and the person didn't love her in return, it would destroy her.

That she would always be left wanting more. Worried that it wasn't enough.

That she could never be enough.

If she slept with a man and he gave her brilliant pleasure, the memory of that pleasure would never go away.

He's your husband.

But what did that even mean?

"Here's the problem," she said. "The way that I see it. How do I know I won't fall in love with you?"

He stared at her. She supposed she should be embarrassed to ask the question, but she wasn't. Because it wasn't as if she was on the verge of falling in love with him or anything. It was a pure hypothetical. "It's a very serious issue," she said. "From what I've been told virgins often equate sex and love."

"You're a virgin?" he asked.

"Yes," she said. "I've had a very irregular life. I have a very irregular brain. I have to worry about things that other people don't have to worry about. My memories once impressed into my mind do not go away. Not ever. They're always there. As vivid as they were the day they occurred. So you tell me, why would I give myself an endless stream of sexual images that I can't escape? I suppose some people might want that. But I never did. And I've always been very cautious. And here I find myself confronted by a very handsome man who thinks he can just sweep in and demand access to my body."

"You will forgive me. I did not anticipate that you had never…"

"You made assumptions. You know what they say about assumptions."

"I don't."

She was satisfied that she got to say it. "They make an ass out of you and me. So in this case only *you*. I'm not an ass. I didn't cause this issue."

"You didn't read the almanac," he pointed out.

She planted her hands on the table and stood abruptly. "I never got it," she shouted. "I never got it, and you acting like I was irresponsible in some way is outrageous. I didn't create this situation. You're the one that's bound and determined to take the title. Why do you even need a baby?"

She felt annoyed with herself for getting so angry. It reminded her of bad times growing up in her father's house. It reminded her of the explosions between her parents that had eventually made it so her mother went away.

"It's heritage. Lineage. It is about ensuring that the future of my family is greater than its past."

"Philosophical for *you*. It is personal to me. I would like a baby. That's the thing. That is the reason that I haven't stabbed you."

"Stabbed me?"

"Have you paid attention to nothing that I've said? I had a very irregular life. My sister and I…" She supposed this was the part where she had to talk about her father. "My father is a madman. Flat-out. Well, he was. He's dead now. But that's the problem. It's the *memories*. He feels like he's right here with me even when he isn't. I think of him, and I can see everything that he ever did. He was a criminal warlord kind of guy. And when my sister and I ran away from him, when we refused to continue to be tools in his arsenal, we had to live in fear. We tried to protect ourselves at all costs. So yeah. If I had to stab you, I would. But the only reason that I'm sitting here listening to this is that I'm tired of being alone."

He didn't look shocked, or even all that aggrieved by

her revelation about her father, and she wasn't quite sure what to do with that.

"You have mistaken me," he said. "I don't actually need a running commentary on your thought process. What I would like to know is if we are at an impasse or not. If you don't agree to this, I will challenge your ownership of the castle. So it's entirely up to you. What's more important. Your virginity, or being a princess?"

"Being a princess, obviously. I didn't expect to keep my virginity for my whole life. I was just being cautious about it." It was amazing how easy that answer was. But it made her heart beat faster. Just then, the waiter came in holding pizza entrées.

The food was set down in front of them and he looked at her, somewhat surprised. "Pizza?"

"Yes," she said. "It's what I wanted. I'm the Princess. So I asked for pizza."

He reached out and took a slice and she found even that movement was predatory. She'd have hoped that him swooping in for a slice of pizza might transform him into a more manageable creature. Something almost human. Alas.

"You would rather have a baby with me than remain a virgin?" he asked.

And she did her very best not to imagine it. Thankfully, she'd never done it before so while she knew all about sex in theory, the images of it didn't loom as clear as images of that which she'd experienced.

"Yes," she said. "But we will need to come to a very strict set of rules."

"And those are?"

She took a bite of her pizza and spoke around it. She was amused by the distaste on his face. "Sex for conception only."

"And what does that mean?"

"We will wait until I am at my most fertile, and then you can… Do your best."

He lifted a brow, and pressed his hands to his forehead. "My best."

"Well, yes." She chewed her pizza thoughtfully. "I don't want you to get performance anxiety. I hear men are very touchy that way."

His expression was extremely flat. "I shall do my best."

"It's all we can ask of you."

He looked at her, hard, and she had to wonder if she was really on the verge of agreeing to this. Hell, she supposed she already had.

But she had wanted a whole new life.

What he was offering didn't conflict with anything. And it gave her one thing she wanted. That she wanted desperately. A child.

And that mattered to her. It mattered so much.

"What are your terms?"

"Beyond the conception thing? You said that you don't want much to do with the child."

"I would like the child to know that they have a father. A father who works to provide for them. I am a billionaire. As you pointed out this palace has not come with an exceptional store of wealth. However, you will have access to that wealth through me."

"Oh," she said, feeling dizzy. "I have access to it?"

"Yes," he said. "You do. You are my wife, and I will take care of my wife."

"What else?"

"My mother will be in residence here sometimes. She always dreamed of it. I will be here when she is here. And she will be considered part of the royal line."

"Sure. That's fine."

She didn't see why the titles couldn't get spread around. Everyone ought to get some enjoyment out of them.

"But as for being with one another day in and day out... I've no desire for that."

"And as far as... As I said, I don't want to go falling in love with you. You do not seem like the sort of man who could love."

She didn't need the drama that might come with them trying to cohabitate. It made tension creep up her spine to think of it. It made her think too much of her parents.

Something sharpened in his gaze. "And why do you think that?"

"You're cold. I can feel it. It's the way that you are. It's a strange sort of contrast, because there is something in you that has a spark. That feels hot, but at the same time you... No. You are not the sort of man that I would wish to pin any dreams on."

"You are smart," he said. "You shouldn't. I will mostly live in Greece. That's where the headquarters for my businesses are. I travel quite a bit. I will engage in affairs as I see fit, of course. I'm a man with a certain voracity of sexual appetite. And if you do not wish for the fulfillment of that appetite to fall to you, then you must accept that while I offer my money, my protection, and my support, I do not offer my fidelity. Neither do I expect it from you."

It was easy enough to see how that would hurt. She would take him into her bed over these next weeks to try and conceive a baby. And then he would be gone. But she would have the expectation. None of it would be a surprise. If she wished to take lovers she could, and she could be in control of that. She had the palace. She had money. She would not be in a desperate position. Those were the sorts of things that created situations that were ripe for heartbreak.

She didn't want to be desperate, she didn't want heartbreak. But she was not desperate anymore, and she didn't love this man. So perhaps this was it. That step toward the life that she truly wanted.

The step toward being a new, self-contained person. Someone who didn't rely on her sister to be her emotional support.

Jessie loved her, but she had to make her own life. Just like her mother had loved her, but had to get away from their father. She understood. She did.

Maren needed to make her own life. When she had a child, she would… She would never leave that child. She would never have to.

This man is a stranger.

Yes. And she recognized that coldness in him. But it wasn't the same as her father. There was no cruelty to it.

At the same time, she could see that developing feelings for him would be a fool's errand.

He was a renowned businessman, he was not a criminal. He was… He was as safe as anyone.

"I would like to sign papers. Ensuring that no matter what I will retain custody of our child."

"By all means," he said. "We can certainly do that. As I said, what I'm after is the legacy. And unlike my father, I will not be weak or ineffective."

"You really don't like your father."

"My father is dead," he said. "And when he died, I decided to pick us up and elevate us in the world. My mother spent their entire marriage waiting for him to fulfill promises. While he waited for another man to hand him money. To hand him royalty. I want the promise, but I did not wait to make my mother comfortable. And now she will have the title that she was long promised. She will have no more reason to weep. My father gave her many. From his life debasing himself to his premature death, when all promise of happiness died with him."

"Yes. I relate to that too," she said softly. "My father gave my mother a lot of reasons to weep. Maybe that's one reason I've always been afraid of men. Falling in love with them, anyway. My mother fell in love with the wrong one."

"You are forewarned. Is that not the same as being forearmed? You know that I am not offering love. What I am offering is something better. What I am offering you is security. All of the money to ensure that this castle is run. You can be a princess. And you will have your child."

"It almost seems like there's no downside," she said.

The corner of his mouth tipped upward. "None at all."

"Well, then… Well."

"There is just one thing left to do. We ought to seal our marriage with a kiss."

And before Maren could protest he had risen from his chair, and crossed the space between them. Then he reached out to her, hauled her up and pressed her against the hard inferno that was his body.

Her heart was beating erratically, her body nearly shorting out.

She had been in a lot of different situations.

She had conned men at poker games. And in some of those situations, she had ended up in a bit of physical peril.

Men had tried to steal kisses from her before.

But it had been different. Because she hadn't felt her body respond.

Here and now she did. Here and now, she felt herself leaning toward him. She felt herself wanting.

And that had never happened before.

She did not feel in danger, she felt as if she was standing on the edge of a precipice with beautiful clear water below. Yes, it was dangerous. But all she had to do was allow their mouths to meet, and she would be plunged into something new. Something she had never experienced before.

And then, between a breath and her next heartbeat, he lowered his head, and pressed his mouth to hers.

And she was tossed beneath the waves.

CHAPTER FOUR

HE HAD NOT counted on this. On her softness.

On her flavor being so rich and intoxicating it overtook him.

He was Acastus Diakos, and he was not a man accustomed to feeling out of his depth. In fact, he had not had that happen since he was a boy.

Since he'd been thrown in the dungeon of this very castle, punished and imprisoned by Stavros Argos.

Since his own father had allowed it to happen. A fitting punishment for his crime, which had been designed to ensure that Acastus never got what was owed him.

This was like that. Disorienting. Like fumbling around in the dark.

He had kissed countless women. There was no reason this one should be different.

She was a stranger, and that in and of itself was not especially different for him.

He was a man who enjoyed a one-night stand.

He did not know his lovers.

But Maren was his wife, a woman he was to conceive a child with.

He had never made love to a woman without a condom. Had never slid inside the warm welcome of the female body without a latex barrier between him and that glorious slick channel. Perhaps it was the thought of that.

And yet it was so base.

He did not consider himself that sort of man.

He had appetites, but he was not a libertine. He was not driven by those things. He was driven by something bigger, he always had been.

It was not about his immediate satisfaction. He was always investing in the future. And this should be about the child. This should be about the triumph of winning.

But it wasn't that which made his body so hard that he ached now. Wasn't that which fired flame through his veins.

It had nothing to do with victory. And everything to do with her.

With the small kitten sounds she made as he forced her lips apart beneath his and slid his tongue against hers.

As he moved his hands down to cup the softness of her rear, and grind his hardness against her.

It was simply need.

Simply desire. Nothing more.

And yet there was nothing simple about it. It was an endless well of longing. Of need.

She was just so soft.

He could get lost in it. In her.

His life was hard. Sharp angles in a fast pace.

And she beckoned him to something different. Something more.

He had thought to use this moment to ensnare her. To ensure that he won. And yet she was the one drawing him in.

She was the one making him ache. Pushing him beyond himself.

She was the one.

Abruptly, he drew away from her. But ceasing contact didn't do anything to help the storm that was raging through him. Her eyes were wide, the color high in her cheeks. Her lips were pink and swollen from his attentions.

She looked like a woman ripe for seduction.

"Oh, my," she said, looking dazed.

She was breathing heavy, her eyes glassy, her lips swollen.

"That was…acceptable," he said, his own voice rough.

She slid her hand up behind his neck, looking at him with wonder. She pushed her fingers through his hair. A crease deepened between her brows as she looked at him. He should pull away and yet he found the concentration she was focusing on him to be intoxicating.

"And you know," she said, her voice a broken whisper. "The problem with that is that I will always remember it. The exact moment that you took me into your arms. The way it felt to have my breasts pressed to your chest. The way it felt when your tongue slid against mine. What is a woman to do with such a thing? To know that always and forever that moment will be burned into my mind?"

He knew without a doubt that it would be burned into his as well. But he rejected the way he felt drawn to her now. The way he felt like he'd die if he didn't touch her.

"We will suit," he said. "That is lucky."

"Is it?" she asked, her voice shaky. "If we aren't going

to be together after the conception of the baby… Well then, what does it matter?"

"It matters, because we will be spending the next few days in bed. Will we not?"

"I…suppose so. Though we can make it as perfunctory as we like."

He wanted to laugh at her. Yet he didn't find it funny.

"We shall see. If it's going to be burned into your memory, Maren, ought it not to be a stunning memory?"

"I suppose," she said, capturing one of those swollen lips in her teeth. "I suppose."

"Should you like your pizza?"

"Yes," she said quickly, sitting down in front of her plate. "I'll have to check my tracking app for sure, but I think I'm not fertile for a couple of days. So… Maybe in two days we can… Consummate." She smiled. "That sounds sort of royal. Doesn't it? Consummate." She laughed.

She was a strange woman. There were some exuberant, childlike things about her. And yet he sensed a deep pain. She had said she'd seen things.

But he wondered how…

He wondered if they were a bit more alike than perhaps it would seem on the surface.

"Tell me," he said. "Did you go to school?"

She shook her head. "No. Our education was easily seen to because everything we see we remember. By default, we learn a great many things quite quickly. But we were never around our peers. We never really had the chance to make friends with other people. We were… We were desperately cut off in many ways."

"Older and younger all at once," he said.

In some ways that echoed his own childhood. He had not had friends. He had worked.

He had learned to put his own needs, his own wants aside. There was no room for them. His father was woeful. His mother sad because her husband refused to do anything to lift them out of the dire straits they found themselves in. He had made her a servant, not a princess. He had done nothing that he had promised. And Acastus had to carry the weight of that.

Yes, he understood all too well.

"I suppose," she said. "When we got away we were like children. Eating candy, staying up as late as we wanted. Watching whatever we wanted on TV. We were free. And we took advantage of that."

"And then you took up gambling?"

"It was the best and easiest way for us to earn money using what talents we had. Like I said. We didn't go to school. We didn't have formal education. We didn't have anything when we escaped my father's compound. We didn't want to be outright con artists. But in a poker game, you feel as if people are consenting to being fleeced. At least, that's what we told ourselves. Jessie was the mastermind. For my part, I was the conscience. I didn't ever want us to go too far. Because I've always wondered, what is it that makes a man think he is above the laws of common decency? What is it that makes a man believe that he could hurt other people in pursuit of his own wealth?"

"I wonder that as well," he said. "For my part, I do

not cause harm. I am far too familiar with powerful men who do."

He burned with no great conviction over that. But it was a decision that he had made.

Because he would differentiate himself from Stavros Argos. He differentiated himself from his father by taking action. But Stavros had enjoyed lording power over people, as much as he had enjoyed withholding it.

And that was never Acastus. And never would be.

He had always known this moment would come. This moment when he would marry a woman that he barely knew, and have an heir with her.

And yet now that he was here, it seemed a stranger thing than he had anticipated.

Perhaps because he was so attracted to her.

He had never been attracted in the same way to Elena Argos.

He had known her since she was a girl, but she had the same condescending manner that her father did, and while there had been a certain masculine drive to subdue that, mostly, he had found it repellent.

There was nothing about the Argos family that he liked, and the biggest issue with having a child with that family was that their blood would be mingled with his own.

In so many ways Stavros had handed him something better than he had before. While convincing himself that he was hurting Acastus. It was humorous.

Yes, he had won.

Maren Hargreave was beautiful. She wanted a baby.

And making that baby would be an entirely pleasant experience.

He would have to be slow with her. Gentle. He had not counted on her being untried, but he was happy to train her in the ways of pleasure between men and women.

He would not have to worry about her falling in love with him.

He was not fundamentally lovable.

"So you were robbing the rich and giving to the poor?" he asked.

"If you consider us the poor, yes. I would not call it overly altruistic, however. I'm not certain that we were… I think we were being good on a technicality. But it was important to me."

That didn't surprise him. It was that air of innocence that she had.

She was a beautiful thing.

And that sweetness appealed to him. Because he had exposure to so little of it. He didn't know how she managed to retain it. He certainly hadn't managed any.

"I'm glad," he said. "That you will be the mother of my child."

It seemed like a light had been switched on from inside of her. She positively glowed. "Really?"

"Yes," he said.

"Well, go on. You silly man. You can't say something like that and then not elaborate at great length. A person does like to be flattered."

"It is not flattery, but the truth. I think you will be able to teach the child what it means to be loved. That is something I would not be able to do."

"You don't think that you'd love a child?"

"I've seen no evidence that I am capable of finer feelings. I am driven, though. And I must hope that it is a fitting substitute."

"I do have one request," she said, looking down at her food. And then she looked back up at him. There was something about the way that she caught his eye. Beneath her lashes. Something bold and coy all at the same time. Innocence and sexuality radiating off of her in reckless waves.

"What is it, little one?" He didn't know why he added that tender phrase. He was not tender, and she should not become accustomed to the idea that he might be.

"I think I should like for you to seduce me."

She curled up in a ball on her bed, filled with a sense of cringe that she couldn't escape. Why had she said that to him?

She had kissed him. He had kissed her. But she had kissed him back. He had been… Glorious. Incredible. And she'd been so lost in that haze that then she had…

She'd asked him to seduce her.

"Any special manner of seduction?"

"The seductive kind."

And she shivered with the memory.

The seductive kind. She was an idiot. An outright absolute idiot. What was she thinking? Why was he like this?

She howled into her pillow.

It was interesting, that he hadn't been around children his own age either. But he didn't seem to suffer for it.

Maren was very good at playing parts for short periods of time. She'd had to play the seductress on multiple occasions, but she never had to actually follow through with any of it. She never had to keep anything up for more than a couple of hours. If she put on makeup, and did her hair, or put a wig on, she could functionally make anything happen.

But now she had gone and begged her husband to seduce her. She told him that she didn't have any experience.

Why had she done that? Maybe she could have pretended to know what she was doing.

But why?

She sat up in bed. Yes. Why? This was an unexpected turn of events. Much like winning a castle. Much like becoming a princess. Why shouldn't it be about her? Why shouldn't it be about what she wanted? Her being a seductress might make him feel better, but what did she care about his feelings? This wasn't about him. This was about her. He had his goals, and she had hers.

She wanted the sex to be a good memory. She wanted the experience to leave her enriched, rather than reduced. She wanted it to be a step forward into a different sort of life, a different sort of Maren. It made her excited to think about it. The opportunity to be a woman in these new faceted ways.

To explore her sexuality. To experience pregnancy, being a mother.

To be connected yet again to family.

And even though he wouldn't be her husband in truth, he was legally her husband, and they would be a family unit. He had promised protection. It was more than her own father had ever given. It mattered. It meant something. That was how she had to look at it. An opportunity. What was life if not a series of interesting opportunities? She had experienced a lot in her years. And she'd had the freedom to decide what she wanted to do for the last few years. If she'd wanted to, she could've gone out and gone clubbing every night. She could have sought anonymous pleasure with strangers. She had determined that wasn't for her.

She was much more interested in safety, security. Much more interested in the path she was on.

And so with confidence she could say she was going to claim it.

It was not very often that surprises in life came shaped like a six foot four muscular billionaire.

It was a pleasant one, as they went.

As long as she didn't expect anything from him but... Pleasure. And money apparently. She wasn't too broken up about the money.

She wondered *how* he might seduce her. And when he might start.

She fell asleep on tenterhooks, waiting for that, but he didn't come to her room.

But then, that was for the best. She had the idea that she wanted the seduction to be something more. Something a bit gentle. Something to ease her in.

She dressed in a flowing gown and went downstairs, heading toward the parlor where her large sitting cushions were. She only wanted pastries and some coffee, she did not need the whole dining table for that. But she was surprised to find coffee and pastries waiting for her in that very room when she arrived.

And then even more surprised to see him sitting there, reading a book.

"Good morning," he said.

"Good morning, Acastus," she said. "I'm surprised to see you here."

"Are you? I anticipated that you would wish to break your fast here. And that you would probably want something sweet."

She narrowed her eyes. "I see. And how do you know that?"

"I spent a collective two hours speaking to you yesterday, and you think that you might remain unknowable to me? You asked for a seduction, Maren Hargreave. Did you think that I would be anything less than thorough in it?"

"As seduction goes," she said, taking her seat on one of the large cushions and reaching for a flaky, glazed pastry, "you're not far off that the way to my heart is paved with butter."

"But it wasn't to reach your heart, darling. Just that tender place between your thighs."

And she felt an answering pulse quicken down there. Just where he'd said. It should be crass and vulgar. But there was something about how he said it, while sitting there with his large masculine hands caressing the spine of that poor book, that made her feel... Not offended. Not disgusted. In fact, she felt as if she could feel the way his fingertips might trail down her own spine. And shamefully, wondered how they would feel where she was growing a bit wet for him.

"Well. But it probably works there too."

She took a bite of the pastry. It was incredible.

"It's very sweet the way that you blush."

"I told you," she said, yet again opting for honesty. "I haven't any experience with men. All I know about sex I have learned from books and movies. Don't get me wrong. I have vivid images stored in my mind. And so it will be up to you to reach deep for my fantasies I suppose."

"Too easy," he said.

"Is it?"

"Yes. You are sweet. In spite of all the things that have happened to you. But you're also very strong, and a lesser man might miss that. He might think that you are soft, and therefore easily crushed. I do not think so. You are soft, it is true, but that is a choice. And it's one you've made from a position of strength. You need a man who can match your strength. You would never respect a man who didn't. You also see the difference between a bully and a man who is strong. Truly strong. You do not wish for someone to overpower you. You wish for strength to surrender to. And those are very different things."

Her heart fluttered. "I have never surrendered in my life."

"No, of course not. Because in the past when men or anyone else has demanded surrender of you, they did so because they wished to see you reduced. You want to give surrender joyfully. You wish to place that surrender in the hands of someone who will treat it well. Who wishes to take it and use your vulnerability as a way to access your pleasure. That's what you have protected all this time. Because you know that when you do surrender, it will be total. Complete. You will not lie back and part your legs for a man who would use his strength to dishonor that which you are offering. And I will not. I will see it as the gift that it is. That each and every cry of delight is being given to me freely. A gift that I could never hope to earn, but must take it as something freely presented and given. Any power I have over you, over your body, is because you have given it to me. Even now. Yes, I married you by default. There is power in that. But I could never take you if you did not give yourself. Because that is not the kind of man I am. That is not what power means to me. To physically force is the domain of the weak. True strength is in waiting. True strength is in knowing that the only way to truly win is to have earned a forfeit."

"All very sexy," she said, her throat feeling parched. "And admirable in part. But why is sex a forfeit for a woman and a victory for a man?"

He leaned forward. "It is an exchange. When I strip you of your clothes, when I lower my head to take one of your begging nipples into my mouth, when I kiss my way down your stomach and taste that sweet honey between your legs, I will be revealing myself. My fantasies will show you the deepest part of myself. As I take control I surrender my power. If you do not capitulate, if you do not find pleasure, then I am a failure. The captain of the ship steers it through the storm, does he not?

He is the master, and yet. If the sea overtakes him, if he fails, he goes down with the ship. In that sense, the power goes to you. All of it. By claiming authority, by claiming dominion, in effect, I give you the power to destroy me. You may find me wanting. You may refuse me. And then it is I who have opened up the deep and secret places inside of himself to find them rejected."

His words rolled over her, and she found she had to think on them. Deeply.

And yet they made sense. The greater power a person assumed, the more they had to lose.

By offering her the position of submission, he was in effect granting her the power to wholesale demolish the dominance he tried to claim. And that was to risk humiliation. One thing she did know, was that there was little more devastating for a man. And so she could see that the risk was high.

She was discomfited, by how well he read her. By just how deeply he seemed to understand her concern about the risk of all this. By how deeply he seemed to understand her. When they had only just barely met.

She looked at him, the hard cut of his face. The lean, stock lines of his body.

This morning, he was casual. His white shirt unbuttoned at the throat, his sleeves rolled up past his elbows.

His forearms were delicious, well-defined and muscular.

He was truly a sight to behold. His emotions were complicated. But she looked into his eyes, and tried to pull them apart anyway. Yes, there was a coldness to him, but there was a heat as well. No one could lay claim to this level of sensual knowledge without heat.

"If I were to leave out breakfast for you it would be strong espresso. You do not wish to have sweets in the morning. You would rather have... Nothing, actually, if you took your pick. But if there was a breakfast to be put before you, it would be eggs. Bacon, likely. American bacon. You would not freely admit that. You do not like relationships because you did not learn how to have them. But you do enjoy sex because it allows you to connect with someone. If you put yourself in the dominant position to a woman's needs then you must stop and read her. And that allows you a feeling of intimacy without having actually achieved it. A surrogate for what other humans are looking for in life. But you're comfortable with the surrogacy." She could see disquiet in his dark eyes. "Oh, it isn't that you've never made a connection. You have one. And it is so domineering, so all-consuming, that you cannot afford another."

One of the ways that she and Jessie had tried to make money at first was by claiming that Maren was a psychic. But she had become uncomfortable with that quickly. She was not a psychic. She was simply astute at reading people. And one thing she had never wanted to do was take advantage of someone's pain. And when you got into faux psychic readings you were invariably brushing up against extremely personal things.

But she used those tricks now, to delve into him. Every remark created a microexpression on his face. A reaction that most anyone else would never notice. But that she did.

"You don't have to tell me that I'm correct," she said. "I can see that I am."

"That is quite the parlor trick," he said.

"I know," she said. "It's all just paying attention. I appreciate that you did not bother to deny it."

"And why bother to deny it?" He shrugged. "You are my wife. By default, the closest, most binding relationship I have save family."

"And your remaining family is your mother. Your father was an ineffective fool," she said, paraphrasing his own words back to him. "You had to take care of her. And you still do. You're a good son. Because you love your mother, and also because you're angry at your father. And the better you are at being a son, the more insipid he looks by his inability to do what a man ought to have done. You are twice the man he was. If not more. Before the breakfast that you prefer not to eat every day."

"Well spotted," he said. "That is all true. Except the part about wishing to have intimate connections and not having the energy for them. I don't want them. I don't want them, because love is a cage. My mother was kept in that cage for twenty-five years. Miserable. I do know, the older I get the more I realize my father was trapped in it as well. He loved my mother. He was just far too ineffective to do it well. What is worse than that? To love a woman, and to track her into your poorly constructed facsimile of how you express that love. I would never. And so I prefer honesty. And sex. Bodies are honest."

Her own felt strung out. Sparring with men had always been something she'd enjoyed. It always felt a bit dangerous, a bit like foreplay, if she were honest. Most of the time, her marks were men she did not find attractive, but on the rare occasions when she had, she had found the process invigorating. She had told herself on more than one occasion that her verbal sparring could be a substitute for sex. She had often found herself aroused by it. And so to bring it into this discussion, with the man she had married, a man whose bed she was going to share, put her on edge in a way she never had been before.

It affected her physically.

It filled her with desire.

"And what else is planned for my seduction today?" she asked.

"You are a woman who likes to know things. Everything. I wonder what it would be like for you if a silken blindfold covered your eyes and you had to simply feel."

The image, of being blindfolded while she waited to find out where he might touch her next, kissed her next, flooded her.

And she felt an answering wetness between her legs.

"I have no interest in any such thing."

"You're a liar. And I don't know what you get out of being a liar on this score. Perhaps you are embarrassed. To tell me your true, sensual nature. You repressed it long enough."

"I'm not embarrassed," she protested. Even while a pulse throbbed between her thighs that shamed her, and called her a liar.

Maybe this was the problem. She was ashamed because she wanted to sleep with him. Because she didn't even think she wanted to wait until tomorrow when she was actually fertile to be with him.

Because she was curious. Because she was attracted to him, in spite of the fact that she didn't love him.

Was this her own fear of wickedness?

Her own hang-ups? Why would she think that?

Of course she had grown up taking on board a somewhat misogynistic attitude around women. Her father had not respected them. He had seen women only as pawns. As sexual objects. And she could see the way that he had treated women he thought of as smart, and women he thought of as playthings. She and Jessie had played into those sorts of perceptions. They had made themselves into the kind of women who looked like they could be treated as sexual objects, but who were in fact smart, as if those two things were entirely separate, when she knew they weren't. They were playing games. They were using people's prejudices against them, and yet, she was struck just then by how much it had sunk into her own bones. How much of it lived inside of her.

That she felt she had to be a fake sort of sexy, concealing her brilliance. Instead of acknowledging that she liked to be beautiful. That she wanted to be sexy. And that it didn't make her less smart.

That she could be all those things. And still good.

There had been such a great many traumatic things for her to work out upon leaving her father's compound, that she had missed this one.

She wondered how many more she'd missed.

"All right. Perhaps I would like to be blindfolded."

A luxurious image filled her mind, one that made her blush. "You could surprise me."

Her deep and real fantasy was him pressing the most intimate part of himself to her mouth, and her taking him in deep.

It made her feel overheated.

And she fought against shame.

"You have sex with strangers often, don't you?"

"When it suits me," he said. "I don't know what you would define as *often*."

"You feel no shame about it," she said.

"No. I feel no shame around the way I conduct myself in life, and I have worked hard to arrive at such a place. I am not my father. I take ownership of that which I am. I make no promises I cannot keep. And I act with a clean conscience. When I have sex, it is with a woman who wants what I want. I am clear and I am up front. And so I feel no need for shame."

"I'm fighting shame," she said. "Because your kiss awoke desire within me, and it makes me feel as if I am not good. Because wicked women crave the bodies of men they don't know. That they don't love. I made that rule, for myself and for Jessie, to protect us. Because I didn't want to make love to a man, fall in love with him, and have him leave only to be haunted by the images of us in bed together. But perhaps that was a lie. Perhaps I simply felt dirty. From my time spent conning people. From the time I spent growing up in my father's house. And I was afraid of adding another sin to my roster. But I do not wish to see this as a sin. I want you."

"That must be a record. The seduction has only lasted these past twenty minutes."

"I should like you to keep on seducing me. I want to be mindless with it." She smiled. "I'm never mindless, you see. I am both fascinated by and afraid at the idea that a man might be able to make me so."

"Then the seduction will continue, wife. Until you cannot resist."

CHAPTER FIVE

THERE WAS A full staff at the palace to see to Maren's every whim and desire. But Acastus decided that he would fulfill them himself. He had decided that he would become the fulfillment of all that she desired, because he wished that surrender. More than he would've said that morning. What he had intended as a game had turned into something much more real. Much more honest.

He went over the dossier that she had sent to the palace staff. The one that stated all of her preferences. Her favorite foods, her favorite music.

And he packed them a picnic lunch, in accordance with her wishes. He did all of the preparation for the food himself.

He programmed a playlist to his phone, and packed a small speaker into the bag because that would add to it. To the sense of knowing her. And he could see that it was important to her. She was a discomfiting creature. The way that she had succinctly analyzed him had cut. But it was no secret. He was proud of the way that he had cared for his mother. She read him wrong if she thought that he feared anything, but he could see how with many other people that would be true. He personally just did not find use for emotion.

There was no room in his life for it, and so he did not give it space. That was practical. It was not a weakness.

He prized strength above all else.

And as long as he had strength enough to fulfill his obligations, there could be no sense of failure in him.

By the time he found Maren again, she was back in the sitting room, curled up on a cushion, reading a book.

He could see that it was a romance. The problem with her was that she did seem quite soft. He did not wish to hurt her, in the way that he simply could not respect men who harmed women. Stavros Argos was the sort of man who hurt women with malicious cruelty. He'd enjoyed the despair of Acastus's mother. He'd seen his own daughter as a pawn to be manipulated and his wife as little more than an accessory. His father was the sort of man who hurt a woman with apathy. And both of those things were quite powerful and quite real. He despised it.

But he had laid out his reality to Maren quite firmly. He could only hope that she listened. That she understood.

It was important that she did.

"I have packed us a picnic lunch," he said.

"You did? Or did you have Iliana ask one of the kitchen workers to—"

"I did," he said. "I think you will find that many of your favorites are in there. Come. Let us go outside. There is a lovely spot overlooking the sea."

"Every spot overlooks the sea," she said, the bit of edge in her voice the only thing that betrayed her wariness.

"Yes. It does. This is part of your seduction, do not look at me as if I am trying to trick you."

"I'm sorry. Everything in my life at one time was a con. I suppose I'm always waiting for the other shoe to drop."

"And who could blame you. But I am simply doing as you asked. And if it is working, then I am only giving to you. Surrendering to you in that sense. The exchange. You will recall."

That earned him a slight smile.

She had changed into a rather diaphanous white dress, and it conformed to her curves. When she stood, he felt as if he had been punched low in the stomach.

He really had not counted on her beauty. It was arresting. Magnificent. As was she.

He was seducing her, but one thing was certain, she was doing a fair enough job of seducing him.

He was anticipating the time they would come together more than he had anticipated. He had truly believed that this would all be about conceiving the child for him. But suddenly it had been reduced to this. To her.

They walked out of the palace, and were greeted by the intensity of the turquoise sea.

He had grown up here. He knew exactly where to take her.

There was a small patch of grass up on top of one of the craggy rocks, and it overlooked the ocean. One of the only good places to sit outside. He helped her up the side of the craggy stones, and placed the picnic basket between them when they sat on the pad of grass.

"This is lovely," she said, and then she opened up the picnic basket. "What is this?" She took out the speaker.

"As much as I enjoy the sounds of the sea, I did think that perhaps you would like an aria."

He began to play the music. Her favorite opera. Which he had found she was a fan of, through the dossier.

"You read my file," she said. She dug through the basket deeper. And took out a toaster pastry. "You really did read my file." But she looked delighted.

"I did. I wished to give you an afternoon specifically suited to your desires."

She shook her head and laughed. "And what about yours?"

"I am looking at you lit in the golden light from the sun. What could I desire more? Except that you strip your dress off, so that I could see the glory of your bare body beneath the sunlight. But that perhaps will be for another time."

She turned pink. And he could see that she was annoyed by it.

"You are not subtle at all."

"You don't want subtlety," he said. "You wish to be adored."

He meant to say it somewhat as a joke. But as soon as he said the words, he could see how true they were. Had anyone ever worshipped her? There had been no lover, so she had not been worshipped in that way. Her father had been a cruel man. Her mother had left. She had a sister, but that was not the same sort of relationship. No. No one had ever worshipped her. Adored her. And he could see she was desperately hungry for it.

"Well, thank you," she said. "This is very thoughtful. I've never been on a date before."

She leaned over and bumped her shoulder against his, smiling up at him. It was… Extraordinarily cute and he had no idea what to do with it.

"I don't know this is a date," he said.

She reached into the basket again and took out a grilled cheese sandwich. She was delighted to find it. She took a happy bite of it.

"It is a date. We are on a date. Which is good. Because even though sleeping with you after one date will be slightly promiscuous of me, at least you have taken me out."

"To a patch of grass."

"Indeed."

"I didn't think you were worrying about whether or not you were promiscuous. Besides, I am your husband."

That created a glowing light in her eyes that he had to turn away from.

"Yes," she said softly. "You are."

She was his wife. His wife. And that should mean very little. It was a formality. It was her instead of Elena Argos, a substitute. It mattered not.

And yet he found that he was glad he was here with Maren and not Elena.

What a strange, strange thing.

And perhaps it was merely sexual desire.

Because sexual desire was a powerful thing, and he was only a man.

Maybe it was as simple as that.

"So what's your sign?" She looked up at him, and batted her eyes.

"Are you kidding?"

"Yes," she said. "I googled you. I already know your birthday. You're a Taurus. Obviously."

"What does that mean?"

"It doesn't really matter, it's just fun to watch you react to it."

"You are a brat," he said.

She laughed. "My sister has called me that before. But nobody else. I guess no one else knows me well enough."

And she wanted someone to know her, he could see that too.

This was all in aid of seduction. He would do well to remember that. He didn't need to grow an attachment to this strange creature that he had married.

He took his own sandwich, and ate it while he watched her.

She really was a sight to behold, bright and red and gold against this extraordinary scenery behind her. All that blue.

"Did you live near the sea growing up?"

She shook her head. "This is glorious. I'm from the US, obviously. But we did spend part of our childhood in London, and then most of our years since have been in England. We've traveled. But places like Las Vegas. I have always liked the idea of living somewhere where there was sun. Where it was a bit brighter. A bit warmer. I like this ocean, even if I do sometimes enjoy the stormy gray sea. All of it's beautiful. But mostly, just having something of my own is beautiful. Though I guess we share it." She frowned. "Life is strange. It's never quite as straightforward as you hope it might be."

"Life is filled with hooks. You just have to decide what to do with the particular ones you get caught on."

"I suppose that is true. There is no such thing as true freedom. The only thing that comes close is being a sociopath like my father was. You are free of obligation. Both to society and to anyone who might care for you. Anyone you should care for. But then there is the law. And it always catches up to you. In the end."

"Do you believe that?" he asked.

"I've seen it. My father is dead because of it."

He could not figure out what the appropriate response was to that. "I'm sorry."

She frowned. "In many ways I'm not. And yet in some ways… You know it's very unsatisfying when a villain meets his end. Especially when they never cared if they were the villain. Not even a little. Especially when they were only ever interested in themselves. In their own victories. I find it very unsatisfying to think that he might just be gone. But that was the end for him. And he never once knew what a terrible person he was. I need to believe that there's recompense in the afterlife."

"I suppose I do too," he said. He had never even had that thought fully formed inside of him, much less spoken aloud to another person. "The idea that my father lived and died a weak man, and never truly understood the harm that he caused… And never got to witness the way that I fixed it… It is a deeply unsatisfying one. I reject it. I need to believe he suffers."

"Me too. Maybe they're together. Maybe they're watching us eat very good grilled cheese while the flames of hell touch their feet."

"Probably the strangest date conversation anyone has ever had," he said.

"Probably," she agreed. "But I do not suppose you or I were ever destined for normal."

"No indeed."

"I would like normal. Birthday parties and friends and Christmas."

"Christmas?"

"I never really had it. And I'd like to decorate the palace, from top to bottom. I ordered decorations before I arrived and had them stored for the season. I've always wanted…that sparkle. That magic."

She put her sandwich down, and then surprised him by putting her hand on his face. He didn't move. He simply allowed her to lean in and press a kiss to his lips. It was slow, methodical. Lovely. His whole body burned with it. With her.

He had set out to seduce her. But she was doing something to him. It was the artlessness. And the insight. Such a strange combination of things for a person to possess. Her kiss was cool, inexperienced. Tender. And it ignited him in a way that nothing else ever had.

He took a lock of her hair and wrapped it around his finger. Tested the silken nest of her hair between his fingertips.

"Let me bathe you," he said.

"What?"

"I will not claim you until tomorrow, but tonight… Let me wash your hair. Let me touch your skin, slick with water."

He did not know why he was making this request. He felt undone. And he had never felt undone in his life.

"Yes," she whispered.

He had won a victory. Or perhaps he had not.

The exchange of power between the two of them was so profound, that he realized he might as well be on his knees.

Normally he would turn away from it.

But not here. Not with her. Because it was simply not like anything he had ever experienced. Because there were rules. Firmly set rules. And so at least this would end. Perhaps it was a chance for both of them to indulge, when they otherwise would not.

Tonight…

His body was tight with anticipation. He could not remember the last time he had truly seduced a woman. He wondered if he ever had.

Women had wanted him, that was certain. But this was different. This was about finding her specific desires, her specific needs, and bending them to his will.

Tonight.

And the very thought of it made him feel like fire.

CHAPTER SIX

SHE DIDN'T KNOW what to expect. She had been sitting in her room wearing only a robe for the past hour, pacing. He had not joined her for dinner, and she felt that it was on purpose. He had not joined her for dinner, and she felt that it was because he was trying to heighten her anticipation.

She had not expected the show of…humanity today. The way he had given her her favorite foods. The way he had played her favorite music. Talked to her. Listened to her. And then ended it with a promise to…

To bathe her.

Her heart was fluttering.

He had said that they wouldn't consummate tonight.

She was still a jangle of nerves.

She knew that men liked the look of her body when it was clothed. She imagined that he would like it naked.

But the fact remained this was new territory for her, and it was a bit…

Well, it was more than a little bit enervating.

She hadn't expected this as a seduction. She wasn't sure what she had expected a seduction to be. She only knew that this felt especially… Luxurious. Sensual. Arousing.

He had found it. The way to get to her. He had lavished her with attention earlier, and then withheld it. She was poised on the edge of a knife. She didn't know how to imagine what was going to come next. She had no picture in her head.

That bastard had read her like a book. And instantly she was brought back to the way that he had caressed the spine of the book this morning.

Oh, my.

There was a soft knock at the door and she jumped. It was him, she knew. She hadn't expected him to knock. She had a feeling he knew that, and it was why he had done so. He was trying to get around her expectations. Trying to defy what she might think of him.

She opened up the door. And her heart did a complicated dance in her rib cage.

He still had on that white shirt, but another button was undone. The sleeves were rolled up. His feet were bare.

The lateness of the day saw his jaw more shadowed, rough looking. She wished to touch it again. To touch him.

But she decided to surrender to his power. To give in to him completely. To allow him to direct this. To place her pleasure in his hands, because he had promised it would make her powerful, and so she would trust it. Would give it.

"I wondered when you would come," she said.

His lips curved. "And I wonder when you will."

She blinked. "What? *Oh.*" It took her a second. Her stomach went tight.

"Come, little one, I have drawn a bath for you already."

He led her through her vast wardrobe room, and into the bathroom. Which was a stunning, luxurious space. The bath itself was like a large ornate bowl, with golden feet, and a cushioned place for her to rest her head.

She looked at him, holding the edges of her robe together.

"No modesty with me, darling. Show me all that you are. It will be my undoing."

Power.

To claim power, she had to be vulnerable.

It made sense then. Clicked into place. And she found herself moving her hands to the knot on her belt. Undoing it. And then letting her robe slide off of her body and pool down on the floor.

In an instant, she saw each of his reactions, the way that he sucked in a hard breath, the slight clench of his fist. She could see his midsection go tight beneath his shirt, could see his pulse pound harder at his throat. His teeth were locked together, the fire burning bright in his eyes.

It was as if his entire body had gotten just a bit harder. As if he was holding on to his composure with that much more of a struggle.

They had traded. She had given. And it had taken something from him.

She was exhilarated by it.

"Goddess," he said. "Venus. My culture has for thousands of years had a great love of sensuality. Of beauty. You would be the sort of beauty that they wrote epics about."

"How fortunate for me, though I do not wish to be the start of a war, even a mythical one."

"And yet I imagine you could've started many. If you chose."

"I try to use my powers for good. Mostly. I haven't always."

"Did you make men think that they could earn the night in your bed, but con them into trading their money to you instead?"

"Not as such," she said, almost forgetting for a moment that she was standing there naked until she became unbearably conscious of the ache in her breasts, the way that her nipples went tight. "But I did… I suppose I've used my beauty to distract men before. Is it my fault, though, that they underestimate a woman? Especially if she has…" She cupped her own breasts and took a chance, rubbing her thumb over one of her nipples. He clenched his fists all the way.

"Shall I help you into the bath?"

"Please."

He took a step closer to her, and then he pressed his fingertip between her shoulder blades, drawing it all the way down the line of her spine. The images from this morning were overlaid on the moment, her breasts catching in her chest, her whole body poised on the edge of a knife.

He did not have to speak the words, she could feel them. He had read her like that book. He knew her. What she wanted. What she craved. She was used to knowing other people in this way, but she did not know what it was to be known by someone else. She could not decide if it was terrifying or exhilarating.

She decided it was both.

He picked her up, and the heat of his body burned her through his clothes. His bare hands, one resting on her rib cage near the swell of her breasts, and the other around her thigh, set her pulse on fire.

And then he set her down gently into the warm water, and knelt by the tub.

"Glorious," he whispered. He moved his hands down into the water and took a handful of it, pouring it out over her breasts.

"Oh," she said, the shock of pleasure moving through her.

"Tomorrow, my mouth will be there."

"Yes," she whispered.

But why tomorrow? Why not *now*?

She wanted him.

For once in her life, she wasn't worried about the future. What she would remember. What might haunt her. For once she was only worried about what she wanted. And it was right there. Within reach. But then she did not have a chance to ponder it because he picked up a bar of soap and slicked his hands with it before moving them down over her breasts, down her midsection and back up again, paying special attention to her nipples as he skimmed his thumbs over her sensitized flesh.

"Acastus," she gasped.

"Yes," he ground out. "So responsive. So lovely. You are absolutely perfect. Gorgeous, my girl."

She had never been anyone's girl. Not in so long. And never like this.

She felt small and fragile and protected.

Safe.

And it made her want to weep. How could this dangerous predator of a man make her feel safe?

How could his touch be so gentle when his hands were so strong?

He continued to smooth his palms over her body, and then his hands found that place between her thighs and began to stroke her.

She gripped the edge of the bathtub, arching her hips in time with his touch.

"You were wet for me," he said.

"Yes," she whispered.

"So wet."

"Yes," she agreed.

"Because you are a good girl. And you will get what you want. You will get what you need."

She wanted to weep. The affirmations did something to her, reached inside of her and tangled around all of these needy places that she had never known existed. Or at least that she tried to hide. Even from herself.

Because she had been worried, hadn't she? That she wasn't good. That something was wrong with her.

He was making this feel okay. He was making it feel right. He was making it feel good.

Making her feel good.

She began to whimper.

And then he cursed, moving his hand from between her legs.

"I was going to wait," he growled.

But then he claimed her mouth with his, and she found herself being lifted from the water.

Her naked body pressed against his clothed one, leaving water bleeding into the fabric.

"I must have you," he said. "I must."

She couldn't protest.

He lifted her up onto the counter, and stepped between her open thighs, and she could feel the hardness of him pressing there to the heart of her.

She kissed him, pushing her fingers through his hair.

Then he lowered his head and sucked her nipple into his mouth as he had promised to do tomorrow.

She didn't want to wait.

His tongue played havoc with her, and then he moved his attentions down her midsection, dropped to his knees before her and cupped her backside in his large hands, pulling her toward his mouth.

And he consumed her. He looked up at her, his dark eyes meeting hers. "I gave you your favorite treats earlier. And now I shall have mine." Then he licked her. Deep. Hard. As if he was tasting the most gloriously sweet dessert he'd ever had in his life.

He devoured her.

And she was overcome.

She arched her hips into his seeking tongue, and surrendered herself.

She was lost in the sensations. Lost in him. Whimpering in the back of her throat as he sucked that sensitive bundle of nerves between his lips, as his hand joined his mouth, as he pushed a finger deep within her while he continued to play havoc on her body.

And then she shattered. Utterly and completely. The orgasm that crashed over her unlike anything she'd experienced by her own hand. It surpassed the descriptions of things that she'd read about. It was a breaking apart. A storm-tossed sea. It was fireworks and waves. It was everything she had ever read and somehow more. Coming from deep within her and overtaking her completely. Making her mind, that cluttered, eternally seeking place, into a desolate wasteland. Into nothing more than her need.

Into nothing more than the pleasure that was washing over her.

She was remade.

In that moment.

Not a brain containing endless images. But a body. Seeking, releasing, having.

And then he moved back up and kissed her mouth, holding her fast to him while he pushed his fingers through her hair and held her head steady, kissing deeper and deeper as the last vestiges of her orgasm shuddered through her.

"Acastus," she whispered. "My husband."

"You are so beautiful," he said. "So beautiful." He smoothed his thumb over her lips, and she had never felt so desired. So wanted. So wholly approved of in all of her life. And she did not worry about what it might mean. She simply reveled in it. Accepted it. Became overjoyed with it.

It was like she was bathed in a glow. One that suffused her entire being.

"I did not intend for it to go this far. Forgive me."

"You don't need…"

But then suddenly he was moving away from her. Leaving her.

"Tomorrow," he said. "As planned."

And she could sense that… He was ashamed. That he had deviated from the plan. That he needed to do this, to regroup, to regain some of his control.

And it made her feel bereft. Because she was lost. Out of her mind. And she wanted for him to be as well.

And when he left, she felt like he had taken a piece of her with him.

And all the warmth she felt moments before went out.

CHAPTER SEVEN

HE HAD GONE too far. He had meant to maintain his control. He had meant to make it about her. He had not meant to push her so far. He had not meant…

He was overwrought. And he was never overwrought. He never had feelings that he could not gain dominion over. And here he was. Shaking over a virgin.

He was…

He had to leave her. He had to defer his own pleasure. Because otherwise…

He would fail the test of control. And he could not have that.

He went to the bar in his room and poured himself a measure of whiskey.

And he nearly laughed when he lifted the glass to his lips and the liquor touched his tongue, only to have the door open.

And there she was. Wearing a lace gown he could see through. And even if he could not, he would always see her as naked in his mind.

Pale, glorious breasts tipped with strawberry-colored nipples. That thatch of red hair between her legs. Yes, he would always see that.

But she was showing him anyway.

"I do not wish to stop," she said. "And I have decided that this is a gift, this marriage. That I get to have something that I thought that I would be denied all of my life. I desire you. I want you inside me."

He had lost. He knew that. If this was a war, then this battle went to her.

He would not deny her. He could not.

It was symbolic, anyway. His show of resistance.

But in his dominance he had shown his weakness.

He had taken her and held her and pleasured her, and it only showed his own lack of resistance. She saw that. And she was using it against him. He could not blame her.

He wanted her. Craved her.

And here she was before him, her curves barely contained, asking that he be inside of her.

His body throbbed in response.

This was insanity, but it would be days of it. And then he would go back to his life and wait to find out if she was carrying his child or not. If so he would come back for a few more days of it.

That was all. There were limits to it. There were limits.

And here you are moving the boundaries. Because of your own weakness.

He snarled, and set the whiskey down. He closed the space between them and wrapped his arm around her waist, drawing her up against his body. "You want me like this? On edge? Barely in control of myself? Is that what you want?"

"Yes. It is what I want, my husband. I'm surrendering to you. To this. Your seduction was thorough."

"As was yours," he said, moving his hand down to cup her backside. He squeezed her hard. "I am a man who prizes control above all else. I indulge, but only when I mean to. You have pushed me. I did not need to do this. I did not intend to be with you like this tonight. But I cannot resist you. How does that make you feel?"

"Powerful," she whispered. "And weak at once. What if I don't please you?"

"You cannot help but please me. Please me by your very form. You please me in all ways."

The words tumbled from his lips, as close to poetry as he had ever gotten. "My princess."

She was a princess, and he the Prince. And yet that did not feel like the achievement here. The achievement was holding her in his arms.

It was as if the world had shrunk, to this palace on the rock, but maybe even more so, to this room. To them.

And nothing more.

He grabbed the straps of the lace dress and pulled them down, revealing her breasts to his hungry gaze, and then he revealed the rest of her body. She was naked again before him, but her own eyes were seeking.

"I wish to see you," she said. "All of you."

And there was something particularly laser focused to her gaze, something that reached down deep into his gut and twisted hard. She would not forget a single detail of his body.

He was not a shy man, he was comfortable with himself.

But what a strange moment, knowing he would reveal himself to a woman who would forever remember him like this. Remember this encounter. Every detail of it burned into her brain. It had to be good. Everything. All that he gave her.

He was not a man given to performance anxiety. He would rise to the challenge.

Because she deserved it.

She had not asked for this. And yet she was here. His equal in this moment in a profound way. Seeing all that this alliance offered her and taking it. But more than that, seizing the sensual opportunity that existed between them. It was a glorious thing.

He moved his hands to the buttons on his shirt and undid them, casting it to the floor, and he watched with satisfaction as desire illuminated her eyes.

"Have you seen a naked man?"

"Not in person," she said. "You will be my first. My standard."

She said first in that there would be more, and right then he felt that was unacceptable. But of course, the parameters he laid down for their marriage would suggest that they would take other lovers.

Later. He would deal with that later. He would focus now on being so undeniable that she would never want anyone else.

He moved his pants then, took them off along with his underwear, and watched as her eyes slid over every detail. He could feel her as if she had cupped his length and run her finger along it, so keen was her examination of him.

"You are quite a bit bigger than I expected," she said. "But I find that excites me."

He gritted his teeth against the onslaught of desire that created inside of him. He should find it embarrassing to respond to such a basic provocation. And yet, he found that with her, he was nothing more than an extremely basic man. He was nothing more than his own need. Nothing more than a cascade of desire coursing through him like a storm.

He needed her.

And then, she moved to kiss him, pressing her breasts to his chest, the length of her naked body up against his own creating a maelstrom of need inside of him. He held her fast. Clutching her hips and grinding his hardness against her softness.

She kissed his neck, peppered kisses down his chest, and his heart reacted. His whole body reacted. She moved down, trailing her tongue along his abdominal muscles, and pausing at the head of his shaft. She pressed her lips against it, near featherlight, and all the more impacting for it.

And then she parted her lips and took him inside.

Her movements were unpracticed, unskilled, but glorious.

He arched his hips forward, and pushed himself a bit deeper, and she responded with enthusiasm. Working her hand in time with her mouth, doing her best to take as much of him as she could.

It was an out-of-body experience, a moment he would never be able to explain. It was for her, she had said. And yet it felt as if it was for him. And he had done nothing to deserve this. This was not in aid of making a child.

This was simply them. Need and glory cascading between them. Both of them unable to deny it.

He felt a gathering desire at the base of his spine. Felt as if he would not be able to deny her any longer.

As if he would not be able to deny himself.

"Enough," he said gruffly, moving her away from him and picking her up, carrying her over to the bed.

He laid her down on it, and stood back, looking at the way her red hair flowed over the fine, black silk blankets.

She was so pale against the darkness. So beautiful.

He gripped his own shaft hard and squeezed it. Trying to regain control of himself. Her eyes were hungry on him, and he did not see nerves. He saw only lust. Only need. Only desire gripping her, the same that it gripped him.

He moved to the bed, kissed her mouth and put his hand between her legs, stroking her until he had her in another sensual frenzy. Until she was wet. Until he could easily push two fingers deep inside of her.

He did not wish to cause her pain.

And perhaps a certain degree was inevitable. But he wanted this to be good. For her. He worked his fingers in and out of her body until she was shivering. Shaking.

Until a slow, deep orgasm rolled over her that squeezed him tight.

His name was on her lips as he positioned himself between her thighs and pressed the head of his arousal against her. Then he sank slowly inside of her. Inch by agonizing inch, the control that it took to not burst there and then was something he would've thought beyond him.

And when he was fully within her, he felt something like completion that he had never known before.

Something like home.

He had been a boy on his hands and knees in this place. A boy who scrubbed floors, who had spent time in the dungeon. And now he was in a bedroom, in a big, glorious bed, deep inside the castle's Princess. And he could not make that matter. Because what mattered was her. What mattered was this. And them.

He arched forward, then withdrew, thrusting back inside of her, in a hard, firm stroke. She gasped, but arched her breasts up against him, indicating pleasure.

And then he was lost. In this. In her. He thrust in and out of her glorious body, watching the shifts and changes of her face, listening as her kitten-like sounds of desire began to intensify.

She clung to his shoulders, dug her fingernails into his skin, pain became pleasure. And they became one.

They moved together. In tandem with the storm.

And when his own climax burst over him, hers broke as well. He poured himself within her, as she squeezed him tight, crying out his name.

And when it was done, he felt as if something in him had changed.

But he was made of stone. So that could not be.

She did not leave his bed. Not for the next two days. Food was brought, left outside the door, and she couldn't even be embarrassed by all of it.

She felt like she should be. Maybe. Like she should be ashamed that she had surrendered herself to this thing between them with quite so much enthusiasm, but she could not find the shame.

She could find nothing but joy as he claimed her, over and over again. As he showed her new things that her body could do. New things that she could want. He had shown her a depth of need and sexual liberty inside of her own self that she just hadn't known could ever be there.

They had done things she didn't think she would ever want to do. More than that, she had begged for them.

Her cheeks heated at the memory. They had done things that weren't in aid of making a baby. Just for indulgence's sake. And it had been glorious.

It was why on the third day, when she woke up and found him getting dressed, she felt like she had been struck.

"What are you doing?" she asked sleepily from the bed.

"I'm on my way back to Athens," he said. "You will keep me informed as to whether or not you've conceived."

And there he was, the stranger. The man she had first seen lying in this very bed, when she had first arrived. Not the man who'd become her lover these last days. Not the man that she had convinced herself she had a connection with.

She had lost herself. She was a fool and she wanted to weep with it. Because what had she been thinking?

She had let herself get sucked into all this. She should hope that she was pregnant. She did hope that she was pregnant. That they wouldn't have to do this again.

Because as he packed up and left, no affection, no kiss goodbye, she felt defeated. Small.

She wouldn't be able to endure this again.

Maren remembered being left. Her mother had done it. In some ways, even though it wasn't fair, even though Maren was the one who'd moved to the middle of the sea, she'd felt like Jessie had left her when she'd fallen in love with Ewan.

That spot inside her was sore, and him leaving pressed into it, like someone pushing their thumb against soft, overripe fruit.

She was alone. Again.

After that closeness, that bliss, it seemed especially cruel.

He didn't make any contact with her. Not over the next three weeks.

And when she started her period, she cried. Because she knew that he would come back. And she wanted him to. Because she was both upset and happy and she would never be able to sort those things out. Never be able to fully understand them.

She wiped her cheeks and sent him a text. And forced herself not to look at the phone.

She went downstairs and got herself some food.

Iliana looked at her with softness, and it irritated Maren.

"Are you well?"

"Just fine."

She went back to her room and was about to give in and check her texts when her phone rang.

It was her sister, Jessie. She'd been asking after how

everything was, and Maren had been putting her off. And putting off the little detail that she had acquired herself a husband.

She sighed and answered the phone. "Hello."

"How are things, my princess?" Jessie asked.

"Princessy. How are you?"

"The size of a literal house. But Ewan is making sure all is well. He is a very accomplished foot masseuse."

"How nice for you," she said, feeling bitter and crampy.

"Anything new at the Palace on the Rock?"

And she decided then and there that she was just going to say it.

"I've had quite a lot of sex," said Maren.

She was satisfied that her sister was silent on the other end of the phone.

"With my husband," she finished, dramatically.

"Maren! What are you talking about?"

"Oh, the husband came with the castle. He is incredibly hot. And the decision to begin making a baby with him was quite easy. Though, we have not succeeded yet."

"You're going to have to back up."

So she told him all about Acastus and everything pertaining to the paperwork.

"You're joking," she said.

"I'm not," she said. "But he is not… Emotionally available. Which is fine. It's just that now he's away he's completely away and not in contact with me at all, and I sort of find it mean. Given that I gave him my virginity and everything."

"Oh, Maren," said Jessie. "You were so self-righteous

with me. And I can't help but feel that you deserve this a little bit."

"That's very mean, Jessie," admitted Maren. "I'm fragile."

"I know. But you were not anything but meddlesome when it came to me and Ewan so I find that this is deserved. I'm sorry, darling."

"I don't think you are," said Maren, feeling hard done by.

"Well, I am. It's just that I also think it proves that you're human like I am. And maybe you can have a little bit more sympathy for me. I couldn't resist him."

Now she understood that, that was for sure.

"Gorgeous men are a pox. A scourge." Her phone buzzed. "He just texted me."

"Put me on speakerphone and read the text," said Jessie.

"Oh, lovely. He's sending me dates for our next booty call."

"Tell him no. Tell him to get screwed."

"That is what he's trying to do."

"You know what I mean."

"I can't tell him no," said Maren. "We have an agreement."

Jessie sighed. "You don't want to tell him no."

"Fine," she said. "I don't want to tell him no."

And that was the crux of the problem. She had missed him while he was away. It had been as much of a pleasure as it had been a torment to have those memories. To wonder what he was thinking. To wonder if he thought of her at all. The memories of his hands on her body were so sweet, and so terrible. She didn't want to let them out of her mind. She wanted to cling to them. To turn them over.

She felt wounded, regardless of the fact that she knew exactly what this was supposed to be. In some ways, it was terrible that she had been so right about herself. And in other ways… She almost enjoyed the way that it hurt.

She was not going to tell Jessie that bit of information. It was a bit too intimate.

And she had a week to look forward to the return of her husband.

It pained her how much she anticipated it. How much she wanted him.

But this was a situation she found herself in, and so… Why not enjoy it? When they were through, she would have a baby on the other side. She wouldn't feel quite so lonely. She would be whole, in many ways, like she hadn't been since her own mother had gone.

This would be another chance, after all. At a mother/child relationship, though this time with her in control of the outcome. This time with her being there, for always.

It would be well.

It would be.

And in the meantime, she would have wonderful sex.

The memory burned bright. But no matter how vivid her memory, it couldn't replace the real thing. It was her first experience with that. With it being so profoundly true.

It was a little bit frightening.

But she wanted the pleasure too much to turn away from it now.

CHAPTER EIGHT

WORK HAD BEEN nothing more than a hideous grind. He had been waiting—more than he would like to admit—to hear from Maren. And when he had, it was all he could do not to go to her immediately.

But he would wait. Wait until the prescribed time.

Though he found that he just wished to be in her presence. Which was a strange experience, he had to admit.

Finally, it was time.

He left Athens behind without a backward glance and found himself looking forward to being back at the Palace on the Rock. As his boat approached the dock, he marveled at that.

He had hated it here as a child. And now... Was it not the sign of his triumph? It was, he supposed. But... It was more than that. Right now, it was about her. Right now, it was about having her.

Acastus clenched his fists in anticipation as he disembarked the boat and began to approach the palace.

He wondered what mood he would find his wife in.

She had seemed short on words when she had informed him that she was not pregnant.

But then, what words did they need?

He fought back against that slightly.

Because they had shared a great many words between them, and he had enjoyed that aspect of their
relationship. She was wonderful in bed. But she was
more than that.

When he arrived, he tried to think of where he might
find her.

He checked in the room that had the cushions, because he knew that she liked those. But he did not find
her there.

He looked in her bedroom, but she was not there.

And for some reason, he knew. Just suddenly.

He went into the dining room, and there she was,
with a glass of orange juice, a cup of coffee and a piece
of toast.

"Turn away from me, husband, for this is an intimacy
too far. You said you did not wish to have toast with me."

He took a step toward her, picked up the toast, and
took a bite out of it.

She looked up at him with outrage.

"Well, there. We have shared toast now."

"That was *mine*."

"It is ours now. A gesture of romance on my part, I
think you'll find."

"That was…"

"Are you playing games with me?"

She shook her head. "No games."

"It seems as if you are, little one. I should not like to
think that you are attempting to freeze me out of your
bed by using toast as a weapon."

"Is your masculinity not up to the threat of toast?"

"I think I made my feelings on toast quite clear."

"Yes. By *eating* it."

"Is that not how one usually expresses their feelings regarding breakfast foods?"

She sniffed. "I wouldn't know, Acastus."

"I have waited," he said.

"You have barely spoken to me."

"It is our agreement. No toast and orange juice. And we will see to our lives in the meantime. Here you have all this glorious freedom. What have you done with it?"

"I have read many books," she said. "I watched whatever TV I wanted. And when I lay in bed at night, I parted my legs and put my hand between them and I thought of you."

She stole the toast back and took a bite.

"Thanks," he growled.

And it was as if he had never been gone.

He hauled her out of her chair and picked her up, carrying her to the bedroom.

He had her stripped bare before him instantly.

She was his. His.

It had been terrible being away from her.

Terrible.

He blocked that out, or he tried to, the memory of how his chest felt like a cavern without her. But the problem was, he kept on hearing that word echo over and over again. He kept on thinking about the way his *life* had felt like a particularly empty cavern without her.

He had known her a matter of a week. And in the time in between they had barely spoken.

Yet his life did not feel normal without her.

It did not feel right.

He kissed her neck, down her lovely body, down between her thighs.

He was starving for her.

She came apart in his arms, and then she kissed her way down his chest, down to his shaft, taking him deep inside of her mouth.

He gripped her hair, guided her movements. Luxuriating in the feel of her. In her touch.

In the fact that he was the only man that she had ever done this for.

Mine.

He arched his hips upward, and gave himself over to the need rioting through him.

She lay back on the bed, smiling up at him when they were through. "Well. I'm not getting pregnant doing it that way."

He growled at her.

Coming over the top of her and kissing her mouth. Their pleasure mingled in that kiss, and he knew that it would not take long for him to be able to do exactly what it took to make her pregnant.

"Are you spoiling for a fight?"

"Or something."

"Why is it you think you can play games with me?" he asked.

"Should I fear you?"

"Many do."

"I suppose," she said, moving her hands down to his masculinity. "The people that fear you have not held the source of your vulnerability in their hand."

He went hard. "Does that feel vulnerable to you?"

"Would you like me to test it?"

He bit her on the shoulder, and she sighed.

It felt good to be back with her, though he did not quite understand why.

He had made the decision to walk away without saying anything. To keep entirely to their agreement, because it had been the right thing to do. And he had to do that. He had to be strong, he had to continue to carry the boulder up the mountain because if he did not…

Weakness was unacceptable. A lack of control was unacceptable.

It would make him his father and that could never be endured.

Now he was back with her, and violating his own thoughts on the matter.

And he realized that he was far too close to feelings.

He moved away from her, in spite of the fact that he was ready to possess her.

"I wish to remind you, exactly what this is," he said. "We have an agreement. I am not answerable to you. I suggest you get over your pique and get ready to receive me."

She frowned. "I *was* ready to receive you. And now you're being an ass."

"You must be ready for me even if I am an ass."

"I feel certain I don't have to be. Why is it that you feel you get to make proclamations?"

"I feel," he said, "that it is fine and just for me to hold you to the expectations of our agreement."

"I'm a broodmare and you're my stud?"

"Yes," he said. "We've had an easy time slipping into

conversation. But I do not wish for you to have expectations that should not be there."

"Oh, so now you're worried that I'll fall in love with you."

"Not if you actually knew me. But I am worried that you might paint fantasies around the fact that you and I can laugh with one another for brief moments. That we might be able to find enjoyment in each other's arms. That is nothing real."

"Is it not?"

"No. I will never fall in love with you. I will never want this to be a real marriage. We will never sit together in a domestic fashion."

It was brutal, the way that he was pushing her away, and he knew it. And unfair. He had come in happy to see her, and he was pushing back against his own feelings more than hers.

He knew that.

And yet.

He was punishing her for the feelings that she created inside of him because he knew that they were untenable.

And by twisting the knife he was reminding himself. That he was his father's son, and that feelings were a prison of their own construction. And he would not fall into that trap.

"Get out."

"You don't want me to leave. You want me to take you. Admit it."

"Did you not hear me when I said I'm more than capable of pleasuring myself? Anyway. I already got mine."

"You want *this*," he said, cupping his hardness. "You and I both know it."

"Trip and fall into the sea," she shot back.

"You need to make a baby with me."

"I think I'll skip today."

"Suit yourself," he said, growling and walking from the room.

In a fury, he took care of his arousal on his own. So that it would be impossible for him to go back to her.

Except he found that impossible with Maren was not what it had previously been defined as.

He lay awake hard all night.

And he regretted the enmity between them.

Even though he should want it.

Maren was sulky and unhappy the next day, and she did not pursue any kind of interaction with him. If she talked to him, she'd only yell at him.

He was infuriated. But he was infuriating. So really, his fault.

He was being awful. Unreasonably so. It was as if she had gotten too close to his heart, and he had felt bound to pull away. Determined to be cruel to her so that she wouldn't get any ideas. Or perhaps so *he* wouldn't.

He was there in the castle, and it was one of her precious fertility days, and they never spoke.

They didn't make love.

And it was true the next day.

And that following day was even one of her most fertile days.

She felt wretched. Pulled apart.

She didn't know why a fake marriage should be quite so difficult. It shouldn't be.

It should be easy. They should be easy.

This uncertainty reminded her far too much of what it was like to grow up in her father's orbit. When he and her mother had still been together and they had taken strips off of each other all the time. She'd seen love that had looked like hate. She'd been the child who'd watched her soft mother cry and cry. She'd felt it echo in her bones and she'd not been able to do a thing to fix it. It had carved out a sadness in her own soul that had never gone away.

She'd been the child whose mother had to run away because of how things were. And perhaps because she'd felt her mother's pain…she'd understood even though it hurt.

This was different.

They weren't in love. So why wasn't it easy?

She had no idea why in the world it wasn't. Why they weren't.

Because you do have feelings for him. Because when you speak to him you feel like maybe he understands you.

She decided to call her sister.

"I am having a fight with my husband," she said.

"Me too," said Jessie happily. "I'm looking forward to the makeup sex."

"You and Ewan fight?"

"Oh, yes. Thrillingly. He is such a stubborn, hard-headed man, and all of his healing has done nothing to eliminate that hardheadedness, but I wouldn't want it gone. I like that he is difficult. And he likes that I am. We are extremely compatible that way. We like it in or out of bed."

"I don't."

Jessie sighed. "Of course you don't. What's the problem?"

"He came back and I was teasing him, and at first he seemed to find it charming. We had a very… Satisfying interaction, though not one that's going to get me pregnant. And then he got distant. Strange. Mean."

Jessie snickered. "Sounds like a man."

"And now we're not speaking, and I… I want him."

"So have him, Maren. You don't need to wait for him. You don't even need to wait to not be angry at him. You can have him while you're furious. Sometimes that's fun."

"But I'm… Afraid of it. Of the intensity of it all. You know how things were with Mom and Dad…"

"What does that have to do with him?"

"It could be like it was with them, if we let it."

"If you let it, I suppose, but you aren't them." But how did you become them? That was what Maren didn't know.

This wasn't what she'd signed up for. She'd wanted to make a baby, not get obsessed with an infuriating, unknowable man with a cold aura and a hot body.

"I think it's best if you embrace it," said Jessie. "I think the very marvelous thing about relationships like the one you're in with him is that they're not like anything else."

"I'm not supposed to be in a relationship with him."

"He's your lover. You've never had another lover. How many people on this earth would you want to be close to, make love to, even while you were angry with them?"

"So far only him."

"*Exactly.* So embrace it. Be with him. Be with him because you want him. Be with him because it's wonderful, and you want to make love with him. And don't worry about the rest. Because it's already sharp and spiky, isn't it? Dangerous."

"Well. Yes. That it is."

"Great. So please yourself. Take risks. See where it takes you."

She pondered that for a while, and then found herself going into her closet to choose an elaborate piece of lingerie.

She would have him. But she wouldn't let it be… It didn't have to be like her parents. She was too self-aware for that.

Because she wanted him. Yes, she was angry, and yes, it was difficult. She didn't understand why her feelings for him were so… Big. When in reality they barely knew each other. Except she couldn't escape from those moments where they had connected. Maybe the issue was she hadn't had friends growing up, and he was maybe the closest thing to one other than her sister. But they had complicated it with sex and need.

Whatever the issue, she liked him, and she missed him. Even when she was furious at him.

But she could make this work. She knew that it wasn't love. She *liked* him. When she didn't want to eviscerate him with her teeth. She wanted him. It could be straightforward if she wanted it to be.

She put on an entirely see-through lavender chiffon gown that went all the way to the floor, but showed the silhouette of her body beneath.

And with boldness, she walked the short distance down the corridor to his room.

She knocked. And it was like that first night. When she had come in and found him about to have a drink. Shirtless and barefoot and sexy.

"You are quite routine oriented," she said. "And perhaps I am too."

"What are you here for?"

"You."

"You want a baby that badly?"

"I want *you* that badly. I'm furious at you. You're impossible and difficult. But I want you. I will be very disappointed if you go away tomorrow without me having you." He moved to her, his eyes hard, his expression stern. He gripped her chin, held her fast as he looked into her eyes. "Finally," he said, and then he leaned in and kissed her. Hard and deep.

And she was a prisoner to it.

In that moment, she was held captive by her desire for him.

Domination. Submission. Strength. Weakness. She was all of it.

She kissed him like it was the only thing. Like there was an endless sea of kissing to swim through, and she would never find the end of it. Never find the depths.

She kissed him, and she was made new.

Suddenly all of the anger that she'd been sitting in the last few days seemed shallow.

Clearly, he had experienced a life like hers. Complex facets of tragedy and hope and family and disappointment.

So of course he felt like pushing away from whatever this was between them. She could understand the impulse.

But maybe it was up to her to persist.

To what end?

Maybe just this. Right now, maybe just this. Because the connection that she felt with him was profound, and felt as if it could not be accidental. She didn't want it to be.

With shocking strength and swiftness he pushed her up against the wall, captured her wrists and pushed them up above her head. She gasped.

And she allowed him to take the lead.

His movements were ferocious, and hungry. And she reveled in them.

He stripped the gown off of her body, leaving her naked before him.

Then he wrapped his hand around her thigh and lifted it up over his hip, grinding his cloth-covered arousal against where she was wet and aching for him.

She wanted him. Just like this.

Her hands were fast and furious on his belt as she freed him and positioned him at the entrance to her body, then he pinned her against the wall as he took possession of her.

He thrust hard into her, grunting like an animal, and she loved it.

The lack of control between them.

If she could capture and hold on to each and every moment of this she would count herself lucky, not cursed.

Maybe she was a cliché. The sad virgin who was catching feelings for the first man she'd ever been with.

But he was also her husband.

And she was also her.

Someone who had been kept separate from others for so much of her life, and now she had found a brilliant and blinding connection that surpassed anything else she had ever known.

There was nothing cliché about her. Because no one else was really like her.

Her sister, Jessie came the closest, but Maren was Maren.

And in this moment, Acastus was Acastus. And he was the only man, the only thing, who could ever satisfy her.

Their race toward the climax was quick, their peak triumphant. And when they collapsed into the bed together, they were both spent and exhausted, but unwilling to release their hold on each other.

He turned to her many times that night, and she willed herself not to fall asleep, because she didn't want to miss it if he decided to get up and leave.

But eventually sleep claimed her, and in the morning he was gone.

She didn't have to search the whole castle to know that he had left.

Again.

She sent him a text, and she knew that he wasn't going to respond.

It disappointed her anyway.

CHAPTER NINE

THE WEATHER TURNED colder as August became September, and Maren missed her period.

She wanted to mourn, in a strange way. Because that meant that he wouldn't come see her this month.

Then she cleared her head.

She was having a baby. One time. They had been together one time during that week, and it had been a lost and furious sort of night. How had she managed to conceive?

It didn't matter how, just that she had.

She was awash in so many feelings. A rainbow of them. So strong she could nearly see them wrap around her like a glowing aura. Fear, anguish, joy, excitement, worry, anxiety, elation. Opposites and shades of the same tone. All brilliant and a bit too much. It took her breath away. She had to sit quietly with it, for a while, letting all bloom within her like a garden.

She didn't tell him. Not the first day.

But she texted him the second day.

I'm pregnant.

Good.

That was his only response. No indication on when she would see him again.

So Maren put her phone away, and determined not to obsess about it. Not to obsess about him.

She called Jessie and told her the news—from a different number, one that he didn't have.

Jessie was pleased for her, but also nearing giving birth herself, so couldn't make the trip out to see her.

"After your baby is born," she said. "But how nice that the cousins will be so close in age."

It was about the only thing that made her happy right then.

The only thing that made her feel like things were going to be okay.

And then her morning sickness started. Furiously. September rolled into October, and she was still ill. She took classes on her computer, business and marketing and all manner of things to keep her brain busy. And felt ill.

November was art classes and being sicker.

And then finally December, and she was round and angry and thought of Acastus far more than she would like.

It had been months. She shouldn't care. And she did. So much it hurt. She waffled between outrage, vomit and sadness.

She got tired and settled on sadness the first week of the month.

She found herself lying in bed most days, feeling miserable.

Her feelings had always been far too big and volatile. She hated them. She hated the way they felt close to her parents and their drama. She hated the way she couldn't imagine this baby. That she'd been putting off a doctor's appointment because she was too afraid to deal with it all.

She escaped into her mind palace, perhaps too deeply. Trying to find comforting, familiar images. Old feelings of happiness, images of old picture books, or favorite scenes in childhood cartoons.

She was a princess, and wholly lost in what that was even supposed to mean.

Her life had been upended entirely when she found out that she was married to Acastus, and she had become obsessed with him. She had forgotten why she was here. She had forgotten that initially what she wanted was a baby.

And now her pregnancy was making her utterly physically miserable.

While she sat around missing a man who likely never thought of her.

She wept a lot.

It was December, and she had such fantasies of what she was going to do for Christmas.

And now she didn't have the energy to do it.

She stopped leaving her bedroom.

She would just lie there and read, and drink tea.

She was hard-pressed to find anything she wanted to eat.

She forgot why she was here. She forgot why the castle mattered.

She wished that she had simply walked away from him rather than taking him up on any of this, because here she was grappling with the consequences while he…

She turned over in bed and put her pillow over her head. She wasn't going to think about him.

She wasn't.

And he would never know about her despair. And that was how it needed to be.

When he received the call from Iliana he was incensed.

"She is ill?"

"Yes, Your Highness, she never gets out of bed. She has sunk into a terrible melancholy."

"Why has no one reached out to me before? Why have you not called the physician?"

"She did not wish for us to call anyone. She wished to handle it all on her own. She's very stubborn. But she's gotten worse this month and I can no longer bear it."

He was familiar with her stubbornness.

"I will be there soon."

He had avoided her. And he knew it was wrong of him.

His phone rang again, and it was his mother.

"Acastus," she said. "Will you be joining me in Palermo for Christmas?"

"Why don't you come to the palace, Mother?"

"I'm not sure that I can stand going there."

His heart froze. "I thought that you wanted it?"

He knew she did. She'd been unhappy forever because of the lack of it and now she didn't wish to…claim that happiness?

"I'm deeply appreciative that with your marriage to the Princess I am now Queen Mother." Thanks to the unconventional rules of the very strange, tiny country that was a rock in the middle of the sea. One he'd fought for. One he'd made it his life's work to obtain for her. "And that you will make me a grandmother, what a legacy. I'll be able to tell everyone. But why should I leave my shiny life with all of my friends? I have nothing but atrocious memories associated with that place. With that country life…"

He'd built that glittering life for her, and she'd been clear then it hadn't been enough. He'd carved it out from blank stone from nothing, his blood and his sweat in the foundation, and yet it had never been enough then.

So he'd gone on. To make sure the promise of her being royalty was fulfilled, and now she was acting as if that was only ever a trinket she was after? Like a new diamond to show off to her friends? When she had acted for all this time as if it was the air she breathed?

He had done this for her. And the way she took only the part that was easiest and most convenient for her galled him even as he made excuses.

He took a breath and tried to reason this out. Tried to find control.

She had been unhappy for so many years. If Palermo made her happy, why should she go to the palace?

There was no point getting mad at his mother. Not ever. She was far too fragile, she could never withstand the weight of his anger, and it only upset both of them in the end.

"Whatever suits you best, Mother, but I'm going to have to spend my Christmas there."

"Why?"

"Because I must be with my wife."

"Don't tell me you've gone and fallen for her. You don't wish to be tied to that place. Tied to one person."

"I have not," he said. "She is ill. Her pregnancy... I must go to her."

"You always did do a very good job of taking on responsibility," she said.

And *that* pleased him.

That was a reminder of who he was. What he was.

He was a man who did not let those in his charge twist in the wind.

He did not let them sink into unhappiness. He was not his father. And he never would be.

He would take care of Maren because it was the right thing to do, and then he would return to his life in Athens.

When he got to the palace, it was dark.

He didn't know what he had expected... Yes he did. He'd expected the place to be all lit up for Christmas. Because Maren had spoken of that, with shining eyes. Of everything she'd wanted to do, and she hadn't done it yet.

He found Iliana, and stopped her in the hallway. "Ready the palace for Christmas," he said.

"Yes sir but..."

"Top to bottom. Every room. I wish for it to be unquestionably bright in here. It must be a Christmas fit for a princess."

"Yes sir."

"Is she in her room?"

"Yes. As she ever is."

"Then I will go to her. And while I am with her, find all of the decoration she had ordered and make this place a fantasy for her."

He made his way up the stairs, and he went into her bedroom without knocking.

He was surprised to see her lying there, so pale and small in the center of the massive bed.

"Maren."

"And you must be the Ghost of Christmas Past." She shook her head. "Because you certainly aren't actually here."

She had staff. An entire staff of people and none of them could be moved to care for her better than this? He was appalled. And he shoved aside any recriminations he had for himself.

He had done exactly as he had told her he would do. Nothing more, nothing less. He did not make promises that he did not fulfill.

Her staff, on the other hand, was clearly not caring for her as they ought to.

"You are not well," he said.

"No indeed," she commented. "I am not. How astute of you to observe."

"It is all well with the baby?"

"As far as I know. I was told there was no reason to see a doctor until—"

"Unacceptable."

He opened the door and thundered out into the corridor. "Iliana," he barked. "Contact a physician for my wife."

"The Princess has said…"

"I am in residence now. I will decide what is to be done." He shut the door and turned back to the bed.

"This place is mine," said Maren angrily. "You are

only here because of our marriage. I'm the one that won a castle."

He felt like he could hear the foot stomp embedded in her voice.

"And I'm the one that earned a billion dollars and has real power outside of this place. Do you not understand?" He thundered toward the bed. "I am the one who has real consequence here. I am the one. You are carrying my child, and you will do what needs to be done to keep that child safe."

He hated seeing her pale. He hated seeing her diminished. He could not find it in him to say that. So he railed about the pregnancy because it was what they were. It was why he was here. At least that was what they had agreed upon.

"I'm surviving," she said.

"This is not survival. Have you really lain down in your bed because of my absence?" He had said it largely to make her angry. To test her.

It worked.

She sat up in bed, red spots of color appearing on her cheeks. "I feel sick. I'm hormonal and I feel depressed. Your absence has nothing to do with anything." She lifted her hands and hit the top of the comforter. "I spent twenty-two years without you in my life, and I would happily spend twenty-two more without you. Except the twenty-two on the other side of this will be me caring for a child that we created together. And that is probably the most involvement that we will have with one another. Do you honestly think I'm such a giant baby that I took to my bed because you weren't here? That I'm depressed without your penis? It's *morning sickness*."

"It seems a damn sight more than that. When I tried to get a hold of you—"

"I'm in contact with my sister. All the time. I'm not in contact with you because I put that phone away. There was no reason to sit by it. Tell me, until recently did you try to contact me once?"

"No…"

She was like a little teapot now, sputtering fury as the fire beneath her raged. "Does it bother you, Acastus, that actually I have been thinking of myself since I found out that I was pregnant with my child? Does it bother you that I did not sit by the phone and wait? I think that you *want* me to be in love with you."

Her eyes gleamed with triumph, and he was shocked to find her words hooked into something inside him. And pulled tight.

He shook his head, the denial coming from deep within him. "I don't. I don't want love. Not yours, not anyone's."

"*Yes*. Sure. So you've said. Because of something to do with your mother. I'm sure the therapist would have a lot to say about that."

"I don't need a therapist to say anything about it. I have my mother to communicate with still. She is fragile. She always has been. The way that she loved my father was a prison. She was stuck with him, in spite of the fact that he could fulfill none of his promises to her."

"She was unhappy," said Maren. "That much is clear.

You know that she was unhappy, because she told you. Why was she unhappy?"

"Because we worked here," he said. "Imagine it as it was then. Stavros, his wife and daughter, and my family. Working in clear servitude to them. My father practically licking his boots to beg for me to be allowed to marry his daughter. My father clinging to that promise because he had told my mother she'd have a title, when he could have gone away and provided better for us. But he knew it was all he was worth and so we remained. In misery. And Stavros continually moved the bar. We simply had to complete this task or that. Serve another year, and then her hand would be granted. And then... And then I stole from him."

He watched Maren's face carefully as he began to tell the story. "There was something my mother wanted desperately and she felt we were owed because of all the time Stavros tarried with his promises." He looked at the wall behind her now, unable to look at her. "For my sins, I was beaten. Thrown in the dungeon. His daughter came to tell me herself that she would never marry me. She said I was nothing. Nothing but a servant. Little better than a slave. A poor boy who would never amount to anything, and whom she would never marry.

"He made it known that I ruined everything. I stole the chance for my family to have this place. My father died after that. His heart gave out. After years of him keeping us in poverty waiting on unfulfilled promises, he had the temerity to die, not to fight. Not for me, not for my mother, not for anyone." His heart thundered erratically as he recounted the story. It always did.

It always got to him.

It always made him feel like a failure.

He could remember his mother saying as much in her despair. Because this had been so important to her. It had been.

And now it was not?

He pushed that to the side.

It was all his father's fault.

He'd put them in the position where they were desperate. And then had the nerve to leave them by dying.

To leave them as lowly as they ever had been. To leave them with nothing.

"It was up to me. It was up to me to save us. To fix this. To redeem all of it for my mother. For her great sacrifice. The way that she stayed with him."

"Why did she stay with him?"

"Because she loved him," he said.

"You say that. You continue to say that. But if she was miserable, and if she was miserable because of what they didn't have, then how much could she have loved him? Or did she just want to be royalty?"

"You sacrificed everything to be a princess. Your freedom. You signed yourself over to me."

"Yes. I did."

"How can you act as if it's not a compelling piece of bait?"

"I'm not. I'm not acting as if it's not compelling at all. But I've never pretended to love you."

"And yet you have wilted in my absence."

"Again!" she nearly shrieked. "*I'm pregnant*. And we have gone in a circle. Why is it that you wish to believe that love is a cage? Were you simply looking for confirmation?"

"Because it holds you to another person when good sense would have dictated you leave long ago."

She looked so angry it would have been funny—so fluffy as she was—f the anger was not clearly so real. "I think the pregnancy is a cage."

"Do you not want the baby?"

Right in that moment he felt like throwing the offer out there. A challenge. An offer for her to cut ties with him and with all of this. What if they decided to simply…not do this? To walk away from it and each other.

"No," she said quickly. "I want the baby."

His breath caught. He hadn't realized that he had been afraid of her answer.

"I just don't feel well." She sounded less angry now. Mostly tired. "You're the one catastrophizing it." She laughed. "Or even worse, making it somehow about me being in love with you."

If he could take back one thing he'd said, it would be the implication she loved him. It felt somehow far too exposing.

"You need to arise. And eat," he said.

"I'm not feeling very well," she said.

"And you think you'll feel well if you continue to lie here? At least go into your study. Sit there. Have a change of scenery."

"You don't get to tell me what to do."

"You will have a bath." He'd decided it then, and he was certain he was right. She looked drab and gray in pallor. She needed to warm herself. He went to the bed and picked her up.

She howled, and he carried her straight through her closet and into the bathroom.

"I do not need to stay. But I will be nearby if you need help. Bathe. Put on something new, and I will meet you in your study."

And he turned and left her there, disliking the tangle of feeling in his chest. Disliking everything.

Everything about this, and everything about the words that she had lobbed at him.

Of course he didn't want her to love him. He could think of nothing worse. The problem was, he worried she might, because it looked so like the love his mother had suffered at the hands of his father.

She had loved him, and he had not seen to her needs.

Would Maren be like that? Would she need to lean on their child because he wasn't here?

It wasn't his mother's fault.

And by extension it could not be Maren's fault if he was absentee and he created the situation.

He was going to have to rethink. Everything.

What a fool he'd been.

He had been in charge of his own destiny from the time he'd been old enough to seize control.

He had believed that it meant something. He had believed that it meant he would be in control always. He had thought it would be the easiest thing in the world and yet he had not counted on her.

Yes, things would change.

He would see to it.

CHAPTER TEN

MAREN WAS FULMINATING the entire time she took her bath. She had to stop scrubbing because she was doing it so angrily it was leaving red marks.

She had no idea what he was thinking. Coming in here and taking charge, carrying her into the bathroom. As if he knew what she wanted.

As if he knew what she needed.

She did end up taking a bath, though.

And she enjoyed it. Felt like probably it was a good thing that she had paused to do something to take care of herself. She was angry at him. For coming in and accusing her of sinking into despair because of him. When he was exactly as he had promised to be, and she really didn't even know him.

It was a pity that it was so easy for her to like him. A pity that when they spoke they seemed to have so much in common. And even worse that when he touched her they had so much chemistry. Because when it came to the specific amount of time that they had actually known one another, it was ludicrous to suggest that she might have feelings for him.

But sometimes it felt like the connection she had to him transcended sanity.

It was deeply problematic.

Deeply.

He was tangled up about emotion, she could see that. And she wasn't really any better. They were both a disaster, and she was going to have a baby in a few months' time, so she couldn't afford to be disastrous.

She thought of her mother. She had gotten herself tangled up with the wrong man, and she hadn't been able to…

She'd had to get away. Maren understood that. She didn't judge her mother. She didn't. She understood that her mother had had to take care of herself. The thing with their father was toxic and horrible, and her mother had wept all the time. He'd never hurt her physically but he wasn't a safe man. Her mother had loved a dangerous man far too much and she'd had to leave.

If she had taken Jessie and Maren with her she might've been pursued.

Maren understood that. But it was also why she truly believed that a person could not afford to get sidetracked. Her mother had been in love with her father, and that was why she had made a decision and linked herself to someone dangerous.

She did not believe that Acastus was dangerous. She just had a feeling. And maybe it was foolish to put so much stock in her feelings. Given all that she knew and didn't know about men. But she had to put her trust in something, right? If she didn't, then she would simply be a tragic human being. She did trust that he wouldn't hurt her. But she also knew that she did need to keep herself from getting tangled up. And unfortunately there was a little bit of truth to the fact that she had taken to her bed because she was upset about him. About the leaving and the fact it was a pattern in her life she couldn't escape.

This was not the first time she'd been bruised, that was the problem.

It was this persistent pressing where she was already injured. Again and again.

She had to stop. She had to keep her head on straight. He was everything that he had promised her. He was not in love with her, just as he had said he wouldn't be.

That was not a failure on his part.

She had asked for him to keep distance. She should be glad that he had honored that promise. She should be.

And she needed to get a hold of herself. It was a hard wake-up call, his return. The way that he had responded to her.

It had drawn a stark line beneath just how much she had let herself get swallowed up in melancholy.

She had been in touch with Jessie. Frequently.

Her sister had been concerned. But Jessie's pregnancy hadn't been as difficult as Maren's.

Maren was very sick. Feelings notwithstanding. And she did think that her hormones had kicked her specifically in the rear.

She went into her closet, and selected a dress. Red and glittery, and far over-the-top for a midmorning visit with her estranged husband.

Was he even estranged? When everything that had occurred between them had been exactly as planned. It was just her feelings. And this was the problem. She just had a lot of feelings.

She was trying to do something about them. But the truth was, she was going to become a mother. And it was bringing up a lot of things.

Things from her past.

But it should serve as a reminder.

A very timely one.

She put on some red lipstick and a bit of gold eyeshadow, and some blush so that she didn't quite look like the specter of death she felt.

And then she walked out into…

A flurry of activity. There were ladders up in the corridor, and staff hanging greenery from the rafters. There were crimson bows and reeds going up in three-foot intervals with the garlands.

There was Christmas music playing. Being piped into speakers that were installed up at the top of the walls. It was a very merry explosion.

"What's happening?" she asked.

"Princess," said one of the men. "It's so good to see you up."

"Thank you," she said. "What's going on?"

"The Prince has demanded that we ready the castle for Christmas."

She'd wanted that. A Christmas in this castle. She'd told him so.

They'd never had Christmas growing up.

And she had tried to establish little traditions with Jessie, but Jessie really wasn't sentimental about that. Maren had always felt like she wanted to be sentimental, and had never been allowed to.

And she'd been so sick that she hadn't gotten around to doing the Christmas that she wanted.

And here it was. Going up all around her at Acastus's request.

"How… Beautiful."

She walked slowly through all the chaos, her eyes widening.

And by the time she got to her sitting room, she was absolutely stunned.

There was a massive Christmas tree in the sitting room. The fire was roaring, and the tree was twinkling with white lights and brilliant decorations.

"This…oh, my…" she said.

And there he was. Wearing a dark suit, looking as stunning as ever. He was not lounging. He was standing by the fire, his hands in his pockets.

"Is that suit jacket a bit warm?"

"Don't worry about me. You are…up."

His dark gaze swept over her.

She found herself blushing.

Her pregnancy was beginning to show, and she hadn't felt much about that at all until right at this moment. When he looked at her with hungry eyes that seemed satisfied by the change in her figure.

"A little bit of scrubbing has done you well," he said.

"Well, thank you," she said, waspishly.

"I am having a tray of food brought in."

"You know I like food," she said cautiously.

"I do know that."

"You know you give yourself far too much credit," she said, because she had been roiling with these thoughts and feelings and she felt that he ought to as well. "The idea of becoming a mother is bringing up a lot of my own childhood issues. I should think that every person faced with impending parenthood has a thought or two about how it links to the way they were raised. You're right. Love is a cage. My mother experienced that. And she escaped the cage. But she left us in it."

"What do you mean?"

"My mother was beautiful." She felt herself softening even as she thought of her mother now. "She had a closet full of beautiful clothes. She was always dressed up. I have her hair. She used to let me play with her makeup and her jewelry. She said that I was beautiful. She said that I was a princess. And I believed her. She was the best part of my life, and when I close my eyes and call up those memories I can still see her. So clearly."

"You said you have an eidetic memory," he said. "So that means that you have perfect recall of that time spent with your mother."

"Yes. And equally of the time spent with my father. My sister… I know she protected me from much of it. She's very strong. She had a head for numbers, and while I'm good with them too—it's a side effect of the memory—Jessie is a little bit of a genius. And she flung herself in front of me in a way that no one else did. She had something to do, though. And I just felt sad that our mother was gone. I have always felt sad about that. I just wish… I wish that she wasn't gone. And I miss her. I never want to be in a position where whatever relationship I have with you impacts the way that I parent our child."

He straightened abruptly. "It is strange that you would say that, because I was just thinking the same thing. I... My father was absent. He was focused on serving here at the palace. He was almost awash in his own self-pity over the fact that he did not achieve what he wanted in the time frame he wanted it. My mother was lonely. I cooked for her. I was her listening ear. It is not her fault, of course. He abandoned her to that fate."

"That sounds like an incredibly intense amount of pressure to put on a boy," she commented.

"I did not mind. I have never minded stepping up and being the man that my father refused to be. I have always accepted that I needed to be the one."

He turned and faced the fire again, and she felt an intense squeeze in her chest. Her own mother had abandoned her. His had... Had taken from him. She could see that. Love was a cage, but for who? Was he in a cage of having to care for his mother?

She didn't want that either. And look at the way that she was behaving. The way that she had allowed herself to get so... Bogged down.

"I will be there for our child. Always. I promise. I would never leave," she said.

"And I will not put you in a position where you must lean on the child."

"I don't blame my mother," she said.

"Neither do I," he returned.

And yet the air seemed filled with heavy feeling, and things that they could not say. His own unhappiness, the weight of it, of all that he'd carried for so long bore down on her. And she had to wonder if anyone had ever felt what he did.

She wondered if even he felt it. Or if he simply shrugged like Atlas, and carried on, holding an insurmountable weight.

She found she wanted to help him carry it. But she might have to set down some of what she was carrying to do it and that just seemed…well, it didn't seem possible.

So she tried to push past it, tried to breathe past it. Even thought it was hard.

"I really just haven't been feeling well. But I did notice in the last few days that I was beginning to feel better."

"The doctor will be here to visit you. To look you over."

"But I told you I shouldn't need to see anyone…"

"I feel that I would be remiss if you were not wholly cared for and looked over. You are having my baby. And you need to be cared for."

"I did make sure that I wasn't missing out on any appointments. I haven't had any bleeding or anything abnormal. I'm not concerned."

"But I am."

"Yes. And now you're here so you're taking over."

"We are at an impasse. I have decided that our original agreement is untenable. I fear that it will put our child in the same position that I was in. And it will make me my father. And of all the things that I refuse, that is the one that I refuse the most deeply. I am not my father."

"Well, I am not my mother. And I will not…" She stopped herself. Her heart felt sore. She loved her mother.

She didn't tend to blame her mother for what had happened. Her father had been a criminal.

And yet… And yet she could not say that she wanted to be like her mother. In some way she did want to be. If she had a daughter, she wanted to share in her love of soft things. Jewelry and makeup. If she had a son, she wanted to sit and talk with him.

She wanted to make her child feel special. She wanted to be able to say you are a prince or princess. And mean it. She had made this life for them.

And those things, those assurances, the way that her mom had made her feel special, that was real.

But at the same time, she wished to never have her child feel abandoned. Ever. "My mother was good to me."

"She hurt you," he said.

She shook her head. "My father hurt me. It was only that… I guess sometimes it's impossible not to think that perhaps I wasn't important enough."

It was like she had reached down inside of herself and pulled out her deepest, most concealed fear. Like she had shone a flashlight on something that shamed her. She didn't want to think badly of her mother. She had been the kindest person other than her sister ever in her life. She was the source of so many good memories. So many.

And when that realization, that feeling, opened up the door on a different memory, one that she kept behind the tallest, thickest door in the mind palace, she couldn't look away.

The day she had discovered her mother gone. All the beautiful clothes gone with her. All of her jewelry.

And the way she had cried in the emptiness.

The way she had felt all the emptiness in that room fill her up.

The way she had been certain she would never be happy again.

A child abandoned and left in this harsh world.

"I just don't understand why she couldn't take me with her."

"She should have," he said.

"It would've put us in danger."

"Didn't leaving you put you in danger?"

His words were harsh and stark, and they twisted something deep inside of her.

She wondered if Jessie felt that way, but never said it because Maren loved their mother so much.

Jessie didn't talk about their mother. Not in the same way Maren did.

Not often.

Was she the only one that didn't see this?

She felt beset.

In pain.

"We lived. We survived. We…"

"So did I," he said. "So did my mother."

"You blame your father for all of your unhappiness. Well, so do I. If my father hadn't chosen to be a criminal…"

"Your mother chose your father."

"Well, at least I have the very real truth that I didn't choose you."

His lip curled. "Indeed."

"But the same could be said for your mother anyway."

"He bait and switched. He promised her a lifestyle that he could not provide."

"But did he behave like a different man? Was it simply that the man wasn't enough if he didn't come with money?"

"You don't know what you're speaking about."

"I know well enough," she said. "I know well enough. What you're talking about is love."

"And you know what love is?"

She wanted to say that she did. But…

"I don't know. I love my sister. She loves me. She has protected me. And I did my best to return the favor when she needed it. I believe that her husband loves her. And she loves him. But they speak in a language that I don't understand, and looking at them is painful. I do know what love is. I have only ever felt it in the smallest of ways. But I did feel it when I was with my mother. I did."

"You will love your child," he said. "You have no need to worry about that."

"I've never worried about that. Do you?"

"I'm not worried about it. What is love, anyway? What is it but care? My father failed to demonstrate his love for his family. Whatever he said he felt, how could it ever be true? When he left us to fend for ourselves. When he left his son to serve time in a dungeon."

She looked at him. "What did you steal?"

He looked down. "Jewels. For my mother."

"Jewels. That's… Incredibly high value."

"Yes it was," he said. "It was a foolish thing to do, and not something she asked of me."

Except it was far too easy for her to imagine based

on the clues that he had given her about his mother. She was fragile. She longed for fine things. His father wouldn't provide them. And so he had done what any bold teenage boy might do.

"Was your mother angry? When you lost that marriage bargain."

He nodded. "Yes. She was very angry. She was really angry at my father."

"I think it sounds like your mother was miserable. I think she's one of those people, she's unhappy and she makes it about everyone else around her. It was your father's fault, and it was your job to fix it."

She could see so clearly that his mother had taken advantage of him. And it made her wonder what he was seeing so clearly with her.

It was like they were both holding pet trauma to their chest, and they didn't want to release their control over their own perception of that trauma.

Seemed fair, really. Their trauma had been with them a lot longer than each other had. Why should she tear herself open for him? Why should she respond to what he was saying?

Still. It made her want to talk to Jessie. Ask her what she was thinking about in regards to motherhood, and their mother, and all the things really.

"Should a son not work to bring happiness to his mother's life?"

"I suppose, Acastus. Hard to know, since I'm not a son and my mother left me. But I do think maybe there's a difference. I think a mother should take joy in her son. Because he is. Because he's there. And anything he does should be admired and appreciated, I suppose, but you should not be…treated as if her tears are a problem for you to solve."

"You don't know what you're talking about."

Her chest ached. "Unfortunately, I do. I feel it. I feel how heavy this is for you, and the way you describe her…makes sense to me. I can see it. I can see exactly what kind of person she is, and what she did to you isn't fair."

He said nothing to that. He simple stared at the wall, his breath heavy, his jaw set.

She decided to change the subject.

"Why did you have them decorate for Christmas?"

"You said that you wanted it."

"I did. I do. But it seems… Well, it seems out of character in terms of being thoughtful."

"Did I not just put you in a warm bath?"

"You set me down in the bathroom and demanded I draw my own bath."

"I would've been perfectly happy to strip you naked and put you in the bath myself, however, I suspected that it would not be well received. All things considered."

"Specifically that we had an agreement to have sex only to conceive?"

"Seeing you naked is not sex."

"With the two of us has it ever not been?"

Her tongue tingled at the intimate sentence. *With us.*

It spoke of the history that stretched back more than just the last six months, but it felt like so much more. It was days out of all that time. But she had been naked with him, and they had confided in one another.

And now there was all this… Acreage of hurt between them. All of this nonsense. Everything that they were.

"When will the doctor be here?"

"In an hour or so."

"Fantastic. I can be examined while being surrounded by Christmas cheer."

"And I will be there. There is something that you must understand. Things have changed as far as I'm concerned. I must be a more involved father than I originally intended."

She looked at him. And she felt a deep tension rising up inside of her, because she was afraid of that. Afraid of what it would do to her. And the simple truth was, she didn't want for the relationship with her child to become tangled because of him. Because of her feelings for him.

"If you wish to be an involved father I will not stop you, but you and I must have very clear ground rules. Our marriage has to be in name only. From here on."

"If that's what you wish."

"It's what must be."

She was tangled up in him already. That was the truth of it. She had already allowed his absence to wound her.

She had already bent herself into impossible shapes, she had already been tragic and lost without him.

She had to maintain distance and sanity.

Because she could see…

If he broke her heart, if she needed to get away from him…

No. She would never do that to a child, but she would simply make sure…

She would make sure.

"That's how it has to be," she reiterated. "That is how it will be."

A large tray of food was brought in then, and his eyes flickered over it, and then to her. "Eat your food. The doctor will be here shortly, and you will need your strength."

She would like to argue with him. Coming in here and being so autocratic, but the truth was… The staff worked for her, and they listened to her when she said that she didn't need to be taken care of. They listened to her when she said that she didn't need encouragement to get out of bed.

She had, clearly.

She needed someone who wouldn't just listen to her.

That was how Jessie had always been.

Maren would say something in a huff, and Jessie would challenge her.

Acastus challenged her.

She didn't want to need him. It was inconvenient. But he was here.

Perhaps she could make that be all that mattered.

Perhaps she could remind herself that it was more of the family dynamic. Like her sister.

Maybe they could be like family. Maybe she could do something about the endless pain in her chest when she thought of him.

Maybe there was a way to fix all of this. Just maybe.

Keeping their marriage in name only was a start. An important one.

And she was bound and determined to stick to it.

CHAPTER ELEVEN

EVEN AFTER COMING and finding her ill everything felt theoretical until the doctor arrived. With official medical equipment and credentials and not a small amount of concern.

"You do look a bit poorly," the doctor said.

And it made Acastus angry, because who was this person to come in and say that Maren looked poorly, as if it was an indictment of her and the way she had taken care of herself? Or the way that he had taken care of her.

"She has been unwell," he said to the doctor.

"So I gather," the doctor said.

In the bedroom, there was medical equipment set up. He didn't know what any of it was, and he hated that feeling. Of being out of his depth. Of not understanding. It reminded him of being a child. It was something that he had gone out of his way not to experience as an adult.

He had become powerful. He had become the one with money. The one with the power to dangle a sword over someone's head like the blade of Damocles. He didn't. He chose not to. But he also never allowed himself to be in situations where he might feel that way again. And suddenly his whole life had careened out of his reach.

Suddenly, everything seemed mysterious. Seemed like something he could not grasp hold of.

He didn't like it.

To say the least.

He also didn't like it when Maren stripped down to nothing, then put on a gown that tied at the back, and seemed fragile beneath the sheet. When her beauty became something clinical, and he felt as if she was not being touched with the reverence that she ought to be. And perhaps it made no sense, but he did not care.

It made sense to him.

He felt like if anyone was going to put their hands on her it should be in the context of the idea that she was the most beautiful creature in the world.

Even if he was not allowed to put his hands on her at all.

His focus was on her face, and it took him a moment to realize that the doctor was performing an ultrasound.

And that the noise that filled the room was the sound of the baby's heartbeat.

His own heart slammed against his rib cage in response, when he did realize.

It was… It was miraculous in a way that he had never thought before. In his mind this idea of having a child had been about legacy.

He had not thought about the magnitude of it. That he and Maren coming together, touching, kissing, being intimate with one another, had created this heartbeat.

That it would grow into a child, who would become a man or woman in their own right, independent of their parents with their own desires, hopes and fears. Their own scars from their childhood.

It suddenly felt impossibly high stakes.

How could he know what the right things were? How could he figure out how to minimize damage? Because didn't parents always cause damage?

So how could he do his very best to not, especially when he didn't even understand…

He had no connections. He had his mother. He had his money. He had business associates. And there was Maren.

He had felt something upon his first meeting with her. And it had only increased in the time they had spent together. It was, he realized then, their loneliness that allowed them to speak. That allowed them that connection. But loneliness was not something they could pass on to a child. It was no real legacy.

There had to be something more. Something different.

And he did not know how to find it. And that heartbeat, pounding through him, echoing his own… That heartbeat was the most terrifying sound he'd ever heard in his life.

And then he heard another.

"Is that hers?" he asked.

"No," the doctor said, his eyes on the screen. "That is Baby B. The other is Baby A."

"What?" he and Maren both asked in tandem.

"Twins," he said. "Not identical."

"Twins?" Maren asked. "You're kidding. It can't be twins."

"It is twins. Definitively. That is likely why you feel so drained. And why you are so round."

Maren frowned deeply. "No one likes to be called round," she said.

"It is a shape not a judgment," the doctor said.

"I feel strongly most would disagree with you," Maren grumbled.

"You must eat more," the doctor said. "You have two babies in there. You have to work hard to support them. It is your only job." He looked directly at Acastus. "And your only job is to ensure that she can do hers."

"What can I do?" Acastus said, reeling from this revelation. It felt impossible. It felt unreal.

He had wanted a child to carry on the legacy, and after one very memorable night, they'd made two.

There had been other nights, of course, but there was no doubt in his mind which night had created these twins.

"Feed her. Help her get plenty of rest. There does not seem to be any reason you cannot engage in intercourse." He looked over at Maren who practically bared her teeth at him.

"She does not seem especially high risk. Only fragile for the moment, and there is the usual risk of twins, which is slightly more elevated than that of a single pregnancy. But I will ensure that she is cared for. I will make sure that she gets all the checkups that she needs, and in the in-between, I am trusting you. A man who made a fortune quite so efficiently should have no trouble seeing to the care and keeping of his pregnant wife. She is more important than money, after all."

"Agreed," he said, the words coming out hard through his teeth.

"Then I shall see you again in two weeks. Call me if there is anything unusual."

"Is that it?" Maren asked.

"For now," the doctor said. "And congratulations."

He gathered up his equipment, and vacated, and Maren was still lying in the bed beneath the sheets looking perturbed.

"Twins," she said. "That can't be."

"It is," he said. "You heard yourself."

"But that's not what I… It's not what I imagined," she said.

"It's nowhere near what I imagined either."

"I was trying to imagine one child. But two?"

He decided to keep his own thoughts to himself.

"It will not be terribly different. Will it?"

"I think it will be. It will be twice as much. This child…"

"These children," he said. "I will be here. The truth is, this is not going to be what we imagined. But we must…"

The impossibility of it all, of the things that they believed about their own childhoods, of the thing that he told himself about his mother, and what she told herself about hers, hovered around the edges of his consciousness.

It was a story. Because of course it was. A story that he told himself that his mother was wonderful and the things that she struggled with could not be helped, because he did not know how else to survive it. He had a father who had been apathetic. Weak. And a mother who… Who had demanded too much of him. And when he thought of his own child, that was when he could see it. His own children. He could never be the kind of father his father was, but he could never be a parent in the same fashion his mother was either.

Had he not realized that he needed to be here because he had envisioned his own child having to take care of Maren in a poorly state?

When he shifted the vision of it, onto his own child, when he changed his perception, that was when he saw just how toxic it was.

Just how wrong. And what Maren said echoed within him. Would his children not be enough all on their own? Healthy, and beautiful. His. They would never need to perform for him, they would never need to contort themselves to the puzzle piece that might complete him. It was his job to give them the world, not the other way around.

"You are right, Maren. What my mother did to me was not right," he said. "I was not allowed to have feelings because they could not be supported. Not when hers had to be the most important. I cannot let my father off the hook for what he did. For the way that he relegated her to the back burner of his consciousness. The way that he was content to wait on promises and allow us to be uncomfortable while he pursued them, but you are correct. If my mother had loved him then she would've found contentment in her life. What she wanted was royalty. And she could not attain that, and therefore could not find happiness. Even now she is happy with the title, but does not wish to leave Palermo. She did not come here to thank me. She still blames me, I think. For the long delay of the title. She's not grateful at all, because she always felt as if she deserved it. And for what? She didn't work for it, my father tried. I did, but we were not earning it. We were waiting for a man to give it to us on his whim or not. And then in the end we got it through the means we did. It is yours. I acquired it through marriage, when in contrast at least my riches came from my own work. I lowered myself to take this title. And it still doesn't matter. It still isn't enough."

"I'm sorry to have been so lowering for you," Maren said.

"Not you. The pursuit of it. That I was willing to have it at all costs. Why? Why. It is all tied up in this anger that I feel. Toward him. Toward my father. And never toward my mother. Not ever. But as I tried to imagine parenting these children, I realize that I can no longer shield her from the truth, even in my own heart. She could never be a parent that I would emulate."

Maren stared straight ahead for a moment, and then looked at him. "You're right. You're right to do this. To pull it apart. My father was a psychopath, and it's so easy to blame him for everything. You're right. Our mother left us. Her love couldn't have been that strong if she could leave us. It simply couldn't be.

"She was content to leave us when she had to. To never check back in with us. To never... I'm afraid to get in touch with her. Terrified. Even with my father gone, because what if she rejects me? What if I no longer have the excuse of my father? It just makes me want to remember her from when I was a child. When I can have a simplistic thought on it. Simplistic feelings. It's foolish, I know. But that tells you everything you need to know. I already suspect all of this. But I'm afraid to have it confirmed. I could not... I could not bear it."

"So we no longer believe the story. The fairytale. We

must believe the truth. Because it is the only way forward." And they were having twins.

And he felt the same way she did, he could sense it. That they had perhaps had to destroy a cathedral to preserve something greater than a monument. To preserve something sacred. Their children.

They had to be united. They could not be at odds, and they could not be in halfway.

It was far too important an endeavor. Much too much. They could not falter.

"On my life," he said. "Whatever happens between us, I will be there for the children."

"As will I."

The magnitude of all of it settled around them. This could no longer be theoretical. It could no longer be dynastic. It felt far too real now. The stakes far too high. He had made these children along with her, and they owed them a debt. Because when you did not care for your children, he was the end result. The tangled-up wreckage in his chest was the end result.

And Maren was right about one thing, they could not afford to touch one another. For the sake of the children.

This thing was precarious. The peace they might find, the happiness, for the sake of the children. But they had to be careful not to disturb it. Not to introduce anything too volatile, too dangerous.

This was a sacrifice he could bear, to ensure their children had all they needed.

That would be worth it. And maybe it would go a long way in healing him and Maren both.

CHAPTER TWELVE

MAREN FELT QUEASY as she dialed her sister. Jessie wasn't going to believe this. Maren still couldn't believe it.

"Hello," Jessie said, her voice chipper and bright. And Maren was happy that her sister had occasion to sound that way. She was glad that her sister was happy.

She really was.

"Hi. I have news."

"More news! Good grief," said Jessie.

"I'm having twins."

The silence on the other end was deafening. And satisfying.

"No way," Jessie said.

"I know," she said, covering her face with her hands. "Twins. I can hardly believe it and… He is shocked, you can tell. Like, completely losing his mind, which is fair, because I am too."

"That's… That's big. Good thing the father of your baby is a billionaire, I guess. Your *babies*."

"Yeah," she said, huffing. "Good thing."

But of course he was also an emotionally damaged billionaire, and the problem was, she wasn't entirely certain that she was… Fine.

She went back to the conversation they'd had that morning. About their mothers.

"What do you think of our mother?" she asked Jessie.

"I don't," said Jessie. "She left us."

There was a bit of brittleness in her voice.

"But you're about to be a mother yourself. You must be thinking of her."

"I'm thinking about how I would never do that to my child. No matter what. She could have taken us with her, Maren."

"He would've gone after her."

"I know you're not as far along as I am," said Jessie. "So I know that they aren't like fully formed. I know that you can't feel them move yet. But they're helpless. Growing inside of you. They need you. Now imagine them outside of you, small and vulnerable. You would just leave them? You never ask after them again. Never check in on them. And we know that our mother is out there, that she's fine. She's a socialite, she has a new husband, new children. Half siblings, and she doesn't care."

"I always told myself she had to make herself not care. I always told myself that must be how she was surviving it."

"Maybe that's true," said Jessie. "But it was more important to her to figure out how to survive it than to help us survive. And that's something that I'm having trouble getting over. Truly."

"I really wanted to hold on to her. To my memory of her. But I'm afraid now that I can't afford it. I'm having two babies. I have to… I have to be the best mother that I can. And I think that's going to mean very directly examining what I believe about our childhood. Because I just don't ever want to repeat what our mother and father did."

"I never worried about being Mother. I worried about being our father. Because I'm the one that's a little bit more detached. Or at least I have been." Jessie sighed. "You have always seemed like the conscience, Maren. I always felt like I did good things to make you happy. To try and make myself believe that I wasn't like our father. I felt like you did them because it was easy."

"No, I did them to prove that I was good enough," she whispered. Suddenly her throat went tight. "I did always wonder. How she could leave me. I was her princess. I was so good. I… And all of this. The softness. The way that I dress, the way that I wanted this castle. The way that I am, it was about proving that I was everything she said I was. So that part of it was real. But that was just me. Reaching out and trying to touch a woman who left so long ago that she might not even ever think of me."

"I'm sorry," said Jessie.

"Why did she not love us enough?"

"I don't think either of our parents could."

That echoed inside of Maren for a long time after she got off the phone. Their mother and father hadn't loved them enough. Why?

It made her ache.

She put her hand on her stomach. "I love you both. The most. Enough. It doesn't matter what the relationship is between me and your father, I'm never going to leave you. You will always be mine. I promise. Always."

On shaking legs she walked down to the dining hall,

hoping that it would be time for dinner. And when she walked in, her jaw dropped. The long table was covered in a glittering table skate. A Christmas town that glittered and shone with candles and lights, gold reindeer all around. There were Christmas trees set at different heights on the table, gold and green and red. And all around the room were real trees, lit up with white lights.

"Oh, my," she said.

It felt like magic. It felt like the sort of fairytale she was trying to tell herself she didn't need. But, oh, how she felt like she might need it.

"I hope this is to your liking."

She looked up, and saw him standing in the doorway, dressed spectacularly for dinner in a dark blue suit. He was so beautiful it made her hurt.

He was the fairytale. Standing there in the middle of it, gloriously handsome and surrounded by all of this holiday sparkle.

But she couldn't afford to indulge.

She had to be practical. Because she couldn't turn away from the truth.

He didn't love her. And they were tangled-up messes of people. Who needed to find a way to be good parents for their children.

And this was just him following the doctor's orders.

With Christmas decorations. It was the season, after all.

"This is beautiful," she said.

"The staff did it, of course, not me."

"I know," she said, holding back a laugh at the image of him up on a little ladder putting a star on top of the tree.

Except then suddenly it didn't seem so funny. Except then suddenly it made her ache just slightly.

What kind of father would he be? Would he want to do domestic things? Silly things?

Their twins weren't identical. They could have one of each. A boy and a girl. How would he be with the daughter? Would he be soft? And with the son, would he be too rigid? Or would he model strength in an interesting way? Would he teach his son that he could have feelings as well? How could he do that when he didn't have any of his own?

"What?"

"Just thinking about the fact that we're having two children," she said. "It's unavoidable. I am... Overwhelmed by it."

"You have no need to be overwhelmed. We will of course get nannies."

But she knew that nannies wouldn't solve the issue of their needing to be parents. They might be able to have this, but they would have to work for it.

They were both wounded adults, who wanted badly not to wound their children in the same fashion.

They didn't have time to move straight into that discussion, though, because the meal was brought out. A spectacular array of roasted meat and vegetables, orzo and pitas.

She was so hungry, she thought that she could eat all of it without help.

It was amazing how her appetite had turned around... Since he'd arrived.

She pushed that thought to the side.

She piled food onto her plate, and he did the same.

She took a bite of a dolma, and chewed slowly. "The thing is," she said. "It's so much easier to see the issues in our childhood when I began to think of them being done to… Well, a child. One that isn't me. I had Jessie, and we survived, so it was easy for me to think that what was asked of us wasn't too much. But of course it was. Of course it was. We were children being asked to work with a violent criminal. Children who were left to live with a violent criminal. And while I will always carry some sympathy in my heart for my mother, the truth is, she loved herself the most."

"Yes," said Acastus, looking down at his plate. "The truth is, I have spent my life protecting my mother because no one else did. It is hard for me to condemn her in any fashion."

"But who protected you?" she asked.

"I would've told you that I didn't need it. I always felt like a man. More of one than my father. I was always so angry about what he wasn't doing, that I felt I always did. I always felt as if it was my calling, my responsibility. But when I think back on the time spent here. The time in the dungeon."

"How long were you there?"

"Two months, I think."

She gasped. She thought he was thrown down there for a couple of hours as a performative gesture. It never occurred to her that he had been kept there. Like a real prisoner.

"Over jewels that they recovered?"

"Yes," he said. "But this is it. My mother was so

upset. Weeping and wailing over what we lost. She never acted as if she cared about my time spent in the dungeon. I accepted that at the time because it seemed... I was willing to take everything on board. I was willing to let it be all my fault. Anything to counteract the way my father made her feel."

"You were a child. Stealing jewelry for his mother, and the fact that she made you feel as if she needed that to be happy and not your safety, that you needed to do things for her and not... Simply be her son, that says everything."

"I do not like to think of it. I do not like to accept it. It is only because we are having children of our own that I am even..."

"Because you know it would be wrong," she said. "You know it would be wrong to do that to them."

"I think of the ways in which my parents live their life. The way my father was a husband, who lived as though nothing had changed. He acted as if he had no wife and child. My mother acted as if her husband and child existed to serve her. And that is why I recognize that we cannot just expect to do this right. We cannot."

"I agree," she said. She looked around the palace. It was so isolated. It sat on a rock. It was beautiful. And she loved it. But she realized something.

"We cannot raise children here," she said.

There was a strange sort of glint in his eyes.

"Why not?"

"Think about your childhood. I'll think about mine. We were so isolated. We were cut off."

"Yes. But..."

"A title isn't going to make our child happy. They need to have friends. More than just each other. They need to have something normal. You and I both know what it's like to not have normal."

"Spending time in a dungeon is a little bit beyond that."

"I know. But I don't think… I don't think we can make a life here."

"But the title…"

"It's ceremonial. We'll still have it. We can spend time here. But our children need to be able to go to school. They need to be able to be around friends. To go to their houses."

"We will discuss that later."

She could feel his resistance to it, and she did understand. Of course, his life was defined by the pursuit of this place. She could understand why it felt too painful for him to let go of it.

And suddenly it all felt a bit impossible. This endeavor.

Their marriage.

How could they make a life together and never touch? How could they make a family?

"Of course… We don't have to live together," she said.

He looked up. "We don't?"

"Why? We aren't a couple? It would be entirely possible for our children to come here every weekend and be with you. You can have whatever you want, and I can give them normal during the week. We can coparent."

There was something thunderous on his face. *"Coparent?"*

"Yes. It's… It's a very modern thing to do, really. There's nothing wrong with it."

"No," he said.

"No?"

"No," he said again, definitively.

"But that's insane. We're trying to make something functional and…"

"And we will not do it by breaking apart the household."

"What good did it do your parents to stay together? What good did it ever do you? I think you know that nothing good came of it. Your mother stayed with your father, and for what reason? So that she could use him continually to manipulate you?"

"Enough," he said. "Don't forget—"

"What? The foundation of this is that I was manipulated into this marriage, into this conception?"

"I believe," he said, "the word you're looking for is *seduced*."

And it was as if all the civility from the last few hours evaporated. She remembered. The passion. The intensity between them. Everything.

She remembered it, and she craved it.

Suddenly, it seemed like a joke that only moments ago they had been trying to construct a mature and careful plan for how to raise their children. That they had been attempting to pull apart their past pain. Because suddenly it all felt so close to the surface. Suddenly they had hit a disagreement, and it was like they had been lit on fire.

They were not friends, that was the problem.

There were moments where she felt like she liked him, but the truth remained, he was the man who had forced her into a marriage. She ignored the voice inside of her that reminded her she had a way out. Several. That she had caved completely when presented with choices she didn't like, and that she had been happily under his spell when she had allowed him to seduce her. That she had pushed him for sex the first time, and had pursued him for it after that as well.

That she was the one who lay around full of malaise when he was gone.

Yes, she conveniently forgot all of that. She focused on what an autocrat he was. On how he had done something no sane person would ever do.

She focused on all of that. Because it made her feel good. Because it made her anger feel justified.

"We're going to do what's best for our children. It isn't going to be about your legacy."

"I told you from the beginning…"

"Yes. And everything changed today. You know that it did. You know it changed."

"Enough," he thundered. "Perhaps you're right. Perhaps something does need to change. We tried. We tried to do it your way. We tried to do it my way. I left. And you dissolved."

"Don't give yourself all that much credit. I was ill. And pregnant. It was hardly my fault."

"Whatever the reason," he said. "You were reduced. I cannot stay away. And we…"

He shook his head. "This cannot be ignored."

He pushed his chair back, and came around to her

side of the table. "I think the real problem lies between us. You speak of coparenting as if this is deniable. As if when we are part we're not miserable."

"Look at us now," she said. "Are we less miserable when we're together?"

"I burn for you," he said. "It is not happiness, but when I am away it is unendurable. And I cannot... I cannot be here, I cannot stand here next to you and not have you."

She shook her head, her heart thundering wildly. "No. It was never what it was about, it was..."

"I know," he said. "But it doesn't matter. We never set out to have twins either. And when we were together it was never all about conception, and you know it well."

"But we're dysfunctional."

"Yes. And we are dysfunctional even when we are not lovers. We will live together. And you will be mine," he said. "You will be in my bed every night. I will have you until we are both mindless with our passion."

"What about the children?"

"They will be there. Of course. As you said, this is for them. But why engage in this farce? Why act like it was not our passion that created them? It was. It is a miraculous thing. We were never lying there thinking of England."

"But if we burn each other to the ground, our children will be caught in the flames."

"You were just here. There should not have been flames, and there were. You are acting as if we can go to a moment where we have no feelings for one another, and I believe you and I both know that isn't true. That isn't reasonable. They're already there. There is no protecting us or the children from what already exists. So let us burn then."

And with that, he lifted her from the chair, and claimed her mouth with his own.

He knew that it was counter to anything logical. To anything reasonable. He did know that.

He knew that he was accomplishing nothing through this proclamation. He knew that it was wrong. That he was putting them both in a more precarious position than should be allowed.

But he could think of nothing but the need roaring through his veins. Could think of nothing but the insult of the two of them living separately.

It had become clear to him the moment that he had first touched her that there would be no other lovers for him. And that he would not be able to abide there being any other lovers for her.

It was clear.

It was clear that whatever their intent they were not what they had hoped.

He didn't know how this fit into anything. Into the swirling mass of emotion that tangled in his chest like a bramble and threatened to destroy him. He didn't know why he was doing this. Except there was no other choice. Coparenting. This idea of living separate. This idea of…

Of being a man who cannot keep his family together. That was what it was. He could not allow it. He would give his child everything because what other option was there? He would give his child everything because his parents had been lost in all of these unfulfilled promises. He would make a promise now. To her. To the children.

By God, he would be a man who made things right.

So he kissed her. And he ignored the truth. That there was a monster inside of him who needed this for reasons that had nothing to do with their children. That there was something in him crying out for fulfillment.

This made sense now, and he needed it to. Wanted it to. Was desperate for it to.

This was everything he had ever needed. Ever wanted. This was something…

That made him feel so far away from the helpless boy he'd been in this place.

And he kissed her. Kissed her because he wanted to. Because he needed to. Because perhaps all along she had been the promise to be fulfilled. Because perhaps from the very beginning this had been what he needed.

Perhaps from the very beginning it had been her.

Maybe this was destiny.

Perhaps he owed his father thank you.

And that nearly made him want to laugh, but instead he growled into her mouth, and allowed himself the satisfaction of swallowing her cry of pleasure that climbed up her throat.

"Tell me you want me," he growled.

She looked at him, a wildness in her eyes. He took a step back. "Tell me," he said.

If she no longer wanted him, he did not know what he would do. He was Acastus. Never, ever, had a woman not wanted him. And if Maren did not want him, then nothing else mattered. None of the previous women, none of his previous achievements. Nothing mattered at all. If he had succeeded in taking her desire for him and extinguishing it with his actions, then…

He felt something helpless scrabble in his chest, and it reminded him of being in a dungeon. Of being at the mercy of somebody else. He was. Now. He was that child with a mother who threw things, who wailed and cried and needed him to be strong. He was that child. Who had done something in an effort to appease the person that he loved most, and found himself imprisoned.

He was helpless. Storm-tossed and wrecked.

And then she said, a whisper, barely audible, "I want you."

And triumph roared through him. A need fulfilled like he had never before known.

He wrapped his arms around her, holding her firmly to his chest. "Mine," he growled.

They were no longer talking about the future of their children.

This no longer had anything to do with custody arrangements or anything he had told himself before.

This was about him. Her.

This was about this great, aching need within him that he could not see the end of.

This was about a deficit in the very depths of his soul that he could not grasp hold of. That he could not explain, but with all the money that he had attained in the years since he had left this place, he could not erase.

So he kissed her, because there was nothing else.

And he carried her out of the room, into the fireside room, and set her down on a blanket beneath the Christmas tree.

"Tell me," he said roughly.

"Acastus," she said, putting her fingertips on his cheek. "I want you."

"You do not wish to live separate from me," he said.

She shook her head.

"You wish to live with me," he growled. "You want me."

"I want you," she said.

He could not stop the words that were pouring out of his mouth. He could not stop the need. The hunger, that rolled inside of him like a dragon.

He couldn't.

There was nothing that he could do to staunch the desperate flow.

He stripped his shirt off, everything else, and looked down at her. She was a present. One that he would unwrap slowly.

He began to undo the intricate knots around her dress. Loosened the silken material and exposed the pale curves of her body to his eyes.

She was wearing a red lace bra, and matching underwear, that fired an inferno in his gut.

The roundness of her stomach was a glory. And he touched her with all the reverence he had felt that the doctor had not given her.

He moved his hand slowly over her curves, watched the contrast between them. The rough masculinity of his hands over that soft femininity.

It was a glorious contrast. It made him feel strong and weak all at once.

And he would've said that he could not glory in any sort of weakness. And yet before her, he did.

She arched her back, and he answered her, pulling the lace cups of the bra down and exposing her breasts to his gaze.

He bent down and claimed one pale, tightened bud with his tongue, sucked her deep into his mouth.

He teased her there until she cried out. Until everything was his.

Until she was his.

He stripped her bare, gloried in the feel of her, the taste. Pushed her further, harder, higher than ever before.

He brought her to the edge repeatedly. Until she was sobbing his name. Until she was a mess of tears and pleas and somehow it still wasn't enough to appease that beast within him that had woken up. That had decided it wanted everything. Needed everything. All that she was.

All that she would ever be.

When he finally thrust inside of her, she shattered. Calling out his name. And she pulled from him a climax that nearly decimated him. That shattered a piece of his soul he hadn't known still existed.

They lay there like that, beneath the tree. And he had never thought much about Christmas, or the miracles that people professed to find that time of year. Had never known magic, spiritual or pagan, beneath the Christmas tree, and in that moment he felt both. In a way that he could not explain.

At that moment, he felt her, in a way he would never be able to understand or articulate.

But he knew there would be no more discussion of them living apart. Of them not touching one another, because it would be impossible. Because it was untenable.

Because they were this. Whatever else there was in the world, they were this.

He had not set out to find this. It had never been an idea in his head.

But when he had seen her for the first time, he had known that she was beautiful. In ways that he had not anticipated. In ways he could have never guessed. And it was only more true now. Beauty had not even been a scratch at the surface.

He had looked at her, and he had known she was his. It was a gift he had not anticipated, and yet it was one he would not question. It was one he would take. Without reservation.

She looked up at him, her expression soft, something deep in her eyes that he wanted. That he wanted to claim. That he wanted for his own.

"You will move into my room," he said.

"I like my room," she said.

"Then I will move into yours," he said, because suddenly compromise did not seem so difficult.

"Okay," she said softly. "That would be acceptable."

"There will be no more discussions of us being apart," he said.

He picked her up then, and she grinned.

"What?"

"I like it when you carry me."

"Well, then I will make sure to do it more often."

She snuggled against him, and he struggled to fully comprehend the whiplash of the last hour. Calm rational discussion, burning over into a fight, which had then become… This.

And his heart felt like it might be two sizes larger than it had been when this had all begun.

He wasn't sure if he liked it. But he couldn't deny it either.

She was a singular woman. This woman who had been raised by a criminal, and remembered every single thing.

Who had been abandoned by her mother, and who had tried her very best to love that woman anyway.

He could understand needing to care for a flawed parent.

She was such a strange and singular creature and somehow, she was the one person he had ever met who recognized something within him. That made that thing in him raise its head and look. For connection. For something more.

He had come into this cold. Acting out of a sense of duty.

And then they had tried to pull everything apart and rationalize it.

Now he felt like they were in a fast-moving vehicle careening toward something. Whether that be a cliff or safety, he didn't know.

And it filled him with a sense of disquiet to realize that connection to another person could create this level of uncertainty. For he was a man of control. A man who had done his level best to always feel certain in his life.

And this thing with her undid that.

And yet he could not go back. That measured conversation they'd been having had been false.

But he did not know what this meant for their future. The future of their children.

It was quite impossible to say.

He laid her down in her bed, and he lay beside her.

He had not truly allowed himself to sleep with her the nights when they'd made love before. Instead, he had dozed just barely, then turned over to take her when the need arose within him again.

And this time, he just pulled her against him, swathed them both in blankets and allowed himself to sleep.

Because later he would find out what they were careening toward. Later there would be consequences for this recklessness. Maybe.

But for the first time in his life, he was putting them on hold.

He was releasing his control.

And giving it to her.

CHAPTER THIRTEEN

SHE LAY THERE, awake in the wee hours, feeling the best that she had for a very long time.

Acastus was there with his arms wrapped around her.

Maybe that was it. Maybe that was why.

Suddenly, an aching cavern opened up inside of her chest.

This was not how it was supposed to be. It wasn't supposed to be about them. She had tried so hard to... To minimize her feelings for him. She had tried to be rational, after all, what was the point of having a brain like hers if she couldn't be logical with it. Rational. Reasonable.

But she was a dreamer. She always had been. She was the one with the mind palace. The one who longed to be a princess. She wished she could be different. She wished her fantasies hadn't rushed away from her.

She had wanted to be logical for her child. Because she had wanted to avoid...

She just didn't want to be hurt. That was the bottom line. It wasn't really about avoiding being like her parents. He was nothing like her father. She wasn't her mother, she knew that too. She wouldn't leave. But she had been left. Abandoned. Hurt. And it was what scared her now.

It was just she knew what it was like to simply not be enough. To not be enough to keep a person with her. To not be enough at all. Ever.

And the idea of being that for Acastus, it terrified her.

She wanted to be logical. She wasn't.

She was in this moment a creature of absolute need. Of feeling. That she had no control over. That she couldn't rationalize or con her way out of.

She turned over and looked at him. He was beautiful when he slept. But not softer.

The man was carved from granite.

He had been thrown in a dungeon here. His mother had depended on him to be strong, and he had fashioned himself into something impossibly mighty, but how did a person reach a man who'd had to build himself up that way?

She had always been far too easy to reach. Her life should have made it harder. She had never managed it.

And right now, she ached with her own softness.

A tear slid down her cheek and she dashed it away. Even as she sat there, taking in the way that he looked in sleep. Because she would have this image with her for the rest of her life, and she would call upon it whenever she missed him.

The idea of missing him made her want to howl in pain. She also knew that she couldn't discount that it might happen.

She knew that.

"You're staring," he said without opening his eyes.

"Well," she said. "You're very handsome."

"Thank you." She heard a smile in his voice, even though his lips did not form one.

"Acastus," she said. "Tell me about being in the dungeon."

"Why?" He did open his eyes then.

"Because I'm trying to imagine it. You here and… Captive."

"It's exactly as you would think. This was its own sovereign nation, and Stavros Argos was the master of it. He put me in shackles, had his security guards lead me down there. He kept me chained. He was afraid of me, as he should have been. I was seventeen and could have easily overtaken him even then."

She felt as if she'd been stabbed. "You were a child," she said.

He shook his head. "I was a man. I had to be one. Because my father…"

"You're very angry at your father."

"She was his responsibility," he said. "It actually does not matter if she was difficult. My father married her, I did not. But I couldn't let her sink into despair. I had to take care of her. Because he wouldn't. He was about what he felt Stavros owed him and nothing more. He could not see past the fact that it wouldn't matter in the end if the promises had been fulfilled because of all the damage he had done. All of the damage… It was so much. I understand that. I was in chains long before I was in chains here. I had to take on the responsibility of being the man of our family because my father would not."

Her chest ached for him. She didn't know what it was like to have to take responsibility. That hadn't been her life. That hadn't been the particular trauma that she and her sister had endured.

They had simply been manipulated into being their father's things.

"I wanted to be good," she said. "And from the time I was a child I was aware that I was… A villain. It was really difficult. To want to be something else. And I did. I wanted it so much. So badly. But I couldn't choose it. My father was in charge of us. Of what we could do. Of how we used our minds."

"And if you could choose," he said. "If you could choose what to do with your mind, what would you choose?"

She felt hollowed out and sad in that moment. Because she wasn't sure how to answer the question. She wasn't sure of so many things.

"I knew that I wanted to be safe. I knew that I wanted to not be alone. I won this castle, and I wanted to be a princess. But none of that's doing anything, is it?"

"You don't have to do anything," he said. "If these are your dreams, then they're fine dreams."

"Sure I want to be a good mother," she said. "I know that. Beyond that, I'm not really sure. I do wonder sometimes what I might've been if I hadn't started life in that compound. Though the reality is, a brain like mine is most useful to a criminal. Someone who is trying not to leave paper trails. I can store everything in my head instead of in files. Practically speaking, in the rest of the world, it's more of a party trick than it is anything necessary. So I don't know. I'm probably deluding myself thinking that I could have contributed something if I had a traditional education. A different life. The truth is, I like to believe that I would've been good. But what does that even mean? Look at what I've done with my life since we've escaped. I engaged in cons to better myself. My station. And even though I can justify it all, because of the kind of men who were making those bets, even though I can tell myself I was being like Robin Hood, and not just a regular con artist, I don't have a lot of evidence that I'm actually good. Left to my own devices, who knows."

"You are good, Maren. I think that's apparent. I don't think you need to worry. In fact, I think a truly bad person doesn't worry at all whether or not they are good."

"I suppose. I guess the real question is I don't know if I'm good or just sad. I don't know if I'm especially aching to be a good mother, or if I just want these children to love me. I just…" Her own longing took her breath away. "It's so difficult. Really. I loved my mother so very much. And she left me. She walked away from me when I needed her. It has always been hard for me to believe that there weren't just some things about me that made me easy to leave."

"You were not easy for me to leave."

His words came close to healing something inside of her. Begin to mend a crack in her soul that she hadn't realized was there. She couldn't respond. All the words just got bottled up in her throat. And she let them sit there. She let herself rest.

Because right now they were together. Right now

she didn't need to know what she wanted to do for evermore. Or if she was good, or if she would even be a good mother. Right now, she knew that she was being held by Acastus. And right now, that was all that mattered. Just this moment. Just their breathing. Just the Christmas decorations outside, and the passion between them. The rest… The rest would be for later.

But this was now. And it was good.

And there had been spare few moments in her life for which that could be said.

So she just decided to rest. No con, no catch, no waiting for the other shoe to drop. It was the best sleep she could ever remember having. And maybe, just maybe, they could make a family. Maybe she could begin to have dreams.

Maybe they could begin to make something new.

She would cling to that hope. And cling to it hard.

CHAPTER FOURTEEN

AS CHRISTMAS DREW nearer Maren began to feel lighter. Perhaps it had nothing to do with the holiday, but maybe it did. She was so happy with him. So happy with this life that they were building for themselves.

And some of her fears about whether or not they would be like her parents had abated. They did fight sometimes. Because Maren was dramatic. And she owned that. She enjoyed a good fight, it turned out. She liked to be seen and heard. And one thing that was apparent, one thing that mattered quite a bit was that Acastus was a safe place for her to vent that anger. He was safe. In general. And that was a gift, she knew.

Her life felt full. The impending birth of their children feeling like a gift. She had Jessie now, and Ewan. Their baby. She had Acastus, and she had the promise of impending motherhood.

Jessie and Ewan came for a pre-Christmas dinner and Jessie was thrilled to see her niece and her sister.

She held her, on her hip, and snuggled her soft baby head.

"She only gets more beautiful, Jessie," said Maren.

"She looks a little bit like her aunt," said Jessie, stroking the baby's downy red hair.

"I guess she does."

"I can't believe that you're going to have twins," said Jessie, putting her hands on Maren's stomach, the only person who would ever be allowed to do that, other than Acastus of course.

She looked up at her husband. "Neither could we."

"That doesn't run in your family, does it?" Ewan asked.

"Who cares if it does," said Jessie happily. "You are absolutely loaded, and we can afford it."

"I'm not sure that my nerves could take it," he said.

Jessie waved a hand. "Your nerves are fine, Ewan. And you and I both know it. We're both gamblers."

"That is true," Ewan said.

Then Acastus asked about their gambling, and off the two of them went to the races, talking about their triumphs and losses in casinos.

Both of them had been playing a game, Ewan working to disgrace his title and the name of his father in order to get revenge, Jessie to make a life for them apart from their father.

It was amazing the way that their own issues were parallel, much the way that hers and Acastus's were.

They were both circling this idea of love and passion, and yet they had found passion, it couldn't be denied. And in all of these little ways she was seeing how it was different. Even this, welcoming her sister and her sister's husband, spending time together, it proved that they weren't the same as their parents.

It really did.

She had lived in a home, too. A rather large one. But it hadn't been this.

This place that was decked out in Christmas decor, and filled with warmth.

This place that was utterly and completely safe. This place that promised her healing and family.

She had never experienced anything like it before.

She wondered if he had.

He had been held in the dungeon here. He had been treated like a servant. And yet it was different now. They had staff for the palace, but they treated no one like they were beneath them. It simply wasn't in either of their characters.

And that, she was beginning to understand, mattered.

It wasn't passion itself that was bad, but the people the passion was between.

That was the potential issue. That was the thing that you had to worry about.

She had married a good man. Through no merit of her own really. She had shown up, and they were married. And over the months, even though there had been time with little contact between them, she felt that when he needed to prove that he was good, he did.

She had spent a lot of time worrying about being good. She had spent a lot of time worrying about a great many things. She didn't worry about that anymore. She felt good. She felt happy. And she accepted that as the truth of the matter more than anything else.

Because hadn't she and Jessie endured enough? Endured enough wickedness and pain to know something good when they saw it? She might've questioned it before. But not now. She hadn't planned this. And she had planned so many things in her life. Masterminded so many things. But not this. Never this.

She hadn't been able to manipulate it, con it, none of it. They had met purely because she had won that poker game. It was chance and fate all rolled into one, but it was them that had made it something real.

The electricity between them. It was not something that could've been planned. Never in a thousand years. She knew that. And it was what made this feel like perhaps it was something she could trust. Just maybe. Just maybe.

She wanted to talk to him about it. She wanted to tell him. She proposed to wait until Christmas, because it was… It was her gift to him.

A laying bare of her soul.

It was the day before Christmas Eve. She and her sister had both agreed that they would have actual Christmas at their own homes. A chance to establish tradition for the first time.

They both understood each other, and the need to do that, because they understood where they had come from.

Before she and Ewan left on Christmas Eve morning, Jessie leaned in and gave Maren a kiss on the cheek. "He's gorgeous," she said.

Maren shimmered inside. "I know," she said. "He really is."

"Be happy with him," said Jessie.

"I want to be," she said.

"What's keeping you from total happiness?"

"I'm afraid. I'm afraid because I think I'm falling

in love with him, and I want to tell him, but I'm afraid that it's going to make him… I'm afraid that he'll run away from me."

Maren looked at her, considering. "He might. But that doesn't mean that you won't be able to get him back. Ewan had such a difficult childhood, and you know that he turned away from what we had. More than once. Because it was difficult, to accept that no matter how much he had wanted to run away from emotion. From love, it had found him anyway."

"But I don't know how to get away from the fear… Because our mother didn't love us enough, Jessie. And I can't bear the idea that he might not love me enough. To get over his pain."

"You can't think of it that way," said Jessie. "I get that it might feel that way. But the truth is, that wound that you carry inside of you, all these things that we remember with perfect clarity, people feel all those things just the same, even if they can't recall the situation in as perfect detail as we can. It doesn't mean that the pain of whatever he's gone through has faded. It lives in his soul. An imprint and a memory. You can't be afraid that he doesn't love you enough, because even if he rejects you, that isn't really what's happening. Even with our mother, I don't believe that's what was happening."

"You don't?"

"I think people run from pain. If the house is on fire, you're going to try to escape, and maybe later you'll regret the things and people you left behind, but all you can think about is the way the flames are burning you. I think that's what our mother was dealing with.

She was leaving a burning house. She left us to burn. That's the truth. But she could only think of her own pain. It was the pain that was bigger. Not the love that was too small."

"So what's the solution? I ignore the pain? I ignore the fear?"

"I actually think that's all you can do. And in a year, I trust that I'm going to be standing here with you, your beautiful children, and your husband who loves you very much. But you're going to have to take the risk."

Maren felt desolate. "Why can't he take the risk?"

"He could. You could wait. You could wait so that you're not pushing him off of the cliffs into a pool of your feelings. But do you really have the patience, Maren? I don't think that's you. You're the one that went and got Ewan for me. You're the one that couldn't stand to see me upset. You pushed both of us before we were ready. If you don't do the same to Acastus, that just makes you a hypocrite, doesn't it?"

"You're very annoying," said Maren.

"I know. But it's out of love. The same that you have for me."

"Maybe I'll just keep it to myself."

"You could. There is nothing that says you have to be the brave one."

But she knew that she would be. She knew that she had to be. She didn't know why, only that she did. She and Jessie had been unloved long enough, that was the thing. She wanted what Jessie had. And she wanted… Most of all she wanted her happiest memories to not be ones that lived in her mind palace. She had this palace. They were having children. It was Christmas. She wanted her happiest life to be in front of her. Not just reliant on those images that she carried with her.

She couldn't fix that thing with her mother. But perhaps she could make something new.

She could have that love, that imperfect love from the past, and she could have love now.

Maybe Jessie was right. Maybe that was worth a fight.

"I'll let you know how it goes," Maren said.

"I have no doubt you will."

She waved them off as they got into a plush boat that would take them back to the mainland.

Jessie didn't like the idea of flying in a helicopter with the baby, and Maren really couldn't blame her. She would be defaulting to a boat from now on too.

It was funny how everything felt precarious and precious now. She and Jessie had spent their lives risk-taking. Gambling. So much of it not being of their own choice, but then later some of it being of their own making. And this would be the ultimate gamble. The ultimate gamble on a secure and lovely life. On the things she wanted most.

If Acastus were to ask her now what she wanted, being a princess or having his heart, she knew the answer.

That morning, she had toast and orange juice put out at the table. And when he came in, she looked up at him. "Have a seat," she said.

He arched a brow. "Are you asking me to have toast and orange juice with you?"

"I believe our goalposts have changed, don't you?"

"I suppose they have," he acknowledged, sitting down across from her. "Not really a holiday spread."

"Well, dinner last night with my sister was a very rich affair, and unfortunately, even though I need to eat all day, I can't eat very much at once these days."

"Poor Maren," he said.

But then he did sit down, and he did pick up his toast.

And her whole heart went tight.

Because maybe this was it. Maybe it was something. Maybe this was a sign.

A sign that he had changed his mind about what their marriage would entail. Well, she knew he had. She didn't say anything, not then, because she had a plan.

"I wish for you to open a present tonight," she said.

"Okay."

"I would like to have dinner in my study, as you call it. By the fire. By the Christmas tree."

"If it suits you," he said.

She spent the day jangling with nerves, and when she came down to meet him for dinner, her heart nearly stopped. Because he was stunningly beautiful in his tuxedo, his olive skin a glorious contrast to the crisp white shirt, his dark hair pushed back off his forehead. No one would ever know that he had been a servant in this place. He looked every inch the immaculate billionaire. And yet he had been. He carried the scars and the pain. He had done all this for his mother and she wasn't here.

Maren knew that pain.

She understood it. She understood him.

She loved him. It was that simple.

And she was willing to risk for it.

For her part, she was dressed only in a short silk robe.

She delighted in that. The mismatch in their attire. She often liked to be naked while he was fully dressed. Liked the feeling of being pressed against the fine fabrics that he wore. Of the power that he had in those moments.

And in turn, the power that she had. To drive him wild.

"I have overdressed," he said.

"You're perfect," she said.

Dinner had already been served, and she sat down with him on the floor by the Christmas tree and served him. Watched as he ate fruit and cheese.

"I thought tonight that it would be my turn to draw a bath for you."

She already had some of the household staff seeing to that.

"For me?"

"Yes. I rather enjoyed the experience of you taking care of me. I thought you should have it in kind."

His eyes were alight with erotic interest.

She loved the way he made her feel. About her changing body. She was never insecure when it came to him, because he made it so clear how deeply attractive he found her.

She led him to the large bathroom, and began to slowly strip his clothes from him. She undid his black tie, his shirt, pushed his jacket from his shoulders.

She knelt down and untied his shoes, removed his socks.

She devoted herself wholly to the erotic art of undressing him. Of unveiling every strong, sinewy line of his body. That golden skin, the rough hair on his chest and stomach.

She kissed him there. Then down further. She curved her hand around his stunning arousal and took him into her mouth, unable to wait.

He gripped her hair, guiding her movements as she swallowed him down.

"This is not a bath," he said, his voice rough as his hips flexed, driving him to the back of her throat.

"Is that a complaint?" she asked, moving away from him to ask the question.

"Never," he said, and she swallowed him again.

Then she stood, satisfied that she had teased him enough, removing her robe, and exposing her curves to his gaze. "Now get in, regrettably I can't pick you up."

He smiled, and slid beneath the water. She nearly groaned as the ripples covered up her view of his body.

But she was equally satisfied when she began to move the water over his hard muscles, making him slick.

She worked his hardness beneath the surface of the water, her hand moving up and down over his impressive length.

And then she abandoned the intimate touch, and moved to his shoulders, stroking him, rubbing him. Easing the tension in his muscles.

She moved her hands down his chest, up beneath his jaw. She kissed him. She showed him how much she cared with every stroke of her hands over his body.

He had always taken such care with her. With her pleasure.

She wanted to do the same for him.

"Join me," he said roughly.

He pulled her into the bath, and she positioned herself over his hardness, sinking down onto him and taking him in deep.

Her breath hissed through her teeth as they began to move, cushioned by the water, the buoyancy helping make her feel lighter. More able to move.

He gripped her rear and brought her down hard onto him, establishing a hard rhythm that challenged them both.

And when they came, it was together. Gasping and panting.

And what happened next just seemed right. Seemed obvious.

What happened next was nothing less than her speaking the truth. "I love you."

She could feel him go stiff. Could feel his denial.

"Let's get dressed," he said, his voice hard.

They did, and went into the bedroom. The one that they shared.

"Perhaps I will stay in my room tonight," he said.

The words sent a trickle of dread through her. He was separating himself from her. Because she had not given him a burden to carry, she'd given him her love. And he had no idea what to do with it. Or perhaps he didn't know how to see love as anything but a boulder, and he had to shun it.

He was doing it. Pulling away. Exactly as Jessie had said that he might. And it had always been incumbent upon Maren to decide if it was worth the risk.

Was he worth it?

Was the ultimate happiness they might find worth it? *Yes.*

A painful, twisted answer bloomed in her soul. It wasn't a simple or easy answer. But it was honest.

She had wanted to be a princess. But that had been a simplistic metaphor for wanting happiness. Protection.

She couldn't have that without him, she realized now. But not half of him. All of him. All that they could be, and if she allowed him distance, if she pushed down her feelings and denied them, she would be a princess with a castle, yes.

But she would not live happily ever after.

He was the one thing she had to have.

All of this could slide into the sea. It was him she wanted.

His love.

"If your intent on pulling away from me, don't do it by inches," she said. "If that makes you want to leave, then I would prefer that you leave. At least that would be honest."

"You're my wife," he said. "I will not leave you, nor the children."

"You will just condemn me to a life of your ambivalence?"

"I'm not ambivalent. What about any of this gives you the sense that I don't care?"

"It feels…"

"Enough. It is not about what it feels like. I… Love is a prison, Maren. And it is not one that I will step into."

"I didn't think you were worried about yourself."

"Well, I am," he said. "I was imprisoned here. For love. How can I forget?"

"And it earned you nothing. But I'm not asking you to go to prison for me. I want you to open yourself up. I want you to be my husband. Really. We signed the paper. We didn't speak about vows. We didn't pledge undying love. But I want to do it now. I promise myself to you, Acastus. I promise to love you, to honor you, to obey you as you do me. I promise to give you all of myself. For better or worse. Even if somehow we fall into poverty. I would never price being a princess over being your wife. I would be your wife even if we were here scrubbing floors."

"No," he said. "I just… I can't…"

"Why? What are you afraid of?"

He looked at her, and she could see the fear in his eyes. Real fear. She would never doubt it or question it. She knew it to be honest. He was not trying to hurt her. He really was trapped in a burning house. She knew that it was real.

"I am your wife," she said. "And you are my husband. We are having children. If you leave, then what? If you leave like my mother, to escape this, the big feelings. Then what?"

"I'm not leaving," he said.

But she could see that he wanted to. "Stay with me. Your mother used you. She manipulated you. Your feelings. You didn't get a chance to have them. Tell me. Tell me everything. Everything you fear. Everything you desire. Tell me. It matters to me."

He sat down on the edge of the bed. "I… I am angry. My father did nothing to protect me. To protect me from his wife's emotions, and my mother did nothing to thank me for all that I did. Everyone around her was at fault. Including me. It didn't matter how hard I tried. It didn't matter what I did. I couldn't ever be enough. Even now, this isn't enough. I married you for her sake. Conceived children because it was what she wanted me to do. I earned billions, to keep her in a lifestyle to which she wanted to become accustomed, and it was clear that what she actually wanted was the lifestyle. Not me, never me. I… I was never enough."

"But you are," she said. "You are. We are together. We are married. If we separate, what end does it serve? If we turn away from this, then we are our parents. I refuse to be. I refuse. I love you. I want that more than I want to be safe. I want you more than I want things to be easy. I have chosen to fight for this even though I knew that you might not be able to say that you loved me yet. But I want you to know it's what I want."

"We never had a chance," he said, his voice rough. "What if I'm unable to give you all the things you dream of? What if I can't give you what you need, then shouldn't I set you free to be with someone who can?"

"I don't want someone else. You are the father of my children. And that is a cop-out."

They talked. Endlessly. Until their voices were hoarse. About pain and loss. About the ways in which their parents had failed them.

"It's Christmas morning," she said, croaking out the words.

"Come with me," he said.

She took his hand. They were both naked, but the

palace was asleep, and they slipped down to a part of the palace she'd never been before.

The dungeon.

He didn't dress to go to the dungeon. It was symbolic of everything that he'd been through here. The humiliation. The pain. But he needed her to understand. He was exhausted from fighting with her. From fighting himself.

He needed her to see. He needed her to understand.

The weight of it.

The great, inglorious burden.

"This was the biggest gesture I could give to my mother. It was not yet enough. I wanted so badly to be enough for her, and I could not be. And I... This has been the prison I remained in. You're correct. Because I thought by staying in it I could somehow keep myself from ever being locked up against my will again. I don't want to be in here anymore. I want you. I want whatever life we can have. Whatever life we might make. Maren, this is no longer about legacy. It is no longer bigger than the two of us. It is us. Us and our children. And if I deny us, it is because I'm carrying on the legacy of pain. I do not wish to do that. Not to you, not to the children. Not to myself. It is simply not worth it. Nothing is worth the cost of losing you. Nothing. I want... I want your love. And you did not ever have to worry about whether or not I love you enough. I am miserable without you. You should've seen me while I was away."

"Why did you stay away for so long?"

"I was trying to prove to myself that this was still about legacy. That it was about the way I could control the world around me. That it wasn't about feelings for me. Because how could it be? I had thought always that I was fated to marry into the Argos family. I had never thought that I could have love. Because nothing in my life was about it. I realize that now. I thought that it was. I thought I was motivated by my love for my mother, and that she survived because of my love for her. But it is not that. I simply gave her what she wanted. I thought that love was the cage. But it's greed. Greed is an endless well of dissatisfaction. And that is my mother's real problem. You were right. All along. And you are right about this too. I don't need to live in this palace. I want to give our children a good life. A life with friends. A life surrounded by love. Because that is truly what matters. I want them to understand that our love for them is based on nothing like giving to us."

"Acastus," she whispered, putting her hand on his face. "Thank you for showing me this place. Now let's leave. Because this is not us. And you're free."

"Yes," he said, his voice hard. "We are."

"My love is free," she said. "I don't need a palace. I don't need glorious stained glass windows, or marble halls. I don't need pristine seas and an endless closet and being a princess. I need you. Your love. You are my joy. Just as you are."

He held her tightly, afraid his heart might burst. Afraid he might unravel.

Finally, he spoke, around a tightness in his throat that was nearly unbearable. "You are my heart. And I… It is the strangest thing. I feel like I am no longer carrying the burden I once did. I feel like…"

"I want to be with you. Carrying all the emotions you have. Whether they're sweet or sour, or sharp or soft. I'm yours. You're mine. And this is love."

"Yes, love," he said, because all other words were beyond him.

They walked out, and went to the room, where they dressed.

And then they went into the study for their Christmas morning. And there were presents, piled high, but as lovely as they were, they weren't what really mattered.

What mattered was her. What mattered was love.

And he would never have to question if what they had was enough. Because it was everything.

He sat there with her, his hand on her stomach, their future before them. More interesting than anything left in her past.

And she kissed him on the mouth. "And they lived happily ever after."

EPILOGUE

THE NEXT CHRISTMAS was bright and glorious.

He and Maren had bought a house near Jessie and Ewan in Scotland, and they also had one in Greece for when they wished to go to sunny weather. But at Christmastime, they had all decided that the castle was the place to go.

The twins—Athena and Diophantus—were sitting crabbily beneath the Christmas tree, overwhelmed by the festivities, while their cousin toddled around them.

It was a warmth and happiness like Acastus had never known. Ewan had truly become like a brother to him, Jessie a very real sister.

Family was something he was beginning to understand in a way he never had. And love could never be a cage. Love, and his new experience, was an ever-expanding resource. One that grew exponentially with each passing year. Every time one of his children did something new. Every time they looked at him. Every time Maren kissed him, or smiled.

He had told her once that he sometimes felt like he had a grave responsibility to her because she remembered everything.

"It's funny," she responded. "Because it matters less

and less. My memory. What matters most of all is what I feel. And every day with you I simply feel loved."

Love, he was discovering, was enough in all cases.

"A real Christmas present to you," Jessie said, grinning, "is the news that we are having another baby."

"Oh, good," said Acastus. "Then you'll finally understand the trials and tribulations of having two."

They laughed.

And when he took Maren to bed that night she looked at him sheepishly. "It is entirely possible that nine months from now, you and I will understand the trials and tribulations of three."

He stared at his wife. "You're joking. The twins aren't even six months old."

"I know. Someone needs to talk to my husband about it."

He smiled, and he felt the love inside of him grow yet again.

"The problem," he said. "Is that your husband is desperately in love with you."

"I don't consider it a problem," she whispered. "In fact, it's the greatest joy of my life."

* * * * *

COMING SOON!

We really hope you enjoyed reading this book. If you're looking for more romance be sure to head to the shops when new books are available on

Thursday 23rd November

To see which titles are coming soon, please visit

millsandboon.co.uk/nextmonth

MILLS & BOON

MILLS & BOON®

Coming next month

A BILLION-DOLLAR HEIR FOR CHRISTMAS
Caitlin Crews

'What exactly are you trying to say to me?'

Tiago sighed, as if Lillie was being dense. And he hated himself for that, too, when she stiffened. 'This cannot be an affair, Lillie. No matter what happened between us in Spain. Do you not understand? I will have to marry you.'

Her eyes went wide. Her face paled, and not, his ego could not help but note, in the transformative joy a man in his position might have expected to see after a proposal. 'Marry me? Marry *you?* Are you mad? On the strength of one night?'

'On the strength of your pregnancy. Because the Villela heir must be legitimate.' He looked at her as if he had never seen her before and would never see her again, or maybe it was simply that he did not wish to say the thing he knew he must. But that was life, was it not? Forever forcing himself to do what was necessary, what was right. Never what he wanted. So he took a deep breath. 'We will marry. Quickly. And once that happens, I will never touch you again.'

Continue reading
A BILLION-DOLLAR HEIR FOR CHRISTMAS
Caitlin Crews

Available next month
www.millsandboon.co.uk

OUT NOW!

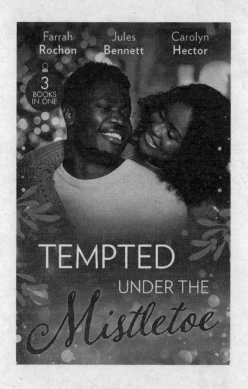

LET'S TALK

Romance

For exclusive extracts, competitions and special offers, find us online:

f MillsandBoon

t @MillsandBoon

O @MillsandBoonUK

♪ @MillsandBoonUK

Get in touch on 01413 063 232

MILLS & BOON

THE HEART OF ROMANCE

A ROMANCE FOR EVERY READER

MODERN

Prepare to be swept off your feet by sophisticated, sexy and seductive heroes, in some of the world's most glamourous and romantic locations, where power and passion collide.

HISTORICAL

Escape with historical heroes from time gone by. Whether your passion is for wicked Regency Rakes, muscled Vikings or rugged Highlanders, awaken the romance of the past.

MEDICAL

Set your pulse racing with dedicated, delectable doctors in the high-pressure world of medicine, where emotions run high and passion, comfort and love are the best medicine.

True Love

Celebrate true love with tender stories of heartfelt romance, from the rush of falling in love to the joy a new baby can bring, and a focus on the emotional heart of a relationship.

Desire

Indulge in secrets and scandal, intense drama and sizzling hot action with heroes who have it all: wealth, status, good looks…everything but the right woman.

HEROES

The excitement of a gripping thriller, with intense romance at its heart. Resourceful, true-to-life women and strong, fearless men face danger and desire - a killer combination!

To see which titles are coming soon, please visit

millsandboon.co.uk/nextmonth